THE

WIFE

BEFORE

LAST

DAVID PALIN

Published in 2024 by
Matthew James Publishing Ltd
(an imprint of Andrews UK Limited)
West Wing Studios, Unit 166, The Mall,
Luton, LU1 2TL

www.matthewjamespublishing.com

ISBN: 9781837916252

*My thanks to all at Matthew James Publishing and Andrews UK
for having belief in me and to Sarah Mayhew for her amazing support.*

I hope you enjoy!

THE
WIFE
BEFORE
LAST

Very best wishes

David Palin

Chapter One

He liked to joke that he was a man who really could become lost in his work; enjoyed saying it out loud to his imaginary audience. Because of course no-one was listening – not at this time of morning – except for the early bird and other foraging wildlife disturbed while he endeavoured to keep the maze pruned to perfection.

There was frost on the branches. Autumn was struggling to resist winter's rather violent advances, but it wouldn't be long before she was stripped bare. He paused, admiring for a moment the poetry of his thoughts, before the rather predatory nature of the image unsettled him.

However, it couldn't be denied that something about solitude stimulated one's creative juices and after all, he was an educated man, indeed a man of education. Not a gardener by vocation, but through expediency. Too many divorces could play havoc with your retirement plans.

But what a garden! Reginald had visited countries smaller than this. Fanleigh Hall dated from that time when money poured into Britain from all corners of the Empire and gentlemen of means had sought to mimic the great classical landscapes of France and Italy. He was truly grateful to Lord Evesham for valuing the tuition the college had given his son and possessing the grace, the savoir faire, to make its former headmaster feel like his employment at the Hall was a blessing to the family rather than a favour.

However, the Lord did get his old money's worth. Sometimes, when Reginald looked around at the sheer scale of the grounds, he had to remind himself that it was a pleasure to be in such surroundings. Often a hard day's work appeared not to have registered on the tranquil landscape, as if it existed through its own effortless serenity, and it was easy to feel your labours had achieved little.

Lord Evesham was nothing if not a true English eccentric and this maze was proof of that rather studied quirkiness. Of course, Reginald didn't ever really get lost in it. Like most logical thinkers – and after all, he had specialised in the sciences – he knew that if you kept the hedgerow to your left shoulder, no matter what, even if it led you down cul-de-sacs, you would reach the centre of the maze and find your way out again. Not that he needed to follow that rule any longer; by now he knew every stone and shimmy of the pathways and had learnt that even conifer hedges had quirks that individualised them, though there were also some of his own makings as he amused himself while trimming the twisting yards of greenery.

It was always his first port of call early every morning, because tourists came at all times of day to attempt the famous maze, often not bothering to go into the grand house itself, which was a National Trust property. He needed to be sure that no litter had blown in, or indeed that no-one had remained overnight, whether by intention or otherwise; alive or dead.

Despite the early starts he valued the privacy the evergreen walls afforded. It was his own fortress in another man's kingdom.

Which was why he knew this morning that something was different, perhaps even – whisper it who dare – wrong. It wasn't that the birds were silent; on the contrary they seemed a little agitated. After all, they were his troops in this fortress and helped him to maintain it, so their darting and fluttering suggested a disturbance.

He couldn't put his finger on it, but he just knew, and when he reached the centre of the maze a non-functioning psychic finger was the least of his worries.

There was no horror at first. That only followed as he stepped forward, trying to understand what and then why.

Chapter Two

Twenty-seven months earlier

She glanced down the table in disapproval towards her English counterpart, Bob Bevan, who had flown in for the meeting, and Marcus saw in that look, heard in Bob's silence, that the door might already be closed; that he had blown the deal; that he owed the wrong guys money now, a lot of it, which he didn't have, or at least wasn't prepared to admit to or cough up, as the British put it. He picked up her unspoken admonishment of the colleague for having brought such an ill-considered lack of opportunity to her and thus wasted her time.

Behind her, through the window and dominating the distant town he saw the twin spires of Villingen's church. Heaven help you if you called the place by its full name, Villingen-Schwenningen. It was said that, though the towns on the edge of the Black Forest had been twinned some years ago, they still couldn't stand each other, one being over a thousand years old and proud of its history, while the other was a business and industrial hub which had been imposed on its older partner. For a second, his mind wandered back to Berlin, his birthplace. If ever you wanted the ultimate example of divided values and principles, you had it there, back in the day. Even now, he couldn't judge whether he had grown up on the correct side of the Wall.

As he contemplated the history of his country, the knowledge and attention to detail was ironic, because a lack of it was costing him now, in more ways than his hosts could ever know, and that was always the problem for someone like him – a non-specialist; someone who had overcome Imposter Syndrome, fighting his way up and through.

It was time to see whether this could still turn out to be money well spent.

She was addressing him. He wished she was undressing him. Was she wishing it too, behind the inevitable woman-in-a-man's-world power suit? Would she throw him a rope? They always threw him a rope – women; they always threw him a rope.

"So, from what I understand, our existing stock will fill your warehouse." He opened his mouth to speak, but she continued. "Populations are growing and ageing. Medication, pharmaceuticals – they have always been and remain growth industries. We would have no room for expansion."

No rope then. Not even a thread. Didn't seem to fancy that fuck either.

He chose humour; as so often an attempt to buy thinking-time. "So, in a way death is a growth industry. Getting older is the new black." Did her face crack at his riposte? Maybe, maybe not. The far-off church bell chose that moment to chime, or perhaps toll, ten-thirty. "Frau Kopsch, we'll find another warehouse for expansion."

"You are already a third-party warehouse," she responded, followed by another glance at her wordless colleague, Bob Bevan. "I don't want a fourth party in our supply chain. Besides, I doubt there are too many buildings of the required standard just waiting around empty, with the necessary MHRA licence."

Marcus sat up, leaned forward, resting on his elbows, hoping the sweep of the new wool of his Boss suit-sleeves over his biceps might win him some points.

"Frau Kopsch – may I call you Katja…?" He saw in her eyes that perhaps he might not. "… I believe that I can resolve this with a quick phone call or two. I think the short-term gains of storing that amount of stock so cheaply – I mean, we're talking a thirty percent saving – would outweigh the little bit of time it takes to find a suitable warehouse for your growth stock. Could we perhaps reconvene tonight over dinner…" he looked at Bob Bevan, "… I mean the three of us?"

She appeared to be considering something, jotting notes down on her pad. Was it the savings, or the dinner? When she looked up again, he tried not to overdo his winning, you-know-it-makes-sense smile.

"There's some merit in what you say," she said at last, "but you have also been a little bit, shall we say *cloudy* about your distribution arrangements. Would these thirty percent savings be negated by delivery costs?"

"Absolutely not!" He hoped his clenched jaws accentuated just his cheekbones, rather than his tension.

"Where are your courier tariffs?" The slight Germanic infusion of a 'V' in her 'W's had lost its slight sexiness to his ear and gave her the air of a Gestapo inquisitor. He was grateful time had rid him of that phonetic curse but left him with enough inflexion to render him exotic to the British girls.

"I didn't bring them with me." Her eyes and another glare at Bob Bevan, who in turn deflected it in his direction, said it all. Things looked even less hopeful from the airspace where Marcus was now flying by the seat of his pants.

Frau Kopsch raised one eyebrow. "Well, for someone who came thinking we were going to discuss only warehousing, you don't even seem very well prepared for that topic, Mr Lammet."

Bitch. If he could have leaned across the table and smashed her in the face, he would. Fucking West German, trying to destroy his dream. And what was the matter with Bob Bevan? In the UK he'd been all in favour, but here he sat mute, no doubt already preparing his excuses for having brokered this meeting.

She pointed to his iPhone. "Surely you can get your colleagues to scan and email a copy."

"They're out on customer visits today." He didn't sound convincing, even to his own ears.

"So you do have happy customers?" She grinned. Bob Bevan just looked at his notebook. He was a lost cause. "One of the warehousemen then?"

Marcus smiled, hoping it reached his eyes. "Oh, you know what those guys can be like when they're asked to use a scanner or some other hi-tech piece of equipment."

"A massive logistics operation like your warehouse has never scanned a POD, or an invoice, or packing list before?"

He leaned forward again. "Thirty percent savings, Katja; thirty percent. Sometimes in business it pays to think short-term. Money in the bank. Nowadays more firms are seeking to control budget and cash-flow…"

"I'm not about to allow this discussion to become clouded by a debate about capital allowances or business expenses and I sense you would be out of your depth, Mr Lammet."

Frau Kopsch closed the folder on the table in front of her and with a gentle but irrevocable motion of her fingertips slid the paperwork back to him before continuing: "Our Service Level Agreement states quite clearly – twenty percent growth, year on year, in stock-holding, to cover five years. The fact that you are sitting opposite me without even a plan for that is enough reason, I'm afraid, to say no." She rose from her seat. "I'm sorry that this has proved a wasted trip," she said, glancing at both men, "for both of you."

"Could we at least discuss this over dinner? I've reserved a table at the Marie Antoinette restaurant at the Hotel Adler where I'm staying in Hinterzarten."

Her slight nod and pursing of the lips might have registered something close to approval but were a million miles from it. "You have expensive tastes. Who knows whether our thirty percent savings might have been thirty-five?" She glanced out of the window and downwards. "Or forty. I see from that impressive rental car that there is no need for us to book you a taxi. I hope parking such an S-Class monster didn't cause you too many problems in our rather modest, outdated car park." She turned back to face him. "There are other parts of Germany where they ridicule us down here in the south-west for our Catholic ways. You might have done well to take note."

He was already no longer listening; all thoughts bent towards escaping this other monster of his own making. The most sophisticated S-Class would not be enough to get him away from his financial backers; a rather dignified, understated description masking the reality of the money-lending world he inhabited. Katja Kopsch had proved to be the hardest of German nails in what might now be his coffin. Despite appearances in this fiasco of a meeting, he was a man seldom without a Plan B, but this would be a test.

Chapter Three

The phone echoed in the cavernous space. Michael didn't even bother to look at the number. No-one else would have been calling him now; no-one would have dared, even if they had the number.

"Richard."

"Where are you?"

"Inside the big white elephant; the great fucking pit which has swallowed our money."

"Unless Marcus is hanging from the rafters, I assume you've found no sign of him returning to England."

"No – not as far as any of my contacts can tell. But you know what a slippery fish he is. We should never have let him back into the fold."

"Come on, Michael; once in the cabal, always in the cabal… till you betray it – and if he had managed to pull it off, getting our hands on those drugs would have repaid our investment ten times over."

"So, you're telling me you don't think he's screwed us over. Why hasn't he called then?" Treachery whistled in the ensuing silence through the eaves of the empty warehouse, till the flapping wings of squatter pigeons broke it. "No sign at your end either?" Michael found himself talking in a whisper, disliking the way his voice resounded in that shell of a building, as if it reminded him of the potential failure of their venture and the emptiness of their former friend's promise.

"No. The woman he was meeting – a Frau Kopsch – has been out of contact too for a couple of days. But you know Marcus; you know how he works. He's probably fucking her brains out somewhere. She's not exactly going to tell her colleagues, is she?"

"All I know is he's fucking us up the arse!" The last word was barked and sent more wings fluttering up in the roof-space. He lowered his tone again. "I mean, you should see this place. There aren't even any rats. It's just a shell, apart from the old racking. At least it's got that – we can put it to some use, even if it's just to hang him from, as you suggested. It would need plenty of work to pass the pharmaceutical inspections. Doubtless he'd have been milking us for more money for that too – not that I'd mind if he had succeeded." He kicked in absent-minded frustration at a dog-end. "You've no idea where he was staying?"

"No, but I will find out – you know me. Can we sell the place; get our money back? Milton Keynes is just down the road – there seem to be a lot of big companies there. The real estate must be worth a bit."

Michael looked around at the walls; took in the crumbling, uninspired, prefabricated structure. For just a moment he might have been back in some old Eastern Bloc factory; perhaps one of the empty, remote ones that tended to be used for destruction rather than production and often resounded to other cries. What excuse did a town with new money have for this relic? "Don't forget where we came from, Richard." In a better mood he might have smiled at that – after so many years away from the former DDR, they had even started pronouncing their German names in the English way, but some things would never change. "In East Berlin, we would cut throats before we cut losses."

As ever, Richard's calming voice prevented one of Michael's fuses from blowing, offering understanding, support and a more rational viewpoint. "I'll keep searching. This isn't just about some warehousing contract. Our own credibility is at stake. Getting hold of some of those pharmaceuticals would have opened doors. It's not just our money – it's our reputation here. I'll find him."

Chapter Four

Jack Jeffries loved his overseas business trips, but unlike a number of the other executives and entrepreneurs he knew, it wasn't about the business-class travel, the lounges, the pampered long-distance flights to the Far East. He preferred the short hops – Amsterdam, Paris, Bruges, Frankfurt – though they made it more difficult to justify an overnight stop. One had to be careful when one's wife was a major shareholder.

And whose fault is that, Jack?

Maybe she had a lover and couldn't wait for his nights away. He reflected for a moment on the arrogance of some men, who too often assumed dark desires lurked only on their side of the secret door.

Whatever the reality, for Jack, his betrayal of his wife was still painful and always worst on the morning of any departure; seeing her curled up in bed at some ungodly hour, cute as a dormouse, while having to leave the warmth of being beside her to head off and catch some red-eye train to St Pancras or Heathrow. All the love he had ever had for her – had for her still – after twenty-five years of marriage came bubbling up.

His predilections were not her fault. Making love with her had been a genuine thrill, but a less frequent one as the years and familiarity had taken their toll. It was lucky for him that she appeared to have accepted the last couple of fallow seasons as par for the course.

Their love remained strong, as far as he could tell, but he had found increasing difficulty in holding the mask in place. His suppressed appetites had surfaced and now he wandered down a different aisle in the metaphorical supermarket, seeking out the oestrogen-free products.

That was what he loved about western mainland Europe. There seemed a greater intrinsic acceptance, which meant less exhibitionism and in-your-face camp showboating that often seemed to go with the suppressed ideology of the UK. He had his favourite bars, in which he would sit happily with colleagues and clients for a post-meeting drink, the only difference being that when they wandered off, he would hang back and stray.

As he had done this evening, though on this occasion his colleagues from the Stuttgart office had recommended the watering-hole, despite both being, as far as he could tell, in happy heterosexual relationships. Had they read him? He was intrigued; this wasn't one of his usual haunts, although a previous dalliance had mentioned it in glowing terms.

He liked to think he wasn't an unattractive man for his age, but right now, in the SonderBar in Freiburg, even he was flattered by the looks he believed he might be getting from the blond Adonis in the corner. That such a specimen was sitting alone – that was a conundrum in itself.

Jack moved from the table where he and his German counterparts had been chatting. Heading to the bar, he ordered a Disaronno and coke.

It might have been two minutes that passed; it might have been ten. Time seemed to have developed a capricious mind of its own, its sole purpose being to stop you counting the seconds and instead measure your life by your pulse. He sensed, rather than heard, the stool next to him being occupied and didn't dare to turn his head. A surreptitious glance at his watch showed it to be just gone 11pm. The night was young.

The bar was busy enough to be convivial and ensure no-one was paying any particular attention to what was happening, though a few pairs of eyes had been observing him with subtlety. Besides, he had noticed that there were only men in there, and they were mostly in pairs. Under the circumstances, it seemed natural enough that two lonely guys might strike up a conversation.

It was the barman who spoke first: "What's it to be, Dimitri?"

"Vodka – rocks."

Wow! The guy's voice – was that a Baltic accent, so faint it was almost an aroma?

When the drink arrived, Jack allowed himself to watch the hand reach for it, enhanced by the Tag Heuer that was worn without show or effort. There was just a hint of the arm's strength before it disappeared inside the sleeve of a biker-style leather jacket. Jack was now powerless to stop his gaze travelling along that arm, across the muscular chest enhanced by a well-fitting T-shirt, then all the way to the guy's face, where he was met by piercing green eyes. He couldn't be sure that he liked what he saw in them, but then the guy smiled and lifted his glass. "Skol."

Jack raised his own glass – "Prost" – was lost for anything further to say and grateful that the deity called Dimitri filled the silence.

"Where are you from…?"

This had to be a misunderstanding, or a set-up by his German colleagues. The guy gave off no single vibe of being gay and looked at least ten years his junior. Either Jack had aged even better than he thought, or perhaps this was a guy on his own in a foreign city just looking to chat. But in the SonderBar? Yet surely the alternative couldn't be the reality; the one in which Jack would make small talk before being fucked by a muscular, saturnine Latvian, Lithuanian, Estonian, whatever, who could have had his pick of anyone in the bar.

"Well?"

He realised that his companion's silence at the end of the sentence had been a tacit request for his name. Blinking, he gave a slight, confused shake of the head.

"Oh, sorry… Jack. I'm Jack."

This was met with a laugh; a hearty mellow sound that might have melted the ice in both their drinks. "Dimitri… as I'm sure you heard." A hand was extended his way and they shook on their new-found acquaintance. "So, did your meeting go well?"

"It's that obvious, is it?"

Dimitri gestured up and down the length of Jack with his hand. "Everything about you speaks English businessman, but the big giveaway is the suit." He laughed again at his own playful sarcasm. "I hope the fact that your two acquaintances walked off doesn't mean that your…" he hesitated, "… tastes have screwed the chance to do business."

"Oh them!" Jack gestured over his shoulder towards the table he had been occupying. "Actually, they work for me. The business is a done deal. This was just a quarterly review meeting."

"Your quarterly escape." He pointed to Jack's wedding ring. "Do you think she knows?"

Jack wanted to protest but found he didn't have the will; longed to give a truthful response, but realised he couldn't face the answer. "I…"

Dimitri laughed again. "The shortest of all possible answers in the history of language – apart from silence of course — yet it says absolutely everything."

"But it doesn't." Hearing a petulant tone surfacing, Jack cut short his protest. Who was he to feel affronted, when here he sat in a known gay bar, once again seeking the thrill of deception and concealment? Different city, same story… except it was more than that. He pictured Christine, her disordered brunette hair and warm forehead, her weary but beautiful face peeking out from under the duvet as he kissed her and left in the morning. He looked down into his glass. "It doesn't."

He felt a hand rest on his arm. Every inch of his skin and each tiny hair responded, a wave of sexual chills seeking to drown his guilt and confusion.

"I didn't mean to offend," said his new-found Father Confessor, "but…" The pause was emphatic rather than hesitant. "I ask again, do you think she knows?"

Jack was too scared to look up from his drink. He shrugged. "Perhaps she guesses."

The hand released its pressure. How he wanted it to return, only more insistent. He reflected on the curse of conscience, as impactful on the human condition as a Victorian corset. He had been here before, almost unable to breathe through its restrictiveness. However, it did feel different this evening. How could that be? This Dimitri – in a matter of minutes he had laid Jack bare with his charming perception. Yet maybe *charm* had more sinister connotations. He continued to avoid those green eyes. Who was playing the pipe and who was the cobra? Jack sensed danger slithering towards him.

It was as if Dimitri sensed danger too; the possibility that this potential… *lover?… fuck?…* might get up and walk away, because the hand returned and it did squeeze. Such was the impact, that pressure might as well have been placed directly on Jack's balls.

At last, he looked up again and into the man's eyes. They remained just as piercing. Surprising even himself, Jack burst out in sudden laughter. Who was he, to think that this Baltic god might be in the slightest worried if this middle-aged, slightly out-of-shape businessman were to get up and walk out into the night? He was a beautiful man; why not enjoy his attention and see what the night brought, even if it turned out to be only darkness?

He attempted to picture Christine's face disappearing under the duvet again, leaving the dyed brunette hair fanned out across the pillow. She was a natural blonde and had only just coloured it in recent months, saying a few more greys had started to show through.

Why brunette?

"Perhaps she's deceiving you too."

God, was this guy for real?! Did he read minds, or simply use these lines on every latent gay or bisexual he approached? Was there a paradigm when sidling up to men in a bar, or was there a specific facial gesture that indicated your mind had wandered back to the false security of the marital bedroom?

Did it matter?

The hand squeezed slightly as Dimitri continued. "I mean, she might be fucking someone right now." He relaxed the grip a touch and tested the texture of Jack's suit fabric between his fingers. "Nice; Super 180 wool — expensive stuff, maybe eleven or twelve ounces. Perfect. I'm guessing she enjoys a good lifestyle with you." He winked. "You have good taste… and she's a woman; she's not going to sacrifice the dolce vita. Let me guess something – at a certain point, did she start insisting on protected sex?"

Jack frowned. "Well, now you mention it…"

"Is there any sex at all now?"

Jack leaned away a little bit. "Now look, there are a lot of marriages—"

"Oh sure, sure – I'm just saying."

He leaned forward again, dropping the touch of defensiveness. "Well, as I say, it's funny you should mention it, because I was only thinking a few minutes ago, we guys are a bit arrogant. We like our secrets, but you know, for every man having an affair, there's a woman helping him to have it."

"How nineteenth century of you." Dimitri pursed his lips in a caricature of gay pique. Jack wanted to correct himself, but Dimitri laughed; an unnerving response, which was then replaced at disorientating speed by seriousness. "For every guy fucking a whore, there's a whore being fucked."

Jack was still absorbing the misogynistic bluntness of the statement when Dimitri raised a hand, perhaps misconstruing something in his features and said: "Oh, I'm not talking about your wife; my apologies if that came across the wrong way."

Jack took a sip of his drink, but as he did so, Christine's dyed hair, which his imagination appeared to be painting with an increasing number of grey strokes, disappeared beneath the duvet.

"So, what do you do, Dimitri? How does a handsome…" Jack felt his tongue floating away on a stream of alcohol and decided to follow it to liberty. Dimitri interrupted the flow with a raised, self-deprecatory hand, but Jack forged ahead. "Oh come on! – how does a mature, handsome man like you end up sitting alone in the SonderBar?"

Dimitri nodded his head, thoughtful. "I'm a businessman who got really screwed over today and I decided to drown my sorrows. I had no intention to come here on the pull… till I saw you."

Jack grimaced a little and responded with heavy irony while looking around the bar. "Oh yeah – and me being the only guy sitting on his own had nothing to do with it. I'm guessing if some Ryan Gosling lookalike wandered in now,

I would pretty quickly become this evening's fish and chips wrapping." He took in Dimitri's puzzled frown-smile. "Sorry, an old English joke – it means yesterday's news."

"What the hell has that got to do with fish and chips?" The god was smiling.

"It's a long story, out of date and not worth explaining. I just mean—"

"I know what you mean." The hand had moved to the shoulder. This time it rested, both men seeming comfortable with that. "And away with the false modesty, Mr… um…"

"Jeffries." Jack didn't really understand why saying his name should make him laugh, but laugh he did as he extended a hand again.

Dimitri was smiling. "The English; so polite and formal. Such a part of your charm – part of the attraction. I was watching you in your conversation with your German colleagues – I assumed they were German; you can always tell."

"Indeed they were."

"Still, they've gone… and here you are, in a gay bar in a foreign city."

Jack held his inquisitor's gaze. "Here I am."

There was a silence full of promises, some full, perhaps some empty, before Dimitri continued: "Anyway, don't underestimate yourself. You're a good-looking guy. I'm guessing from your demeanour you're late middle-aged, but from your looks…" He looked Jack straight in the eyes with an unwavering stare. Cobra? Charmer? Perhaps both, because Jack felt one way lay danger and the other, control. That suited him; he wanted to lose it.

What the hell did they put in their Disaronno in this place!?

With that unnerving timing once again, Dimitri picked up Jack's empty glass. "Looks like you're well on your way to drowning something too." He caught the barman's eye, gesturing with the glass as he approached. "Same again for my friend here."

"Of course, Dimitri."

The guy wandered off and Jack leaned in closer to his admirer. "This a regular haunt of yours?"

At first Dimitri frowned, but then realised what was being asked. "When I'm in Freiburg." He gestured towards the barman, "But I wouldn't expect him to remember my name. I'm flattered"

"Now you stop with the false modesty." Jack suspected that the alcohol was racing untamed in his veins for a variety of reasons, doubtless accompanied by adrenaline. He couldn't remember feeling this uninhibited before; aware of his English skin shedding by the second. Did that make him the cobra?

An image was recurring; Christine's dishevelled, deceptive brunette hair re-emerging from beneath the duvet, but now turning into snakes, Gorgon-like. Dimitri was right – women were perceptive. She knew his peccadillos; the safe sex; now he thought back on it, the encouragement for him to stay away overnight.

And then, as if someone had taken the ice from his glass and thrown it down the back of his shirt, he jolted as he remembered; one evening, about five years ago, an unusual one for them in that she was drunk and he was not, they fell into one of their increasingly rare sexual clinches – and she had offered him… yes, she had offered him entry to a portal, which had remained closed throughout their marriage.

He had refused, saying she was drunk, but now, on reflection, could he be sure he wasn't being tested, perhaps even ridiculed? How had he forgotten, not just the incident, but her words? Had he chosen to wipe it from his memory; her looking back over her shoulder, slurring a bit as she said: "*What, are you a taker, not a giver?*"

Oh my God!

Dimitri was staring at him. "Are you okay?"

Jack thought about it; nodded. "A trick of memory."

"Your wife?"

The Disaronno arrived. "Enough. Tell me about this issue you had today with your business."

"Quid pro quo, as Hannibal Lector once said." Dimitri smiled. "Tell me about your life in England. Like I said, judging by your suit, you're pretty successful."

"Well…"

"Again," Dimitri interrupted, "one word that speaks volumes. You're a successful guy and modest. As you said, your fellow drinkers a few minutes ago were your employees."

Jack shrugged. "I own a software company."

Dimitri straightened up, his eyes widening. "Nice to meet you, Mr Gates."

They both laughed.

"I wish, I wish – but we're pretty successful. We're called *Mighty*. It's a poor play on My IT."

He moved to take a sip of his drink. Dimitri reached out to stop the progress of the glass. "Actually, I feel some sense of responsibility here. Are you driving? You've had a few drinks already. Despite everything, I wouldn't like to think of your wife as a widow and your kids without a father."

"Ah… no."

"You're not driving? Good."

"No, I meant there are no kids." He paused, frowning, "But no, I'm not driving. Actually, the hotel is…" Jack pointed with a vague gesture, having no idea of the actual direction. He laughed, feeling a certain giddiness. "I don't know where it is, but I do know it's fifteen minutes' walk from here."

Dimitri's mouth turned down. "That's a real shame."

"I thought you said you felt a sense of responsibility." He took a large swig of his drink. Was he being coquettish? It felt liberating, in a shameful way.

"Oh I do," Dimitri nodded, "I just meant that I'm staying in Stuttgart."

"You're not staying in Freiburg?"

"No, my hotel is about one hundred and eighty kilometres…" Dimitri laughed as he mimicked Jack, pointing in a haphazard way, "that way."

Jack could tell the alcohol was loosening them both up. This was promising to be a night of booze and taboos. He was about to congratulate himself on his little play on words when the penny dropped. "So how were you planning to get back tonight?"

"A late train – or early, depending on your point of view." Dimitri glanced at his watch. "My hotel's the Loewenpick, right by the airport."

It was like watching someone else's hand as Jack reached across to touch Dimitri's arm. "I won't hear of it. Why don't you stay with…" God, what was the matter with him? "… take a room at my hotel and I'll drop you at Stuttgart in the morning when I'll be sober. My flight is out of there too. That way we can continue our conversation tonight."

Dimitri looked down at the hand resting on his arm. "I've got a better idea. Why don't I walk with you to your hotel. We can pick up your car and I can drive us over to Stuttgart."

"Why?"

"I think, for the sake of your reputation, it would be better if we were away from Freiburg and any possible interaction with employees or acquaintances of yours." Dimitri drew his gaze from the hand and into Jack's eyes. "Besides, you'd be closer to the airport in the morning."

Jack swallowed hard. There was a sudden panic. Had he stepped into a minefield? "You've been drinking too. There's a great bar at my hotel – and they serve food through the night; my treat."

Dimitri raised both hands. "I couldn't possibly."

Fuck me? thought Jack. *Oh yes you could.* "Oh yes you could," he said.

Chapter Five

Visitors to the maze at Fanleigh Hall on the morning of Reginald Wood's horrific discovery found an additional obstacle blocking their attempts to get to the centre; blue-and-white police tape, preventing them from entering at all. Of course, this didn't stop a small crowd gathering on the off-chance of seeing something gossip-worthy, but it was less than a faint hope, absurd in fact, as it would have taken rubber-necking to a new level, given the object of their interest was at the heart of a labyrinth.

Detective Inspector Morris turned to his junior officer, DS Billings, as they watched from the windows of the Hall, its elevated position giving them line-of-sight across the massive grounds.

Billings responded to his DI's question: "I did, sir – I told them to leave. I said the maze would remain closed and that any attempt to enter it would be potentially interfering with a crime scene."

"That's the weird thing," said Morris. "I doubt it is the crime scene, given the lack of blood and…" he paused, "… a body."

Billings glanced across at him. "I take your point, sir."

Both now turned their heads at the sound of the door behind them opening. Into the living room came the head gardener accompanied by Lord Evesham himself. They watched as His Lordship directed his employee to a seat by the fire and proceeded to pour him a large brandy, after which he gestured to the two officers to take a seat.

Morris took up the questioning: "Mr Wood—"

"Reginald has had a traumatic experience," Lord Evesham interrupted. He had remained standing, hands clasped behind his back, and he rocked onto his toes as he spoke.

"I just have a couple of important questions," said the DI in a reassuring tone. "There is no suggestion that Mr Wood is in any way involved in any wrong-doing."

Morris suppressed a smile as he took in this upside-down vignette of English aristocratic life; a vast living-room, a roaring fire by which sat an elderly, less well-to-do man looking rather pale, glass of brandy in hand, having happened upon an Agatha Christie-esque crime, while another white-haired quintessential English lord waited on him. He found the role-reversal amusing but remembered himself and carried on at a faint nod from Lord Evesham.

"Mr Wood, you found these, shall we call them unusual artefacts upon your arrival at work this morning?" Reginald Wood merely nodded, so he ploughed on. "And you can be one hundred per cent sure they weren't there when the maze closed at 5pm?"

"No sir! I mean no, they weren't there."

Morris turned to Lord Evesham. "Is there any CCTV footage? I'm guessing not, as I didn't see any cameras near the maze."

"No, the cameras cover the house and the gates," replied Lord Evesham, "but if someone were determined to enter the grounds via the fifteen-foot walls, then there's no footage."

"Can you think of any reason—"

"Gentlemen," interrupted their host again, "if you can think of any reason at all for such an obscenity, I'm all ears."

Under the circumstances, that last comment contained an unfortunate, cruel irony which appeared to have escaped the gentry in this instance, but not Morris, nor Billings it seemed, who was staring with great intensity at the floor, doubtless hoping his slight smirk would go unnoticed. Morris tried to chastise himself in silence for his black humour and a lack of professionalism but was failing miserably. He frowned, needing to focus. A dreadful crime had been committed. Somewhere, someone was suffering.

* * *

Twenty-seven months earlier

Another senior detective, wearing a coat and frown similar to his *unbekannt* English counterpart, likewise approached police tape that flapped in the breeze, albeit in different colours from the UK version. Jauch wasn't one hundred per cent sure why he had been called from his warm bed. It had sounded like a common-or-garden fatal road accident when Polizeiobermeister Maier described it on the phone, except the sergeant had imbued it with an air of mystery. He guessed some of these uniforms just didn't like taking responsibility – or maybe they took a secret delight in the idea of dragging their seniors out; misery liked company. In that sense it had backfired, as it was a beautiful late autumnal morning and Jauch had no issue with being out in it.

He was met by a busy scene. The Kartauserstrasse, the road along the north bank of the River Dreisam where the accident had happened, was now closed off and all traffic was being turned around, having to head back to cross the river and continue along the Schwarzwaldstrasse on the opposite side. He watched with a wry grin – the streetcops were certainly good at making their presence felt when it came to bossing around motorists and the general public.

He ducked under the red-and-white tape and then took in the ordered chaos; a tiny universe of pain, swirling, inexorable, drawing ever closer to the travesty of normal life lying at its centre. Even if he hadn't spotted the boot of the car poking out of the water, the dark tyre tracks leading from the road and into the river would have directed his gaze.

He turned to the uniformed officer who had approached and saluted him. "Polizeiobermeister Maier."

"Sir!"

"Drunk driver?"

"My thoughts exactly, sir. There's nothing on the surface of the road that might have caused the car to skid."

"Could have been avoiding an animal, of course."

Across the river, Jauch noticed, despite the earliness of the hour, that there were already onlookers gawping from the grounds of the Strandbad — the lido and restaurant complex on the opposite bank.

"Someone beat them to the early plunge." His comment was directed at Maier and he didn't bother checking whether his graveyard humour, a necessity sometimes in his line of work, offended the officer or not. "Guess he wasn't after the sunbeds."

Jauch strode to the riverbank and noted from the number plate that this was a rental car. He saw that it was also empty. "I assume there was a body."

Maier gestured towards the back of a nearby ambulance. "Time of death appears to have been around 3am."

They made their way over and, at a gesture from Jauch, one of the medical team pulled back the sheet covering the victim's face. There was a livid mark on his forehead, to which Jauch pointed. "From the steering wheel?"

"We'll know more once Forensics have had a chance, sir."

"So, the airbag didn't detonate."

"There appears to have been no collision with a solid object, sir."

Jauch looked back towards the car. "Lucky him." He glanced back at Maier and saw his dry humour had evinced the slightest of smiles. "And the identity of the victim?"

"That's why I called you, sir. It's an Englishman," Maier said, consulting his notebook, "name of Jack Jeffries, here on business. Owns… owned an IT company called *Mighty*. Records show he flew in yesterday morning and was due to fly out again from Stuttgart today at around midday. He had a room booked at the Best Western Hotel in Freiburg. Initial observations are that he drowned, though Forensics will confirm whether he was conscious. I'm guessing we'll find he was over the limit. I remembered you telling me, sir, about the time you spent working with the British police, here and in England, on a previous case, so I thought you would like to know."

Jauch nodded his approval. Maier was right – in instances like this it might help to know the English mindset as well as the language. "You've found out a lot already. Was that via the car rental company?"

"No, sir – part of the reason I say he's probably over the limit is that there appears to have been no foul play, in the sense that all his ID, passport, his wallet, money, phone and so on were still on his person, including a keycard for the Best Western Hotel. Of course, he might indeed have swerved to avoid a rabbit or something…"

Jauch frowned; looked around. "So why is he here, heading technically away from Freiburg? You say he'd checked into the hotel."

"Yes, sir."

"Strange then that in the early hours he's driving to… where? I could have understood if he was heading back towards the city. So, was he off to Stuttgart? It's not exactly the most direct of routes either."

"Maybe he had a… liaison, sir. It's not unknown for businessmen."

Jauch shrugged. He reckoned he had underrated Polizeiobermeister Maier. The man had been hard at work and had only called on the detective for fear there might be delicate conversations to be had with people in Britain.

He gave a curt nod. "Good work, Maier. Let me know what the blood tests and Forensics say. I'm sure you're right."

As the uniformed officer moved away, Kriminalkommisar Jauch returned to the riverbank, watching the Dreisam stream sweep by and wondering whether the fate of Jack Jeffries, however great or small its importance, was already flowing away forever in the famous runnels of Freiburg.

* * *

Once again, when the phone rang there was no need for Michael to look at the incoming caller ID. He did sometimes wonder whether Richard took this unbreakable bond of theirs a bit too far at times, but it was just a millisecond of impatience. Deep down he knew his friend was like the stock market – he never slept, certainly not with anyone, whereas Michael had specific needs in that area! At such moments of annoyance, he remembered how the same finger that pressed with such eagerness on the dial-button had more than once reacted with similar speed to save his comrade's skin. Besides, during their formative years on the other side of the Iron Curtain, back when the steel of their brotherhood had been forged in the ice and heat of Communism, whether down ill-lit streets or behind the façade of law-enforcement, speed had often been of the essence, in action and in thought; whether to secure contraband, or in nineteen eighty-nine, to seize opportunity and make it, along with their funds, into the West as different people.

Michael glanced at the slumbering features of the Eastern Bloc slut beside him, their true nature emerging in the absence of make-up and a smile; yet another wannabe, whose flawless complexion, slim body and cheekbones would doubtless snare an unsuspecting loaded Brit at some stage along with her tales of the unkindness and alcoholism of Russian men, of how she wanted to be a good wife – at least until that longed-for passport arrived.

But she was wasting her time with him. Eve would fail in her temptation. He had enjoyed her fruit, and sometime soon another Slavic temptress might find her way into a hotel bed with him, but there would be only one snake and the only Fall impacting on him would always be that of the Berlin Wall, with all it had brought, good and bad.

He extricated himself from beneath the duvet. The girl murmured but slept on, still processing enough coke and vodka to render an army comatose. Picking up the mobile phone, he moved into the bathroom.

"Richard."

"Not a sign of him."

"Scheisse!"

Michael leaned on the washbasin and stared at his dishevelled features in the mirror.

"Let's face it, Michael, he was spending enough time away from us for long enough to have made his own contacts. I've spoken to all our best forgers, but we have to accept, we've been out of that market for a while. There are new kids on the block. There are new means. We've lost him for now."

"Not even a hotel anywhere?"

"Oh sure – I was able to find where he booked in as Marcus Lammet at the Hotel Adler in Hinterzarten the night before his meeting; just his cup of tea, the big-time Charlie. I saw where another chunk of our money went; likewise, I found the Mercedes he hired, because he had to give the registration number when he booked in." Michael sat on the toilet, still listening. "He was out of there and the car was returned as soon as the deal went wrong." He paused. "Let's face it – we fucked up. You were right; we should never have taken him back, but old cabal ties and memories were still strong." Richard paused. "We fucked up in other ways of course."

"How so?"

"We're old school. He was unpopular in the Stasi because he wanted them to buy into new ways. Once we got into the West, perhaps we should have bought into him and the online world more; trusted him more to make it work."

Michael snorted. "Look where that trust has got us."

There was a longer silence before Richard continued. "There was one thing, a couple of days ago."

"Go on."

"A car went off the road and into the river just on the outskirts of Freiburg. It's a long shot, but Marcus' hotel was between Freiburg and Stuttgart."

Michael stood up. "It's him!" he hissed.

"I wanted to think so, also because the dead driver was an English businessman. They were a similar height and build. With the right hair and make-up…"

"The name?"

"It doesn't matter."

"What do you mean?" Michael was pacing now. In the restricted space of the bathroom, for just a couple of moments he was taken back to the Stasi cells.

"All the guy's papers were still on him; his plane ticket, passport. I checked the flights to the UK and no-one flew back under that name – and how would they without the documents? He was just a dead drunken bum – and a dead end." Another silence. "It's pointless to continue looking."

"He's got to be over there somewhere."

Michael ended the call. He stood by the washbasin again, staring at his tired features.

His fist lashed in the direction of the mirror, angry with himself for having allowed this situation to arise through a misplaced nostalgia and then irritated for drawing attention to this room through his violent temper.

Once dressed, Michael left the usual wad of notes on the bed next to the snoring whore. She'd been worth it for the sex; they always were.

"Go find yourself another mug," he whispered, pointing at the money, "or maybe use that to try forging your new life."

He left in silence, apologising in Reception for having slipped and cracked the mirror in the bathroom, while another wedge of cash assured it would never be spoken of again.

Chapter Six

As a wise woman once said: never do anything that leaves you fearing a knock at the door. There is something visceral in our response to it at certain times of day, or when it is unexpected; an illogical, but not necessarily false assumption that it is a harbinger of doom. If the knocking is insistent, so much the worse. As for a hammering, that both pre-empts and echoes our fearful heart.

On this occasion, although there was just a simple rat-a-tat, it still caused Christine Jeffries' head to spin like a ventriloquist's dummy towards the sound. Her stomach lurched. The way the kitchen knife slipped from her fingers, clattering onto the granite worktop, told her something about the state of her nerves, even though nine months had passed since the ditzy melody on her smartphone had proved a totally inappropriate herald of terrible news. Perhaps smartphones were a blessing; maybe one day she would smile at the memory of *You Spin Me Round* being the prelude to such awful tidings, the irony all the more dreadful for the band's name being *Dead or Alive*.

She made her way to the front door, pretty sure the visitor would not be one of Jack's many siblings, with whom he had never had the closest of relationships in a family riddled with dysfunctionality. Jack's will had left her, but no-one else, sitting pretty where finances were concerned. Perhaps because of that, she doubted his brothers and sisters would resurface anytime soon, having done their duty by attending the funeral. Instead, the visitor was much more likely to be another board-member, wearing a mask of civility that failed to conceal his or her frustration at now being answerable to a novice; having to explain the complexities of the balance sheet, management accounts, or the profit and loss account to a grieving woman who lectured in the history of French Art. More than once, she'd wanted to point out that anyone who had studied the excesses and arrogance of Louis XIV and Napoleon was more than well-enough placed to understand the dangers of ill-targeted investment and the importance of cash-flow, but she had held back, not wishing to subject herself to the vacant, idiotic expressions that would have greeted her observations; reflections of an ignorance of world history that was beyond her.

Hearing the way her flat shoes echoed on the wooden flooring as she made her way through the house, she wondered whether her memory was playing tricks, her overactive imagination imbuing with mawkish emptiness the space in which she now lived alone. Surely it had always sounded this way. The sad truth was, although she did miss Jack's friendship, that there had been a void in their marriage for way too long. The ghosts that haunted her space now were as nothing compared with those which had lurked in the shadows in recent years, in particular on the eve of his business trips. There were matters avoided, ignored by two people settling for a comfort blanket instead of writhing in ecstasy beneath one.

Christine possessed enough self-awareness to know that her current tension and grief were exacerbated by the dreadful way in which Jack had died, plus the possibility that each knock on the door might be bringing the revelation that he had been murdered. The police on both sides of the Channel assured her that was extremely unlikely, but they were keeping both a lookout and an open mind. She had felt actual sympathy for the officers in their evident discomfort when they advised her that there were suggestions Jack had been the recipient of some attention in a gay bar in Freiburg on the night of his death. It was proof of nothing, but they were nonetheless keeping a watch at ports and airports for a man of the description given by one or two patrons of that bar. So far they had drawn a blank, but they would give it more time.

She had loved Jack, truly she had, and it brought her to tears almost every night to know that she was moving on, overcoming her grief way too fast, but there were games in which she needed a chip now, before she forgot the rules. Whisper it quietly – a woman had needs.

She opened the door and was shaken by the extent to which she had been suppressing, or ignoring, those needs.

How readily she smiled, while her stomach lurched at the sight of the stranger in a suit. She had to resist a crazy impulse just to step aside and invite him in.

He responded to her smile with a hint of embarrassment. She glanced at his left hand, the ring-finger, saw the dreaded glint of gold – God, what was the matter with her!? Had someone pulled out the cork while she wasn't looking? The concatenations of all her desires for the immediate future seemed to stretch out beyond his shoulder and down the road, past what she assumed was his

Porsche Macan, a vehicle that told her this was no fortune-seeker after her newly inherited wealth.

She wanted this man to take her to bed; *now* would have worked well, but under the circumstances she would have settled for *sometime soon*, knowing that, as with all our deepest desires, it was never going to happen.

She wondered whether this short history of her life to come was written all over her face.

"Hello?" In that single word of greeting from her lay all the absurdity of repressed womanhood and human life in general, as indeed it did in her sudden concern about the state of her hair and whether she, as a recent widow, should have been smiling with such ease.

"Mrs Jeffries?"

She guessed that would still be her. "Yes?"

He couldn't be police, could he; not in a Porsche Macan?

He extended a hand. "Joost de Boer." There was the faintest of accents – from the name she took it to be Dutch – almost non-existent, but just enough to set the hairs on her arms and neck on end. "Please excuse my intrusion at this difficult time. I knew your husband. It's possible he never mentioned me. My sincerest condolences for your loss."

That little thrill of anticipation turned to the chill of dread. Many of Jack's overnight stays had been in Amsterdam… but no, surely not. Her gaydar just wasn't registering. She tilted her head and frowned, waiting for the data, but her instinct was telling her otherwise.

She held back from inviting him in and he seemed to pick up on her reticence, continuing: "I'm not surprised you don't know or trust me. Jack and I talked on a few occasions about going into business together in website design. It was a little side-project of his. In the end it came to nothing, but we stayed in touch; met up from time to time in the City for a beer."

"Which city?" It came out with more mistrust than she intended.

He responded with a shrug, a smile and a hand extended as if towards some mythical site of pilgrimage. "The City – London."

"Oh… you live here."

"Yes, have done for many years."

There was a silence that edged towards awkward. He broke it. "Anyway, I have only just heard the terrible news and wanted to offer my condolences." He paused. "I'll be on my way."

"No." She cringed at the over-eagerness of her response. Something in his eyes suggested it hadn't escaped him. She gestured towards the hallway and, given the awkwardness of some of the exchange at the door, found herself wondering whether her first response to seeing him, a wordless invitation to have sex, might not have been the best plan after all. "Please, you've been kind enough to come over. Forgive my ill manners. Would you like a coffee?"

He inclined his head. "If you're sure – only if you have time."

"Please, come in."

As he stepped past her, his athletic bulk and the smell of him filled her senses with such force it sent the edifice of widowhood crashing; the friendship that had replaced passion in her relationship with Jack lay in fragments. The settling dust failed to conceal the foundations of her relief – she still had it in her to feel and long for something. With that in mind, she had to question, only half in seriousness, who might be in the greater danger as she allowed him in; the unexpected stranger or the frustrated, predatory widow?

He was speaking as she followed him into the living-room: "And who's this lovely fellow?" Joost had crouched down and was fussing Tyson, a genial Labrador whose name had been chosen with massive irony. He was curled by the open fire and lifted his head in acknowledgement before resting it again on his paws and enjoying the fussing hands of the stranger.

"He's missing his dad."

Joost stood. "Yes, I was shocked. What exactly happened?"

"It seems simple enough. Jack was massively over the drink-drive limit and appears to have lost control of his car. He ended up in… I think it's called the Dreisam River that runs through Freiburg. It looks like he didn't have his seatbelt on…" she said and paused, "… which is odd given the horrendous, insistent noise modern cars make when you forget to wear it."

Joost seemed to weigh up what she said. "A fair point. Maybe he had the radio on."

"Anyway, he seems to have struck his head on the steering wheel and then…" She needed to pause. The edifice might have crumbled, but that didn't make the images of her husband's death and the loss of his friendship any easier to take. "Death by drowning was the initial verdict."

"I'm so sorry to hear that." He paused as if doing a double-take. "Initial?"

"Yes, they are still keeping an open mind in the light of him possibly having been picked up in a gay bar that night." She couldn't tell whether his look of bewilderment was for her benefit but pushed on. "On reflection, I would be less upset to hear that he did die by misadventure rather than by murder."

Seeing the utter discomfort in her visitor's eyes, she gathered herself together. "I'm sorry – too much information."

"No, I—"

"It's okay. I'll just go and make that coffee."

"Again, only if you're sure."

She felt the sadness of her smile. "The only thing I'm not sure about is whether it shouldn't be something stronger."

* * *

He was turning out to be remarkably good company; also a Father Confessor, though whether in anticipation of sin rather than penitence, she didn't yet know. Her family and friends had proved singular failures in helping her to unburden herself, but then again, perhaps that was always a role best filled by a stranger – no precondition or prejudice; neutral eyes that saw you without the entanglements of history.

He listened well and boy did he need to! She had turned to the 'something stronger' much earlier than might have been wise – gin; mother's ruin as it had once been known, though under the circumstances, given that she was unburdening herself to a man called Joost she preferred to think of it as Dutch courage. Even Tyson had moved from the fire and decided to curl at her guest's feet; if ever there was a nail in Jack's coffin – she shrank inside at that unwelcome image – that was it.

There was only one thing stopping her inviting this man into her bed – she wasn't yet sure that desire was mutual. She had been out of the game a long time and yet… and yet, did you ever lose that instinct? However, in the light of her doubts, she pushed on.

"So, were you actually friends? It's unusual that he never mentioned you – at least not that I remember." Something in his eyes told her the question was clumsy at best and she raised a hand in apology. "I'm sorry – that sounds insulting. I'm a bit paranoid."

He just smiled. "Why wouldn't you be? I'm well aware you're in a sensitive place; I mean, recently bereaved, still in shock…" As he paused, his frank stare jolted her. "… I assume. Have you been left holding the baby? Jack did once tell me you're a major shareholder. I'm guessing that's changed to *the* major shareholder." She nodded but said nothing. "A man you've never heard of turns up at your door claiming to know your husband. If you trusted me at this moment, I'd have to question your previously undoubted intelligence."

Again, he smiled – *disarming* didn't do it justice, *disrobing* might have done.

She didn't know what hormones were messing with her, but she wanted nothing so much as for that smiling mouth, trustworthy or disingenuous, to be paying lip service on her whole body. Was this a symptom of the shock he had just referenced; some primal equivalent to the need for a comforting hug, pared down to sharp-edged desire by five years in a sexual wilderness?

She shifted just a little in her seat, aware that, if he had any ability to read women, then she had opened the book of her life when she opened the door.

He took another, perhaps rather studied, sip of his coffee and the fates chose that moment to mock her as the glow from the fire glinted on the wedding ring. If ever there was a light warning a ship away from the rocks, that was it.

She sailed on regardless and he continued, "We were business acquaintances first and foremost, but he would often give me a call if he was going to be near Camden – that's where I live." There was a discordant note somewhere, but his next question pushed them on past it for the moment. "How are you handling things? From what he told me you're an academic; a PhD, not a CEO."

She took another sip of her gin and then laughed, gesturing with the glass. "As you can see, I'm not handling it very well. I'm as well-prepared as any lover of the history of French art can be for running a software company." She gave a slight snort, though whether with laughter or derision wasn't clear to either of them. Hidden in there for sure was the sound of self-pity, but she believed she was owed a bit of that.

There was sympathy in his eyes. "More cultural exchange than currency exchange then." It was a try-hard play on words, but somehow it made her feel better. Sometimes in gentle humour lay an antidote to heartbreak.

"There are a couple of…" she looked long at him; felt tears stinging, "… pricks – people I'm sure he thought were friends – who've been on at me pretty incessantly to surrender my shares and get on with what I really want to do in life." He didn't respond, so she continued. "If they had just waited, shown a little more savoir faire, then that's probably what I would have done. But there's a stubborn streak in me, so now, as the major shareholder, as the owner of the company, I make them dance to my tune a bit; you know, report to me. Effectively, they have to run the business — it's not in their interests to let it go down the pan – and I let them continue to drop broad hints." She took another sip of her gin, aware it was affecting her speech pattern a little, but willing to make the sacrifice of a loose tongue in return for the release of tension. "I haven't decided what I'm going to do yet. All I do know is, the new university term is about to start and I need to finish my preparation for that. Demands of selfish undergraduates wait for no-one."

He leaned back and laughed, a movement and sound that sent tingles to all the important places. "The unsympathetic minor shareholders of the future." She echoed his laughter, while he appeared to be contemplating something. "French art, eh? Well, what could be more appropriate? As Suger said, *L'esprit terne se lève à la vérité à travers les choses matérielles.*"

She knew her mouth had opened in astonishment. In the midst of this intellectual repartee, the only word that summed up how she felt was *gobsmacked.* However, Joost just lifted his coffee mug in salutation. "Well, kudos to you. And look – as one company owner to the other," he said, the downturn of his mouth suggesting massive self-deprecation and not a little irony, "if you ever need any advice, or just want to compare notes, let me know." He hesitated before adding, "untrustworthy though I am. I have some knowledge of the IT world; not to the same extent as your… Jack."

The single dark syllable of her husband's name moved across the sun and a black shadow seemed to fall across a room which had just been lit by laughter. With it returned the discordant note from earlier.

"Why would Jack head to Camden?"

Joost's frown told of many things, none of them easy. The relief she felt on seeing that was something of a contradiction; one of those moments when the thing you've been fearing turns up to give that bony-knuckled knock on your door. The ghost had arrived; exorcise it.

"As I said, it's where I live."

That was his first evasive response. She looked him straight in the eyes and he held her gaze, before appearing to come to a decision and continuing: "If you're asking me whether he was there because he was gay, then I'd say yes – but then you knew that, didn't you?" Her complete stillness must have told him everything he needed. "It's written in your lack of despair. It's there in the fact that you have gone back to being the blonde you are, rather than dyed brunette he told me you had become. Is there a woman alive who's completely unaware if her husband bats for the other side?"

The sudden mercilessness threw her, repeat blows doubling her over. She needed to retaliate. "Does that include your wife?"

36

Even before she had completed the line, she hated the weakness in her rather sulky response.

He raised his left hand, fingers spread wide. "This…" he said, removing the wedding ring and pitching it on the wooden floor, where it rolled for a moment, protracting the tension, winding it up. Tyson looked up at the source of the disturbance, before resuming his dozing. "A relic from a dead past. I wore it in case my sudden appearance at your door caused you concern. I am a loyal, one-team man."

He stood, a sudden movement that alarmed her, but the situation was defused somewhat as he crouched and muttered to Tyson. Still stroking the dog, he continued: "There are certain clubs in Camden, which he liked to frequent." He smiled. "Where he wouldn't feel out of place in his Super Wool suits. They were harmless enough drinking venues, but at a certain time of evening I used to make my excuses." He stood up again. "As indeed I will now. It's been…" he paused, "… mostly a pleasure. I do apologise if the Dutch in my nature means occasionally I'm a little too direct. My offer of help still stands."

He reached into an inner pocket and produced a business card, which he placed with care on the mantelpiece. Then he moved towards the door of the living room.

She had remained seated. As he passed her chair she reached out. "Please wait – don't go; I'm…"

He did indeed stop and her extended hand hung in the air for a moment, unsure which nettle to grasp, before coming to rest with a misleading gentleness on his arm. He looked down at her. "Shall we leave that sentence unfinished, or try to find it a suitable ending?"

Chapter Seven

The true gauge of the destructiveness of any storm on the island was whether the wheelie bins were still standing or not, so on that basis, this one hadn't been as bad as the forecasters had predicted. Margot could have told them that they'd been overreacting; it had only taken her fifteen minutes to cover the four-hundred yards to the bin collection point. Call that a storm brewing? Thirty minutes was something to make you think about bringing in the washing.

Much more of a surprise was hearing her iPhone ringing as she stepped back into the cottage. Bins might have been movable, but high winds often brought down cell towers. There would be those who assumed, of course, that any sign of a signal would be a shock, but actually the service was pretty good these days according to the longer-term residents. Nevertheless, the internet continued to redefine *slow*, though that, naturally, was part of the attraction of this beautiful spot.

But it was the very fact of a call that threw her.

Her retreat from society had been an unqualified success; no morons with lenses here, camping at her garden gate – no gate in fact; just rugged stones, deformed trees and the pounding sea. Nipping out unnoticed for a pint of milk caused no problems. No-one cared who she was; no-one knew anything. She was just Margot at Banntraich Taigh; the surname Foye meant nothing to them, as far as she knew. In truth it meant nothing to her, as she had grabbed it from the air, throwing it across her identity; a protective cloak in case fame had ever decided to come calling – and had it ever!

Popping out for any groceries had a different interpretation on this island anyway. The milk, for example, involved a quad-bike trip of fifteen minutes to the dairy farm, which sat in isolation almost as magnificent as her own. If Hamish Innes, who owned the farm, had any idea who she was, he hid it well. That journey was as far as her adventurousness stretched. She had a boat but found fishing wasn't for the soft-hearted when, on the odd occasion casting a line had brought her success, she had returned her catch to the sea.

Perhaps life on Harris was indeed so insular that even people who had read her work didn't understand half of what she had written, or at least the concepts involved. Maybe they had sussed who she was but were just being polite; after all, there was a high percentage of Catholics on the island. She found herself hoping the raunchy, dark deviance of her multi-million selling novel hadn't reached these shores, at least not in any way that would draw a link to her. There didn't appear to be any copies in the local library. Then again, perhaps the story had found huge popularity as a salutary lesson in the pitfalls of sin and was therefore always out on loan – at least, that might be the excuse for those using it as an instruction manual! The thought caused a momentary grin.

All joking aside, the success of her novel had been a double-edged sword, hacking to pieces the life and friendships she had once held dear, but then – huge irony – providing the financial wherewithal to escape. Harris might not have been for everyone – not on days like this – but when the storms passed it was God's own garden.

Only three people from her former life knew about her sanctuary on this island; her mother and her agent were two of them, but the toy dog showing on her phone now, the profile picture of the third person, set her heart racing more than any wild weather. As usual, she wanted to ignore his call; as always she saw her hand reaching for it, unable to resist.

How dare he? Weeks, months, she had heard nothing and then up he had popped again – and as much as she wanted to dismiss him, she had welcomed him with open arms; with open everything. The fact was that she could never erase from her memory the technicolour images of that couple of nights in London, one against the outside wall of a bar, one in a hotel. Sex and room service – she'd been able to disappear, already fleeing the uncontrollable monster that had ridden in on the tsunami she had created. Sixty million copies and counting; proof that the hunger, in particular the female appetite for a good pornographic novel, was whetted and in need of feeding. In fairness to him, his absence spoke of someone not interested in eating her out of house, home and fortune.

The one benefit of being an author was that few people recognised your face. For sure, he had seemed unaware who she was as he'd talked with her in that bar, though his opening line had then suggested otherwise. For her it had been a breath of fresh air not to be asked anything about writing, her characters, fame; she had allowed herself instead to become lost in the beauty of his face, the slight exoticism of his indefinable accent and the almost hormonal intensity with which she fell in lust with him.

She had not hesitated to fuck him and oh boy… nothing she had envisioned in *Kingdom Cum,* her monolithic contribution to the underworld of literotica, had prepared her for their two nights of unbridled passion.

She wondered now whether she had retreated to this island because she knew he could never be hers – could never be anyone's – in perpetuity and she would never replace what he gave her, so she would put herself beyond the temptation to search. Such unbridled physicality was not the stuff of cosy relationships; it was a flower on a mandrake.

It seemed the flower was about to bloom again.

She lifted the phone with care, using such parts of her fingers as were not covered in muck.

"Well hello… I'd be lying if I said I wondered whether you might call." She listened to his lies; was glad there were some things she could rely on, including the proof, in that ache between her legs, that her body's age had not yet betrayed her. "Yes, it's been a while… oh, I don't know, I lose count… it's strange that a part of me misses worrying about money, how perverse is that? So when will I see you?… I look forward to it… you know…" she hesitated, "you know… I need you to know, there's been no-one else."

The call ended. As on every occasion, she hoped never to hear from him again and despaired that she might not. Like a creation from one of her books, she both longed for him and feared what might happen if their paths ever crossed again.

As usual, she hated her continuing need for him only a little less than she hated herself and, once again, the island sounded desolate for a few minutes, while the devil hurled his spite at her windows. Her world seemed barren and in need of a storm.

***

You could check the time on your phone but nothing spoke of elitist disapproval as much as an impatient glance at an expensive wristwatch.

Natalie Savage suppressed her smirk and watched the arm sporting that Jaeger-LeCoultre timepiece return with ill-concealed annoyance to rest on the boardroom table, where the fingers resumed thrumming a tattoo.

As Lancelot Greene's PA, she would never let him see the pleasure his discomfort gave her. He might have been an arsehole to work for, but she wasn't about to kill the goose that laid the golden egg. Salary-wise she was punching above her weight. Life for her boss had been intolerable enough answering to Jack Jeffries; an Etonian having to doff his cap to an entrepreneur. Besides, in that respect she and Lancelot had a certain kinship. He, too, had swallowed his true feelings for his boss, concealing the hatchet beneath the considerable wedge the company's success brought him. Even the families of those who attend Eton can fall on hard times, courtesy of a drunken disgrace of a father.

However, impossible though it might have seemed, the situation regarding Lancelot's answerability had worsened after Jack's tragic death – and it *was* a tragedy for he had been well-loved by nearly everyone else – when his wife, a *"bloody academic"* had assumed control, in the loosest sense of that final word.

She was out of her depth. Everyone knew it but Lancelot had now brought that aforementioned hatchet gleaming into the daylight again. In the nine months following the dreadful news, having allowed what he considered a suitable period of mourning, he had tried everything to persuade her to relinquish control in favour of the two other directors who sat at the table now, prodding at their respective iPhones and tablets in the uncomfortable silence; the offence they felt at the late arrival of the new non-executive director, whose appointment had been the last straw for Lancelot, barely concealed.

Then, as if he had read Natalie's mind, he spoke: "For God's sake, can't he be on time for once? The client's going to be here in ten minutes."

Various pairs of eyes glanced up, before returning their attention to the devices in front of them. Everyone had said everything their consciences and vast pay-packets would allow. Lancelot pressed on, "I still don't understand his appointment; his presence."

Gwen Beardsmore looked up: "If you don't, Lancelot dear, then you're not the intelligent man we assume you to be." Lancelot looked affronted but stayed quiet. "You pushed her too hard. Now one of her husband's... one of Jack's old acquaintances has stepped forward to represent her best interests." She paused, her eyes fixed on some distant point. "He's not without his uses for us as a company," a further beat of silence, "and I'm not talking about his software knowledge, which is adequate, but from a PR perspective."

She turned back to her tablet.

His uses, thought Natalie, again suppressing a smile. She knew the exact point in the distance on which Gwen's eyes had fixed for a moment. *His uses*

– a good euphemism. The guy was gorgeous, even to her younger eyes, and if Lancelot couldn't comprehend why a woman like Christine Jeffries had appointed Joost de Boer as a non-executive director, then that was his failing as a human being.

Oh yes, they had checked him out; he was a consultant. His CV, for want of a better term, seemed to stack up. Yet Natalie would have sacrificed a portion of her salary to have him in the sack, even though he was a good few years older than her. He was hot, clearly kept himself in shape and though the board members were somewhat dismissive of his business acumen, when it came to *the business,* she was sure Christine was not being disappointed. Natalie didn't know whether Joost was installed in Castle Jeffries, but she could sure as hell guess where he parked his car every night, in both a literal and metaphorical sense. All of which made him just the man for the job, reporting back to her, protecting her shares and giving AOB a new meaning. There wasn't a part of Natalie that didn't understand Christine's motivations. There were lessons to be learned.

As if she had rubbed a lamp, or equivalent, up he popped. There was a tap at the door and in walked the man of her naughty dreams.

"Oh man, I do apologise!"

She loved the way that Dutch accent had the paradoxical effect of rendering his idiomatic expressions utterly charming; but the fact that he had directed his apology towards her first might have played a part in that. What was she to read into that, if anything? She smiled but dropped her gaze and glanced at the others; noticed that the fact wasn't lost on Lancelot, who was struggling to retain an air of civility.

De Boer continued: "I lost an earring." He moved to his chair, having rendered the others speechless. "I mean a cuff-link." He sat and then made an apologetic gesture with his hands. "I'm joking on both fronts. Again, I'm sorry; I'm just late."

With her head still bowed, Natalie took surreptitious note of the impact of his words on the others. Lancelot's face had continued to redden and he struggled to maintain his impassive air. Duke Burgess burst out laughing. He was American – what else with that name? – and he got it; the irreverence was so out of place in a British boardroom. Besides, he was old, wise and intelligent enough not to feel threatened by the upstart. Gwen Beardsmore remained sphinx-like. She was of the woman-in-a-woman's-world school; the one person with whom Natalie never risked sharing. Csilla Molnar, on the other hand, would be leaving a stain on her thong right now. When Joost had glanced across at her and winked she'd shifted in her seat; always a giveaway. Had he already? Well, much as men thought with their dicks, she doubted he would be so stupid as to jeopardise his status as long as Christine Jeffries ran the show, or rather, as long as he was her locum. The male of the species was driven by one overwhelming, overweening need, but still, surely he wouldn't.

Would he?

She sat stroking her chin with one finger and looking at Csilla. The woman did have everything, didn't she? The Slavic cheekbones, no hint of cellulite peeking from beneath the short skirt of her power-suit. No husband. Still, he'd looked at Natalie first. She wondered whether no conscience and no boundaries could compete with no cellulite.

Lancelot's words interrupted her reverie. He seemed to be offering an olive branch, which was a surprise, but then again they did need to gather themselves together before the visitors arrived. "I suppose no harm done."

Joost spread his hands. "Hey, I'm sure no harm would have been done even if I hadn't turned up. You guys have all the expertise; I'm just an observer."

It was clever, leaving Lancelot nowhere to go.

The boardroom phone rang. Natalie answered and then turned to the others: "They're here."

Joost inclined his head. "Nick of time, eh?"

* * *

A couple of explanations had already been rebuffed. Right from the outset the meeting had been tense, small-talk minimal to non-existent after the acceptance of a cup of coffee. Biscuits and, it seemed funny-bones, had been left untouched. They had all dealt with Glyn Rose before, Operations Director of Cache 22, IT and software security specialists, but he had brought the owner, Mike Parfitt, with him. It would have been easy to label him as unyielding and pedantic, but he had a point. Most of the detail had gone over Natalie's head, which was now bowed again as she focussed on keeping the minutes and tried to ignore the latest silence. She found herself critiquing the choice of name of the potential client, yet another example, to her ears, of someone looking for an ear-catching solution, but unaware of the nuances; a cache of weapons sprang to her mind or a problem inherently unsolvable.

43

Doubtless this latest silence lasted no longer than five seconds but had them all feeling like the accused awaiting the jury's verdict.

Parfitt broke it. "So, the bottom line is you have no solution."

Now everyone joined Natalie in staring with disproportionate interest at their biros, embossed with the word *Mighty*. A chair creaked. Natalie looked up to see Joost lean forward, elbows on the table, fingers knotted. One index finger disentangled itself to point in the direction of Mike Parfitt. "Well, that could be because we don't know the problem."

Both Parfitt and Rose frowned while the sudden lifting of heads by the others spoke of wary meerkats, their attention drawn to an alarming sound. These were Joost's first words since the opening pleasantries.

"I'm sorry?" It wasn't clear whether Parfitt's response was one of challenge or genuine inquisitiveness.

"You're asking for a solution to something that doesn't exist."

"Terrorism exists." Parfitt's truism sounded rather weak; a playground riposte to an accusation. Natalie watched fascinated. It was the first challenge to his authority during the meeting and he seemed thrown by it.

"That's like saying cancer exists and expecting someone to provide a cure-all." Parfitt opened his mouth to respond, but Joost continued over the top of him. "Look, the security forces and their IT systems are always a step behind the hackers and the terrorists. For example, the shoe bomber; now we all have to remove our shoes, but only a delay at the airport, during which the lighter fluid on his laces dried out, prevented Richard Reid from blowing up that plane. One hundred millilitres limit for fluids in hand luggage; do you think a symposium sat down and came up with that one? It's always reactive. We, this company, are looking to help anti-terrorism organisations plan better. And allocate the right funds and resources. You've seen our cost benefit analysis." Joost tapped the manila folder in front of him; his was the only one that remained unopened on the meeting-room table. "That's exactly what you need in a marketplace where emotion can sometimes rule."

"And in the meantime, it might cost three hundred lives." Parfitt wasn't taking it lying down. However, his features suggested he was welcoming someone standing up to him, like all true entrepreneurs.

"You mean in the same way that it costs dozens of lives sacrificed taking placebos so that cancer researchers can save thousands of them?" As rhetorical questions went, it was tight.

Natalie glanced at Lancelot long enough to see him mourning the death of his dream. She didn't share his total pessimism; though her opinion of Joost was not one of complete objectivity, she felt he had put forward a balanced and eloquent viewpoint.

"So…" For a moment Parfitt seemed lost for words.

Joost leaned further forward. "Look, it's always shits and giggles until someone giggles and shits."

Had she just thought of him as eloquent? Natalie had to admit though, as she stared open-mouthed, there was no denying the balance in that statement!

That morning, she had learnt something about silence – there are so many ways in which an absence of sound can dress an occasion, but the words and actions that precede it are the tailors. This particular moment suggested a cloak concealing a dagger… until Mike Parfitt threw himself back in his seat and burst out laughing. He pointed, wagged a finger at Joost and could only shake his head.

Joost grinned. "Am I right?" He moved the folder that lay in front of him towards the centre of the table. "You wouldn't have come here if you weren't impressed by what our guys have done. But ninety-nine percent is nine percent ahead of the competition. I know you want that extra one percent, but there is no such thing as one hundred percent certainty in life."

"Unless you're North Korean," ventured Parfitt.

Joost inclined his head and made a gesture with his hands that might have been a flower opening or a bomb exploding. "I rest my case."

Parfitt and Glyn Rose exchanged a glance and the latter spoke: "Okay, we need to go away and think about this so…"

"You don't," said Joost.

"I think we do."

To Natalie, the frisson of irritation in Rose's response suggested Joost was now pushing his luck. He didn't seem to have read that the look exchanged by the two customers was the passing of the baton back to the Operations Director. Winning over the owner was one thing, but it was rare they were the decision-makers in the day-to-day business. Jack Jeffries had been an exception to this and she'd watched visiting would-be suppliers make errors there too. However, in the case of Cache 22, Parfitt might have owned the ship, but out on the turbulent waters of business Rose was very much the captain.

It seemed Joost was determined to plough on nonetheless. "You don't, if only because…" Joost looked towards Lancelot, and Natalie could have sworn she saw the old Etonian's mouth slam shut in the nick of time, gathering himself together. "What time are Holmes Security due in today?"

To his credit, Lancelot didn't hesitate and gave a smooth response. "Two-thirty."

He looked back at Glyn Rose. "It's just that time is of the essence. We're a small team taking huge steps. We need to prioritise and if we're to push on, we need to look at our resources too." Now he addressed Lancelot again. "And Holmes are happy with ninety-five percent?" The director nodded.

"I thought you said you were nine percent ahead of the competition." There were no flies on Rose.

"We are. You never play your full hand."

"So you have that other one percent we just talked about up your sleeve and all's well."

It seemed the flies had nowhere to settle.

Joost just grinned at Rose. There was something wolfish about it; likewise the smile with which Rose responded.

Natalie glanced first at Gwen Beardsmore and then Csilla; the fact that the former's lips were struggling to suppress a smile said a thousand times more than Csilla's doe-eyed adoration, though there was ambiguity too. Was she enjoying Joost's occasional discomfort? Natalie toyed with the idea of Gwen as a dominatrix. Her smile remained that of the sphinx.

Never in doubt was Joost's love of being a showman, enjoying the spotlight. Though Lancelot remained less than impressed by the man, there was no question that if this deal could be closed, even he might be for turning.

Rose was looking at his own manila folder, which he now closed with a certain emphasis. One hand rested on it and he tapped a finger in thoughtful percussion. He looked back at Joost. Their eyes locked and, Natalie could have sworn, so did their horns. "Okay look, on the whole what you say makes sense and if you can clarify one thing for me, then I'm sure we can come to an arrangement."

"Fire away," said Joost.

"Well, like all companies considering taking on a new supplier, we believe in due diligence. I was just curious that your last company accounts haven't yet been filed, given that the deadline has passed, whereas before, they appear to have been filed on time. I was hoping the captain of the ship might have been here to explain, as it's happened on her watch following the unfortunate passing of her husband…"

Lancelot interjected: "I'm not sure captain is the right word; she owns the vessel."

"Well, we're just hoping there's no water in the hold, bringing any risk of sinking."

The cup of coffee from which Gwen Beardsmore had been about to take a sip had stopped halfway to her lips when mention was made of the non-filing. Now she replaced it on the saucer. "I signed off those accounts in plenty of time. I'm sure there's just been an administration error."

She turned to Csilla, whose face had been reddening anyway without the addition of the Company Secretary's piercing gaze.

Natalie wasn't very well up on Egyptology, but could tell the sphinx had been replaced by whichever of their gods was the most vengeful. Csilla looked after the accounts; any mistakes in the entries were down to her alone. Any anomalies should have been reported to Gwen, including failure to submit in time, which was pretty much unforgivable given the window was ten months. Of course, as the person responsible for ensuring that the company complied with standard financial practice, Gwen would not come out of this smelling of roses either and that would have been her main concern now. Pieces were already moving on the board of the blame game.

And then there was a tell-tale second when Csilla glanced at Joost.

Oh my God! The question of who would bed him first had been answered. It was a fait accompli. So that raised the question — what was she covering up? Had he been playing fast and loose with the company expenses? From the places he took customers for dinner, the clothes he wore, the car he drove, Natalie knew he enjoyed the good life – what she liked to call a Bertie Big-Bollocks – though she'd assumed he could afford this through his other business interests. She looked at him; he too had a face like an obelisk, but not so granite-like that the slight clenching of his jaw wasn't visible.

The meeting was once again rewriting the book of standards for silences; this one was deep, dark, perhaps dangerous. Joost broke it once more but this time the impact was lacking. "Look guys, we'll check into this. Miss Molnar and I will take this up straight after the meeting." He raised his palms. "I realise a question isn't answered if the answer is a question. But look, the key point is – we're profitable. Don't forget we've invested heavily in R&D for this programme."

Natalie checked out Duke Burgess. If one face told of the monumental fuck-up this accounting revelation now represented, it was his. He, too, was expressionless and that was something rare.

Mike Parfitt sat up straight, his smile redefining the impact of that gesture in much the way a fire redefines wood. "Well then gentlemen and ladies," he nodded around the table, finally towards Glyn Rose who returned the gesture, "we await your clarification and hope that we can continue discussions." He tapped on the manila folder and addressed Duke Burgess. "It looks like an amazing piece of software."

The compliment sounded genuine but no-one was listening. Observing, on the other hand, was seriously in fashion. Natalie couldn't help herself; despite the implications for the company of failing to secure this business, she was fascinated. Lancelot looked in disbelief at Gwen, who glared at Csilla, who glanced with pleading in her eyes at Joost, who watched Mike Parfitt and, Natalie sensed, just about controlled an impulse to punch Glyn Rose in the face; perhaps wipe off the smirk that had formed.

Parfitt got to his feet, preparing to leave and, everyone knew, taking his business with him. It wouldn't matter what revelations Joost and Csilla brought back with them to the table; the customer wouldn't be there. They had been ill-prepared and for that, much though Natalie hated to sanction the reality, Joost had to take huge blame. He should have coordinated this. He was Christine Jeffries' chosen representative at this table. For such a key discussion he should have ensured all the pieces were in place.

It would be fascinating to see how he responded. Natalie hoped it wouldn't be by pointing a finger of blame. Under Jack Jeffries the musketeers' credo had ruled – all for one and one for all.

Yet through it all, Natalie's racing mind saw opportunity.

Chapter Eight

She screams, shedding her skin, discarding something worn out and faded for more glorious colours, and as she does so the distracted thought occurs: be careful what you wish for.

She sees now, to her astonishment, just how comforting and anodyne sex had been before; not just in recent years, but forever. How had she become the person who had settled for that? Surely, we were all born with the same drives and instincts. How did we allow them to be tamed?

Enough of that – she is here and she is now. Guilt and false nostalgia could be sloughed off with that old skin.

She screams again, taken by surprise. I could die now, she thinks – at which point, with obtuse timing, a horrible flash image of Jack's eyes staring from a watery grave tries to impose itself on this moment. So instead of pushing Joost's head away, as she had been about to before the pleasure could kill her, she entwines her fingers into his hair and pulls him onto her, letting his tongue exorcise everything except the ecstatic agony of her nerve-endings.

When at last she pants "Stop... stop... stop!" the past has also drowned beneath waves of frenzy.

She looks down at his smiling, glistening face and hears what must be another woman speaking, not her usual studious, rather dry self. "Be my gigolo." Her heart thumps; her breath is ragged. He laughs. "No, seriously – you need no other skills than that in life." She spreads her arms on the bed in exhaustion and cranes her neck again to look at him. "I'm a wealthy woman – name your price."

He says nothing, but as he rests his hands on the end of the bed, she marvels at the shape he's in. Doubtless, at some point she will find out his age, but right now it is just an abstract concept. His upper body is that of a fit man in his early thirties, the wonderful lines of character on his face speak of someone in his fifties – but the pale blue eyes are ageless.

He pushes himself up onto the bed and slumps beside her. God, how long has it been since she has felt the primal joy of that weight dropping exhausted next to her, if ever? She is about to curl an arm around him when he turns her onto her right side. Now his lips, his breath are tickling by her ear. He runs one finger up the outside of her left leg and on over her hip. "Here's my price," he whispers.

A litany of mild perversions follows, by the end of which her hips appear to be moving with a will of their own. She responds with just one demand of her own – two words – which he duly meets. As she screams again, she wonders who she has become. Only one thing is certain – she will deny him, and through that herself, nothing.

* * *

How different that had been. How long ago it seemed, yet it was just one little year. She lay now, her arm across her forehead, a foolish drama queen. The thought of him showering when he returned from walking the dog and climbing into bed beside her had lost its power to provoke involuntary movements in her pelvis some time ago. She had put it off too long; needed to know. Because a man capable of turning a head as he had turned hers would know he possessed a weapon and would use it for as long as there were needy, foolish, heartbroken women in the world. She had been all of those things, as well as an idiot!

But now it was not just about sex, with its shadowy entourage of wasters and deceivers. Lancelot Greene would no longer be denied and he had been implying things that played on her own selfish fears. He wouldn't elaborate over the phone. Christine was no businesswoman but having read the information her Etonian nemesis had sent through after she cancelled yet another showdown meeting with him, things looked iffy even to her untrained eye.

Poor Csilla! The girl's suicide letter was not something to which she could relate, but that seemed to make the paradox of her own pain all the more poignant. Did coming from a stable, middle-class background mean one's sense of sadness at someone else's desperation was also infused with guilt? If you had never struggled for money it was perhaps not possible to sympathise, in the fullest sense of the word, with someone committing a dishonest act out of financial desperation – or were we all just one ill-advised investment, one threatening letter away from dipping our fingers in the till?

Still, a sixth sense was indeed telling her something else was at play. Added to this were Lancelot's words – it *was aberrant behaviour and a total shock* to him; something he found simply too hard to believe.

She reached across to the bedside table, picked up the iPad and reopened Lancelot's email. This she read for perhaps the twentieth time. The two attachments potentially held the key; two sets of accounts, or rather two versions of the same accounting year, with different details.

According to Lancelot, this was the danger of entrusting one person with the book-keeping. Csilla controlled the day-to-day administration of accounts receivable and payable, payroll and banking. She was also, he implied, completely besotted with Joost. This last fact, he assured Christine, was not something of which he had been aware, but his attention had been drawn to it in the last few days by someone else. He declined to reveal his source or to comment on whether he believed it to be true and Christine might have been grateful in a certain way for his old-fashioned civility, if it hadn't smacked of Lancelot holding an ace up his sleeve. However, he did point out that Joost had been using a company credit card for meals, clothing, fuel and indeed payments for leasing his beast of a car. Csilla controlled all payments to the credit card company and should have flagged up this increasing profligacy.

None of that might have mattered – after all, Christine had not exactly controlled herself when indulging Joost – if the expenses, which totalled almost twenty thousand pounds, hadn't miraculously reduced to only three thousand pounds on the later set of accounts; the one Gwen had signed off and which had not yet been submitted to Companies House.

But there was worse, uncovered by Lancelot once he decided to delve further. It seemed that Csilla had taken out a personal credit card at the same bank used by the company and had been using company cheques to pay it off, while paying off the other company credit cards by bank transfer. That card had been used for meals at exclusive restaurants, rooms in expensive hotels in Central London, trips to the theatre; in short, to finance the good life.

Lancelot concluded by writing that he needed to speak urgently with Christine, insisting his intentions were in her best interests, given her 'close friendship with Mr de Boer' and the fact that Csilla's apparent Machiavellian behaviour coincided with Joost's time in the company. He found the wording of her suicide note, her supposed confession, distressing on many levels. With unexpected eloquence, he remarked how its brevity evoked much more sadness than any lengthy, rambling confession might have done. However, he implied that in his opinion not one of those few words reflected the truth of Csilla's end.

Christine contemplated all of this. How she wanted to believe Joost had no part in it. But while there were compelling reasons for believing Csilla had become desperate – after all, at twenty-five her career was potentially finished – it was hard to take. Yet surely Lancelot couldn't be suggesting Joost had a hand in her death! It was possible she was misusing funds to support his expensive tastes, but he had his own company, plus his salary as a non-executive director of a middleweight company, all topped off with the indulgence of a middle-aged, sex-starved widow who should have known better.

Should have known better. Oh boy! Allied with Lancelot's description of her *'close friendship with Mr de Boer'* this was certainly one of the evening's understatements. Their clandestine marriage would have to be owned up to now. He'd sworn her to secrecy. What a fool. What a bloody fool! She had it coming to her; pressed her eyes with thumb and forefinger at the thought of the sheer humiliation and despair heading her way. Her only consolation, though slender, was that she had arranged for a pre-nuptial agreement to be signed. He hadn't objected. Doubtless he had already planned the manifold ways that he would get his hands on what was hers – from bedsheets to balance sheets in one easy grab.

However, the piece of paper that protected her from embarrassment and shame hadn't been created yet.

At the sound of the key turning downstairs, she slammed the iPad shut, wishing she could have done the same to that front door, and waited.

Despite the tragedy, thirst and trauma of the past twelve months, it seemed almost surreal that one anomalous fact was weighing with her, shaking her out of denial. Yet again this evening he'd walked Tyson, a task that took him two to three hours a few evenings each week…

… and the dog was gaining weight.

* * *

Natalie had to face it – she had a sick mind; surely that was the only explanation. Either that or months of celibacy had driven her lust across a border into a forbidden land. After his role in Csilla's fate – never mind his role, what about hers, getting him access to the accounts so he could cover his tracks, or rather make them seem like Csilla's? – she should have felt repulsed, either by him or by her own needs.

She would have been fooling herself.

On the day of the meeting with Cache 22 she had sensed something below board had been going on, seen it in the look he and Csilla had exchanged; known that if she could help him disentangle himself from it, her bed might seem a safer haven than that of her Hungarian rival.

Was there a risk that he might now turn on her; that her life was in jeopardy as the keeper of his secret? Was this somehow turning her on too?

Natalie was old and wise beyond her twenty-eight years. There was a contingency in place, just in case anything should happen to her; a safe deposit box containing copies of documents. Oh, she was worthy of him! She'd let him know – hinted at it. He'd fucked her harder than ever that night. She'd asked him to choke her a bit. It had been too long since anyone had indulged her. She had dropped to her knees and gestured with the dog-lead. He had refused and there was a look in his eye that told her oh so many things.

God, she was sick. Her only consolation was knowing she was far from alone.

* * *

She peered over her reading glasses at him as he entered the bedroom; didn't want him suspicious as to why she was still awake.

It was all a bit pointless really; there was no delicate way to start this discussion.

"Another marathon tonight; I'm surprised Tyson hasn't wasted away."

"Ja, for sure." He peeled off his jacket.

"He doesn't seem to be though; putting on weight if anything."

"Oh, we just amble. That's why I'm out for so long. Besides, I like the thinking time. You know how Labradors get those bad hips as they get older." He gestured towards the book. "Research for tomorrow?"

"No…" Oh this was pointless. "Lancelot's a bit concerned."

He kept his back to her as he hung up his tie. "Oh yeah? What about?"

"Well, he's concerned that for the first time ever we didn't submit our accounts on time to Companies House, which never gives off a good vibe."

"Ah man, I'm always late with my accounts. It's not going to set any real alarm bells ringing unless you need funding."

"But he's found another set of accounts, on a memory stick he happened upon, which seems to suggest there might have been some anomalies and that might be the reason poor Csilla…"

Even ice-cool Joost couldn't manage it; she watched him with a gaze of microscopic intensity as she made that statement and there had been enough of a pause in his actions to know a nerve had twitched.

All of a sudden, she wanted to get out of bed. Just sitting there was making her feel exposed and her nakedness, for once, added to her discomfort. A terrible thought crossed her mind, try though she did to dismiss it; was that how Csilla had felt, right at the end? She stood up.

"Look, what is going on?" He turned. There was no smile; no pretence. "You put me in there. Lancelot has disliked me from Day One. Csilla looked after the accounts, Gwen signed them off, so why weren't they submitted? Are you asking me?"

"Yes, you! The non-executive director who's supposed to look after my interests. As far as I can see, you haven't. The company's not made the money it should, we've lost a big deal with Cache 22 and…"

He raised his hands; an aggressive motion, though not directed at her. Still, she flinched. "For God's sake, that deal wasn't in the bag. It would have been, thanks to my intervention, if your fucking accounts person had done her job properly…" He stopped himself, looked skywards. "May God rest her tortured soul."

Christine thought she was going to vomit. Though she hadn't been at the scene, there wasn't a day since when she hadn't pictured Csilla swinging, her belt digging into her beautiful neck.

"Were you and she…?" The words were out before Christine knew it.

Joost's eyes blazed. "Don't be so fucking ridiculous!"

She had to fight back. "You and Natalie then?"

"What?" He stepped towards her. Any dust from the embers of what they'd once had circled in his wake. "You're going to say I'm taking Duke Burgess up the arse next."

The spell had broken for good. "I'm beginning to think nothing's beyond you."

He took a further step; she backed away and it seemed her fear made him think better of it. Nevertheless, some obtuse corner of her refused to surrender and she decided to call his bluff. "I followed you one night. I was growing suspicious of your long walks. You were walking Tyson a few blocks to that…" she hesitated – *there but for the grace of God* – but pushed on, "to Natalie's house." He said nothing and there wasn't a single thing she would have wished to hear. "I believe Lancelot, when he comes around tomorrow, will be asking me to step down. If I do…"

He shrugged his jacket back onto his shoulders, retrieved the Tom Ford tie she had bought him from the hook. "I'm gone."

And he was true to his word.

As she heard the front door slam, she sat down heavily on the bed, put her head in her hands and wept, thought whether in sadness or relief she couldn't tell.

"I'm so sorry, Jack; so sorry."

The sound of Tyson whimpering downstairs brought her round. Someone would genuinely miss him. For her, she didn't know what damage had been done and its impact further down the line.

Late though it was – and the irony wasn't lost on her – she took Tyson for a long walk. He had some weight to shed. She chose to go past Natalie Savage's door. Looking up at the windows, she saw the blinds were drawn. Why was she here? Was it to put some flesh on the bones of the bluff she had just called, when she lied about having followed him before?

Reaching into her coat pocket, she produced the wedding ring Joost had discarded on that first visit a year before, in what she now saw had been a melodramatic but shallow, dishonest gesture. She did the same, without the drama, pitching it into the PA's garden. For all she knew, it had found its rightful home.

The next part was much tougher. She found herself many more blocks down the road before she was able to slip her own wedding band from her finger, though it came away easily enough in the cold night air. Given she had hidden their clandestine marriage from the people around them – at Joost's insistence, supposedly for her sake, but oh the gift of hindsight! - the ring hadn't had a chance to carve a groove. Perhaps there was symbolism in that, and the ease with which it slid off, but heaven knew it was still a hard task. He had given her something she'd never had; an awareness and love of her primal self in all its vivid shades.

So it was not without regret that she stopped to drop the ring down a drain. Even then, she found herself laying down some conditions. If it struck a part of the grille and bounced back… but no, that was ridiculous! Still, there were tears as it plunged with unerring accuracy into the sewer. She had to hope the recent months were not already down there to welcome it. Worse still was the thought that the future might have trailed in its slipstream.

Tyson, as was the way with dogs, seemed to sense her sadness and pressed against her legs. Stooping, she hugged him, her only confidante; the one soul, apart from the registrar and two random witnesses, who knew the true extent of her liaison dangereuse.

Chapter Nine

She clung tight to him and he reciprocated, which made her feel good about herself. She doubted Christine Jeffries had satisfied him like this and as for Csilla… well, she had the body and the face, but the poor girl had been too in love and clearly mentally unstable, whereas Natalie was just in lust – always a healthier stance to take.

Now, of course, she had the key to his, well, pants she supposed. It wasn't a very good metaphor, but she wasn't interested in his heart. Yet key was all too appropriate a word. First there was the function key, which had enabled her to access Csilla's emails and delete all those incriminatory words of admiration with which Joost had wormed his way into her affections and then via her bed into the company's profits. Then she had the good old-fashioned metal key to the safe deposit box in which hard copies of those emails now resided. What a stupid, tragic girl young Csilla was. For someone so well qualified, she had provided yet another sad illustration of the power of hard flesh over hard fact.

The strangest part was that once again Natalie had dropped enough hints to Joost that she held said documents, yet it hadn't stopped him fucking her. In fact, it was as if he saw in her a fellow traveller along the road to Hell.

Natalie wasn't from the wrong side of the tracks but there had been no privilege in her life. She reflected on the word *power*. As a philosophy and literature student, the words of Nietzsche had found embodiment in her when he talked of *The Will to Power*. Jack Jeffries' death had been unfortunate on more than one level. As with Joost now, she had also been the keeper of his secrets and then, just like that, there had been no-one left to betray. Not that she would have done; she had loved Jack like a daughter loves a father, but that didn't stop him knowing what side his bread was buttered. She'd never wanted a directorship, with all the hassle it might involve. No, the above-average salary was more than enough compensation. Ironic how Csilla had once questioned, over a quiet drink, how Natalie had achieved such remunerative status. *Look and learn*, she should have said. Look and learn. If anything symbolised Csilla's abject failure to do so, it was the cold place in which she now lay, rather than this hot bed.

"I have to leave for a while."

The explosion from the bursting balloon was almost audible.

"What?" She released her hold. He withdrew and lay next to her. She propped herself up on her elbow. For perhaps the first time as they lay naked, his face was the sole focus of her attention. "What do you mean *for a while*? Define *a while*. Why?"

And then it was as if, for the first time, it registered that he hadn't brought the dog. From the moment of his call saying he was on his way over, she'd thought of nothing but sex and they had not even made it to the bedroom for the first helping. The lack of a dog hadn't featured in her fantasies. But it was Wednesday; Wednesday was always dog night due to Christine Jeffries' out-of-hours commitments.

Natalie put two and two together, hoping she was making five: "She doesn't… hasn't…?"

"I'm afraid yes is the answer to both questions. She confronted me tonight; said she'd followed me a few nights ago and saw me coming here. She'd grown suspicious about the long dog walks."

Natalie slumped onto her back. "Oh my God!" Around her she could almost smell dust, feeling the walls of the mighty palace starting to crumble. She didn't know what had hit her the hardest, but it needed only a brief reflection; Joost was one of the statues in that palace. That above-average salary, upon which she had just been reflecting with such satisfaction, might now be nothing more than a handful of loose banknotes lying in the debris and stirring in the breeze of the coming storm even as she watched.

She sat up. "But you didn't admit it… didn't tell her… weren't stupid enough to—"

His hand on her throat cut her short. "Shut up and calm down." His voice stayed even and was the more menacing for it. "Stop fretting. Be a good girl and I can make sure you're not dependent on the bitch for this." His eyes took in the luxury of her bedroom.

Now he released her. She put her hands to her throat and thought of Csilla. She remembered the times his hands right there had made her orgasms more frenzied.

There was something else – his accent seemed to have taken on a slight change; grown a bit more guttural.

Who was he, Joost de Boer — a name is merely the title of a book – this guy capable of stripping her bare with one fell swoop, leaving her feeling naked, vulnerable and alone? Perhaps the most telling thing was the way her mind wandered again to the copies she had kept of his email exchanges with Csilla. How to pick the moment to remind him she had them, just in case?

In case of what, Natalie?

Was this an admission that she'd known, all along, he might be dangerous? Had that been part of the appeal where the sex was concerned? But there was danger, too, in telling him. He might see her as a threat. The papers and memory stick were in two separate safe deposit boxes at different banks. Tucked away in there, they were less of a problem for him, particularly if she wasn't around. Lying that she had a contingency plan in place in the event of her death was tantamount to accusing Joost of being capable of murder. Either way was a mess. She saw now that those pieces of paper could be, best case, her Get Out Of Jail card, worst case, her death warrant.

She refocussed, referencing his comment: "What do you mean *not dependent*? You'll have a place for me in your own company?"

He reached across to the bedside table, took a cigarette, lit up. She masked the irritation this caused her, realising it would now seem sullen at best, but it was symptomatic of just how much the view from her window had changed in perhaps one minute.

"That was just a side-show. I have money invested; big money. That's why I need to lie low, in the UK at least. I can't afford to be embroiled in any internal investigations. So, like I said…" He sat up and put a finger to her lips, "… keep your mouth shut – about everything." His eyes brooked no contradiction. "Csilla did what she did. I knew nothing about the credit card but I did know that she was, shall we say, imaginative with my expenses. I can claim I know nothing about it; that she did it out of love – after all, I submitted all the bills. Technically, I haven't been fired. They have no grounds to do that. I've just been thrown out of the boss's bed. I think if I stay away for a while, it will give them a chance to let things settle."

His accent was disturbing her, in the sense that she couldn't nail it down. Who had she been fucking? It did not, however, distract her from her main concern. "What about me? For fuck's sake, the owner thinks I've been sleeping with her lover."

She saw his mouth open, knew he had been about to say something of which he then thought better.

"She can think what she wants; she can't sack you for it." He put a hand on her shoulder. How she wished it brought her comfort. "I'm telling you, stay calm. If she tries firing you, she has no grounds, whether in terms of your conduct at work or your performance and she's hardly likely to want to broadcast her shame to the world. Besides, as you once told me, there are things about Jack Jeffries she wouldn't want getting out and not only to spare her own embarrassment. We might be in a more permissive age, but there are still plenty of hard-nosed homophobes out there." He looked her in the eyes. "I'm one of them, so believe me, I know." His gaze grew more intense. "Look, play it right, wait for me to return and I will make you richer than Mighty Software ever could."

In the midst of everything, her own greed shocked her. The thought that she might end this whole affair wealthier than ever excited her, as did the fact of his having understood her needs. He had laid himself bare too. Perhaps they were meant for each other after all. Sex and money – did it really ever come down to anything else, this life?

He dabbed the cigarette in the ashtray, turned and pushed her firmly down onto the bed. For the next few, wild minutes she marvelled at the pull of danger – its all-consuming fire – and when she found herself placing his hands on her throat again, she knew that, no matter what she told herself, she was the one in chains, he the one with the key.

A random thought came to her – she had once contemplated joining up to a dating website. On reflection, just what the hell type of guy would she have described herself as looking for?!

Chapter Ten

Bella took the child-sitter's hand in both of hers and hoped her guilt wasn't transmitting itself.

"I'm so grateful. Sorry it was eleventh hour like this, but Adam doesn't get up to Manchester very often; usually only when there's a business opportunity."

"So, what time do you think you'll be back, Mrs Fisher?"

Bella wasn't sure she didn't see reproach in Mrs Brady's eyes, though she did feel it in the withdrawal of the hand. Fine for those who believed the marriage vows were sacred even after death, but after divorce… forget it. She wanted to appear to let it pass, keen not to antagonise when she needed help, but then thought better, or worse, of it: "I can't guarantee. Did I misunderstand when you said you could stay overnight? Do I need to pay you double?"

To an extent she regretted her sharper tone, but the thought of being in Adam's arms always made her… she settled for *hasty* rather than another word starting with *h* and ending with *y*.

Mrs Brady looked slightly alarmed. Her husband had left her on the lower side of comfortable at best. This money was a godsend; both women knew it. She backtracked: "Not at all, Mrs Fisher – I just didn't know whether to stay up or go to bed and I wouldn't want to panic hearing a noise at three in the morning. You enjoy yourself."

I will, thought Bella. "Thank you," came out.

* * *

She was so busy rooting in her handbag for a lighter that the sound of her name made her jump. Turning, she was astonished to see the sporty car parked more or less beside her.

"God, you scared the hell out of me. I never heard you arrive."

"You wouldn't," he said. "This is a Tesla; pure electric."

"Looks expensive," she said as he got out and came round to open her door, having first planted a gentlemanly kiss on her hand, the old smoothie.

"Fifteen hundred pounds a month to lease," he said. She whistled. When he climbed in again, he leaned across and his breath on her ear made every hair on her body stand on end, even in places she thought she had waxed! "You may not have heard *me* come…"

* * *

After such an *amuse-bouche*, it had been hard for Bella to concentrate on the actual meal as her mind had raced ahead to the dessert of her choice! Matters weren't helped by the nature of the establishment with its über-attentive waiting staff. She had never had time for those shoals of pilot fish, complicating the process of eating a meal; over-egging the pudding, you might say, and with it the cost of the entire experience. It was why she tried to steer clear of such places, despite the privileged financial position in which she found herself, courtesy of her entrepreneur ex-husband, who seemed to have found it difficult more than once to keep his smoked eel in his pants.

Bella was an intelligent but unpretentious Manc. For her, Michelin was to do with tyres. She wasn't one who needed a gold hook on the table for hanging her handbag and preferred to feel full from the meal she ordered, rather than needing to top it up with endless helpings of poncey bread. Indeed, she had only agreed to go there that evening because Adam had insisted. She had to admit though, as a treat – a pagan ritual – it hadn't been unpleasant, just awkward.

However, the real Bella was the one currently shattering the Tesla's silence; the woman who had lost all sense of time and place; over whose mouth Adam had needed to clamp a hand as she came.

"Bella, it's a very…" he hesitated, "… public place."

"A very…" she spoke between panted breaths, "… privileged one… that's why I… came here… so to speak." She started to recover. "No street-lighting here. We'd see a car from a long way off. Besides, I like the thought of them all…" she looked through the windows, "… barricaded behind their big iron gates and security systems, not knowing what this trollop is doing on their doorsteps." She laughed, threw her arms around his neck and looked him deep in the eye. "And apart from that, I couldn't wait."

Indeed, they hadn't gone far from the restaurant.

Now the frustration hit her. "I'm so sorry we can't go to my place. It's just… the children, the child-sitter. How far is your hotel?"

She thought the look in his eyes would break her heart and felt suddenly exposed sitting there on him – a fool's whore.

"I'm not staying overnight."

"Really?"

"I've got to be in London early."

How damned early did he need to be? "We have an airport in Manchester, you know. You could fly down." She dismounted him. After the ecstasy of only moments before, the pain was intense. "And you were going to tell me this when?"

He zipped up his pants. "During those minutes when you decided to jump me."

Once again silence reigned in the Tesla.

Then the car moved forward as if by unspoken command. Adam faced ahead as he addressed her. "That's the way it works."

She was stung by the simple brutality of the statement. "Well I don't like it. Makes me feel like a slut who you'll call on and bang every now—"

"No, I meant the car," he interrupted. Now he turned to her for a moment. "There's no handbrake to release either."

He smiled. As always when he did so, she couldn't help but become a reflection of it. She faced forward now, fighting hard. "I see you once in a blue moon, you tell me you love me, we have great sex and off you go."

"I can't help that you have children."

She could almost feel the blaze in her eyes. "They're great kids."

He raised one hand from the steering wheel. "I'm not saying they're not!" Now his tone changed. "Look, I'm on a hectic schedule. I need to be in London bright and early, but I made time to meet you; to have a meal. I never said anything about staying overnight." The hand returned to the wheel with a slap. "For Christ's sake, I'm doing things that will be to our advantage."

In an instant of abstraction, she noticed that Germanic tendency to pronounce the word *adwantage*. It had always puzzled her; they had no *W* sound in their language. The distraction was momentary; over as soon as his words bit.

"Our advantage? You talk as if there's a future for us."

Once again, his hand moved and rested this time on her arm. She resisted every impulse to pull away; couldn't deny she was intrigued and was unable to dismiss, as ever, the tingle in his touch.

"Interesting choice of word – future. More appropriate than you know."

"How so?"

"That's what I deal in – futures. It's why I need to be at the stock exchange first thing. I'm meeting someone to have a discussion about grain prices, before going on to meet someone else who might want to buy a contract from me. I stand to make a lot of money."

He had lost her already – her speciality was languages, not finance. "Well, that's fine and dandy, but I'm wealthy enough – for my needs anyway."

"I don't doubt that." His eyes narrowed. "But I guess you're also a chancer."

"A what?" Whatever he meant, the word sounded offensive. There might have been an element of guilty conscience in her pique. Was he making some veiled allusion to her social position being down to the efforts of her ex-husband?

"I mean I see in you someone who's just a bit bored. I know you drive a Land Rover, but I don't see you as one of the Chelsea Tractor brigade. You crave a bit of excitement, hence fucking me in this car in this road. That certainly wasn't love, but then that four-letter word takes many forms."

He put both hands back on the wheel again.

Under other circumstances, there was something about Adam's excellent English, delivered with the faintest of Germanic accents and, as observed before, the occasional misplaced 'W', which always fuelled Bella's engine. Right now, however, she felt just inadequate, as if someone from overseas having such a command of her own language placed him several steps above her on the intellectual staircase. The tension in the car overrode desire.

"So, what are you suggesting?"

"That you take a small portion of your wealth and invest it; ride the markets. Let me speculate on your behalf. As I say, just a small portion. It's a zero-sum game – whatever someone wins, someone else loses. I promise you, it will hook you. And then, whatever we do, we can be equal partners."

When she didn't reply he continued: "Just think about it. There's no need for any decision now."

Yet already she knew that any anchor thrown into the mysterious sea that was his hidden world would at least give her a hold. Plus, what he said was right; what was love – and what was life – without great sex? Besides, she had one massive ISA into which she never looked or dipped. Why not live a little?

"Send me through some information once you're back in Berlin." She moved her hand. "And stop this damn car."

She would have sworn the devil had climbed into the backseat of the Tesla.

Chapter Eleven

Funnily enough, it was the part where he wrote *not necessarily looking for commitment* that had hooked her. Of course, Tanya was assuming he was a he, but given his profile picture was a toy tiger – was there any symbolism in that? – the profile could have belonged to anyone, considering the gender fluidity of the times. Some of them had a point but increasingly Tanya found the whole business tiresome.

Back to Tony the Tiger, as he called himself; a bit of snap, crackle and pop wouldn't have gone amiss in Tanya's life at that moment.

She stole a guilty look at the back of the photo frame on her desk. Heaven knew what warped sense of decorum always prompted her to face it away from her whenever she was on 1-4-Me.com, her dating website of choice. It wasn't as if the kids were walking in on her *doing it* or anything, but even though she knew she wasn't a wonderful parent, she just didn't want to see their faces when she was… well, to be brutally honest, looking for some excitement.

There had been a fallow period of over a year after she and Dan had agreed to go their separate ways. For a woman of her appetites, that counted as an eon. Since then she had, from time to time, found herself harbouring the perverse wish that Dan had caught her having an affair. Perhaps then he'd have ended up with the kids and she'd have had the visiting rights.

For a moment she slumped forward, head in hands, the knowledge that she might actually have been a bad mother overwhelming her. But what was she to do? She had needs. She'd quietened the beast for a time – actually six months following the divorce – but then there'd been that moment when it refused to be tamed, in that club in Windsor. The irony of it; in a toilet cubicle only yards from a different type of seat, namely that of the Royal Family… but hey, there was enough depravity in that family tree to fill a service station's worth of loos. Anyway, the monster had reawakened – except people had no right to label it that way.

She lifted her face from her hands at the soft sound of an alert from her computer.

Tony: You've gone quiet. Have I upset you?

She regathered herself.

Tanya: No, one of the kids was doing what teenagers do – assuming I'm on this earth to serve her.

Tony: I don't envy you. I couldn't handle that. Never wanted kids.

Shit!

Tanya: Oh – does that mean this thing has crashed before it's taken off?

Why the fuck had she mentioned kids, or, to use the technical term, baggage? Here it came; he'd replied.

Tony: No, no, no – sorry. I didn't mean it that way.

Phew!

Tony: I just wouldn't have been a good father.

Tanya: Why not?

Tony: I travel too much – love my job. Love my life.

She closed her eyes while those words, which could have been hers, resounded. Still, it all meant something here didn't make sense.

Tanya: So, why did you wink at a woman who mentions her two kids in her profile?

Time to turn this around; stop being the victim.

Tony: It was you who took my fancy. If you have kids, then so be it.

She didn't know whether to throw up at the excess of cheese, or weep with gratitude; decided on the latter, minus tears, in the hope he felt guilty. Besides, it was true, he had winked first and on 1-4-Me.com, to adapt a phrase, a wink was as good as a nod.

Tanya: So tell me Tony – why won't you show your face? What's with the stuffed toy?

Despite the smiley, Tiggerish face, there was something vaguely creepy about its anonymity.

Tony: Practicality – it's not just for the sake of the woman that I suggest, for a first date, meeting in the middle of the day in busy venues. I want to be able to check them out too and walk away if they've lied or don't take my fancy.

She smiled.

Tanya: Thank God for that. I was hoping you weren't going to come up with some deep philosophical bullshit. You type very quickly, by the way. That was quite a long answer. Are you in IT or something?

Tony: No, I just cut and paste from a Word document containing all my standard answers.

Now she had to laugh.

Tanya: Charmer!

Tony: So look Tanya, are we going to meet? Are you going to take your chances with the tiger?

That threw her. Her fingers hovered above the keyboard…

* * *

The cafe was busy and he was late. Then something occurred to her and she looked around, but no eyes studied her. She hadn't sat where he'd requested, knowing he would have been able to see her as he approached the open entrance. She reckoned now, he'd have to walk in and there would be a tell-tale scanning of the clientele, which would give him away.

Again, a dissonant thought – what if he'd looked in already, seen the table empty at the preordained time and assumed he'd been stood up? Tanya tried to shove that crow from her shoulder. This guy didn't strike her as someone who feared, or indeed expected, a no-show.

Her phone chirruped; her heart leapt with it. They had exchanged mobile numbers.

Shit! It was Dan. She wanted to ignore it, but…

A sigh of relief. It was just a picture via WhatsApp; the girls and him at Legoland. She responded with two perfunctory smiley emojis, those retreats of the lazy or lying.

The phone vibrated again. She opened WhatsApp to find another face smiling at her – except the backdrop was…

She looked up. *Fucking hell!*

There he stood in the doorway. She swore again in silence, but this was an oath of admiration. This couldn't be right; he was gorgeous. Beautiful green eyes peered at her from beneath blonde bed-head hair, set against a bone structure that belied the fifty-four years he insisted he had lived and loved.

She wanted him.

Now she imagined peeling that skin-tight grey T-shirt from a physique… no, she had to stop. It was time to push the bottom jaw in place again; deaden the eyes a little before their *please take me to bed* expression ceded all the ground to him.

She stifled a grin as a random image entered her head – the barista asking: "Would you like special Columbian beans with that?"

He wandered over, plonked himself down opposite her and pointed to her phone. "That's always one way of telling whether you've found the right person – I mean, the right date." He extended a hand towards her. "Hello Tanya." They shook hands and as she released his, he gestured towards the empty spot on the table in front of her. "May I get you something?"

It was weird hearing a voice and, of course, nationality didn't necessarily always translate into typed text. She could remember nothing that suggested where he was from, and his accent was a hybrid of inflections.

"No, please allow me," she responded.

"I wouldn't dream of it. Just make yourself more comfortable than you looked when I walked in. What would you like?"

Special Columbian beans crossed her mind.

Macchiato and latte in his hands, he sat down, leaned back and scratched his head. "Y'know, I don't even remember whether I expected you to have the kids with you or not." Now he leaned forward. "Can't say I'm disappointed they're not here."

"They're with my husband... ex."

"Okay – and his name is?"

"Dan." For her the word seemed to ooze into the space and drop onto the table like pus. It had no place in this moment in her time.

He picked up on it. "I'm sorry; I just thought it might be easier to use in the conversation than *my husband.* That seemed to cause you some unease."

"It would suit me if it's never mentioned again actually, if that's alright with you." He raised two palms towards her, part defensiveness, part apology, but she felt the hammer in her hand still and the need to use it. "While we're at it, I always like to put a name to a face."

He seemed taken aback for a second but recovered his composure. "Actually, my name is Tony... well, Teunis, which is a Dutch version – but the inspiration for the profile picture came from that, not vice versa."

His smile defused her and she found herself wondering what obtuse streak had prompted her to be so confrontational. Had she been raging against the light, frustrated that she found herself drawn to it again with such helplessness? Hadn't things started like this with Dan, or indeed every other guy who'd broken her heart?

But he was looking at her and she needed to move.

67

"So where are you from?" As opening gambits went it wasn't inspirational, but she had to start somewhere.

"Originally Rotterdam, but for the last few years I've been based in Boston."

"Ah, hence that occasional American twang. And what are you doing in the UK?"

"I'm on a business placement. I work for McKinskey Sutch. They're a major futures trader."

She made a gesture with her hand over the top of her head and laughed, which felt good, the more so as he appeared to relax too. "Beyond me already."

He sipped his macchiato. "Well, that's good. I kinda want to remain an international man of mystery."

She looked at him for a moment and he stared right back. "So what's a high-flyer like you doing on 1-4-Me?"

He laughed. "Oh thank you, thank you. High-flyer! That should be defined in the dictionary as long hours, large salary and no time to spend it."

"My heart bleeds. You should try large divorce settlement, loads of time to spend it and absolutely no motivation to get off your backside and do so."

He tapped the table. "Well, you're here, aren't you? Isn't that a first step?"

"Back to my question."

He pulled a face that might have been surprised appreciation. "You should be the tiger." There was a pause. "What's that famous line? – *a lonely impulse of delight*? I don't know; you find yourself in a foreign country, wonder if there's a lady out there for you to help the early days pass a bit more quickly." There was an apology in his eyes as he looked at her and raised a placatory hand. "Hey, no way do I count you in that category. You asked about the motivation, is all."

Something wasn't adding up here. "So why choose a woman with two kids?"

He didn't hesitate. "Because that suggests somebody more mature," he grinned, "in the most positive sense of that word; somebody with a more balanced outlook on life." Now he leaned forward. "And if I'm honest, somebody who'll appreciate the attention – maybe doesn't get it that often."

She inclined her head slightly. "No saucy pun intended."

"If the cap fits." He had recovered himself; stared at her. It was hard to define the resulting physical sensation. Was it discomfort or desire? *A lonely impulse of desire.*

She diverted him: "So excuse my ignorance, but what are futures?"

He wasn't having it. "The things we use to replace dirty pasts." Now he smiled. "I don't intend to waste the precious time I have with you today boring you with financial issues. Not that it is boring; the chance to win big with money usually isn't. To cut to the chase, I get entrusted with large sums of other people's money and look to turn them into even larger sums. I'm good at it and that's why I've been sent here to the UK. But tell me about yourself instead; your kids; why it didn't work out with Dan."

"Have you been married?" Back went the ball. She would play these opening rallies without risk from the baseline.

"Sure."

"What happened?"

"She died."

Strange how the first point didn't feel like any sort of a victory.

She lifted her cup, aware that reflex was a signal of discomfort in the body-language, "I'm sorry. May I ask what happened?"

"It was a car accident. Drunk driver."

Her cup returned to the saucer. "Oh my God, I'm so sorry! To me it's akin to manslaughter. They should throw the book at bastards who destroy lives like that."

"The Fates did – she was the one over the limit."

Tanya was reeling and realised she would need to redefine the rules of this game.

First change — it wasn't a game.

Then there was the paradox of someone's vulnerability seeming to leave their opponent at a disadvantage. She had noticed that about dating websites. Yes, it was true they were a valid forum for those of a certain age or situation; people who were not going to or were unable to hang out in pubs and clubs. However, they were also a sanctuary; part psychiatrist's couch for the broken-hearted, part foot-pump for the deflated ego. She had held a couple of therapy sessions on previous dates! How she had been hoping this wouldn't be another – and perhaps it wouldn't if she didn't allow it to be.

Time to move on. "Well, as you said, the book was thrown. I'm sure you want to rake over those embers as much as you want to talk about futures, so can we maybe drink up and take a stroll by the river?"

He smiled: "I'd like that."

***

"Oh yes," she said, placing a hand on his arm and feeling no awkwardness in doing so, "the clam chowder, there by that... oh, what's the market called?...

Quincy! Quincy Market. That was so good – and I needed it as well; it was bloody freezing! We'd gone to try to see the replica of the ship involved in the Boston Tea Party, but they were still renovating it, so it had been moved elsewhere and all I got was cold! The wind was icy!"

She realised she was talking too much, but he laughed and then reached into the pocket of a fleece he was carrying to produce a packet of cigarettes. "Do you mind if I…?" He gestured with it.

She was surprised, but not unpleasantly; at least he felt relaxed enough to unmask his demons. "No, go ahead. In fact…" She reached over and pinched one of the cigarettes.

His eyes widened. "I didn't have you down as a smoker, especially not with two kids."

"That's when you need it most." She laughed. "But it's a guilty pleasure rather than an addiction. The odd one down at the end of the garden."

They stopped as he fished in his pocket for a lighter. As he lit her cigarette, his hands cupped around hers. They all but touched. Somehow, the intimacy – the sharing of a bad thing – was almost unbearable. Had her life really been that empty?

He was much taller than her. As her head bent to accept the light, the most wicked of thoughts danced in the flame. She looked up at him. He gave a knowing smile before lighting his own cigarette and they moved on in more than one sense.

Somewhere a bell struck two.

He glanced at his watch for confirmation. "Hey, what time did you say you needed to collect the kids again?"

"God, I didn't realise the time had gone so fast!"

He stopped; put a hand on her shoulder. "It's been a blast… for me anyway."

"For me too."

They turned and started to head back towards town. She hoped it symbolised nothing.

"Shall we…?" They started the sentence together; likewise both then laughed.

"You betcha," he said, "I mean if you want to… which I'm guessing you do."

She didn't find anything even remotely presumptuous or arrogant in that assumption. "So where are you staying?"

"I'm in the Runnymede-on-Thames Hotel."

She whistled. "Very nice."

"That's why I'm busy this afternoon – I've got a few properties to visit with a view to renting. Can't expect the company to pick up the tab for the Runnymede forever."

"I'm guessing you're a busy guy."

He stopped, turned her to face him. "Are you around Wednesday evening, or is it difficult with the kids?"

She hoped her pulse rate wasn't communicating itself through his fingertips. "Ah, the more I'm out of the house, the better the kids like it – till they need something!"

"Well then why don't you come to my hotel? It's got a great restaurant and…" He raised his hands, part apology, part defensive. "Hey look, I didn't mean… I mean, just a meal."

She frowned. "Why do you feel the need to explain yourself?"

"I'm sorry – I thought I saw a look in your eye."

One corner of her mouth tilted up. "You might have done… and you might have misinterpreted it."

They walked on in silence. She wondered whether their thoughts were tiptoeing along the same path. Tow-path, toe-path. She shook her head as her mind wandered.

At last, she gestured. "Well, here's my car." That awkward first date stand-off ensued, till at last she craned her neck and pecked him on the cheek. "Don't be a stranger in the meantime. You have my number, but I won't take huge offence if I don't hear from a busy man like you. I don't want you to feel guilty if they find me hanging somewhere."

There was an immediate, peculiar look in his eye. She thought of his wife; no direct correlation, but that had to be it. Had he found himself driven to thoughts of ending his own life in the aftermath? Then she realised she was overcomplicating the nature of her misspeaking – she had simply reminded him of a dead woman. Great! She flushed. "I'm sorry – that was a bit tasteless."

He smiled. She might have been imagining it, but it seemed a tiny bit forced. "Hey, no harm done. Enjoy the rest of your day."

And with that, he was gone. She wondered whether Wednesday might now never come.

Chapter Twelve

In the darkness she sat, her face lit only by the website screen, giving it an almost vampire-like appearance in her bedroom mirror. She could see from the company website that his organisation was huge. Many times that day she'd been so tempted to call him but he had warned her, with perhaps a touch more foreboding than it deserved, that under no circumstances should she attempt to contact him there. Given the nature of the business, security was paramount. He didn't want his connection with her known. Despite the logic of that, it had made her feel excluded, as if he was ashamed of her. How desperate she felt; how she wanted that voice in her ear right now.

Had events in the car – her brazenness – been too much for him after all? Had it not quite sat with his Germanic reserve?

He'd told her that they were not allowed to switch on their personal mobile phones in the office, but there was a problem with it anyway and he needed to take it in for repair. Great! Otherwise, she might have texted him.

Bella flicked to the other screen she had open; there was nothing to stop her transmitting her passion in the written form of this private email. Still, halfway through the first sentence she bent forward, putting her forehead to the backs of her hands, which were resting on the desk. God, she wanted so much to be a part of his world, particularly the part where they fucked.

Realising what she had started to write was an irrelevance and not the purpose of her wish to communicate, plus the fact that he might want to print off the email to show someone, she started again:

Hi Adam, how are you? Listen – I looked at that stuff you sent through, and I want to invest. I can't say I understood it all, but enough to know I could win big, plus it's money I could afford to lose. Please call me. Let me know where to transfer the money. She paused. *Bye.*

* * *

Tanya knew something was wrong the moment she stepped out of the bathroom.

She had expected to find her new lover sprawled like some sculpted depiction of a Dionysian reveller across the bed, the sweat of their passion cooling on his skin and that beautiful, bad cock still somewhat engorged. Heaven knew it hadn't faltered during the full hour that he had fucked her – though technically it was half an hour, given just how much she had fucked him back. She had felt the express train of her hunger emerging from a long dark tunnel; a not inappropriate image under the circumstances.

But that was all by the by; what she found instead was his broad back turned towards her as he sat on the edge of the bed. From his body language, she sensed she had caught him unawares and further furtive moves suggested he was trying to hide something — given events of the last hour, she assumed not masturbation!

Something fell to the floor. Perhaps it was irrational, but she felt betrayed and stepped forward with intent. He bent to pick up what looked like a piece of paper. She stood, just waiting; noticed his wallet was in his hand. Was he taking something of hers? A glance at her bag suggested it was exactly where she had left it, undisturbed.

"What's going on?" she demanded. "If we go no further than tonight, I want to know why; you owe me that at least." Even as she uttered the words, fuelled by a touch of despair, she wondered at her own thought processes; why she had made this quantum leap of potential illogic and destructiveness.

As he looked up at her, there was great sadness in his eyes, which threw her. He held the piece of paper towards her and she could see it was a photograph. "It's just Gina and the kids."

Kids! "Kids? I thought you said…" It was out before she could stop it and she felt a sudden chill, laden with guilt. Oh my God; assuming this was his wife, had she written off their children too in the madness of a drunken drive?

She took the picture from him with gentleness. He buried his head in his hands. His nakedness and, by a strange paradox, his muscularity rendered him the saddest, most poignant of sights. Looking at the picture, she took in the stunning redhead, arms around a boy and a girl, both of whom might have been younger than ten years old. She assumed the picture was taken some years ago, but now was not the time for questions.

He started to sob. Tanya untied the towel from around her freshly showered body and sat naked on the bed with him, arms around him.

"I'm sorry," was all she said. In truth she was fighting against the beast whispering in her ear: *"Just your luck – another messed-up date with a messed-up guy!"* She tried shoving the interloper aside, but he held his ground. *"So what was all that stuff on the dating website about him never wanting kids; not having the patience? Sounds a bit screwy to me."*

It seemed he had read her mind as he spoke into his hands. "I wasn't a good father. That's the last picture I have. They were about two years older than that when… well, let's just say I was part of the reason she was drinking."

"So why do you keep the picture?"

He lifted his head and looked at her. "To remind me of the person I never want to be again."

Well, that's a relief, spat her demon. She found herself almost screwing her eyes up to shut him out. Nevertheless, this presented a chance she was not too proud to take. It was time for honesty. The irony of it – who was the basket case now?

"To be honest, Tony, I'm a selfish person. I'm not a good mother. I do try to be, but it's not…" she struggled for the words.

"In your nature." It seemed he knew and understood.

"That's right. I try to hide it and most of the time I think I succeed, but Dan is a good father, the kids love him. Getting them to be together tonight was no problem." She paused. "But I am bored. Rich – Dan has done very well for himself. I'm bored and a pragmatist. As long as I'm supposedly looking after the two girls, the pay-outs keep coming my way." She stared out of the window across the immaculate grounds of the hotel towards the Thames. "My life is empty. I have a big house in Bray, a big empty bed and an empty head." She put her hand on his back. "What we had this evening was the most excitement I've had in years. I'm not foolish enough to believe it can be this way forever, but I want to live it with every nerve-ending and I'd love it to be a part of my past that I remember with a tingle. On that basis alone, if the future means just futures, then I'm game. I'm truly sorry for what happened to Gina and your kids; imperfect mother though I am, I wouldn't wish that on anyone." She took a chance and allowed her hand to start wandering. "But I can't lie – I didn't know them and I want more of what I've just had."

To her soulless delight she saw his body respond to the movements of her fingertips.

* * *

An hour or so later, once the door had closed, he allowed himself a big grin. He had her, but he would bide his time till she was completely hooked. He would play her the opposite way to the others; deny her a chance to invest. He knew she would want what she was denied, even though she had denied him nothing – perhaps, in fact, because of that.

He placed a hand on his manhood; sore, but worth it! He was the bear – the Russian bear — with a sore head. Geographically, of course, it was stretching a point as he was East German, but the reality of history and politics was that if you had grown up in the Stasi regime, in Berlin, you were nothing if not a Russian.

He rolled out of bed, dug out his laptop and logged in. While he waited for it to power up, he touched the photo, now lying on the table; had to laugh out loud, perhaps with more than a touch of hysteria, at the thought of what might have happened if by some ten billion to one chance Tanya had known Bella Fisher. He wondered if Bella would miss this picture; whether it was a special one and it consumed her that she couldn't find it. Shouldn't have been so intent on eating him alive then. He had a rule — where possible always take a picture… literally. You never knew when or how it might come in handy.

Different cities, different women – same bored bitches. Perhaps on that basis these latest two might well have known each other; they both belonged to the BBC – the Bored Bitches Club. He laughed again.

Speaking of the devil – here was an email from Bella. Wonderful! She had transferred her money. And there it was, in the body of the email; that question – the one they always asked. Three words that spoke of their deep insecurities; the superficial enquiry – *Are you okay?* – which, if you typed it into Google Translate said: *I haven't heard from you. Where are you? I'm suspicious? I'm jealous. I'm lonely. I want you to fuck me. I hope you're not fucking someone else.* They were to be commended for managing to say so much so succinctly. However, as she had just made him a touch wealthier, he thought it best to reply. He typed: *I'm good. Just heading into a meeting. Don't forget, as the old saying goes, the stock exchange never sleeps. Thank you for the money. Let's make it happen.*

Next, he logged onto 1-4-me.com. Seven comments or winks greeted him. The power and mystery of a stuffed toy! They had it coming to them really, given their apparent willingness to interact with a man they couldn't see.

He flicked through. Ugly; too young; hot, therefore an attention-seeker who was doing what-the-fuck on 1-4-Me; nice but sounded poor; if that was this one's best photo, heaven help her.

Then the message he'd guessed he would get after the first date. This one had been a little crazy, a bit needy and hooked from minute one; no kids; a successful entrepreneur living alone in a big house in Bath.

He started to type a reply and felt his balls aching. He'd had to fight this one off pretty much on that first encounter. Better make it two days' time. This was a nice hotel; a decent place to hang out. A shame he'd had to pick up the tab, but he needed to keep up the pretence of the business trip. Then again, they were picking up the tab whether they knew it or not.

He liked where this mad one lived. Bath oozed wealth in a subtle way and so did she. It was a less dangerous place than London; more genteel and seldom in the news for the wrong reasons. The odds on being spotted were longer.

Basing himself in the hotel for an extra twenty-four hours was certainly not an issue for him. It was probably best to keep out of sight. Even though he was starting to feel out of immediate danger, he knew that was the very time you made mistakes and stepped into a man-trap.

He looked in the nearby mirror and felt his hair. It wouldn't harm him to have a break from colouring it either, but it needed to be black again before he headed north.

One thing was certain; Richard and Michael would never stop trying to find him, but he was almost starting to get a buzz from the knowledge that he was ahead of the game and frustrating them.

He smiled. He had adopted new technology; they were old school, relying on contacts – that euphemism for thugs. His own contacts existed in the dark web. Passports, visas, bank accounts, mock-websites – all at the key-tapping fingertips of his rebellious IT-savvy, anonymous friends. They wrote the gospels of a new creed.

Looking again at the face of Jessica in her 1-4-Me profile, he smiled, realising just how much he was actually enjoying this now, including the dangers. Just laundering money and beating up a few objectors, or buying silence from figures in authority – where was the thrill in that old Mafia stuff? Twisting bored, desperate women around your little finger, often your middle finger, feeling their need, satisfying it. Fucking them… and then fucking them again as you disappeared thousands of pounds better off, knowing they considered themselves deeper and more complex than men, yet observing how their carnality betrayed them as much as any man. When it was all over, their shame stopped them from broadcasting their stupidity to the world. In fact, he felt he was also striking a blow for all those guys who had been screwed over in divorce cases, hit twice as hard by the insistence of most courts that children stay with their mother; perhaps he was single-handedly redressing the balance for them and benefitting financially in the process. In most cases their money hadn't bought them any happiness, mired in the asexuality of suburban motherhood and the children they so yearned for had turned from gemstones to millstones.

Easy pickings.

The smile faded for a moment as he remembered that bitch Kopsch in Villingen-Schwenningen, but that had been a different type of combat. One day he would still look to renew her acquaintance. He liked a challenge. In many ways his new game had become too easy. He turned his attention back to the screen – perhaps that was what fascinated him about this crazy bitch Jessica. There had been something about her in the bar. He'd scented danger. She was a paradox – seemed fragile, despite the successful business she'd described, which he had checked out online. He wondered what would happen when he broke her. When he had walked her back to her car, she wanted to go on somewhere; didn't want to return home, though it was strange, because she could have invited him back. Standing by the car, she'd allowed her hand to press against his groin.

Perhaps more than the money, he wanted to take her – take her down even – but suspected that she might be capable of dragging him with her to depths he hadn't plumbed, certainly where sex was concerned.

He shook his head a little. This was dangerous. *More than the money!* Had he really just allowed that thought? That sealed it; he needed forty-eight hours for sure before seeing her again, to regain his equilibrium.

He started to type. A quick line to keep her tuned in, then breakfast and see what the world had to offer.

Chapter Thirteen

Detective Inspector Morris looked up as Billings tapped on the door and wandered in.

"It's the same man, sir."

At least ten cases popped into DI Morris' mind before he remembered where the DS had been that morning.

"So pretty much as we guessed then – I mean that it is a man."

"Yes, sir. From texture and collagen content they're pretty sure."

"And that it's the same man makes this even more weird," Morris mused.

"It's pretty weird already, sir."

Morris looked puzzled. "That's what I'm saying. Two body parts; no obvious message from them. So what are we up against? Are there more parts in places we haven't yet discovered?"

"I don't think so, sir. Perhaps in future, but…"

"Yes, you're right Billings; these were left where they would be found. So assuming at least one person, the gardener if no-one else, was going to reach the centre of the maze, we were meant to find these early."

"So do you reckon we can expect some sort of a demand, sir – you know, for a ransom or whatever?"

"I wouldn't have thought so. How long's it been now?"

"Forty-eight hours, sir."

"If it's a message, I don't think it's for us."

"So really we should be looking for a body, sir."

DI Morris knew what was expected of him next. This was how he and DS Billings worked, completing each other's thoughts, two halves of the same guy, their own recipe for avoiding being considered mad and talking to themselves.

"The fact is that anyone mutilated like this would have arrived in agony at a hospital, so either he's being kept alive, heaven help the poor bastard, or he's gone into hiding, left alive by them as a message for someone – perhaps for the victim himself. Whichever, we're talking some pretty sick puppies. Given the DNA isn't on the database, we're looking for a misshapen and very bloodied needle in a haystack."

"Which leaves us trying to define the haystack, sir."

Chapter Fourteen

Katherine's pulse raced as she heard the key in the door. Then came the *thock* of the Louboutin heels, her sister's one concession to the vanity of brands, on the parquet flooring of the long hallway, while hard on the heels of those heels came the pitter-patter of dread.

The lounge door opened and in walked the immaculate, but inexpensively suited figure of Jessica, her arrival conveying an aura of intimidation that had everything to do with the favour Katherine needed to ask. She took in her sister's blonde hair, identical to her own, but forged into a thick, waist-length Rapunzel-like plait, whereas Katherine's was loose and twisting in her fingers.

"What now?" Jessica's two words carried reprimand and foreknowledge quite out of keeping with the brevity of the question. Yet wasn't that always so in life? Did any word that wasn't invective carry quite the same intensity of accusation as 'What?'

"Why do you say that?"

"Because I know you and I know that when you're sitting in that chair, in that posture, waiting for my return, you've got some bad news for me."

Katherine sprang up from the chair. On another day she might have assumed her hair falling across her face gave her an air of madness, but the words – his words – from their wonderful evening together rang in her ears, when he had complimented her on her thick locks. How she wanted to feel his fingers entwined in them, stroking them, pulling them.

"Why do you always have to assume the worst of me?"

Jessica put down her bag with a weary sigh. "That line has been the precursor of everything that's ever gone wrong in your life." She pulled off her jacket with an unconscious allure her sister could only dream of matching and headed across to the drinks tray. "So I repeat, what now… or who?"

Katherine paced across the room and then back, her flatties making no sound – in contrast to the Louboutins – a ghost in a place she would have loved to call home. She heard her own silence, wanted to break it, but lacked the steadiness to keep it rational. Standing there, she took in the glorious view across Bath from the elevated position of the house, seeking a place to anchor, but instead turned and drifted back to the centre of the room.

There was the clink of ice in a glass; just one glass. Clearly her sister wasn't feeling amenable. Then again, there was a positive in the fact of her pouring herself a drink. She always drove, never took a cab — Jessica was fiercely independent, but then with that beautiful new X-trail who wouldn't want to provide their own wheels? – so this meant she was probably planning on staying in.

Which suited Katherine.

His image came back to her and for a moment she felt the injustice of life, picturing the rather worn, patched-up clothes and even more weather-beaten jalopy in which he'd turned up for the date. It had touched her that he'd wanted to pay for everything that evening when it was very apparent he could not afford it.

However, she was also angry for reasons of her own. She tried to push it aside; after all, she knew well enough how hard her sister worked – had always worked – to make her business the success it was now, with the sort of commitment to professionalism that would have been beyond Katherine, who knew she was the apple which had fallen and got bruised.

She put her hands to either side of her face; tried to gather her thoughts and stop the tears.

"Well?"

She turned to find Jessica holding two glasses, one of vodka on the rocks for herself, the other a brandy – no ice; no clinking in the glass. Katherine continued fighting back the tears, wandered over and took the proffered glass.

Jessica raised her eyebrows in continued expectation of an answer.

"Oh, um, it's Max."

"Is he the guy from the other night?"

"Yes – why do you say it in that tone?"

Jessica made a quizzical gesture of helplessness, but it looked disingenuous. "What do you mean *that tone?*"

Katherine paced away again. "You know exactly what I mean; that air of condescension."

Her sister took a sip of the vodka, seemed to savour it. "It's not condescension, it's concern."

81

Katherine turned towards the window again and wandered across to it once more, taking in the glorious interplay of sunlight on the sandstone houses and green parkland, buying herself the time to swallow the peevish response, which was surfacing like bile. Again, the inadequacy of her own words frustrated her. Dammit! – she had a degree in English. Once more, her ship, with its one silent passenger, her soul, was caught in difficult waters; torn between the calmer seas further from shore and dangers of trying to land.

There, she could conjure the images. Why couldn't she express them vocally?

How she wanted to be her sister.

"We had a lovely evening together. He was charming."

"Aren't they all?"

"He didn't try anything."

"Because he knew he wouldn't have to."

Katherine spun round. "You bitch!" The words were out before she could stop them. She regretted it, but also because she had cast the first stone. The lack of an immediate angry response from Jessica made it all the worse.

"You do fall in love…" her sister paused, as if thinking twice, but then forged on, "… and into bed very easily."

"I'm passionate – I can't be…" she gestured with her hand towards Jessica, so wasn't quite able to stop before it was too late, but the latter raised a palm of her own; a placatory gesture on this occasion.

"I know, I know. I just worry about you."

She could give no response to that. Katherine threw herself down into the nearby armchair. The next words came softly: "Do you think it's fun being like this?"

Jessica sat on the chair opposite. "Being passionate – yes, actually, but I admit your lack of a parachute when you throw yourself out bothers me."

Both of them took a sip of their drinks and sat in momentary silence, broken by Jessica: "So what's the plan for this evening?"

Katherine swallowed hard, remembering the reason for her trepidation at the sound of her sister returning home. She knew the wheels were about to come off. Her teeth clenched with the fallibility of her being, but on she ploughed. "He wants to take me to see a play in London." She read all the usual signals from Jessica but carried on. "I'm not sure what time we'll be back."

Katherine waited a moment. "But you'll be back." There was once again no suitable response that didn't sound like a lie. "Because know this – I have a very important meeting in Gloucester in the morning and I will not be late. I'm not prepared to sit here, unable to sleep, wondering where the hell you are."

"Okay – okay." She hated the sound of her own petulance, but it seemed the need to be on fire overrode all shame. The desire to be looked at again as if you were actually hot. It was a brutal fuel.

Jessica leaned forward. In a moment of dislocation, Katherine observed the way she sat with her legs slightly splayed, not folded together to perfection, while the blouse that should have moulded to curves stretched somewhat across shoulders strengthened by several years in the fire brigade. Above it all, balanced on a neck that had remained, rather incongruously, worthy of Nefertiti was a face that lacked the encumbrance of prettiness and all its dangers, possessing instead a wonderfully sexy combination of intelligence and confidence. How was that possible with a twin sister? Surely it should have been like looking in a mirror...

...except of course mirrors presented you with a complete opposite of yourself.

How could we possibly be so different? Katherine was sobbing in her gut. *Why are you just so good at everything?* But she knew what was coming – out of the good cometh forth evil.

Jessica gestured with her glass towards the ceiling. "Up there, as I seem to have to keep reminding you, might have been two very good reasons why it's not okay most of the time."

"I just knew you'd have to…"

"Stop right there, Katherine. You knew, because it's a universal truth. We're lucky that it was only two abortions."

Someone's hand slung the brandy glass across the room where, in one of the luckier moments Katherine had enjoyed, it struck wall instead of glass and shattered.

Much like the bust of the Egyptian queen who had entered Katherine's thoughts moments before, Jessica sat expressionless, staring towards the amber stain on the wall and the chip in the plaster. Katherine believed she would have dealt better with things if her sister had got up and simply punched her in the face, rather than this eerie calmness, but Jessica didn't move nor utter a sound. The same hand of violence now was clasped across Katherine's face, gathering her sobs and the tears from her screwed-up eyes.

"Do you think those… surgeries were easy for me?" she gasped.

She could tell from the strange softness of her sister's voice that Jessica's gaze had turned away from the scene of wanton destructiveness and was fixed on her. "No – I never thought it would be and I never said it was."

"I was young." Even in her genuine despair, Katherine disliked the self-pitying tone of her own voice.

"So you are still. So am I. We grew up together and that's why you're here with me." Katherine heard movement, the click of heels, felt her sister's weight settle on the arm of the chair. Between her shoulders came the pressure of a hand that she hated yet longed to feel. "And you know I'll always try to help you, but you have to try to help yourself. Perhaps you need to talk to someone."

Katherine stiffened; knew that Jessica had noticed it because the hand that had been rubbing her back stopped. She turned, feeling anger rise again. "Who, if not you?"

"I'm not a professional."

"You mean a shrink; or more medication?"

"No, I mean a counsellor."

"A shrink."

"No." Jessica was getting impatient. "You just need to understand how to control your… urges; desires. We can't just wander through life doing whatever we want."

"You do." It wasn't said with malice.

"Well, I want things that I believe aren't ruining my life. But you're destroying yours." Here Jessica looked towards the ceiling again. "And maybe others in the future. I warn you now, I won't allow my career, my business, my future to be stymied by your indiscretions. If you had decided to keep those…" there was an awkward pause, "… children, they would probably have ended up not recognising you. They'd have been calling me mum and not just because we're twins."

Katherine was out of her seat, propelled by the fire of truth in her self-loathing. "Maybe you're right. Sometimes I feel I have no value in this world. Maybe I should just leave it."

Jessica raised her hands, palms outwards. "Oh no, don't start that now."

"What do you mean?"

"Poor me, poor me. Always we come round to the suicide thing. I love you, Katherine, but I'm not going to have that Sword of Damocles over my head. I have my life; you're a part of it, but only a part."

Did she imagine it, or was there some hint of regret in Jessica's eyes as she said those words?

But now her sister had got to her feet. They hadn't quite drawn sabres yet but they had exchanged a gauntlet and Katherine had enough sense to know who would win that fight. Now her desire to just go out that evening seemed safer ground!

"Look, sis, I just want to go out and have a nice evening."

Clearly a nerve had been touched, judging by Jessica's response: "Oh, to relax after the tough day's shopping and coffeeing, you mean."

"Shopping and coffeeing? They're not things I like to do alone and as you're never around... since my friends appear to have deserted me..."

"Given your..." Jessica paused, "... let's call it interaction with their husbands or boyfriends, I'm not completely surprised."

They say the truth hurts, but sometimes, depending on which weapon has fired it forth, it has the potential to kill. At that moment, it was only seeing a frisson of sadness cross her sister's features that prevented Katherine from launching herself cat-like at Jessica.

Now it was Jessica's turn to head across to the window.

Like sister, like sister, thought Katherine.

If only chirruped her ever-weakening good angel.

Still, it seemed Jessica couldn't quite let things pass. "Do you have any money left for this nice night out?"

And there was the reality of it; it was a pertinent question. Max had been struggling since the death of his family. He'd been finding it hard to keep employed and what was left of Katherine's allowance for the current month – given the apparent need for chastity, perhaps she was better calling it a stipend – would cover the cost of a hotel room for that night, but only just, never mind the things she longed to give him, with his worn clothes, his wreck of a car and, above all, those sad but gorgeous eyes – and what lay below!

Jessica's back was still turned towards her. "Well?"

So things were ending as succinctly – as brusquely – as they had started. "Yes, I have money."

Which was when it started, rather than ended. For at that moment, with that half-truth behind her sister's back, Katherine had an idea. It would require her to become even more deceitful and observant, neither of them traits for which she was renowned, but paths down which she had already wandered with her identity theft.

Though she appeared to be calming down, Jessica was still clearly angry, judging by her words as she turned to face Katherine: "Don't let me down."

"I won't – I promise."

Good – that was good. It even sounded genuine and seemed to have the desired effect as Jessica crossed the room and gave her a rather unexpected hug before placing her hands on Katherine's shoulders. "I'm going to get changed. Please believe me sis, I just want what's best for you."

Katherine smiled. *So do I sis,* she thought, *so do I. And I've just realised how you can make good on that.*

Chapter Fifteen

This was just the pits, mooning around like a lovesick girl. She was better than that; it wasn't who she was.

No – she was a lovesick woman! Evidence – the way her heart had leapt when his response to her email had come through, thanking her for the money and promising her a rich return on it, as far as promises could be made in the futures market. Then there was the despair at the lack of any gushing sign-off.

Bella had tried looking up some more background to that particular area of business, but had ended up feeling worse about herself; stupid and worldly-unwise after she'd found everything beyond the second sentence went over her head. She'd reasoned that a better understanding of his world might make her feel a bit closer to him. Instead, it had ratcheted open the distance, introducing her to a universe where he had power and she none, her mind a punctured tyre that only he could change. Her investment had never meant that much to her. Now it made her feel cheap; just an attempt to buy her way into his affections. There had really only ever been one return in which she'd had any interest. Now even their lingua franca mocked her – *return, interest* and most ironic of all, *futures*.

This was no good. She was getting angry, mainly with herself, though that rather frigid response to her email had fuelled it. Okay, he was German, but still…

It wasn't sitting well with her now that he had forbidden her to ring his place of work. Plus, what did that say about her that she was going along with it? Sod that for a game of soldiers!

She reached for the phone.

Passion, a furious passion, got her as far as ten digits, always assuming her fingers hadn't been as scrambled as her mind. Eleven digits. Her thumb hovered over *Call*.

Which was when it struck her that she was dialling numbers at all. Why had she never saved him as a contact on her phone? Had she, right from the beginning, seen the truth; the classic tale of a flame burning too brightly, to be extinguished all the sooner, or destroying everything in its path?

"Press it," she muttered. Press it and be damned? Press it or be damned? That seemed to be the choice.

All of a sudden, it felt like pressing *Call* would be saying *Candyman* for the fifth time.

Having cut off her attempt before she started, she was furious with her perceived weakness when faced with the possibility of losing him through her disobedience.

What about his mobile?

A second blow landed, this time in the pit of her stomach. She didn't have his mobile number. A big part of 1-4-Me.com was that people could set it up without giving out their phone details, holding back that bit of security and privacy until they were really keen – so all that stuff she'd been thinking before about sending him a text; it was nothing but a concept. He'd never given her the number – and she had been so fixated on his other equipment, she'd not even clocked it! What did that tell her?

Unbelievable! If this latest punch in the solar plexus caused her to bring up anything, it would almost certainly be stupid pills. She had handed him every card. So, she had his email address – so what? On reflection, most of their interaction had been on the dating website. She'd given him everything, including licence to run.

She stared around her as if with fresh eyes, and on the walls danced the shadows of all the beasts he had unleashed in her, though they were growing motionless in the dawning cold light of reality. He'd dropped his mobile and it was in for repair — that's what he had told her. Oh yeah! For security reasons she couldn't phone him at work. Of course – everyone in international business could get by without a mobile, particularly if prospective customers couldn't call their office. She had screwed up. They had never actually spent a night together anywhere and she had perpetuated that with her monstrous, untameable libido, fucking him in cars and down side-streets, determined to have him before business took him elsewhere. She was no scholar, but even she remembered a line from Shakespeare, learnt at school and never forgotten. It mocked her – *frailty, thy name is woman.*

Then the knock-out punch landed and somewhere in the distance, she heard the countdown. Was it too late?

Attacking her laptop, she tapped frantically at keys, swore at the inevitable typos. From her desk drawer she took a card reader. Cursing, she rooted through the chaos that is the contents of a handbag till she found the correct card. Wondering whether dementia had set in overnight, she struggled to remember her customer number, likewise her PIN, but got there after groping through her limbic brain for birthdays. As for the internet – God, it was so fucking slow! It took all her self-control – a quality she realised now was not hers in abundance – not to hurl the machine at the wall.

At last, she was in. For once, her hope lay in bureaucracy. For sums like the one she had transferred, the process had been known to take up to seventy-two hours. She stared at the screen; Classic Saver Account... View statement?... Yes... *Click...*

"C'mon!"

Then, just like her internet, she froze, before slumping back in her seat. Too late. The twenty thousand pounds had already gone.

Perhaps she was over-reacting; after all, this was just a response to a lack of warmth at the end of an email; a lack of communication over a very short space of time. He was a busy guy. He worked in futures. They say the stock market never sleeps but clearly she had been dozing.

Wake up, Bella!

She got up, stalked across to the drinks cabinet, pausing for a moment at the sight of the red-headed idiot framed in a mirror. She resisted the urge to smash her fist into this portrait of a moron in a world of fools, pitching away twenty thousand pounds of her children's inheritance. Moving on, her hands shook as she poured a drink. Then she had to place it back on the tray with a sudden bang. Ice cubes rattled in a mocking tribute to her cold-running blood.

The photograph of her and her children! The one in her bag. One of those pieces of personal memorabilia that, like the eyes of a loved one, you stop taking in till one day they are no longer there.

Like now? Had she imagined that?!

She hurried back to the desk where she'd slung her bag, fumbled in the pocket where she kept the credit cards and that picture. Digging around, she shovelled things backwards and forwards, a mole burrowing its way to hell.

The photo wasn't there and she'd had no reason to move it. It had been on the desk for years, having been taken by the father of those children at a time when her love for him had been at its strongest and then removed from the frame when his infidelity was a pain almost beyond bearing. She had put it in her bag, unable quite to tear it and him from her life via the shredder.

There was no sense, no logic to her quantum leap of deduction that her lover had removed it, but by instinct she knew. She remembered having insisted on paying her way that recent evening at the restaurant. He had spotted it when she dug out her card – eyes that keen now made him worthy of suspicion – and asked to see it, much to her discomfort. Showing images of her children to the man she wanted to fuck made for a muddy battlefield with her conscience. Why had he asked to see them? She couldn't imagine.

She reached for her mobile – no power on earth was going to stop her calling his place of work now.

"Good morning, Square Mile Serviced Offices, how can I help?" Bella looked at the phone – the number was correct. "Hello?"

"Hi, may I speak with Adam Hartmann please?"

"Certainly – which company does he work for?"

Something else she didn't know! Serviced offices. Of course! You could rent one of those and never visit. "Don't worry – thanks for your help."

Bella cut off the call and sat with a thump. Perhaps there was a storm heading her way. Because who was he? To what had she exposed her children now? Had she endangered their lives or her own? Perhaps all of them? Ruined them?

* * *

He pulled up at the barrier, entered the code, drove through.

Without fail, he enjoyed this drive of a mile or so across the farm towards the office and storage units, where no-one asked any questions. He loved it not only for the peace of mind from the open land and the sense of leaving a dangerous world behind for a while, but also for the sight of the eastern Europeans picking in the fields; no strangers to the hard work, but their pathetic wages a comparative fortune which they would send back to their families. To an extent they believed they were in some sort of Shangri-La; had found nirvana. It made him feel good about himself. He'd found a way to succeed behind the Iron Curtain and continued not to struggle since it had risen.

Was there just the tiniest part of him that envied them that satisfaction with their humble lot?

He dismissed the thought. There was envy enough in their looks as they watched his Qashqai drive past, into which he had changed en route, from his rental Tesla. It was the only journey this car ever made, playing no part in his activities except to bring him here. A good car, but unremarkable. However, in the light of what was about to happen, he was glad those workers were busy breaking their backs, unable to pay detailed attention to everything and also too far from the road to do so.

He stopped now in front of his storage unit. No-one ever saw him, and no-one cared. He paid the money, cash in hand, and that was all that mattered. Pulling on the heavy up-and-over door he parked the car and locked it away.

The unit next to it now became his focus. Inside, behind the closed door and beneath a light that lit flickering memories of times in Stasi cells, where he and his former blood-brothers had displayed their state-driven skills, the changes began. It was unfortunate that didn't include the hair. He felt its rough texture and frowned in irritation. Black was his natural colour, but when the meeting in Villingen had gone pear-shaped, he had headed back to his hotel quickly and gone blond, knowing that soon two former Stasi eagles would be circling on the lookout for their dark-haired prey. He'd allowed it to grow a bit longer over time as further camouflage. A smile formed for a moment as he realised how like his cabal brothers he had been in many ways, given he had then headed out from his hotel in search of his own victim at the SonderBar.

He would be glad to take a little break for a while, once his two remaining bits of business were concluded. Time to disappear. His randy author friend Margot, having performed that illusion herself, was the perfect magician's assistant to make it happen. He would need to be back to black-haired for her. It was a pity she chose not to live the life of luxury, but then again, neither did he in essence. Sometimes the thought that you could have what you wanted was enough. Anyway, recharging the batteries on Harris would be perfect before starting afresh. He had not yet been, but online it looked like everything he needed right now – stunning, majestic and remote.

In went the contact lenses. Next came the clothing he had acquired from clothes banks; the shiny trousers, frayed shirt, jumper and tweed jacket; all clean of course – he was a man who had lost his family but not his pride.

Transition made, he turned and grinned at the other car; the old Mondeo, as reliable as hell, with one hundred and eighty thousand miles on the clock, a few dents and scratches.

He heard the sound of tramping feet outside; laughter. Lunchtime for the workers. They seemed happy. Was he?

Again, that gave him a moment's infuriating pause. But was anybody really? One thing was certain – the money was bringing him a greater happiness than it had brought those divorcees.

He took a deep breath, trying to clear from his chest the irritating and unusual anxiety which was refusing to be expelled. Was this what the West did to you? In a world where far more people had, well… far more, did your loss of uniqueness drive you to question why you wanted material things? Behind the Iron Curtain, those who could did. It was simple. The state told you when you could take a piss. Any chance to be your own man was grasped at and the motivation for that, the opportunity to indulge in a little luxury or power, was understood by all. The difference was you didn't wave things under the noses of others.

He laughed out loud at the thought of Facebook or Instagram in the old Eastern Bloc. *Here's what I'm eating tonight – the same as every other fucker. Look at my new Trabant – oh, you have one on order; how many years till delivery?*

Shrugging away his thoughts as best he could, he waited a minute or so till the footsteps and banter outside had faded, then drove out. Just as he was closing the unit door, he felt a mobile buzzing. He recognised the number – Tanya. What the fuck did she want? Had the girls in the East been this needy, or demanding? He'd had power and status, but the women over there had it too, if they worked as hard as the men. He couldn't help thinking he'd become more of a misogynist in the West. Women here were more complicated; it seemed the more they had the needier they became.

That had been a mistake in Windsor. For once he'd been cocky, got careless, taking her picture in the café and sending it to her. So now she had his number.

There were a few seconds of rage at his stupidity. When he next went online, he would cancel the account. Not that it mattered – all the details were false, though his hacking skills and those of his contacts on the dark web meant they would get him everywhere and everything he might need – but it was the inconvenience of needing to buy another phone, a proper one for when shit really mattered. From now on, for everything else, only the unregistered phones would be used.

The call ended and soon the voicemail pinged. He listened; the usual clichéd rubbish. Didn't they have an original bone amongst them… apart from his? He barked a laugh. Now the text – *Are you okay?* Ditto his previous thoughts on that question. Maybe in the case of Tanya it was a genuine question. After all, the death of his family had moved her.

Hadn't stopped her wanting him in the midst of his grief though.

Stepping back inside the container, he took the hammer he kept for matters requiring crude and immediate effectiveness, thought about smashing the pay-as-you-go phone, but decided against it. Nevertheless, he would pick up another at the next motorway services, just in case.

With that he locked up, nipped onto junction 6 of the nearby M4 and sped off to Bath, though never over the speed limits. While he trusted his hacker contacts and his ID documents, why tempt fate?

Chapter Sixteen

She was feeling both shameless, which was his fault, and guilty, because that shamefulness was infused with rejoicing that his family's fate meant he was hers, at least for now.

One hand clutched the pillow, the other his hair, preparing to push him away when it became too much, but for now pulling him towards her, never wanting him to drag her away from where she was at this moment, teetering at the rim of the crater.

He had been gentle, more than she liked if she were honest. She had been shocked by his body, the muscularity of it, given how depression had taken its toll of him in recent times, but she hadn't thought it through, because he had ended up as a labourer once he lost his high-paid executive role.

She wanted it all; to eat him up yet have him on the menu every night, every day – but he was so much more than à la carte. More than anything she wished him to be again the man she imagined he might have been before. Her heart had ached at the sight of the slightly shabby clothing and his rather battered car, though it had rendered the gift inside the wrapping all that much more pleasant a surprise.

She had disliked the way the man at the front desk of the hotel had addressed her and not him; after all, parental allowance enabled her to at least dress the part for a place like that. She was determined to change things, allow him his 'Pretty Woman' moment, where he could return here and confront the bumptious prick with a *"Big mistake."*

For a moment she had slipped away from the crater's edge, but now he brought her back again and her body returned her mind to the moment.

* * *

94

When they were done, she lay exhausted, sweat cooling on her while he seemed to have drifted into a post-coital slumber. Hard though she fought, thoughts of the future tormented her as they always did. This could be different though, couldn't it – the path towards a tomorrow she would shape? The deception would have to continue. Worse, the lie would need to grow. She was too scared to admit the truth and run the risk of losing him.

Founder of Fire-Dawes, the booming equipment and training provider, she had claimed to be and such she would need to remain.

As this supposedly successful entrepreneur, how could she leave him driving that old banger and wearing his Help the Aged wardrobe? Her allowance was generous but it wouldn't stretch to changing his life.

There was always the marriage option. Their parents, God rest their souls, from whom the allowance came and which Jessica managed as executor, had built a clause into their will stating that Katherine's complete inheritance would come to her if she married. However, even then it would need authorisation from Jessica, since their mum and dad had recognised pretty early on – as, to be fair, did Katherine herself from time to time – that she might not always know her right mind. Besides, she had learnt enough about men to know that any sort of suggestion of commitment seemed comparable to placing the north poles of two magnets together.

No, she would play this another way; continue to tread ever so carefully – dare she say sneakily? – along the path down which she had set off a couple of days before and if her luck ran out, or indeed the money, then hopefully a decent man like him would acknowledge that she had done it all for him and love her for it. Because…

She turned on her side, laced her fingers in his hair and watched a smile form on his sleepy face.

Because he was beautiful and surely her luck had to change.

She would start with the car. That was more of a bloke thing, though perhaps only marginally these days, judging by some of her previous dates and things she saw on social media. Besides, it was much easier to tell a guy he needed a new car than that he needed new clothes! Should she lease one? Jessica had explained it was the way to go where controlling your budget was concerned, which would be key for someone in Max's position. Once he was on his feet, strengthened and supported by her love, he could take over the monthly payments himself.

She glanced across at her phone and was overwhelmed by sadness on noticing that it was almost time to head back. However, it gave her pleasure thinking of him enjoying once more a touch of luxury, as he was staying for the night.

Once home, she would continue her own illicit activities. The thought filled her with adrenalin and dread.

* * *

The door closed and he allowed himself to breathe, a long exhalation, part relief, part fatigue. She was exhausting! Not just physically, though that for sure. It was as if every past wrong in her life, every beat of her broken heart could be exorcised through sex. He found it a paradox how someone as successful as her should seem to be channelling so much despair. Surely her appetite couldn't be accounted for by a lack of feeding. A woman with her looks – not pretty, but alluring – and enough drive to found her own business was surely not short of potential lovers. Then again, if he was an example of the Machiavellian types drawn to her success, love might have been difficult to find.

Still, who needed love, which was just sex with Ts and Cs? She had certainly surrendered in haste to her carnal needs. When he'd gone down on her, it hadn't been long till she had gasped that she was coming, but when his tongue had started to cramp and he had begun to despair of it ever happening, she had screamed and shoved his head away. *"I'd begun to wonder if you'd ever come,"* he'd said, only for her to inform him that she had already – twice.

If it wasn't for the fact that he'd researched her online, he might have decided to cut and run; too much hard work, even out of bed. He had checked her out on her company website, seen her picture and read her vision for the company. Then, courtesy of his hacker contacts, he'd looked on Creditsafe. She was doing very nicely, thank you. Her address tallied. It was all he needed for now to make him hang in there. Nevertheless, his upcoming vacation on the island of Harris was beginning to seem like some very necessary R&R. The irony of it – fleecing women had developed into a business which was literally and metaphorically wearing him out.

He had made progress today. His alter ego, Max – his broken self – had worked a treat, as he had guessed it would. Again, he marvelled at how someone so successful could be so naive and malleable. Tomorrow, the new Jaguar F-Pace – a snip at seventy-eight thousand pounds – would be his, or at least the funds to make leasing it possible. Of course, he'd protested it was ridiculous to be taking such a chance on him, but she had insisted. She'd hinted at clothes too and they would follow in due course; for now, she had baulked at suggesting he needed to update his wardrobe, but he knew, deep down that despite her troubled spirit she was kind.

However, one comment in relation to his sartorial appearance had frozen his blood; made him realise why perhaps there appeared to have been no solid relationship in her life for some time. In the discussion about her two miscarriages, there had been no mention of the children's father. He was the empty chair at the table, remarked upon by no-one and in truth he couldn't work out how they had come into the conversation. He gave a guttural laugh as the thought came to him that perhaps he could have shown her his stolen picture after all. He had abandoned his plans to play the bereavement card once her story emerged. Who knew; perhaps she had raised the topic to bring herself down to his level – *I too have suffered.*

Now he felt a slight chill. Had this been her way of letting him know she wanted children? Was he a means to this hundred-miles-an-hour businesswoman taking a step towards the nuclear family? Was he, Max, the missing piece?

Enough of that – back to the money. He had expressed concerns about such a sum moving in an online transfer. Traceability was the fuel to the flames of his concerns, but he hid that fire with talk of the potential tax hit he would take and, indeed – something that had to be of concern to her – the delay bureaucracy would cause for such a transfer. She had insisted he must have the car as soon as possible; was impatient that it should be so. That worked perfectly for him. She had agreed to cash and said that she would contact the bank the next day.

He spread himself out on the bed, enjoying the feeling of its luxurious mattress and the prospect of a good night's sleep. Eleven-thirty had felt like a strange time to be saying farewell. He would soak up everything the hotel had to offer, including, once again, room service now and in the morning, for which she had already paid. No way was he wandering into the breakfast area wearing those shitty clothes. The looks he would receive for sure might have led to a response from him not heard since his Stasi days.

That gave him pause for thought. As a highly respected and rapidly advancing young member of the former East German secret police, he had enjoyed benefits that he was not supposed to flaunt in that Communist regime. There were ironic echoes of that in this game he was playing with Jessica. He had amassed enough wealth to enjoy a hotel such as this without a second thought but needed to maintain the façade of his impecunious life. He had to question how much longer he was prepared to hide in plain sight, not from her but from his former partners-in-crime, Richard and Michael. During the Cold War, the three of them had looked with envy, despite their positions of relative privilege, towards the wealth and comforts of West Germany. Together they had made provisions for the fall of Communism. Happy to be out from under the yolk of Erich Honecker and the Soviet Union, once the Wall fell, they had kept a low profile at first, but at length the luxuries and the possibility of indulgence had proved too big a draw and they had found a way to achieve that gratification. He had the taste for it now; the cars, the suits; the fine dining; the women. There was only so long he would be denied – and who would be his chip in the game?

Not Jessica. Not any of these sad, desperate women with their pain and the encumbrances they called children. Perhaps Margot, with her literary fortune and no family. Then again, she had chosen exile in the pissing wet of a remote Scottish island. Still, he was looking forward to seeing her.

He picked up the wad of notes Jessica had left on the bedside table, looked at it then replaced it, recalling Jessica's words as they lay in the after-madness of sex. She seemed unable to control her neediness. Surely a woman on a third date would know to avoid discussing marriage, but while she hadn't made overt reference to it, its viperous subtext had woven its way through the long grass that still masked the future. There had been mention of a large sum of money in a particular clause in her parents' will and payable upon her marriage. Perhaps that was why she had never married, fearing the true intentions of any fiancé, but then why mention it at all? Besides, surely she was wealthy enough not to be relying on some inheritance. It made little sense.

Then again, did it represent an opportunity for him? Certainly, risk would be involved. He would have to avoid publicity if the event took place. While Michael and Richard might have downgraded their search, they would never spare him if fate led him across their path.

But he had this woman twisted around his little finger already. The bigger problem for him would be dealing with her manic behaviour. Was she bipolar? She bore many of the signs, her undoubted brilliance and focus as a businesswoman, the discipline required to have been in the fire brigade, as her website had illustrated when he checked, counteracted by the apparent instability of her emotions.

Then there were those children – the ones she had lost and those she still hoped for. Their cries would echo through any marital home simply by their silence.

He sat up; muttered: "Get a grip," but the idea of the inheritance was gnawing already; a worm destroying ripening fruit. There had to be a way to get his hands on the money without the ultimate commitment – didn't there?

He lay back again, started to think, but then decided food could take a few minutes' priority. Yet when he picked up the room service menu, he couldn't concentrate on it and slapped it down on the bed.

He didn't want to burn any bridges. Getting out of bed, he took out his iPad, which had been carefully concealed in the bottom of his rucksack. Time to speed up the first of his three outstanding pieces of business.

He typed in Tanya's address: '*Hi babe, sorry for the radio silence. Did you try to call me? My phone is what's technically known as screwed for some reason and I'm getting it fixed, but I just wondered if you would like to meet up. T.*'

* * *

Tanya knew a grin was spreading from ear to ear. It was ridiculous. How could this be? How could one little email disperse the black clouds which had been gathering, dissipating the storm? He was having problems with his phone and had taken the trouble to email her.

That told you something, didn't it?

Even if it didn't, if a placebo could make you feel this good, then who needed medication? After all, she'd had the real thing, with disastrous consequences. Hence, she would rename it *no big thing*. He'd had it too and lost it in the most tragic of circumstances. If that, too, didn't tell her something, that the man who had been through that terrible ordeal had now been proactive in asking her out for a date, well then there was no goodness in the world.

Her reply was short and sweet in all the right ways.

Chapter Seventeen

Her heart thundered as she approached the bank. Surely her attempt to pick a way through this minefield could only end in disaster. Then again, trying to trace her way out might prove just as perilous. Besides, the need to press on made it feel as if someone else's body was propelling her, which of course in a peculiar way, it was.

The traumatic joys of being a twin sister.

She stopped; took several deep breaths. She could not afford to look or behave like this in there. Channelling her fear and the concomitant adrenalin into activity, she made yet another paranoia-fuelled check of the contents of her bag. They were all there, as they had been perhaps three minutes before. The customer service representative had advised her to bring her passport, driving licence and birth certificate. None of them had been difficult to find. She might not have been organised, but her sister certainly was.

If they asked any security questions, she would know the answers. Her sibling's biggest enemies were, despite the frustrations involved, her love for and trust in her sister, or rather in Katherine's lack of worldly wisdom and acumen. They had opened their bank accounts at the same time, taken by their loving parents and carrying with pride the one-pound notes they had each been given with which to complete that transaction.

It felt ironic and empowering that, for a change, Jessica was the one displaying naivety. The fact that internet issues had once put her business offline for almost two days meant that she liked paper copies as back-up, providing food now being devoured by the death's head moth that, for the time being, Katherine had become.

Just a few more paces. The old Bath Stone building housing the bank in the city centre loomed before her like some dark-powered, ancient edifice. Her mind was taken back to a film which had scared the living daylights out of her a few years back on the TV – *The Omen*. She felt now like the child Damien when he was being driven towards a church for the first time, its tower standing in judgement. At that moment, it would not have surprised Katherine to learn that she did have 666 tattooed on her somewhere, such was her whispering sense of betrayal of trust.

She had to stop again. She squeezed her eyes shut and almost shook her head to free it from that thought, seeking to replace it with the potential good she was doing in helping one depressed man to restart his life.

Is that what you're doing? Isn't it just that you want to fuck him forever?

She couldn't be sure that she hadn't spoken those words out loud; she placed her fingertips against her lips and looked around to check she hadn't been heard.

Such were the disjointed propensities of her brain, some famous words came to her – *if it were done when 'tis done, then 'twere well it were done quickly.* Lady Macbeth coming back to her from her degree days, telling her to get on with it. Hardly an encouraging role model.

At last she drove her feet forward, up the steps and through the revolving door.

It seemed she was expected, but then she remembered she did, in fact, have an appointment.

"Miss Dawes – a pleasure to see you." He extended his hand. "I'm Arthur Gibbons. I look after our Key Accounts."

They headed down the wealthy silence of a carpeted, soundproofed corridor. The insulation didn't prevent the screaming in her head – increased the volume in fact – while images of subterranean torture chambers flooded her mind before they entered a beautifully appointed meeting room.

"I'll go and get you that coffee," said Gibbons. His expensive suit didn't mask the deterioration of his waistline. She thought of Max in his shabby clothes; the sculpted treasure they contained. It gave her strength, as did the stirring in her loins.

Gibbons returned with her cappuccino. His smile had her wishing he'd just looked angry as he continued. "I can't say I'm not sorry that we're losing your business, Miss Dawes."

Was this some sort of a test? "But you're not losing my business. I'm just closing one account, which is sitting earning a half percent interest. Everything else remains unchanged. The cash flow and all related bank charges remain in your control." She had listened well to some of her sister's after-hours conversations in her office at home and had jotted down what she thought might be a useful phrase or two.

Gibbons' smile didn't curve the set line of his lips. "May I ask why you didn't want a straightforward transfer, or look at putting the money in a higher-earning account?"

"I need the money urgently and can't afford the admin delay. Plus, this is a side venture of mine; an investment in a start-up business where – how should I put it? – for both parties a cash transaction is preferable."

"Understood." He tapped at an iPad and smiled at her – this time there was some lateral lip-movement. "Um, may I see the documents please? Passport, birth certificate, driving licence."

Katherine knew better than anyone that her behaviour could often be erratic, but she preferred to think of it as a by-product of intelligence rather than stupidity – or had meeting Max simply prompted her to take a different fork in the road so that she thought with a greater degree of cunning?

No, that latter thought was cowardly of her, blaming someone else for her corrupt and deceitful behaviour.

Either way, she had come armed with her wits today, the sharper version, rather than the blunted one.

"Mr Gibbons, with all due deference, may I first see some proof of your ID? After all, you met me in Reception and led me through to a meeting room; the bank was busy. You could be anyone."

She had enjoyed pulling that arrow from the quiver and his startled expression made firing it an even greater pleasure.

He regathered himself: "Of… of course, yes." He looked puzzled, but tapped on the iPad, turning it for her to read. "My apologies if you didn't receive the email backing up the phone call."

Shit! she thought, *shit shit shit!* What would happen when Jessica saw that? She hoped the horror wasn't registering on her face.

Which address had they sent it to?

"Which address did you send it to?"

"jessicadawes@gmail.com"

Therein lay her only chance.

"That's my only…" She stopped herself in time from falling yet again into the behavioural pattern which had tainted so much of her life – voicing her thoughts; the results of thinking but not thinking through. "That's my only possible reason for not having seen it; that's my private email." She had to hope Jessica was too busy to have looked at personal emails yet today; that her comments in the past about being way too busy with work to have a life still held true!

102

She needed to get this done and get home.

Focus, Katherine, focus!

He placed something next to the iPad on the desk. She realised it had been attached to his left jacket lapel all the time. How foolish did she feel now as she looked at the ID badge? Looking back up at him, she saw he was barely able to conceal his smug delight.

"So if you're happy then, Miss Dawes, we can proceed?"

* * *

It was almost impossible to comprehend. Could this little slip of paper, this banker's draft, really change lives, or destroy them? The problem was that she knew already that it could. After all, it had turned her into a liar, a cheat and an identity thief.

She had envisaged walking out of the bank with a bag full of money – very Hollywood, but not very practical; a reality Gibbons reinforced.

"Even if we had the money sitting here, we would not have allowed you, for your own safety, to walk away from these premises carrying thirty thousand pounds. I would suggest you authorise your, um, beneficiary, by signature," he said, smiling, "the good old-fashioned way, to cash this into their account." He gave that thin-lipped smile again. What it represented was no longer obvious. Victory? Contempt? Defeat? Perhaps all of them. One thing, though, was certain – whichever one, it was its darker manifestation.

As she took the cheque in her fingers, he held it a second or two longer than necessary, perhaps enjoying her evident struggle to stop her hand shaking. Did he suspect her? If so, then surely, he would not have completed the transaction. Perhaps he believed she was indeed Jessica, but knew she was being disingenuous and evasive about the purpose of the withdrawal. Did he suspect she had a lover? What did it matter to him? She was a single woman of means as far as he was concerned. Did he fear she was under duress in some way?

This was not the moment she had imagined. It contained about as much satisfaction as someone getting away with murder. Then there was the bit she had pushed to the back of her mind; how Jessica would react to finding herself thirty thousand pounds poorer. Her need for Max had blinded Katherine to the consequences. She was hazarding everything. The account might have sat there doing nothing for some years, but her sister had not become successful by lacking an eye for detail. Katherine guessed all she herself could hope for was to garner her reserves of strength, lie well and deny all knowledge – before running! On reflection, doing it all online might have been a safer bet, though from what she understood, these days almost anything done in the virtual world left a trail. This way, as long as she stuck to her guns and stonewalled, she could win. Besides, perhaps she could get away, maybe even start a new life with Max.

But what if he ends up in jail, Katherine, for accepting stolen money?

The thought turned her cold, but she dismissed it – he had no idea what she had undertaken.

So, you end up in jail instead. Try feeding your appetites there amongst the criminal lesbian community.

Stop it!

Again, she looked up, trying to read in Gibbons' face whether she had blurted that out. It appeared not. It was also the least of her worries – in fact insanity might have to be pleaded once this all came to light.

There was a further pressing matter, for which she had not allowed – that bloody confirmation email. She had always known she would need to hurry home and replace all the documents she had borrowed, but now there was the little matter of working out the password for Jessica's personal Gmail account and deleting that fucking email before it was too late.

How she hoped her sister retained certain habits. There was still a chance. That way lay salvation. Just destroy any evidence that this had happened today, at least for the moment. Buy herself time to think.

To find some salvation, she tried to picture Max's face when she handed him the cheque, seeking solace in that prospect. She envisaged only joy, but he was a humble man who had become used to having nothing. Perhaps it would make him uncomfortable, this display of generosity. She had to hope a new car would help him get used to the idea of a little luxury.

What if they took it away from him? How much more desperate would it make him feel if they blocked off this particular path to the promised land and a better life?

All this time Gibbons had been mouthing platitudes. They were nearly at the exit. Seeing the street beyond the bank doors, hearing life rather than the silence of the hermetically sealed meeting room brought home the reality of the world, but the closer they got to the doors, the more she expected security guards to pounce on her.

Then, a shake of hands and she was blinking in the sudden daylight of a changed life.

Once out of sight of the bank, she ran.

Chapter Eighteen

The wildness of the storm took her breath away. She collapsed next to him, a sweaty mess on the bed. He too seemed exhausted and she watched fascinated as the tectonic plate of his diaphragm rose and fell. The earth had moved – that much was certain!

"Oh my God, that was awesome!" Her voice was a whisper.

He turned his head and smiled. She wanted to eat him up all over again. They had gone to a different level tonight and there had been a closeness that belied the almost savage intensity of the sex. She was moved by the look in his eye.

"I don't know how to thank you. I can never repay you."

She stroked his hair, turning on her side the better to look at him. "That orgasm was repayment enough."

"No seriously."

"Well, as a businesswoman, I know a good investment when I see one and if it makes you feel better, you can see that as a loan. Think of me as one of the Dragons. Once you're back on your feet..." she stopped for a moment and allowed her coquettish finger to trail down his stomach, "... then again, I might never want you on your feet again."

As always, she had no idea where that beast rose from; the image of three sixes somewhere on her body occurred to her again. Part of her hated the prisoner her appetites made of her, quietly building a cage while she was busy losing control, as her dear sister – the adjective was not without bitterness – chose to remind her time and again.

With Max – well, she felt she might tame it; control it; use it.

She gave an arch smile. It was an eventuality she looked forward to with thrilling immensity.

"What are you smiling at?" He gave a gentle stroke to the corner of her mouth, the light brush of his finger sending a pulse through her which was out of all proportion with the weight of his touch.

"I'm just happy."

Perhaps she could indeed learn to train the monster. After all, being back at the time she'd promised on her previous night out had played a part, for sure, in Jessica making less fuss this particular evening. Whether she would have been quite so amenable if Katherine hadn't managed to work out her Gmail password was another matter. Finding the bank's email unread had been a rare break in her life. It had taken a good few minutes for her pulse to calm down after that. She had thanked such powers, presumably demons, who watched over her for the fact of her sister not being the erratic, capricious person that she herself had turned into. Always the same rotation of passwords – *je551c@,* then that same combination backwards – changed on a monthly basis. Her business emails were probably another matter, but who gave a shit at this moment?

Quite what would happen on the nights-out front if the account closure was discovered… well, she would just have to deny any knowledge, or better still hope she had moved on.

Katherine reached towards the bedside cabinet and took a sip of water. Spotting her phone lying there, she decided she wanted this moment forever. She tapped the camera app and turned to Max.

"Stay right as you are – in all senses."

"No!" His reaction shocked her, both in its vehemence and its violence, his hand sending the iPhone flying from her grasp across the room.

They stared at each other and her heart sank. Then the same hand of anger was raised in abject apology. "I'm so sorry. I didn't mean to…" He reached towards her cheek.

"But you did!" She jerked her head back out of reach.

"Jessica, I'm so sorry. I just…" She got off the bed and stalked across the room to where her phone lay, picked it up and examined it. "Is it okay?"

"The phone might be…" She glared at him.

"Again, really, I'm so sorry. I just hate having my picture taken."

"You're not kidding!"

"No, I mean… I really hate it."

She pushed her swathe of thick blonde hair back behind her ears. "I think that might be what you could call an over-reaction."

Now he got off the bed and moved towards her. For the first time in their short, intensely physical relationship, the sight of his body held no immediate appeal. "It's just…"

She was waiting. It had better be good.

He slumped down on the bed. "When Gina and the kids were killed, before they set off, she took a selfie of us." He looked towards a distant hell. "The phone survived the accident. That image still haunts me. I'm so sorry." He buried his head in his hands.

The only thing for which Katherine might have hated herself more than her weakening at that moment, would have been if she hadn't weakened.

Another glance at the phone; it seemed intact, but what did a broken phone matter when weighed against a broken life? There was a far greater significance in Katherine not knowing what to say, than for most people. Her silence reflected a painful acknowledgement that her love for her own children would not have been this deep. It hurt her to recognise this; that Jessica's insistence both times that she have an abortion was perhaps justified. It wasn't that she was stony-hearted. On the contrary, her need for love raged, but her passion seemed to be ice, not fire, driven forward with an unstoppable, glacial intensity; forging new ways; changing the landscape around her. Those unborn – *terminated* – children, those unfortunates, were the terminal moraine when the glaciers melted. Why ice and not fire? She couldn't be sure, but perhaps because fires brought warmth and light as well as destruction. Deep down, she knew her life had brought the former elements to no-one; neither parents nor sibling, so she had to assume that would that have remained the case for her children.

But in Max, perhaps she saw a way to change this; believed that she could light up the darkness in which he found himself; reignite his ashen life and in doing so find redemption.

Looking at him sitting on the bed, his head in his hands, naked and more helpless for it, she couldn't keep the anger alive.

She sat next to him and he lifted his head. "Please forgive me. I didn't realise there was still so much pain."

She took him in her arms, knowing that was where he belonged. Gently she lay back, bringing him with her.

They lay in the post-coital rest of exhaustion that should have been theirs a few minutes before.

Her eyes opened with a start. Extricating herself from him, she looked at her phone. Thank God for that – still an hour and a half before she needed to be home. There were no missed calls, so hopefully no bad news.

Now she looked again at Max. He lay like an innocent boy, but one assembled with care from the redistributed pieces of Michelangelo's David. His sleep was deep, back rising and falling with a mid-ocean swell.

He would never know, would he?

Chapter Nineteen

The text had confused her – it had to be a mistake. She'd not noticed it the day before, being Jessica Two-Phones on a point of principle, not wanting work to impose on her private life, no matter how well her business did.

What private life?

She shook her head, seeking to ignore the gremlin, though it had a point – the work phone took almost all of her attention and she hadn't spotted the message till that morning.

Even then, it was only by chance she happened to clock the different account number. She was used to her current account being permanently below the alert threshold, which triggered the texts, but again that was because that account was for everyday expenses.

But this savings account – there had to be a mistake, unless, of course, she had been subject to fraud. Thirty thousand pounds to zero – frightening odds!

She wouldn't, or at least didn't have time to go online now and wasn't sure what good it would do to have the big fat zero staring at her. The bank would need to be informed either way, so why not speak with someone face-to-face? Despite her relative youth, it was her preferred modus operandi anyway.

She needed to be into work on time – the contract up for grabs would dwarf the money she seemed to be missing, but the office wasn't that far from the bank and she would manoeuvre a break in the meeting to enable her to get straight over there.

* * *

And here she was, at the bottom of the steps looking up towards the grand Georgian façade of the bank, feeling in no way intimidated and enjoying that fact, as she always did. It was not some über-feminist bullshit; fighting deadly fires simply left you feeling everything else was a breeze.

As she walked in, her Louboutin heels were silenced by the change from marble to plush carpet. She caught one or two of the glances from the staff, the smiles bank employees gave by rote now, post-recession. Only half the counters were occupied by customers. Out of habit she sought out a cute guy who looked intimidated and made for him. She wasn't one hundred per cent sure what that said about her.

"Good morning, madam. How may I be of assistance?"

"I've received a confusing text this morning. I wonder whether you could check the balance of a savings account for me."

"Certainly. May I have the account number and also see some form of identification?"

Jessica saw the slight frown that crossed his features as he studied the details after he had tapped away at the keyboard. "The balance is zero and the account was closed yesterday."

She felt the blood draining and her mouth opening. "Closed? By whom?"

Cute Cashier was now clearly uneasy. "By... you, Miss Dawes."

"Let me see that." She gestured towards the computer.

"I can't turn this screen, madam."

"Show it to me." She heard herself and would have liked to take back that unreasonable response, but the loss of five-figure sums had that effect, she guessed. It was a new experience for her.

"I can print you out a copy."

To his left another female cashier was making a phone call sotto voce.

Cute Cashier continued: "I'll need to see another form of ID, madam." She opened her mouth, but he anticipated her. "It's just standard regulations, part of our FCA security procedures."

"What – I didn't look enough like me on my driving licence?" She knew her anger would have been better vented elsewhere than on an innocent employee, but already something was nagging at her.

As she dug in her bag, she caught his slight shrug of the shoulders towards another colleague. All of them, with bowed heads, appeared to be finding the tops of their desks or their screens of sudden, huge interest.

"Miss Dawes, how nice to see you again."

The voice behind her made her jump. The situation was affecting her nerves. How bloody annoying to find she wasn't the epitome of calmness she strove to be in so much of her life. She turned to find Arthur Gibbons, according to his badge, standing there, hand extended, features doing their best to evince warmth but with something untranslatable in his eyes.

She took the proffered hand, while an unpleasant nagging shaped her next question: "Again, yes – how long has it been?"

The unreadable message in his eyes translated with sudden clarity as *what the hell is she talking about?* "Well, yesterday, of course; when you came to close your Long-Term Saver account."

"Close it?"

"Yes." He saw some movement behind her and gestured.

Cute Cashier stepped forward with her print-out and driver's licence. Clearly, he was uneasy handing over the former, but Gibbons made a dismissive gesture. "It's okay, we'll flout the FCA just this once and I won't demote you." He gave a little snort of laughter.

Cute Cashier seemed to take courage from the attempt to release the tension. "I do remember seeing you in here yesterday, Miss Dawes. My apologies for any inconvenience I have caused." That said, he retreated to the safe ground behind the counter.

"Maybe someone who looked a lot like me," she responded, "but I suspect..." She stopped; her insides frozen by a sudden, horrible thought.

"Someone who looked exactly like you," corrected Gibbons, though the certainty he tried to convey sounded a touch defensive. He reached across and took the driving licence from her hand; scrutinised it. "You... she had all the correct documents as well. Of course, it could be a major piece of criminality, but all the documents passed all the scanning tests."

It was now that Jessica noticed the two well-built men in suits who had stepped forward ever so slightly into the main foyer...

... they wouldn't be needed, unless it was to provide her with support for her shaking legs along the way.

"I do apologise if there has been some mistake," said Gibbons, mistaking her silence. He was caught between a rock and a hard place, needing to reassure everyone that he had done nothing wrong, but not wanting to offend a customer with three other accounts at the bank; one who might just be losing her mind. "Joshua," he looked towards Cute Cashier, "check that nothing untoward has happened with any other of Miss Dawes' accounts."

Gibbons and Jessica stared at each other for a few seconds until, from over her shoulder, Joshua's voice announced: "Everything else hunky-dory, sir."

"Hunky-dory," repeated Jessica with heavy irony, but already she knew rage against the bank would be misdirected; home would be a more appropriate target.

Why? Why!? Until she understood, she would need to tread carefully. There was a lot at stake here – if only she knew exactly what. Reputation was a large part of it, she couldn't deny. Not the only factor, but – her mind wandered to that morning's business meeting – if word got out that a businesswoman couldn't manage her own funds or family…

Gibbons pulled a face of appropriate concern, but she knew he was already in arse-covering territory. "We will, of course, conduct a thorough investigation and believe me, I'm at the centre of this. To me, it was you sitting in front of me."

Jessica tried to beam back to Earth. "Yes." She gave her best impression of a smile, but her mind was lost in the darkness. She had such fears now. "Or rather no… I mean, there will be no need for an investigation." Gibbons looked confused, opened his mouth to protest and she tried her very hardest to look winsome. "You're absolutely right – the mistake and confusion are all mine. I meant to close a different account. I don't know what I was thinking and my mind has been on other things this morning, so I ended up talking rather laterally with you."

"We'll still need to investigate…"

"Will you?" She was still smiling; the toughest challenge of a life strewn with obstacles overcome. "I mean, if I'm happy that the account is closed, then what need? I haven't spent the money yet…" *oh please God please let that be true!* "So I will return it and come back to complete the transaction correctly."

"Well…"

She leaned forward, stopping short of coquettish, but bringing a flavour of the conspiratorial to her softened voice. "What will it bring? As you say, I've closed an account, during which process you followed all the correct procedures. Today I've had a bit of a flip-out, but it's all good. Tell me, Arthur, if you report an incident as a result, what profit will it bring?"

He seemed to relax a little. "If you put it like that…"

"I do." She gestured with her eyes. "You can tell the brutes in suits to stand down."

Gibbons was perhaps a little lost in her eyes for a moment; it seemed to take a second or two for her comment to register, but then he glanced towards the security men and with a discreet inclining of the head sent them on their way.

She strode as nonchalantly as she could through the foyer, catching again the glances of the staff, though this time they were directed back towards Gibbons.

Once outside, she knew what needed to happen before anything else and, hating herself for it, she pulled the cigarettes from her bag. Lighting up, she sent a plume of smoke up into the stratosphere, where she hoped it might overtake her wits.

Now certain things about Katherine's behaviour in the last couple of days made sense, above all the lack of contrariness, the willingness to agree, the punctual returns from her dates.

"And you, Jessica, you bloody fool!" She whispered it out loud. "Despite everything you allowed kinship to get in the way and let your defences down – and in that, you are your sister, just with different weaknesses, different drives."

She took every grain of tobacco from that cigarette and once her head had stopped spinning, reached for her mobile. It wasn't the police she would be calling; not yet. Despite everything – not yet; for the sake of her sister…

… *she wanted to believe.*

And her sister's was the first number she called.

Voicemail.

She knew Katherine well enough to be certain she would have seen the call and be ignoring it.

Her message was as simple as it needed to be: "Oh Katherine – what have you done?"

Despite it going against every screaming instinct, she had to return to the meeting. Business had to continue, as there were other people's jobs and careers dependent upon it, but concentration would, for once, not come easily. This was more than the foolishness of a bipolar twin sister. This was deeper. Like life itself, Katherine was a problem to solve now and it needed to be her, Jessica, who solved it. If she didn't, if she had to go through the authorities, there might be no business, or at least it would need saving along with the family name. There was nothing like the flashing of paparazzi cameras outside a court to send investors fleeing like rabbits.

Chapter Twenty

It was no surprise to Jessica – a first for that morning! – that her sister's phone had just rung out unanswered and just as predictable to find now that there was no-one home. Jessica cursed herself for having given away the fact of her discovery courtesy of the voicemail.

Then again, perhaps it was a blessing. She wasn't sure how she would have dealt with the confrontation at this stage, with Righteous Anger already coming out of its corner swinging; aiming brutal blows at its technically superior, but ill-prepared opponent, Reason. Katherine would now be scared, a victim of immense vulnerability looking for a hiding place.

Having entered the decompression chamber of the house, she closed the door and leaned against it, taking several long, deep breaths. She headed for the lounge and poured a large vodka, though not without questioning that need arising so early in the day.

Thirty thousand pounds! Why?

Katherine's condition made her capable of many acts of selfishness, though often they were just the result of a certain childish naivety or guilelessness, so what had engendered this example of considered cunning; this – there was no escaping the word – crime? Yet even as she asked herself why, Jessica knew the more appropriate question was *who*? The chances were, if she took a guess she would be right. Her sister's defencelessness in the face of the charms of the opposite sex was well documented in the records of various abortion clinics. Jessica realised the expediency of her thoughts might have sounded brutal to an outsider, but she knew it was better for everyone that there were no children in Katherine's life to witness or end up as tragic innocent victims of the consequences of their mother's fragility and appetites.

But Katherine had never before stepped over the line into the dark side of unlawfulness. Who had prompted this? She thought she knew the space that person occupied in this universe… but who the fuck was he, this Max?

She rang Katherine's number again, expecting no answer and receiving none. Instead, she'd been rather hoping that, in her panic, her sister might have left her mobile at home. She wished it was for Katherine's good she was harbouring that hope but knew deep down she might use the phone; that it held answers.

Making her way upstairs now, she was taken aback to feel her legs shaking. Entering Katherine's room, she rang the mobile once more. No buzzing; no ring tone – she had the phone with her.

Now Jessica cursed the conflicted fusion of sibling love and selfishness that formed the spine, the core of her. Aware of her sister's vulnerability, she had always hammered home the need for the GPS to be switched off. While she wished for that to be a purely altruistic motivation, she had also not wanted chancers following Katherine to her home, or tracking her here to see its evident, though not ostentatious wealth; finding in it some sort of target. Of course, that meant there was no way of tracking her phone now.

Still, Katherine was nothing if not passionate and she would almost certainly have some memento of her lover or their time together.

Perhaps, though, he was cunning. If he was capable of tricking Katherine – wait a minute, tricking Jessica by proxy! – out of thirty thousand pounds, keeping his identity would be a no-brainer in his dark world.

It never entered her head that she was being unfair; that Max, whoever he was, was just an honest journeyman whom Katherine had decided to take under her wing, the feathers courtesy of her minted sister. Jessica would not waste a second on that scenario. It might have been a damning indictment of the circles in which a successful woman moved, but she was single for a reason and certainly by choice.

However, she knew her sister well enough to know there had to be some clue, some trace of the path she had followed in pursuit of her lover.

The two, perhaps three or four elements of Katherine's splintered personality were reflected in her room. A homemade bed worthy of Tracey Emin alongside cupboards and drawers of immaculate neatness. She looked under the pillows, in the pillow-cases, beneath both mattress and bed, and found nothing. Next was the rat's nest in the corner.

She struck unexpected gold almost immediately. In a plastic folder full of all manner of bits of paper, it leapt out at her – a receipt for the criminally expensive Walton Hotel in the centre of Bath. It was dated the night before last and had been paid in cash. Katherine didn't keep receipts. For her, for the moment, from the man who probably gave nothing, this served as an ersatz love-letter; a reminder of profligacy and sex.

It was at least somewhere to start. Plus, it occurred to Jessica that, although in many ways her sister was out of control, she was also a creature of habit and would probably believe herself safe back in the hotel; the lovers' refuge in a world which had been unkind to them.

Flicking a little way on in the folder brought further evidence; a couple more receipts, one of them for the night when she and Max were supposed to be at the theatre in London. Jessica shook her head. This was some expensive sex. Her sister didn't ever allow for the fact that the aftermath was potentially costlier.

She glanced at the address details and keyed the telephone number into her phone.

* * *

He ensured the woolly hat was on the passenger seat of the Mondeo beside him, as a reminder to pull it on over his hair when he reached the farm again later. Of late, the changes of identity had been so frequent that he was losing track of who he was and didn't want to draw any attention to himself, given he would drive away from the storage container in the Evoque.

The thought made him smile, but at the same time there was an element of sadness; some false nostalgia for the days behind the Iron Curtain when just being himself had been a guarantee of power, including over women. There had been many a *Nutte* in East Berlin who had begged him to use his cuffs or wear his uniform while she pretended to writhe on the bed. If those stupid girls had known the reality of being locked up or interrogated by the Stasi they would have turned colder than Siberian sperm.

One of his phones was ringing… Tanya. He pressed the *fuck off* button.

"Leave a fucking message." That was her third attempt that morning – yet another reason to stick with the online communication via the 1-4-Me website in future; if there was indeed a future on there for him.

The thing was, he might have been feeling irritated, but he shouldn't alienate her and after all, he had texted her from the hotel in Bath a couple of nights back to suggest they might meet up soon. The weakness that made these women suitable targets became, over time, the biggest turn-off, but he would be foolish to stake everything on any one of them. Though Jessica might have seemed a potential cash cow, who knew when the latter part of that epithet might start to dominate and he would need to turn elsewhere.

So when, on cue, five minutes later she tried again, he answered.

"Hey!"

"Tony! Wasn't sure if your phone was working now. I…"

"Seems to be." What had he said last time? This was the problem when you had too many irons in the fire. He'd just about remembered his American accent and hoped his vague answer would be enough.

"It's just that you mentioned meeting up a couple of nights back and I…"

He didn't have time or the humour for this right now. "I have to warn you, I'm not on hands-free. There's still some problem with my Bluetooth." It had been pissing him off that this old banger and the pay-as-you-go phone were restricting his style, but for now it served as a worthwhile excuse. "Look, let me get back to you later. I'm a bit nervous. There's a few too many panda cars for my liking."

She laughed: "Panda cars! How sweet. Have you been watching Dave on the hotel TV?"

"Who?" At the sound of further laughter, he thought he'd better join in, though clearly he was missing something and he made a serious mental note that he never wanted to stand out for anything other than his love-making. Just went to show, even after all this time, once an outsider, always an outsider. Years of interrogating people had revealed to him the devils which always lurked in the lack of detail.

She seemed reassured by the sound of his laughter. "Okay, well drive safely. I look forward to hearing from you later."

The phone remained clutched in his hand, which in turn rested in his lap. He stared ahead for a troubled moment, reflecting again on the conclusion he had just reached about the nuisance value of these easy prey. It was to be expected, but for the first time in a while he was growing tired of it. That wasn't good. In staleness lay the potential for errors; threads people could grasp, if not the women themselves, then the police, despite their incompetence – and if not them, then Michael and Richard.

He'd been right – it was time to take a breather. Besides, the likes of Bella and Tanya were small fish compared with the sea-monster he had snared in Jessica. One big win under his belt already and there was plenty more where that came from. He had never known anyone quite as hungry as her.

Nevertheless, he needed to recharge his batteries. He grinned – fucking, or fucking-over nymphomaniacs could take it out of you. He thought of Margot and was glad he'd made that phone call. At least he'd have a day's journey to garner his resources for her demands.

Shit! He remembered his hair. The journey was going to be even longer than he had allowed for. He would have to book a hotel room on the way up, pay on arrival, dye his hair black and then just slope off. On the other hand, perhaps he could just turn up blond. Say it had been a bet. What would she care?

Main thing – he was heading somewhere safe, to be with someone whose desire to stay out of the public eye matched his own for now.

At that very moment, as if on cue, his phone buzzed and he recognised the number. He wasn't of a mind to speak with anyone else, so he would wait and then listen to Jessica's voicemail.

It was lucky he was on a stretch of road with no traffic cameras. Despite his desire to keep a low profile, he threw the car into a U-turn, incurring the wrath of at least three other drivers. He took the birds they flipped and other gestures, just wanting them to go on by, which they duly did.

He hadn't got too far away from Bath, so getting back wouldn't take that long.

Words are not the thing; it's all in how they are spoken. Everything Jessica had said in that message told of trouble. He needed to understand why; calm her. The woman remained a puzzle; a paradox – so successful in business and yet seemingly so fragile.

Why was she back at the hotel? They had no tryst lined up for this day. In fact, he had never understood her need to meet there instead of her home, which he had viewed online and seen to be a classy, non-flashy residence. She had said she didn't want the neighbours knowing her business and that being in a hotel just gave everything a feel of forbidden, sinful luxury. Fair enough, but today in the light of the message, it made no sense. Perhaps he should call in on the way to the hotel; find out whether there was anything she was hiding – but no, on reflection it could wait.

In effect, her message had expressed nothing definitive, but the letters reassembled spelled trouble. It had been a rambling request to see him and he had heard the pain; God knew, his life had given him a sixth sense for such underlying meanings – except *pain* in Jessica's world had the potential to radiate.

* * *

On previous visits to the Walton Hotel, he had always parked some way down the road and completed the journey on foot, telling Jessica this was through shame; the thought of his battered car parked amongst the multitude of German brands and, more particularly, being seen returning to it in the morning. There was an element of truth. As someone who had once had official status but been forced to drive a Lada, it irked him to see even sales representatives parked in superior model Audis and BMWs, but the reality was that he never knew how things would pan out and he wanted to avoid being caught on the CCTV cameras that monitored the vehicles.

That need for anonymity had become magnified, the woollen hat now serving its intended purpose in a different arena as he walked towards the hotel, trying not to evince cautiousness but rather a sense of belonging as he strode to and through the door.

Luckily Reception was busy. He was known here. Even if those at the check-in had poor memories, his rather casual clothing would draw attention to him. Doing his best to appear relaxed, he took the stairs rather than the lifts, seeking to bypass human contact if possible. His life was crossing a dangerous desert now, barren but fraught with dangers. Apart from the lack of way-markers, any splash of colour, any reflection of sunlight which marked you as being something other than a part of the landscape might come back to haunt you.

For that very reason he had always tried to avoid using the little gizmo in his wallet, which out of necessity he was about to utilise. Any other common-or-garden burglar might have given their eye teeth to own it, but common-or-garden had never been his thing; a little beneath him maybe, though that sounded like a crooked morality even to his ears. However, now he could see no other solution. There was no way he could have enquired at Reception for the room number or requested a key. Already he had learnt, by dint of her personality, Jessica was the ultimate oxymoron – predictably unpredictable. Assuming it wasn't taken – a further risk of course – he knew she would go for the same room they had been in the night before, in this instance 501, but he really had no idea what had driven her to return this day and leave her static-filled voicemail.

As he approached the room in that carpet-deadened silence so typical of those plush hotels, he produced the keycard; a token of appreciation from one software engineer who had been down on his luck but had grown wealthy through his association with the eastern Bloc, though not – and this was important – with Michael and Richard. He had not yet used the tool and hoped that it lived up to its creator's promise.

Max, as he was forced to think of himself for now in the event that the mad bitch in 501 was still thinking straight, could probably have made a decent living as a petty criminal from use of this entry-card alone, but drawing the attention of the police to any hotel in which he was staying had never struck him as a good idea. Besides, he had bigger fish to fry.

He glanced up and down the corridor. Thankfully, the Walton was the sort of hotel whose clientele would have considered CCTV an insult. He could almost hear the voices of privilege: *Who the devil do they think we are? Beatrice, we're leaving!"*

Having pulled on a pair of latex gloves, he held the card against the reader. After a delay of a heartbeat or two, the little green light went on.

Giving the door a gentle push, he stepped inside and closed it again before semi-whispering her name: "Jessica?"

No response.

The silence was the mere underlining to trouble's signature. He could smell badness in the air already, though its exact form escaped him for a few seconds longer.

There was no sign of her in the suite. Into the bedroom. The bathroom door was open. He stepped towards it with caution and picked up the unmistakable scent; one so familiar to him. Sometimes, the Stasi had left cells at Hohenschönhausen Prison or interrogation rooms uncleaned; a kind of attention-focuser for the next occupier. Diluted and disguised though it was, his nostrils picked it up in an instant and he knew that this moment's contract with the devil had been signed in blood.

It told him much that all his thoughts were born of self-preservation and selfishness. He had gone first thing to pay in the cheque and he found himself wondering now whether the funds would be available.

If she were still alive, would he really want to be anywhere near this active volcano? Second best though she was, was Tanya now his only remaining source of funds? Fuck! He'd been on a good number here. Too good to be true, it seemed. How quickly could he head off north, up and away to Margot – and before that was there anything in this room to incriminate him?

It was almost an afterthought when he looked at the figure in the bath. The colour of the water suggested she had only just slit her wrists, possibly when he had entered. Perhaps it wasn't too late to save her, and in the process the money. Dead, she was of absolutely no use to him at all. He would have to see her as a short-term project. In a moment of supreme irony, his words to Frau Kopsch in Villingen came back to him: *Death is a growth industry.*

He stepped across, extended his hands towards her to see whether he could pull her out – and then stopped, looking at her half-open eyes. Was she smiling? No, impossible! She just had him spooked.

He squeezed his eyes shut. When he opened them again, he placed his ear close to her mouth – there appeared to be no air escaping from her parted lips. Had she truly been that ready to die?

As he reached down again to pull her out, he spotted a smashed glass, part of which he assumed she had used as a blade, and an empty pill bottle on the floor. "You stupid bitch!" It confirmed what he had thought; all of it – the call, the pills, the wrist-slitting – was a pathetic cry for help. She had been too weak to see anything through. In anger he shoved at the top of her head, causing her body to slide a little further into the large luxury bath. As her face dipped beneath the water, there was no response, no reflex.

But then something drained the blood from his veins too for a moment.

The phone rang in the bedroom.

He retracted his hands; observed her lifeless stare. She was gone for sure, and he didn't need to dirty his hands in the blood-tinged bathwater. Entering the bedroom, he looked at the phone for a wasted second or two. Was it Reception? If so – he checked the time – why were they calling her at 2.15pm? Had she perhaps not checked out? He'd assumed she had left after him in the morning but if so, what had happened in the interim to cause this? He glanced around. No – the room looked different from last night, even allowing for the little matter of a corpse in the bathroom. The bed was made; things were clean and straight. Nothing had been hung up. She'd not long been here.

The phone stopped. The pregnant silence that followed was, if anything, worse than the insistent chirruping. They'd be up soon, knowing his luck and the way this day was panning out. If it wasn't Reception, then who was it? Given that he had ignored Jessica's call that morning, who might she have then called in that most desperate of hours?

He took in the room again, spotted her handbag and was about to rifle through it quickly when a thrumming sound, which he recognised as the lift, reached his ears. He had always asked that they take a room at the end of the corridor, so that he had multiple exit strategies; the fire-exit was also close by. If this happened to be someone from Reception coming up, then he had little time to lose. It was all gut-instinct now; you didn't grow up in somewhere like East Berlin without honing the sixth sense that told you, if it sounds like trouble and smells like trouble, it probably is trouble. It helped when you yourself had hand-operated the ruthless mechanism of the Stasi; when you had been the one the timid creatures were listening out for as they stood on their hind legs and sniffed the air in fear. That same instinct was telling him now, the receptionist or whoever, had not called for reasons of benevolence.

He wanted to check through that damned handbag, contemplated stuffing the contents into his pockets, but then knew an empty handbag would tell a tale. He knew how that one detail would turn this from an act of lonely despair into the work of a potential third party. Rather than stuffing the bag into his jacket, he left it, trusting that he had always been careful enough to keep his identity out of this whole sorry affair.

He left the room hurriedly but not so much that he forgot to dry the latex gloves, close the door and check the corridor before diving for the fire exit. The lift motor was purring to a stop. He remembered to push the fire doors back into place, despite the resistance. It took both patience and effort as the doors had been designed to close gently; again, the plush hotel had the customers' well-being high on their agenda and wanted to avoid disturbing their sleep.

He stifled a burst of dark laughter – they would struggle to wake the current resident! For a moment he wondered whether he had been amongst the British too long and absorbed their graveyard humour.

When the doors finally came together, he had just enough time to duck out of sight beneath the wired windows before the lift doors opened. In another of those moments of displacement, when it seems the mind is trying to protect its keeper from harsh reality by filling the head with random thoughts, he remembered the name of Jessica's company, Fire-Dawes – an entity minus an owner as of two or three minutes before.

Immediately he heard knocking, so knew it had to be at room 501. Removing the latex gloves and shoving them into his pocket, he started to make his way with caution down the uncarpeted stairs; fancied he heard the room door opening. Was that the faint echo of a scream, or the wind carrying off the last dust of his conscience?

Re-entering the part of the hotel not designated for souls fleeing in panic, he made his way down the third-floor corridor and headed for the lifts at the far end. The last thing he wanted was to stroll into Reception via the fire escape.

Once outside, it wasn't until he closed the door of his car that he released a rebalancing breath and felt his heart rate returning to normal. It soon picked up and he thumped the steering wheel multiple times in anger when he realised what an idiot he had been. If any proof were needed that he wasn't thinking straight and needed to go off-radar for a while, it was this latest oversight. That last call had been from her mobile. Maybe it was still in her handbag. Fuck! He should have taken the bag after all, or at least dialled her number when he was in the room to hear whether it was nearby.

He took a deep breath. "Calm down, calm down." He had always used a pay-as-you-go phone with her so it wasn't trackable. Nevertheless, if they found her phone, they would know she had been calling someone in her darkest moment; there was someone else in her life. They would be seeking out him or her for some clue as to her distress.

Time to go. He wasn't going to wait around for the police to show up.

He wouldn't bother returning to The Farm and guessed that the container and its secrets were safe enough for now. He wouldn't risk being recognised in his Mondeo by bored workers as he crossed the farmland. It would be a hellish chance but that seemed to be the motto for the day. However, he blessed the anonymity of that old car. Now, from Bath it was just a shortish drive to the M5 and he would head north. M6, A74, M74 bla bla bla – with luck, which was a caveat on British roads, he could be on Harris within, say, twenty hours.

He hissed with sudden annoyance. Make that thirty-six hours. He was going to have to book that hotel room for hair-dyeing purposes after all. The way fate had played him this day, his blonde hair would betray him in some way. He was going to have to go dark in more than one sense.

Knowing that pay-as-you-go phones could still be tracked under certain conditions, he took the first opportunity of a quiet lane to follow through with his previous intention and smash the old phone, then allowed the next stretch of flowing water to swallow its remains.

It was quite something – rather than feeling restrictive, his shutting-off from all means of communication, including the lack of a DAB radio, was liberating; almost like the old days. It added to the feel-less-bad factor – *feel-good* would have been a step too far! – that he found a few of his old CDs in the glovebox and their music took him north of the border.

Chapter Twenty-One

The call to the Walton Hotel had born fruit of sorts; they'd confirmed that Katherine had returned to it, though they were unable to connect her. She had even learnt to play her sister's game, asking for Jessica, in which name the booking was indeed confirmed.

The real Jessica thanked the gods for the proof that a successful entrepreneur did not have to buy into the whole celebrity trap. She knew her niche. Her business was growing and she was doing very well out of it, but had no plans to overstep her boundaries. She couldn't imagine asking whether Sir Alan Sugar had booked into the hotel without causing uproar. Jessica Dawes – not a single head would turn.

None of this raised even a grim smile as she bombed down to the Walton. Jessica knew just how much was at stake. It wasn't the money; that was something and nothing. Worrying about that would have been akin to fretting about a smoker's cough while the house burned down.

She parked up and entered the hotel a few paces behind a man whose jeans and rather grubby waterproof seemed out of place in that swanky foyer; doubtless some slave to shabby chic.

There was a small queue. Nothing for it, she would have to wait. She knew from the occasional stays here that it was hotel policy never to give out room numbers without calling up to advise the guests they had a visitor. As the time dragged, she cursed herself for being very British and continuing to stand in line. She was unable to shake the ominous feeling hanging over her; was caught between the devil and the deep blue sea, not wanting to blurt out to the receptionists that all she wanted to know was the room in which she herself was staying! In addition, if by some freak chance someone did recognise her, the behaviour would seem odd and might delay things; if they didn't, it was drawing unwanted attention to that very name. She hoped she was overreacting.

Nevertheless, the need to keep this from the press was important for more than one reason.

At last she was at the desk and, by lucky chance, alone. It felt like it.

If the situation had not been so parlous it might almost have been amusing. There was a displaced moment of humour, laced with serious regret, as she thought of all the fun she and Katherine could have had as young twins at the expense of others, if their relationship had been anything other than dysfunctional.

"Hello, Miss Dawes." The receptionist gave her a broad smile. "How can I help you?"

Jessica pulled her best ditzy face; it didn't come easy, was anathema to her, but for what she was about to say she needed to give that impression.

"I'm so sorry; I seem to have lost my room keycard."

The responding smile still seemed genuine enough. "Not a problem. I'll give you a replacement. Now, just in case someone else finds that other key, I'll need to raise a new code. Please forgive the request, but may I see some ID?"

"Of course." Jessica fished in her bag and handed over her driving licence. She was taking a chance of course. Was it definite that her sister had booked in her name? The difficulty remained getting the room number, which would not be on the card. That had been the reason for her away-with-the-fairies smile; anticipating having to ask.

It turned out luck was on her side. On receipt of the ID, the receptionist seemed to have lowered her guard and was talking to her screen. "That's fine; so there's the new code for 501…" she hit a key, "… there!" She looked up and handed over the card, her indelible smile still in place. "By the way, there was a call for you earlier. I hadn't seen you go out, so tried to put it through. Sorry, that's a bit of non-news, isn't it? I just wasn't sure whether you were expecting someone and had forgotten."

Jessica raised her eyebrows and tutted. "Oh man! Yes, I was expecting a call. I have such a sieve for a brain. Is there a direct line to each room?"

"Yes, there is. I wouldn't have been allowed to give it to them as it reveals the room number. Replace the last three digits of the hotel number with your room number."

"Thank you so much."

"A pleasure, Miss Dawes."

Once away from Reception, Jessica shook her head. Boy, that had been surreal, pretending to be herself! She headed for the lifts but paused to call the direct line – no response.

* * *

The lift whispered its way to the fifth floor and slowed so gently, there was only a rumour it had stopped.

There was a scent in the air as Jessica stepped into the corridor but things were so fraught for her that it might have been nothing more than the odour of disquiet. As she opened the door and entered the room, that same scent was there.

"Katherine?" A silence full of foreboding. "Katherine?" She pushed the door shut behind her and wandered through.

The bathroom door was open. She saw what she saw; screamed, as any sister would at any age at the sight of her sibling, presumed dead. Rushing through, she took in something, the process of which she couldn't quite understand, but the results of which were all too evident.

In an almost subconscious move, her fire brigade training kicked in. A few years before, she had decided that a life of discipline, ritual and – if she was honest – taking orders wasn't for her, but a desire to protect life was, which she had then combined with her interest in the world of business; something she had inherited from her father. The colour of the water suggested Katherine had not been bleeding for too long yet. She grabbed her and hauled her out of the water. Her body warmth suggested more than just the temperature of the water. Was there still a chance? How long had she been submerged? What to deal with first? A glance at her wrists suggested Katherine had not succeeded in severing an artery, only veins, as did the colour of the blood, which was dark red and oozing from the wounds, rather than the bright red spurting of arterial bleeding.

Jessica made a choice. Pointless wasting time bandaging wrists if the victim had already drowned. She put her ear next to Katherine's mouth and felt no breath. Pressing her fingers to the neck, there seemed to be no pulse.

She launched into CPR; pumping, pumping. "C'mon please, Katherine, please!"

She knew it was no use…

… at least until the moment a spout of water shot from Katherine's mouth, followed by a terrifying gasp and the rise and fall of her chest.

125

There wasn't time to praise or damn. Rolling her sister into the recovery position, Jessica set about dealing with the wrists, wrapping towels tightly around the wounds, applying direct pressure. Checking her sister's breathing again, she decided it might be safe to sit her up and hold her arms above her heart to slow the bleeding.

They stayed like that, surreal statues representing the torments of some Breughelian vision. At last, as the towels had not become drenched in blood, Jessica decided the bleeding was under control. Her sister remained unconscious but her breathing was regular.

Unbelievably, the worst seemed to have passed. Katherine had at last opened her eyes and there had followed a few seconds of some memories that caused her, despite her weakness, to thrash, eyes suddenly wide. Had she, in those moments, relived slipping beneath the water, suddenly not wanting to die but tasting just her diluted blood, breathing in only life-extinguishing fluid? Now she lay calm again, sleeping whilst Jessica stood in a wasteland of selfishness, tormented by the feeling she had betrayed her flawed sister through her decision to resolve all issues herself. Even now, should she not have been calling the emergency services, an ambulance for sure, maybe the police? Instead, part of her wanted to save the family name for all manner of reasons; some of them cold-hearted and related to her business, others deeply moved by the sight of her disturbed sibling and wanting to ensure, if there was someone else involved in driving her to this desperate action, they would pay with a rougher justice than the courts could offer. Jessica was torn in so many ways; she wondered whether she wasn't a gene or two from being as fragile as her sister. Half of her hated Katherine for having deceived her and the other half was horrified to think it was fear of retribution that had driven the unstable girl to flee to this hotel like a child running to her bedroom.

Overriding all of this was an implacable need for revenge against whoever had taken advantage of her sister, causing her feverish dishonesty, most likely this Max, whoever he was and assuming that was even his name.

She looked around and knew that to deal with Max and the future, whatever it might hold, she had to first control the present; understand what and why as well as who.

Turning to Katherine again, she saw her breathing was even. One might almost have been fooled into believing it had never happened, were it not for the towels around her wrists. That was going to take some explaining to the hotel maids.

126

Shit!

Quickly, she took the *Do Not Disturb* sign and hung it on the outside of the door.

She wandered through into the bathroom. In this expensive hotel, perhaps there was a chance… no – not a sign of a first aid kit. She hurried down to her car and dug out her own. It was something she ensured was always available – what chance did you have of credibility in the health and safety world if you didn't carry such basics?

Back in the room she prepared some heavy-duty bandaging for Katherine's wounds. However, there was a bigger problem and like many in life, a sticking plaster would not resolve it. She leaned on the washbasin for a moment and stared into the mirror. What the hell was she going to do?

Then, despite the circumstances she smiled. Of course! How dumb was she being? The answer was literally staring her in the face. As far as the staff were concerned, she was staying in this hotel. Assuming she could keep the room, if she could buy herself a couple of days, she could get both of them out. There was nothing for it. She would take the suite until further notice.

Back in the bedroom, she removed the towels with care from her sister's wrists and saw that Katherine had made the usual error of so many attempted suicides, whether genuine or a cry for help. She had cut with a blunt edge across her wrists, rather than along them. The bleeding was already minimal and the cuts didn't look like they would need stitches.

She could get them through this.

Having applied the bandages, she returned to the bathroom. It was time to clear up – which was when she spotted something that had escaped her in the initial panic of finding her sister; the pill bottle – an empty vessel making a lot of noise and proof that this whole scene was a piece of morbid theatre. That last lot of anti-depressants had, courtesy of Jessica's discussion with the doctor, been placebos; she had used her position as her sibling's legal guardian to ask that favour. No way would they have rendered her weak. Nor had she been in the bath that long. She'd not bled enough for that to be so. So many questions. Had this been a piece of theatre for someone's benefit? If so, was that Max? Had he been here? Had he perhaps pushed Katherine under the water either in a panic or in anger, because thinking about it now, her position suggested some force may have been applied, though she might have simply slid to where she ended up.

This moment of mystery was also a paradox because it brought insight in another way; one that brought some shared pain for Jessica. Had she been wrong to take away the calming impact of the medication? She had argued her sister was bipolar, so the pills were also sedating the good side of her; the intelligent, caring, passionate one, which of course was also the one that got her into trouble. It was – the irony of it – just another sticking plaster solution. As fate had it, Jessica's actions may well have saved her sister's life on this occasion in this room, though knowing Katherine the way she did, the idea of a staged drama was still more likely, set up to try to win the love and force the hand of beloved Max. There was every chance those tablets ended up down the toilet.

Either way, what a fucking mess!

On which theme, she looked at the bath. She removed the plug and allowed the devil's own vino rosado to flow away. Now she watched fascinated but also repelled as two objects were revealed. A shard of glass, some skin still attached. That she had expected when she saw the broken glass, though was no less horrified to see it. The other object, in the context and through its incongruity, was perhaps more repulsive – a mobile phone. She lifted it out gently. Waterproof, it lit up. For a mad moment she wondered whether the lock screen would reveal a picture of Max, but instead was greeted by a picture that could as easily have been her as her sister.

As far as the lock key was concerned, Jessica had the fates on her side – 1111. For someone who had proved so adept at deceit and cunning, Katherine remained as gauche as ever.

She looked into the bathroom mirror again. "Well, who are you to talk, nearly thirty thousand pounds lighter and a sibling down?" When it dawned on her that she had thought of the money first in that moment, she turned away from her reflection, shook her head to dismiss the counterproductive anger and focussed on the phone again.

First stop – the most recent calls. She recognised her own number as the last inbound but felt her pulse race at the sight of the last outbound. She was about to dial it when something stopped her; the howl of a wild beast that rampaged just beyond the horizon, out of sight of her mind's eye but possessing a ferocity that shocked her.

She stared into the mirror once more, almost reeling, and a dark smile formed. Yes, better to wait. Some things were best served cold. She would look at the phone in detail later and see what other monsters lurked, whether in its memory or in hers.

First, there was a bath to clean. Then she would risk nipping out for some more bandages and other medication along with the laptop from the boot of her car, which she would need for a number of reasons. At least Katherine didn't drive – Uber ruled her movements, so there was no car to worry about in the hotel car park.

Although she had not been a party to any of this, she had to assume from Katherine's actions that Max might have had no inkling about the existence of a sister. If she had gone into a bank masquerading as Jessica Dawes, booked hotel rooms in that name, then there was every chance she had been maintaining that pretence from the beginning. After all, if this Max was the chancer Jessica assumed him to be, he would have checked her out, possibly before picking her out as a date, but certainly afterwards.

Oh, there was so much supposition, so much guesswork, but at this moment Jessica needed a path, no matter how muddy, along which to set out and this one would have to do.

As she logged onto her laptop, she knew where she would start. If he thought she was dead, then she needed to be dead. Her website would need to go on hold.

Chapter Twenty-Two

Given that there were more remote and desperate locations in the world, it was strange how places such as Harris still managed to feel like the end of the earth.

He noted how, as a townie, nearing its slumbering form filled him with a certain dread. Its very nature was a paradox; he needed somewhere to hide from humankind but had never been more aware of his love of the shadows, the polluted ways and maelstrom that marked out society. He had grown up surrounded by the very definition of a police state in East Berlin, indeed become a key part of its machinery and witnessed the many ways in which its bastard child, secrecy, manifested itself. For him, life had always been about furtiveness; hiding for real, not in plain sight. Now, like so much of this part of the world, he saw there wasn't even a tree to hide behind.

He shook his head as the ferry approached the land, in an almost literal attempt to clear his mind of the negativity. Recent events had somewhat burst the bubble. He wanted to take a simple, deep breath before blowing another. There were plenty of positives; still lots of money in the bank, irons in the fire. He'd got over worse hurdles than this, the Berlin Wall probably the ultimate example. Okay it had fallen, but many an East German had not lived long enough to profit from that.

He had always learnt his lessons and he would again after this latest shitstorm. Now he knew the difference between feeling unloved, needing attention and psychotic. Still, this place he was approaching – it seemed to have been created for mischief as he looked at the early morning mist that greeted him. He'd watched enough noir thrillers in recent times to know that sparsely populated islands could be places of danger, with crimes born from the seeds of inbred minds, or people simply seeking excitement where there might otherwise be none.

And people hiding.

Hell! – he couldn't shake the sense of foreboding and would have been more comfortable walking through the alleyways he had just been remembering in the wrong part of a town or city. Given that he had been in far darker places in his life, why was he so jumpy now?

He thought he knew. Perhaps he was even in denial.

He had made a mistake; more than one. Since he'd gone solo, this had been the largest sum of money he had squeezed out of a victim in one hit and he'd not allowed for the protracted clearance period. Then the mad witch had distracted him with her needy behaviour before completely destroying any chance they might have had of a life together. He'd not been thinking straight when he had turned and gone back. On reflection, if she hadn't put herself out of her misery, he might have contemplated doing it for her. He would never sniff that money now. No way would the funds be made available when the account holder killed herself the following day! Even if it were, the authorities would be watching its progress; owls tracking a mouse. He'd have to kiss it goodbye.

He punched the ship's rail before looking around to see whether he'd been observed.

There was no denying that he needed to be out of sight – out of mind was probably an impossibility for different people and reasons – for some time. He was confident enough that he had covered his tracks. Having left the Mondeo down an anonymous-looking side street in Portree on the Isle of Skye, he'd made his way by public transport to Uig, avoiding hiring a car, not wishing to leave any trail of breadcrumbs.

Once at the ferry terminal, he had called her from a landline – the breadcrumb principle again. He wanted to avoid interaction with people on Harris as much as possible, based on the assumption that strangers might well stand out, so whereas he might have tried hitching a ride to her place, he dismissed that possibility. As always, the devil was in the detail. Bearing out her comments about the signal – he had called her mobile – he had just about made out, to his intense relief, that she would meet him at the port – a grand word for that little stage…

… and sure enough, there was the battered 4x4 she'd told him to look out for.

Her greeting – her demeanour – seemed to match the landscape, a certain cloudiness in the eyes and a definitive frostiness. Fair enough; he hadn't been in touch for some months till his recent call.

Still, in her welcoming kiss on the cheek – the fact that there was a kiss at all – and the fact that she had come to meet him, there was a thread of hope.

He wondered; had that thread been cast out to lead him in or ensnare him? If the latter, however, in many ways that suited him better.

He felt like he had written the instruction manual for this type of encounter – The Handbook of Desperation.

No word was spoken till they were well on the road back. Though he was fine with that, he could also imagine that silence might well be the lingua franca of this sort of remote settlement. He pictured men coming home after another day of working on the land, whether as farmers or dry-stone wall builders, or perhaps fishermen, exhausted and expecting food. Having communicated with no-one except sheep, rocks or the wind all day every day, they might have forgotten the art of conversation, or indeed have nothing other than their children in common with the wife who had spent her day also battling with discontent, dampness and dust to keep a home.

There was a similarity to life in the former DDR, except there, silence was often the price for working in the secret services or the fee for keeping yourself alive.

He knew well enough that this particular woman's lack of words represented chastisement. It spoke volumes that she hadn't even commented on his blond hair. He had decided against the delay that would have meant him leaving more of those breadcrumbs – hair-dye purchased, the possibility of someone happening to see him check in somewhere as blond and check out very soon afterwards as black-haired. He played at penitence with his own silence. Who would blink first?

Her of course.

"I wasn't sure you were going to make it, Uli."

Marcus turned to look at her as she drove, thanking the gods that she was staring straight ahead, for fear she might have seen the momentary flinch the name caused; thanking them also for reminding him, through her, which alter ego he was supposed to be using. "Look, I know I have previous, but I'm here and…"

"No, I meant they're forecasting a storm, or rather what passes for one for the ferry companies. People tend to view them here as a good day to put out the washing!"

"Well, here I am, despite that."

She continued to stare straight ahead. He wasn't completely forgiven yet – or rather he was, he could just tell, but she was determined not to cut him that slack yet.

"Why?"

His turn to look through the windscreen. Good question – needed a good answer; something better than *I've missed you.*

"I've missed you. I fought against it, but…" He saw her knuckles whiten as they gripped the steering wheel. The ensuing silence was emerging from a different place now into the daylight. He could sense its positivity, despite her best efforts. He pushed on. "Plus, I never got my signed copy of your book."

Her little snort might have translated as a laugh but was still open to interpretation.

He continued, still looking forward: "Look, you know how it can be, to become so wrapped up in something that you forget for a time who and what you are. So you start looking for the sanctuary, where you might find it again. I admit the futures market eats up my time. I'm competitive; not greedy, but I do want to be the best I can."

The lack of response to his serving of humble pie was starting to annoy and concern him. It was time to add some chillies. "And then, the other day, a colleague of mine was killed." He sensed her head jerk to look at him. "Overtired, way too many hours, too many missed meals, too many visits to late-night bars after work, a simple misjudgement in his car. I knew what had caused it. Suddenly, I wanted to live a little, defined differently from my usual take on that expression… and I thought of you."

Marcus waited.

"I'm sorry." One hand moved from the steering wheel and rested on his leg. Now she looked at him, just a brief glance, given the nature of the road. "Particularly about that hair."

There were two or three wordless seconds…

… and then they both burst out laughing. Tension fled stampeding from their respective chests into the air.

When quite some seconds had passed and they had calmed down, he stroked a hand across his scalp. "Actually, so am I." He paused. "It was a bet."

Her next words took him by surprise, in part because of the lack of context, but also in there being no need for interpretation. No turning to the handbook to decipher; no hidden meaning to an apparent statement of innocence. "Will you fuck me? God, I've missed it!"

* * *

133

Something that did need redefining in his lexicon was the word *remote*. On the drive from the port of Tarbert heading south towards Northton, they might have been crossing the landscape of some distant planet. After that, they skirted some of the most picturesque beaches he had ever seen. It was awe-inspiring. During all that time, they had to pull over for perhaps two vehicles on the single-track roads. It was all perfect for his needs, yet even as they parked up outside her cottage he started working on escape routes. Was he paranoid? No-one was going to find him here and when your exit strategy without a vehicle entailed ten miles on foot in every direction, apart from the one cut short by the coast and the sea, then you owed it to yourself to relax a little. Besides, for sure, no-one was going to be able to sneak up on him.

On their arrival, there appeared to be a slight reinterpretation of her request – she fucked him. Almost from the moment they entered the front door she was like some strange beast which had lived alone for too long in this far corner of the island. He could taste her loneliness; saw in the extremes of her need a reflection of his own desire for domestic danger, crowded streets, traffic, restaurants, galleries… money. He wondered whether he was witnessing something unique; if the heroine of her novel *Kingdom Cum* – was heroine the right word? – had not been based on Margot. If not, then it seemed she had become that woman. There was no stopping her. It seemed inevitable that one day she would leave this isolation behind.

At last, she slumped beside him. He stared at the ceiling, exhausted. She turned her head to look at him and said: "Better get used to it. There won't be anything else to do. The internet signal is a bit intermittent. It's just this spot. There's a signal of sorts on the road we came down but we'd need to get back about seven miles to pick up a hot spot or two." She paused. "Actually you called me from a landline, didn't you? Why was that?"

"I've managed to lose my mobile."

"Well, the passcode to my phone is 627468 – it spells *MARGOT* – if you want to try your luck sometime."

He couldn't deny that this left him feeling dependent. The sense of freedom he had experienced in the car deserted him for a moment.

He needed to get a grip. What did he want to do – order a pizza?

Nevertheless, he was concerned at the prospect of being unable to communicate with his remaining cash-cows. It was an issue to be addressed further down the line. At least one matter had been resolved, the one of whether she had forgiven him or not.

She swung herself off the bed. "Would you like a vodka?"

He smiled and determined once again that he would enjoy this time for what it was.

She continued, "I'm afraid I don't have any of that rather camp Disaronno you ordered in that bar where we met."

Marcus burst out laughing. "No, I can't imagine Disaronno on Harris."

As she turned her back on him and headed off to get the drinks, Marcus' smile faded. He remembered Jack Jeffries drinking that in the bar in Freiburg. His wife had also fucked like a wild animal for a time. She had even married her husband's murderer. Life was just a knotted rope.

Chapter Twenty-Three

There were so many reasons why Jessica wanted to take Katherine away and look after her in the comfort of their own home, some selfish, she had to admit, some less so. However, if the seeds that had just planted themselves in her mind were to flourish and bear their necessarily bitter fruits, she needed to tend them well and with patience. There would be less distractions here in this hotel room. The embryonic plan required her full focus. Right now, it lacked structure but not purpose.

The fact of them being identical twins was another obstacle to her taking Katherine home. Trying to make it through Reception without drawing attention would have been challenging. Given the events of the last hours, Katherine was too weak to make her own way and if trying to sneak past the hotel staff with your lookalike weren't difficult enough, having her leaning in distress on your shoulder was a recipe for disaster. Putting her in a disguise would just seem weird when you had checked in alone and might even prompt someone to check the CCTV that was a requirement in the lobby and grounds, though not the corridors.

No, they were best off staying put for now. She could keep the world at bay. Jessica had never fully appreciated the talismanic properties of protection in a *Do Not Disturb* sign in such a five-star establishment – it overrode everything, including that ridiculous ritual of turning down the bed; a latter-day curse on the pharaoh's tomb – *Enter on peril of death to your reputation as a hotel*. Of course, if some overzealous chambermaid did enter during one of Jessica's occasional necessary absences, it would be to find her, to all intents and purposes, tucked up in bed. All very confusing!

She couldn't just sit around; she needed to focus and put some flesh on the bones of her fledgling idea. She had already taken the first steps online. No matter the lack of finer details, the plan had a name – vengeance.

Without ever having met him, she remained convinced that this Max held the key. Never before had Katherine stooped to such levels of deceit. If her mystery man was anything other than a chancer, where was he right now in her hour of need? Surely, he had to be pretty special, this someone for whom her sister had been prepared to turn the world upside-down and then red, willing to incur the wrath of her closest living relative. Much more likely of course, he was a complete charlatan.

Once the bank had confirmed that the thirty-grand cheque had not been cashed, she had asked them to cancel the account closure. She wondered whether losing out on the money would provoke Max into making an appearance. For that sort of sum, four to six days were required before the money would be made available. Did it eat at him that Katherine hadn't been able to give him cash? Mr Gibbons at the bank had wanted to bring in the police but she had played a card to which there was no answer; they both knew she had to be lying when she said she'd suffered temporary amnesia after a blow to the head, causing her to forget on her next visit that she had closed the account. The problem for Gibbons was that he had no knowledge of the existence of her sister. While every bone in his body felt the deception, he had no rational explanation and just had to accept it. Besides, his and the bank's security processes would have come under scrutiny if he knew the truth. He was a man with an axe, but no tree to fell. In fact, its sharp edge probably rather made his neck tingle with fearful anticipation. In the end he settled for letting it go and the compensation of thirty thousand pounds back in his keeping.

But ridiculous though it sounded, saving her sister's life and returning things to the status quo were not enough for Jessica now. She wanted Max on a plate, assuming he was responsible for this. Her instincts told her it was so and she'd learnt to trust those slivers of foreknowledge.

What's eating you, Jessica?

She looked over her shoulder, as if the words had emanated from a presence of flesh and blood, which had sneaked into the room. Instead, her conscience found Katherine, sitting up in the bed, faint marks of blood still staining the fresh bandages around her wrists. The cat seemed to have got her own tongue and she just had to sit, shocked, while her sister continued:

And what if someone had indeed got past your guard; your pharaoh's curse and the other barriers you seek to put in the way? That would be twice in as many days, wouldn't it? Or maybe three times? Someone gets to your sister yet again, despite your best attempts to be the self-appointed guardian. The problem is she feels her passions with a greater intensity than you could ever imagine. A woman who both loves – and loves sex. It's driven her beyond your control so many times already and you're left gathering the harvest each time. But don't you wish you could feel that burning for yourself? That danger? You miss it, don't you? Literally, you miss the burning – those years in the fire brigade, blazing a trail for women, haha! If you can't feel the heat between your legs, then find it another way. Making those decisions that save lives, showing the men who's the mummy! Then you see an opportunity to use those skills and others to become a different type of trailblazer. You have all the contacts and soon all the contracts. Dragon's Fire.

But now a guy gets one over on you, through me. I'm weak, but still my cunning gets the better of you. My weakness becomes yours. You're even made to look a fool at the bank. That can't be allowed to happen. And as I can't pay, he will. You'll see to that – personally. It's the danger again, isn't it? And revenge – for getting past you.

But how will he pay, Jessica? And who else will pay? Will it be me?

Jessica screwed her eyes tight. "Shut up!" Opening them again, she observed Katherine stirring slightly at the sound of the raised voice before resuming the deep, silent sleep into which she had been despatched by her painkillers.

She squeezed her eyelids together again as another dark thought sought entry to her troubled mind – was there any part of her that regretted her sister's failure to complete her bathtub mission? Were the painkillers meant not simply to numb Katherine's distress but to bring peace for Jessica while she was stuck there with her?

"STOP IT!"

Was she just going stir-crazy, trapped for now in this hotel room? It was always possible. If there was a thread of truth in that imagined monologue just now…

Just one thread?

… it was that, despite all her entrepreneurial business success, she did miss the thrill of working with a team in perilous circumstances to save lives, often pushing yourself to your physical limits. No amount of marathon running for charities or buttock-aching repetition on the rowing machines of some swanky hotel chain could create that teak-hard fitness. Plus, unlike business or indeed the current infraction by Max, you knew your enemy, how it would respond to certain triggers, what you could and couldn't do. When it would defeat you and all you could try was to minimise the damage.

Max was not a fire, but just like one, he had destroyed while having no substance.

She shook her head, stretched it to right and left to relieve the growing tension, then turned to her laptop.

Where to begin? There was that number on Katherine's phone; that last outgoing call. Given everything that had happened, the time of the call suggested she would have made it shortly before her failed or faux suicide attempt. Was it a cry of help to Max? Surely yes, almost certainly, but calling that number now might lose her any nascent trail by spooking him.

"Why aren't you handing this information to the police?"

She recognised the voice — her own — so didn't turn this time and simply rejected the self-criticism. It was important for her to accept the truth – she wasn't simply after justice, at least not in its judiciary sense.

So, what other secrets were held on that phone; the four-cornered heart of modern society, worn on the sleeve by far too many people and by means of which many sought public acclaim for their humdrum existences? Where the wannabe sage revealed him or herself to be just an onion?

She flicked open the photo gallery, selected the last picture taken and experienced a kind of demonic excitement at the sight revealed. It had been taken the previous evening, the subject a man, judging by the musculature, though he was face down and had his features turned away from the lens.

Here was indeed danger. In a moment of self-awareness, she had to acknowledge once again the earlier critique of her conscience; that in business she had never replaced the appeal of risk. Even the winning of a big contract never matched that visceral tingle.

But there was more. The sleeping male had slightly too long blond hair and now, with the recall that had served her so well during every element of her career, she remembered the scruffy guy who had preceded her into the hotel. Was she mistaken – she didn't think so – or had there been there a few blond locks peeking out from beneath his woollen hat? Hadn't Max been less than well-off, a little down on his luck and in need of some new clothes according to Katherine; all part of his appeal? Might he be in need of a haircut too? And hadn't he simply walked on through Reception? Perhaps her memory was playing tricks.

She lifted her head and sniffed in vain, but what the olfactory sense now lacked was more than made up for by her memory. There had been a scent in the corridor and in the room itself when she had first approached it; a very male scent like an aftershave or shower gel. The scruffy guy could have been here while she'd been held up in the queue earlier. Nothing like jumping to conclusions, of course, but she had built the pillars of her life from such materials.

She zoomed in on the picture – and now it really had her full attention! Her eyes were drawn to a tattoo on the sleeper's upper left arm; a strange three-pointed symbol, not quite a triangle, nor a letter A. Around the outside was a circle, giving it the air of da Vinci's Vitruvian Man. There were dark decorative lines at what she thought of for now as the corners of the triangle. She tried zooming in further, but they became indistinct.

This had to be Max.

She stared at the picture like a critic in a gallery, seeing a man sated and apparently at ease with his ways. Yet was she doing him a disservice? Was he exactly whom he said he was and Katherine had simply fallen head over heels, losing mind and reason, breaking the law to try to keep him happy? But did it matter? Either way, she needed to speak with him; confront him.

Above all, his absence from Katherine's life in the last twenty-four hours, coinciding with the prospect of thirty thousand pounds coming his way wasn't mere coincidence.

How to find him? This was a hotel that made a point of eschewing CCTV cameras other than in the grounds and lobby. It was almost as if being able to afford to stay here entitled you to – what was the best phrase? – live a little.

Aware that she was becoming transfixed by the picture and needing to remain objective, she returned to the phone's home screen.

On seeing the Instagram app, she had a damascene moment, realising that once again this little rectangle of electronics and the social media forest that fed it, was truly the portal into so much of people's lives now. For certain, it offered her a way to reach out. If Max preyed on women in need of attention and its sometime by-product of sexual intimacy, wasn't there a chance that somewhere somebody might recognise that tattoo? It was a long shot, but one she would take.

Hitting the laptop again, she took a few minutes to open Facebook, Instagram and Twitter accounts under a pseudonym. With that done, she cropped the photo till only the tattoo showed. The pity was that she couldn't zoom in further on it, but she did what she could – and out it went, accompanied by the post: *Cool tattoo – anyone know what it means?* Having hash-tagged every variation of tattoo that might be appropriate, all she could do now was wait.

Chapter Twenty-Four

She had left him for dead and set out for provisions. Judging by last night's performance – her own – he was going to need his strength!

Plus, she needed to be active. Living on your own on Harris, there was always something to do and you forgot how to relax. Not for her cuddling up in bed; she had left that poisoned domesticity behind long ago – or rather, it felt like a long time since *Kingdom Cum* had opened the door to dangers and wonders.

She was grateful that the divorce was already out of the way before this had all happened; that she had released herself from the suffocating boredom of marriage by the time fame and wealth, those two-faced interlopers, had come knocking on her door. Of course, they had introduced a different kind of stranglehold – another take on being unable to breathe – but as she looked through the windows of the 4 x 4 she acknowledged that success was a double-edged sword, enabling her to afford to come there, where life was stripped down to the bare bones.

But oh boy, had she missed sex! While *Kingdom Cum* may not have been based on any element of her life, there was no denying her appetites had been drawn on for source material. At one stage, during the hedonism of the last few hours, she and Uli had exchanged knowledge; a look as they climaxed together that spoke of a mutual understanding: *I understand your needs and love doesn't number amongst them.*

As she approached Leverburgh she knew she would submit to another need. Much as she hated the clawing and cloying grip social media exerted on modern life, it had made her. She couldn't be a hypocrite. Hence, her other reason for heading into what she thought of with knowing irony as the seething metropolis, was to try to pick up a more reliable internet signal. She needed to know how book sales were doing. She might now have been rich beyond her wildest dreams but the critiques still counted, some of them rather painfully so. Plus she was awaiting news from her agent about the screenplay.

Her business in the little supermarket, the only shop in the area, was quickly done and it reminded her of the positives of life at the edge of civilisation. No-one knew her or if they did, they didn't show it. She was treated like any other customer. Back in the days when she could only dream, she had always believed one of the plusses of being a successful author would be anonymity. Who knew what anyone except the most massively successful writers looked like? Some might have chosen to soak up the adulation, but if you so desired you could enjoy the fruits of your labours in relative privacy.

So much for that. She'd been wrong, courtesy of social media and the demands of her publishers.

Back in the car, she parked where she knew there to be the best hotspot. 'Hot' was a relative term as it still involved one bar, occasionally two maximum, but it was enough and the phone fell into a minor fit of buzzing and beeping.

Trawling through the emails, she found a couple from Sarah Kent, her agent. One had an attachment. Was it a film contract? Was it buggery – it was a jpeg. She read on, intrigued.

Hi Gotty,

Miss you and being able to talk to you. Any thoughts about when you might be on the mainland again?

In the meantime, food for thought! The attached tattoo has gone somewhat viral and I had an idea. Given Georgia's fixation with Jude's tattoo in KC, I wondered whether there was some marketing play that could be made out of this. Believe me millions have shared it, thousands have commented.

Intrigued, she opened the jpeg and frowned.

It looked similar to the one Uli sported on his arm, but what did she know? She wasn't a fan of the trend for tattoos – supposed marks of individuality paid for so you could ape everyone else. She wondered how many indigenous peoples, for example Maoris, felt offended by this vain fixation. Anyway, yesterday had been the first time she'd seen Uli fully naked and she'd been more fixated on that dangerous weapon throbbing in and against her than on his tattoo. What had caused her to pay any attention at all was that, for some reason, she hadn't expected a City worker like him to be sporting a tattoo of any sort. There was no good reason for that pre-judgement – she stopped short of calling it a prejudice.

She shouldn't have been surprised; there were so many contradictions about Uli and her feelings for him. Sometimes he didn't seem to quite stack up but maybe that was part of his maverick appeal. Then again, there was no longevity in their relationship, no past, no future, so what was her basis for leaping to assumptions? Was it the author in her, looking for plots when there were none; threats in a smile? Without doubt, for a lot of women it was the latent danger in her creation Jude that held the most appeal. It was why the book had sold in millions, leaving so many men, and women too, wondering whether they should accept defeat and run for the hills or ride in bareback firing arrows.

When Uli had approached her in that bar in London, she'd sensed immediately there was something different about him. His opening line had been a beaut: *Don't worry – I'm only after you for your money.* They had fucked that night but in a way that meant she saw nothing of his tattoo, just the finer details of some cement in the brickwork outside the hotel.

She had never forgotten that. Memories of it and the other night spent in the more luxurious, forgiving surroundings of a hotel room aroused the sleeping beast in her, no matter what the elements or the dark clouds of her own psyche threw her way on this island. It was why there had been zero chance of her refusing to pick him up from the ferry terminal yesterday.

Margot wasn't sure where things went from here. Frankly, she couldn't be bothered to think beyond the next few hours. Perhaps she should consider putting a sign up outside her cottage: *Breakfast and Bed.* She thought again of the purgatory, the coldness, which had been her marriage. Almost thrown into her path by a random gust of Hebridean wind came a memory of a Restoration comedy she had read at university – *The Way of the World,* where a feisty lady, Mrs Millamant, had uttered prophetic words about marrying: *'I may by degrees dwindle into a wife.'* It had stuck with her. Yet despite the warnings, she had done what so many did in haste and repented at leisure.

The recollection of that might have explained the force with which she now gunned the engine as she headed back.

Chapter Twenty-Five

It hadn't taken long, but wasn't that one of the plusses of social media? Within minutes Jessica had turned the alerts signal to silent on her phone, so frequently did it chirrup. How she wished people responded to her business mailers by asking to be friends or be allowed to follow as eagerly as they did to the sight of a tattoo! How could posting this picture on social media have suddenly rendered her a figure of such fascination?

Now started the process of sorting the wheat from the chaff, deleting all the responses that said *Cool!* and those plugging their businesses. A few picked up the similarity to Vitruvian Man, so of course the conspiracy theorists now needed to be weeded out; it seemed if you mentioned da Vinci online these days you attracted weirdos in as great numbers as, if not greater than, art lovers and historians.

Then something of genuine interest cropped up – a post on Instagram from somebody who pointed out that the image might well be an adaptation of the symbol that formed part of the flag of the DDR, the former East Germany, and of the crest of the Stasi, the secret police of that country. The vertical line down the middle of the triangular shape appeared to be, on closer inspection, a hammer and the two longer sides of the triangle might have been a compass. The surrounding circle was possibly rye. Back in the old communist regime this had a strong symbolism; the hammer represented the workers, the compass the intelligentsia and the rye the farmers. However, what the refreshingly intelligent guy was unable to make out with any clarity were the decorative black lines at the three points. If this symbol were in any way related to East Germany, there was a chance that might be Gothic script but it was simply not clear enough to see.

Jessica replied with heartfelt thanks and then sat deep in thought. Max, blond – from the name and hair colour there was a chance he was German, though if he was a conman, he might well have used a false name. However, the tattoo would make sense. In the absence of anything else it gave her something to chew on; a tenuous lead but she would follow it.

Turning back to the screen, two new comments now caught her attention. Both came from females, which gave the seeming vitriol of the words added bitterness and held her attention, given her current mission; well, one was a woman for sure, if Bella Fisher's profile picture was to be believed. She had a winning smile; a vibrant red-head who looked like she enjoyed life. The other, Christine Jeffries, seemed cagier, with just a flower in the picture slot.

Jessica had accepted both friend requests only a minute or so before. Now more than curious, she clicked on Christine Jeffries' profile. Curiosity turned to puzzlement. The account had very few posts or photos and such as there were seemed to relate to art, French in particular. Nor were they very recent. It felt as if someone had opened the account because it was the done thing, and then lost interest. So what was it about the tattoo?

Which made it all the more surprising that the initial comment came from Christine Jeffries.

Once Jessica had finished, she realised she'd stopped breathing.

If I read this symbol correctly, it translates as 'predator'. Would you agree? See my message.

Then there was a line from Bella Fisher, a response to that comment: *Most definitely.*

Now her heart missed a beat at the sound of two alerts and she glanced across to see two messages waiting – from her new-found followers! It told her much; they must have been hovering over their phones or keyboards. Surely only the photo of the tattoo could have been responsible for that tension and prompted such urgency. She doubted anyone was that keen to be her friend!

Much as Jessica wanted to play it cagey, she couldn't help but respond. *I have a sister recovering from attempted suicide who might agree.*

What excited her now was the speed of response to this specific detail. It seemed she had tapped into a productive vein. *I'm sorry to hear that, but relieved it was only attempted suicide. I had an ex-employee who went one fatal step further – or at least that is what we were all meant to believe.*

"Oh my God!" The whispered words reflected a true depth of emotion, lacked so often in the modern parlance of the *OMG!* brigade. She glanced across at Katherine. After all they had been through, the thought of another woman – a presumption of course, but one she believed had substance – succeeding where her sister had failed filled her with deep dismay.

145

Then – a moment of horrified enlightenment.

She typed: *Please call me* and added the number of a Pay-As-You-Go which she had purchased on her brief trip from the hotel.

No more than a minute later, that phone rang.

"Christine?"

"Who is this?"

"My name's Jessica. Thank you for calling me. I'm intrigued. You said *'An ex-employee.'* I take it from that you run your own business?"

"Yes – why?" It was clear the world and all its ills had rendered Christine cynical and suspicious.

"Can we meet? I'd rather talk about this face-to-face." There was silence. "There's nothing to fear from me, Christine. I think we have a mutual nemesis."

"That nemesis is out of my life. I'm wondering what raking over old ground is going to bring."

Whilst they were talking, Jessica clicked on the other Facebook message from Bella Fisher. *Where did you get this?*

She turned her attention back to the phone. "Not quite out of somebody else's life or mind, if another message I just received is anything to go by."

"How is your sister?" Christine's tone warmed for a moment.

"Out of danger – physical danger. How well she recovers from the psychological impact of this… well let's just say my sister isn't the strongest. If we're talking about the same man – and I suspect we are – I don't think she'll make a full recovery until he is dealt with." Jessica knew, in suggesting her motives were purely for her sister's well-being, she was not just diluting the truth, but distorting it. She pushed on. "We need to find this… what did he tell you his name was?"

"My husband… my second husband's name is Joost."

Jessica paused, her breath taken for a moment. "Okay, it went that far! Your husband. Well, just so you know, his name in this relationship was Max." She gathered herself. "Look, Christine, I ask again, as I think we could talk about this better face-to-face, would you be prepared to meet? I'm afraid it might be a bit of a trek. I don't know where you live but I'm based in Bath. We could meet at a halfway house – motorway services or something."

"No, your place is fine, if that's what you would prefer. The drive may give me time to think and besides, I doubt the theme of our conversation is going to be something best accompanied by a Costa."

The droll tone surprised Jessica, but she warmed to her interlocutor as a result. That hint of humour was nowhere to be found in Christine's next words.

"So, it's not your intention to go to the police."

"Uh… of course… eventually."

"Hmmm." The response carried more than a modicum of disbelief, but it appeared curiosity was winning the day. "Okay, yes, let's meet. I believe *where* has been decided, so when – and what's your address?"

"I'll message you the details. When?" Jessica pondered how long it might be before she could leave her sister on her own in the hotel for a few hours. "Soon, very soon."

She'd had to force herself to go to bed after that; her brain was a cauldron and the bubbling of its poisonous contents would mean sleep was probably beyond her.

So it was strange to be woken by the sound of another alert on the laptop. A glance at her watch revealed 3am; clearly someone else's witching hour. She forced herself across to the sofa where she had left the machine and clicked on the message from someone called Tanya. *Whatever's happening, count me in!*

Now Katherine opened Christine's message again and typed: *I think we may have a quorum.* She got as far as thinking about making her way back to bed when she noticed the message had been seen. It seemed she had at least one thing in common with mythical Max – women leapt at her messages! In no time, the response came: *Let's call it a witches' coven, or perhaps a convening of the Furies.*

Jessica laughed at the like-minded sense of humour but was then struck again by how dark things had become. It was a sad indictment of her life that she struggled to remember the last time she'd found something light and humorous. Considering what had just amused her, she had to think about the road she was on and the shadows that hid everything ahead.

* * *

Though she doubted any of them were sleeping, she left it till morning before sending a simple message to Bella Fisher and Tanya – her prepaid phone number and the request: *Call me.*

Chapter Twenty-Six

He was still in bed when Margot returned. Much as she would have liked to believe that her performance and appetites were responsible for his exhaustion, she had to allow for him driving all the way to the north-west Scottish coast and the subsequent ferry crossings.

He didn't seem to have moved. She watched him sleeping for a moment, then moved closer on tiptoes. She looked at the part-obscured tattoo then back at the phone in her hand. Damn, but they were very similar.

She wasn't sure how she felt about this. So many questions bobbed in the wake of his turbulent arrival and, much as she hated to admit it, a spark of jealousy flared. If this was a picture of him, where was it taken and when? That, though, was the least of things at this moment; when you left a light shining in a dark place, you could hardly complain about the moths.

So why had he chosen to visit her out of the blue? Given her own motivations for coming to Harris, namely escape and anonymity, she couldn't help but wonder.

Despite everything, the sight of his muscular torso in her bed stirred her. Whatever was happening in his private life, those questions could wait. She needed to take and she needed to be taken – it was all that mattered for now.

* * *

He woke up and smelt the coffee – and the bacon. Sometimes, amidst the over-complications created by the mind, it was both a source of wonder and a timely reminder that our appetites remained primal.

He turned onto his back, relished the uncoiling stretch of his limbs; took in the square of unblemished azure of the Atlantic sky through the dormer window while memories of abandonment wandered in along with the aromas of breakfast.

When had he last felt like this, warmed by a moment of unadulterated, calm pleasure and an appreciation of simple things? Strange to think that it might have been during his years in what had turned out to be that most claustrophobic of regimes in East Germany, where nothing had been untainted. Yet that was a judgement made only with hindsight. At the time, the world existed as presented to you, certainly for those born under Communist rule, such as he, Michael and Richard, the self-styled cabal; the triumvirate. Had anything ever tasted as good as that contraband packet of fig rolls when he was a boy? Interesting how they never yearned to be in the country that produced those nefarious goods, just licked from their fingertips the fruits of disobedience.

When you were told what to do, life was simple. Likewise, power was uncomplicated. Once you had it, it was yours. People did what you said. No need to change your name or curry favour with some stupid woman for a few thousand Ostmark, in part because they didn't have it to give. Besides, you didn't need money when you had power, nor for the journey there. Your only hindrance would be a conscience.

Hindsight brought an awareness of the reality of repression but even then, that vision wasn't twenty-twenty. As usual, history was written by the victors – and by those who had power.

This was no good. He sat up, his fleeting calmness tainted now by thoughts of the thirty thousand pounds which had slipped through his fingers. Much as he wanted to keep a low profile, he would have to find a way to contact Tanya and Bella; the poor internet signal was a mixed blessing.

Despite everything, that smell of bacon was a lure he could not resist. Getting out of bed, he pulled on his jeans and T-shirt, then wandered down.

Margot was at the cooker. She turned and smiled: "Good morning!"

Their eyes locked for a few seconds that spoke of many things, mostly pleasurable, though he couldn't be sure there wasn't something he failed to interpret. Perhaps she was just feeling some atavistic embarrassment as a result of her unbridled lust of the night before. She turned back to the frying pan as she continued: "I went and got some provisions. Help yourself to coffee."

The fry-up was an island of delights all of its own; the *Nachtisch* even more so as she straddled him there by the breakfast table, gasping and moaning her way to what seemed like a massive climax. Yet all the time, he could sense something, as if smoke had drifted across the blue square of the bedroom window. He wasn't going to ask; she was a woman – she'd tell him soon enough. Perhaps it took someone who had made a habit of lying to recognise it in someone else, or was it just his trained eyes, honed under the Stasi, that helped him see the inflections of deceit or defensiveness? Having said that, he knew now that almost everyone in the DDR, guilty and innocent, had learnt to lie well.

Her words broke his train of thought. "Hey!" Here it came. That single syllable was far more fragile than it seemed. "When I was over in Leverburgh earlier I got a signal. I had an email from my agent, Sarah Kent." Margot leaned back across the breakfast table and reached for her phone. The sight of her doing so, the way her breasts swayed, made his groin twitch again. He turned her to face the table, eased her back onto him. She groaned, but still clung to the mobile. Eagle-eyed, he watched for confirmation of the PIN that she, in her naivety, had revealed to him the day before, as she proceeded to call up a picture. "She said this tattoo has gone viral."

As he took in what she showed him from over his shoulder, it took a huge effort to maintain his hardness. Then, in a moment of disturbing detachment, he had to question whether the knowledge of what was coming helped him. He hoped not, otherwise he was truly a lost soul.

He lifted her hair, placed a gentle kiss on the back of her neck. He let his lips wander down to her shoulders, nibbled where they met the neck and took in her sighing response. Whatever was on her mind, it didn't stop her hips starting to churn slightly. With one hand he pushed the phone away while his other wandered across her breasts. He saw her eyes were shut. He thrust; enough times to make her drop all defences before placing an arm around her throat. Pressure applied. A few flails of her arms that might even have been mistaken for a death orgasm.

And then all was still.

He picked up the phone.

Now he did shrink out of her, seeing again his own tattoo.

So this had gone viral online. Jessica, you fucking idiot! It must have been her who took this. She'd been trying to just before he…

So, who was the fucking idiot really?

… fell asleep. Well if this was out there, you could guarantee, despite their lack of savvy on the internet, that Michael and Richard would see this soon enough. He'd have to stay put for a while now, out of sight. The thought chilled him, lodging here with this deathly hostess.

Having closed the curtains – they didn't seem to go for nets in this sparsely populated part – he turned his attention to her phone. Finding her Yahoo account, he dug out the fateful email. It seemed she hadn't replied to her agent;

good in one way but not in another. A lack of response about something relating to her book sales might raise suspicions. Scanning the inbox he looked through their various exchanges, needing to find some suitable jargon, nicknames, something that would help him mimic her. There seemed to be no coded endearments.

With that, he searched through the WhatsApp contacts and found Sarah Kent on there too. Better to send a response through social media – less wordiness expected. He tapped out a short message: *Saw your email – great idea about the tattoo. Am in KC myself at the moment, taking a few days with a hot Spaniard! Give me a couple of days and I'll get back to you. Maybe put something together. Love Gotty.* That last word seemed to be her standard closure.

He hit *Send,* but the clock symbol on the message showed it hadn't transmitted. Fucking signal! Where did she say she had gone? Leverwood? He would have to head down there, wherever it was, if the thing didn't transmit.

The couple of days he'd referenced were really all he could afford. What if this Sarah sent something through that needed specific approval? What if someone on the island just decided to call by? Above all, and despite everything he had done throughout his life to immunise himself against the betrayal wrought by emotion, he doubted he could stand too much of this accusatory silence.

He looked at her, the mute but questioning face turned towards him. Already the gods who created these moments mocked him as he was drawn to the slight smear of brown sauce on her cheek. He pulled his clothes back on and went to find a blanket. Then he would look on one of the maps she had lying on the bookshelves and find the place with the shops and a signal. He couldn't risk taking the car, but looking again at her body he realised a walk of a few miles, some hours away from this place, would be just fine.

Chapter Twenty-Seven

The sound of the doorbell startled Jessica even though she was expecting visitors. Was it perhaps because the house now felt alien; no longer hers alone, but a den of deceit and a cauldron of conspiracy? She decided to try to dismiss that concept; it was far more likely that her nerves were simply on edge after the events of the past few days. Nevertheless, there could be no denying the presence of the mysterious Max lurking somewhere. His shadow darkened not just the past but the path on which Jessica was now set. She'd not reacted like that to a bell since her days in the fire brigade and back then, she had responded according to a tried and tested process in which they all knew their role. Yet did this represent just as much of a warning; a danger to life?

Also, part of her mind was elsewhere. She had toyed with bringing Katherine back home with her but had decided against that ultimate risk, not wanting there to be the remotest chance of her sister overhearing anything. It meant she was distracted by thoughts of the victim lying in that hotel room. She was on the firm road to recovery, at least in body. Only the gods and the fates knew what the future held for her mind.

Jessica had allowed a couple of days to pass before organising this witches' sabbath, as she was tempted to think of it now. She'd explained to Katherine that she was popping out for a few hours to attend to some business, not wanting her to wake in panic to find herself alone. Then she had taken the chance of administering a sedative. Hopefully all would be well.

She opened the front door. "Christine?"

"Am I the only one you're expecting?"

"No, you just look like someone who runs a company." The attempt at humour, with its self-deprecation, appeared lost on her visitor, so she beckoned her in with an awkward gesture. "Thank you for your time."

Now Christine Jeffries smiled and some tension dissipated. "Someone who doesn't run a company very well. It was my husband's, but he died."

"Oh, I'm so sorry."

"I am, for his death, which was recent enough that I still mourn things about him, even though we were drifting a little, but also because it left me something I couldn't deal with. But for that, our friend Joost might never have come into my life – supposedly a business acquaintance of his who called on me a few months later when I was vulnerable and also…" she gave Jessica a knowing look, "…very much in need of sex!"

Jessica hesitated, all her attention taken by one syllable. "Joost – I think we have a theme here, don't you?" She showed Christine through into the living room.

"Meaning?"

"I'm assuming he has a slight accent."

"Yes. You're thinking he's European and relying on most Brits not being able to tell one vaguely Western European accent from another, hence Max."

"Correct. Do you have a photo of him? I couldn't find anything in my sister's things and I'm guessing he tried hard to avoid being photographed, but as your husband…"

"… he'd have a job explaining his camera-shyness." Christine gave a half-smile. "Thinking about it, he wasn't into selfies, but then again neither am I. It's the obsession of the needy." She paused, looked into the distance for a moment and gave a half-smile devoid of any humour. "Or is that sex?" She refocussed. "But yes, I do have one." She searched in her bag.

"Can I offer you a drink?"

Christine looked up from that onerous task of trying to find something in a handbag. "Unashamedly yes – a very large whisky please. Don't worry, I'll be getting a taxi home." She moved across to the window for some better light and gazed out. "Marvellous view. What business are you in?"

"I'm a health and safety consultant. I was in the fire brigade and I just saw a window of opportunity." She gestured towards the view and smiled. "No pun intended."

"Ironic, isn't it?" Christine continued to stare across and into Bath as she spoke. "You can write all the books, have all the files, rules and regulations you like, but nothing can ever guarantee the well-being of the ones we love."

It gave Jessica pause for thought. "I had been thinking something remarkably similar to that when you rang the bell."

"Very Hemingway – for whom the bell tolls. Hmmm." Christine stared out into the distance again and pursed her lips, seeming in deep thought.

153

Jessica put down the decanter and brought across the drinks. Likewise, she stared through the glass before turning to her guest, smiling and raising her Talisker single malt. "Let's look through the frosted glass for a moment. Your good health."

Christine responded: "Here's to whatever we define as success."

"Was your husband's..." there was an awkward pause, "... your first husband's death suspicious?"

Christine opened her mouth, seemed about to say something and then a strange look came into her eyes, whereby Jessica sensed a change of script. Both of them looked out over Bath again. "Dead in a river in Freiburg, in his car, over the alcohol limit. The German police say... said there appears to be no suspicious motive. All his paperwork was still on him, so clearly nobody seems to have stolen his identity. However, my husband was..." she paused, turned her head and Jessica felt eyes on her. "... unhappy; hiding a secret about his sexuality. Perhaps he couldn't live with it anymore."

They stood a while in silence, sipping their drinks. Then Christine handed across a picture – she presumed this was Husband Number Two.

There was no denying how handsome he was; how the eyes drew you in. Though her inclinations, drives and desires meant that Jessica walked out fifty per cent of the time with bat in hand for the other side, she was aware of her innate response to this image and could imagine how, under certain circumstances, she might have been tempted to change teams for a night or ten.

Once again the doorbell rang, but what startled Jessica this time was her guest's jolting reaction to the sound. It was like those times you watched a horror movie with someone who was on total edge; who jumped even at the non-scary stuff and caused you to do the same. She regathered herself. "To answer your earlier question – we have two other ladies attending. I think we might find some striking similarities in their stories."

Tanya Collison was the last to arrive. Jessica sensed a certain coldness in the looks exchanged by them all. It must have been strange for these three ladies to realise that, to put it bluntly, they had all been fucked by the same man; fucked over by him too. They had been fools to allow themselves to be put in that position in the first place – and they knew it.

As Jessica brought Tanya into the room, she decided to make the introductions: "This is Christine Jeffries, who was married to, I believe, the man I know as Max. In her case, he went by the name of Joost."

Christine Jeffries extended her hand: "Am technically still married, as things stand."

In many ways, this struck Jessica as odd. There was something in Christine's tone that almost suggested she was taking some sort of moral high ground. Perhaps it was just a defence mechanism but a strange one. Of the three women, she seemed the most uncomfortable.

She was still talking: "I kicked him out, but we've not been through any formal divorce. It's..." She tailed off, thrown by Tanya's sudden apparent distraction.

The latter was staring at Bella. Her mouth opened and then a peculiar smile formed as she pointed and said: "Then you must be the wife before last." Bella frowned in response. "And you must also be dead."

"Okay." The word was drawn out and hesitant, as Bella awaited the revelation that had to come.

"Do you have two children?" asked Tanya.

"Yes."

"One a redhead like you."

"You're scaring me." Bella's tone carried that hybrid anger, which is the counterweight to fear.

Tanya raised a hand. "Not my intention – I'm sorry. It's just that Tony..." she paused, "... actually, perhaps we should call him John Doe? Might also help each of us to stop thinking of him in any intimate way?"

Each of them nodded, in agreement with the sentiment if nothing else.

Tanya continued addressing Bella. "Sorry, I was going to say he carried a photograph of you – I'm almost positive it was you. He said you had been killed in a car crash; wept as he recalled it. You were married."

The words of Procol Harum stepped from the shadows and into Jessica's head in a moment of distraction as she watched Bella turn an even whiter shade of pale than her typical redhead's complexion before blowing out through her parted lips and shaking her head: "That photo... the fucking bastard!" She stared at Tanya. "Let me guess – the futures market?"

Bella downed her large whisky, held the empty glass towards her hostess with no hint of embarrassment. "Please." She seemed to take in Jessica's hesitant the look of concern. "Don't worry – I came down by train."

Her three guests slumped into the nearby chairs while Jessica could only imagine their thoughts. Returning to her earlier theme, she conjectured that not only had they been fucked by the same man, it could even have been in the same week. He might have had a timetable for different areas of the country! Her hand shook a little as she poured the drinks, realising she might have underestimated the level of danger involved in dealing with her prey; how the hunter might become the hunted if she took a wrong step.

Tanya was speaking: "Surely we have enough to go to the police."

Jessica spun round in time to see Christine Jeffries open her mouth to speak, before a strange look came into her eyes and she seemed to decide against it.

"No!"

As one, they looked at Jessica, puzzled by the vehemence of her response.

"What do you mean?" Bella's northern accent came through strongly and she seemed angry.

"Well for a start, he appears to have charmed you all into bed and likewise into funding his lifestyle. If you want your joint shame to be broadcast to the public, go ahead." Jessica knew she was playing with fire, reminding them all what naive fools they had been, but she could not afford to display weakness here. She pushed on. "I'm not actually sure what crime he's committed." She looked at Christine. "I assume you have nothing concrete, just suspicions. It could indeed be suicide for your business if news of the ease with which somebody infiltrated it gets out there."

She came over with the drinks and continued as she handed them out. "Above all, to put it bluntly, I want to resolve this for my sister." She pointed towards the ceiling. "She is lying in bed having failed in her suicide attempt; her cry for help."

There were sympathetic shakes of the head, embarrassed whispers of support. She would keep from them for the moment, or perhaps forever, the supposition she was making about Katherine's true fate. She needed personal revenge on Max. Despite Tanya's previous comment, she could not – did not – want to think of him as John Doe, needing instead a definitive personification of this man's evil. So, Max he was. His sitting in a jail would provide no satisfaction and as she had just stated, they couldn't be sure he had done anything, in the letter of the law at least, that would see him punished.

There was another factor here, also playing a part in Jessica's need for thinking time – the question of what would equate to a satisfying and appropriate vengeance.

Of course she, too, feared things going public, just as she had suggested would be the case for Christine Jeffries; in particular the way her sister had closed down that account with such ease. In a public investigation, that would inevitably come out. She thought of the implications for her business, the lack of confidence that easy breach of security might engender, especially in the changing times where data protection was everything. Despite a frisson of shame, she could not deny her concern that she would not be covered in glory. Indeed, her name would be sullied forever, having prompted the bank to forget all about the fraud. Perhaps jail-time would be hers too.

She sat herself down, accompanied by perhaps the largest vodka she had poured that week, and pushed on: "Look, let's just examine what we have. Max…"

"What happened to John Doe?" It was Bella.

"Too anonymous. We need to feel the anger – it requires a target." She pushed on. There was something about Bella that grated; perhaps the risk at which she put her children in order to satisfy her desires, or maybe something else entirely? Who knew? Some people just weren't meant to get on. Jessica's next syllable carried enough poke to emphasise that the floor was hers for now. "Max… well, we're pretty sure he's the same nemesis for each of us. You all recognised the tattoo. Two of you have fallen for his whole futures scenario. You're all women who are, perhaps, susceptible to some flattery, and are definitely well-off."

"What about your sister?" It was Tanya.

"I'm also well-off and I've been her guardian since our parents died. She had an allowance from me and a trust from them. She's more at risk than any of you, suffering a form of Asperger's, not just loneliness, another reason I don't want this going to the press or the police; it could finish her." It had been a fair enough question. The little matter of them being identical twins would have to remain hidden.

"Well if he's not going to be caught or go to jail, why are we all here?"

It became apparent to Jessica that she had talked herself into a corner; given away too much already. These victims wanted justice. So did she, but of a more primal kind. She knew she had a decision to make now and on reflection it wasn't a difficult one – she would have to lie to them too!

Hell might have had no fury like a woman scorned, but four of them? It was a sure-fire recipe for disaster. She would use their anger to bring the cyst to a head, draw out the information she needed and then, when she was ready, apply the cold compress. She would bring Max to book. Vengeance would be hers – they would just never know. Whatever her motivations, she believed she would just work better alone. It was how she had built her business career. Despite that, she reflected for a moment on how much she had loved being part of a team as a firefighter. However, later success had turned her into a lone wolf. Besides, none of the others had possible attempted murder to avenge.

But did she? This gave her further pause for thought before she came to a resounding *yes*. If she could be sure Max had been in that hotel room only minutes before her, then he had seen Katherine in the bath, bleeding, drowning. If he had then chosen to just walk away – well, that was manslaughter at the very least.

If… if… if…

All the more reason she had to find him. She needed to know; to prove.

She realised her visitors were looking at her with a mixture of puzzlement and expectation. Tanya's question remained unanswered. "Okay ladies, we're here because we need to find him. What happens then, happens." Their faces suggested agreement and she pushed on. "So what do we have?"

Christine spoke first. "He's almost certainly from mainland Europe. He may not be Dutch, but not once during our…" she looked awkward, "… marriage did he slip into an English accent without inflection. It would be difficult to maintain that level of deceit. He may well be Germanic."

Again, there was this peculiar undertone to Christine's words. Jessica couldn't nail it but there was something. Perhaps it was just different when you had married someone. Was the hurt deeper, more profound than if you had simply spread your legs for an Adonis? Maybe you felt greater shame at the extent of your complete manipulation.

"He did a damn good hybrid European and American accent," said Tanya, interrupting Jessica's musing, "at least to my untrained ear."

She was staring out through the window as she spoke, a rueful twist to her lips, not dissimilar to the look on Christine's features a little earlier. Jessica saw many things in that expression, some of which shook her. This guy was some player. In the case of two of these women, but perhaps not Christine Jeffries, she had the impression that if he turned up again at their doors full of contrition, they might have had him back, even the angry Bella Fisher. All the more reason to follow a solo path.

She pushed on: "We have Tony the Tiger." She looked at Tanya. "It was his username for my sister as well." Tanya responded with a shake of the head, as if an incipient dream had just shattered.

"We have the futures market," said Bella. "I want my fucking money back." Though that anger might have given the lie to Jessica's thoughts about Bella taking the guy back, the words sounded desperate; a scrap of wood being clung to while the woman tried to avoid drowning. On another day she might have felt contempt for this display of weakness but were they not all living in interesting times?

And then it hit her like a school textbook being thwacked across the back of her head for not paying attention. The way ahead was obvious, wasn't it?

"Ladies, these methods of his are now his weaknesses because we know them." She looked at each of them in turn. "Four women – and I'm sure there have been plenty of others – vulnerable and moneyed, all perhaps easy prey for a charming, handsome chancer who pays them the attention they crave." She ignored the nascent looks of protest and denial in their eyes and ploughed on. "So we draw him in again. Become the black widows. I'll set up a profile on 1-4-Me.com and any other dating websites I can – I'm divorced, looking after two children, recipient of a sizeable settlement from a very successful entrepreneur. I'll find a suitable photograph. None of us will do, obviously."

"Not even yourself," ventured Tanya.

Shit! How the hell to get out of that one?

She took a deep breath… but now Christine Jeffries leaned forward. "You're not thinking of setting yourself up as bait in some way? You're the only one he wouldn't recognise." Everyone's eyes widened. "Don't underestimate what you're up against. He came into my life, taking advantage of the death of my first husband."

Back into the box of secrets went the twin-identity, courtesy of Christine Jeffries' unwitting rescue act.

There was a sharp intake of breath all round. Jessica was interested to see another side of Bella Fisher as she reached out and placed a hand on Christine's arm. "I'm so sorry about your husband."

Christine gave a sad smile of appreciation. "I'm not saying he – Joost – had a hand in things. My husband was found dead in his car, well over the drink-drive limit, in a river in Germany."

Bella's hand squeezed.

Christine continued: "But somehow…" she hesitated, "… Joost knew of that death – knew to step into the breach."

Jessica spoke up. "You're saying we can't rule out that somehow he knew more about the death than he was letting on?"

The look in Christine's eyes was a paradox; both ingenuous and yet laden with the burden of knowledge. "I'm just saying, be careful what you do. Underestimate him at your peril." She sat back in her chair and took a long sip of her drink, an action mirrored in subconscious empathy by the other guests. Now she looked at Jessica and addressed her alone. "If you are proposing playing the temptress, be very careful. Make sure you have some way of communicating to us immediately if you're in any trouble."

There was a thoughtful silence, broken at last by Tanya. "I'm starting to have some doubts." Everyone looked with a greater intensity at her, and Jessica was concerned to see a slight nod of agreement from Bella. "We've pretty much agreed we have no true idea of what we're dealing with here. I was taken in, one hundred per cent. We've heard that there's a chance, however slim, that he had a hand in the…" She paused to give an apologetic look at Christine. "… in the death of your husband as well as potentially in the death, if I read your implications correctly, of one of your employees, managing to disguise it perhaps as suicide." Now she looked at Jessica, who fought to remain still and silent for the moment. "Upstairs is your sister, thankfully in recovery after a suicide attempt." Tanya made air commas as she spoke the last two words. "I agree you should be careful, but are we all perhaps in danger?"

Another wordless, thought-infested silence followed. It was clear to Jessica she needed to lead on. She gave her best attempt at a look of reassurance.

"My feeling is once he's gone, he's gone. He's a grazer, moving to wherever's the ripest harvest. Did any of you feel under threat when he was around?"

None of them shook their head but this, in its own way, answered the question. Jessica pushed on. "What you have said, Tanya, makes me even more determined that we should not go to the police. Okay, if he has seen the tattoo online – and I suspect he does inhabit the world of social media, maybe even the dark web – he may well run anyway, but if the police are openly on the lookout for him, my gut feel is we will never see him again. While that is a result of sorts, it means your money will be gone too."

There was still no particular show of agreement or buy-in – in truth, Jessica wasn't necessarily sure she bought it herself. What she did need to buy was time.

"Don't worry. I don't intend placing myself in any danger. Let me give it a bit more thought. But I am convinced we can be the predators now; turn the tables. I will let you all know if and when I feel we're ready to pounce. The main thing this evening, ladies, is that I think we've found our secret doorway into the life of Max… Joost… Tony the Tiger and he will rue the day he decided to mess with us." She raised her glass. "Here's to bringing him down."

Now Tanya and Bella raised their whiskies with a little more enthusiasm, Christine less so, pausing to say: "The trouble with the unexpected is that, in reality, you could always see it coming, if only you faced in the right direction."

Jessica wasn't sure how to interpret that enigmatic response.

***

What followed were the most surreal few minutes that Jessica had experienced, which in the light of recent events was really saying something! She was sure the others felt the same. With their purpose defined, they weren't sure what to do next, both at that very moment as they stared into their drinks and in terms of how to move forward. They were poker players whose only common interest was the cards. Of course, each could have walked away and decided vengeance was hers, but there did seem common agreement that Jessica was the driving force and, after all, though her sister had been a direct victim, she herself was not so could maintain the objectivity to bring the plan to fruition.

Jessica sensed the relief when she lied that she needed to head upstairs to tend to her sister. It was the excuse they all needed to make their escapes once she had thanked them all for making their long journeys. Perhaps each of them hoped the miles back home would enable them to build some distance from the naggings of conscience and the sour odour of revenge.

In truth, Jessica was indeed worried about Katherine and wanted to make her way back to the hotel to check all was well. But there was no denying the excitement she felt – *did that make her a bit warped?* – as she contemplated her next move; bringing this man into the crosshairs.

She needed a starting point and wondered whether there might be something additional to be found in the dialogue between Katherine and Max that would enable her to strike the right tone in her own version. What might float his boat, or at least cast it adrift in the current?

* * *

She was back in her sister's room. If Katherine had acted true to pattern…

… and indeed, she had! Here was a printed-off version of Tony the Tiger's profile. She switched on Katherine's laptop, logged on with ease. "God, sis, you're so naive with your passwords." The sound of her voice, the admonition in it, gave her a moment's pause; a quiver of introspection as she thought again of the ease with which her own security had been breached by her supposedly artless sister. She pursed her lips and gave a little ironic nod. "Physician heal thyself." Forcing herself on, she accessed Katherine's 1-4-Me account.

Now she skimmed through the shared dialogue. At first it was chilling, seeing a profile picture that, despite them being twins, she knew was of her and not Katherine; seeing her own name being used. Then sadness and a sense of hurt took over, as Katherine expressed how she felt hemmed in by her overbearing family. For family, of course, Jessica read herself and Asperger's; though there was no reference to either, there was little doubting the protagonists. Despite the melancholy those views provoked, they in no way dimmed or diminished Jessica's need for revenge. After all, this was also partly personal.

What do you mean partly?

She shut out her doubting conscience and focussed, made easier by reminding herself of the levels of deceit she was observing. She was tempted to put the fear of God into Max by sending a message as Jessica nee Katherine, but common sense prevailed and her anger cooled to that temperature required for calculated acts.

She wondered at what point she realised she was not there at all to find clues about the online relationship. After all, she had pretty much everything she needed; knew his name, that his picture was a toy tiger, his modus operandi. Perhaps it was when she noticed the tears as they fell on the plastic folder containing the profile. There was nothing that useful or revealing in the conversations, but the very fact of the profile being printed off brought a sadness to which Jessica had long considered herself immune and a stranger. She watched the droplets fall; heard the faint tick as they hit the plastic. To this point she had refused, perhaps subconsciously perhaps not, to be overwhelmed by the tragedy of it all; her sister's defencelessness in the face of a genetic disorder rendering her powerless against the onslaught of her own hellhounds, some of which had once again manifested themselves in the shape of a man.

Feeling now like an eavesdropper, she couldn't avoid reading through some more of the online exchanges, fighting hard to remain objective in the face of further criticisms from her sister, edging her way beyond those thorns and brambles to the hidden lake, the almost mythical place in which the love of two sisters for each other might lurk.

Observing the behaviour of the predator, she saw the smooth circles of his words as he swooped towards his prey. Like all good hunters, he had a cunning camouflage; the impoverished young man down on his luck. The passion of Katherine's responses made the subsequent potential attempt to kill her all the more distressing and surreal, which in itself was astonishing. In fact, Jessica couldn't be sure that killing her sister was ever his intention. Was that his magic, that even now he didn't seem like a murderer to her? The money had always been his motivation and he would have seen Katherine as an easy target, one not requiring the futures bullshit with which he'd ensnared the others.

Soon the words were babbling past Jessica, a stream she no longer observed. Instead, another perverse devil on her shoulder was agitating and needling her.

Though the dialogue was a lie, it was only so from one side. In that, it probably mirrored most of the conversations between the sisters in recent years. Who was the liar? On reflection, that wasn't easy to define, but it would be too easy to point the finger of blame at Katherine simply because she had emptied that bank account.

Couldn't you have listened to her instead of dictating the path of her life? And hasn't she at least experienced passion; lust; joy? Not just with the man calling himself Max, but also on those occasions when she found she was expecting children? Children you took from her because you decided you were the best judge of a purposeful life, namely your own. No childcare duties for you! Wasn't a minute of lust also a minute of true, unbridled, deep love and as such worth more than years of dusty romance?

Jessica gave the plastic folder a sudden shove off the desk as if it had burnt her fingers. Still, she could almost feel the hot breath of the devil as he whispered in her ear: *Who or what are you avenging?*

Turning back to the screen, she tried to submerge herself again in that stream of conversation between two people whom she knew better than they knew each other yet who, in other ways, were both complete strangers to her. She needed to drown out the words of her conscience. As she looked at the text it struck her as being like pages from a script. Yet hadn't plays, works of mere imagination, moved the reader since the dawn of the written word?

She knew she was on the finest of edges when the sound of the doorbell once again made her jump out of her skin.

If she had been someone who liked a bet…

Far too risky for you – too much fun.

… she would have put a lot of money on this being Christine Jeffries. At various points during that day's discussion with the other women she had looked troubled, like she was about to say something before seeming to think better of it and withdrawing; a dormant volcano from which the occasional wisp of steam had escaped, the harbingers of an eruption that never came. At one stage she seemed to have retreated to some far-off place and had needed to be drawn back onto the path along which they had all decided they were heading. As for the state of Christine's nerves during their discussions – each ring of the bell had prompted the same convulsive jerk of the head. Perhaps she had been remembering the day Joost arrived at her door. Her words on departure – *be careful* – had seemed heartfelt, but that heart was clearly heavy.

Whatever the reason, Jessica sympathised and as she headed down the stairs, she promised herself that, once all this was resolved, for better or worse, she would change the damned chime on that doorbell.

Opening the door, she experienced a chilling moment of enlightenment; an awareness that, up to this point in her life, she had never truly experienced terror.

Chapter Twenty-Eight

Two days earlier

It had been the references to the Stasi and the German Democratic Republic, that most laughable of misnomers, which had raised the flag for them. Having come to the belated recognition that all the time spent by Marcus – the hours about which they had ridiculed him while he mastered the trends of social media and gained a deeper knowledge of IT, had given him the clearest of inside tracks and escape routes – Michael and Richard had decided to at least familiarise themselves with the opportunities it presented. Now, in the universe of hashtags and trending, a light shone; not a faint one but a supernova.

They stared, open-mouthed, incredulous, at the picture of the tattoo. If you looked in the right places, it was everywhere. So disbelieving were they at the ease with which this medium had allowed them to find the scent of their prey, they even bared their own shoulders to each other to confirm that the fading symbol, at which neither of them looked any more, was the same.

If they knew nothing else, they realised the existence of this photograph represented a mistake by Marcus. He had let down his guard.

"For this alone I want to punch him a thousand times in the face."

Richard laughed. He knew his friend's propensity for losing control. If the Stasi had played good cop, bad cop, there would only have been one role for Michael. He was always the feisty one. Now Richard's grin became tight-lipped. Feisty – a good synonym but inappropriate; a thin disguise for violence. Memories of certain times came back to him and he pushed them away. They had never sat easy with him. A part of him wished Marcus a safe escape; when you had displayed the complacency of underestimating the cabal brothers, Michael was not going to show mercy. Also, the nature of that brotherhood meant Richard would not really be in a position to stop him!

It was soon apparent that, rather like laundered money, the source of the original post would be too difficult to trace and was beyond their respective capabilities for sure. It had passed through too many hands. However, their years spent in clandestine observation of people enabled Richard to draw certain conclusions: "There's something behind this. Posting this picture screams of ulterior motive. From what I understand, when something goes viral like this, the person posting it doesn't hide their identity. They want the publicity, the kudos in this self-obsessed age." He paused. "I'm guessing this is a woman who's posted this as I can't imagine why a guy would take that picture."

Michael leaned forward to look more closely at the screen. "Whoever she is, she doesn't really think this is a cool tattoo. It's faded and it's not all that cool, not by today's standards. Nah, I agree with you. I might be a million miles out but I think she's trying to find him."

"This is Marcus. I feel it."

Richard smiled. "True."

Michael pushed back his chair in frustration. "Want a coffee?"

"Yeah, sure." Richard took Michael's place in front of the laptop screen. He wanted another look at the image in detail. While not as enraged as Michael, he was angry enough to have perhaps overlooked something in the initial excitement of discovery.

It was as if a moment's calm was all it took.

He frowned and leaned towards the screen before calling Michael back over. "Hey, what do you think about this?"

Michael stopped messing with the cafetiere and wandered over. "What?"

"Am I imagining it, or there, right at the top of the screen, is that very blond hair?"

Michael narrowed his eyes. "Could be... yeah, given the position of the arm; the fact that this cunt is probably asleep after sex, that could well be hair."

Richard zoomed the picture out. "I think it is. Just a few wisps, but to me they're certainly peroxide." He looked up at Michael. "You know what I'm thinking?"

Michael nodded. "That he dyed his hair blond as part of one of his disguises, quite possibly because he knew we would be looking for him?"

"Yes. Do you remember how there were a few jobs years back where we knew there would be CCTV so he went very blond?"

"It doesn't help us."

Richard appeared deep in thought. Suddenly he banged his hand on the table. "It might! Do you remember our contact in the German police told us, when we were trying track down Marcus, about that guy who had been found dead in a car in the Dreisam?"

"Yes, but what's that got to do with it? We decided there was no connection."

Richard was only half-listening to Michael's responses; he was dredging a different river for memories. "Jack… Jack…" he clicked his fingers, "… Jack Jeffries! Our contact said Jeffries had been chatting in a bar in Freiburg with a guy, possibly an Eastern European or Russian, with very blond hair."

"Hardly a club with a small membership, the Eastern Bloc Blonds." Michael wandered over to the window, lost, it seemed in his thoughts.

Richard pushed on, though he was addressing himself as much as his friend. "I don't know; I've never been a hundred percent happy with the fact that Marcus went to Villingen, someone died near Freiburg, and after his failed business meeting Marcus disappeared." Michael remained staring through the window. "Put it this way, it's only a thread, but what else do we have to grasp?"

"Agreed… but the guy's ID, wallet, passport, money – none of it was taken. If not, then why do it?"

Richard wandered over to the cafetiere. "Because it opened a door. Wasn't Jeffries married?"

Michael turned. "I don't know. I never took it any further. I suppose it makes no sense that he'd be chatting up a gay guy."

Richard picked up his phone and gestured towards Michael. "Bear with me. Let's go to the horse's mouth." He dialled a number.

"Which horse are you thinking…?"

Richard raised a hand to silence him and spoke into the phone. "Tillman? Hi, it's Richard. How's the life of crime… no, the solving part? We're the other side of the Iron Curtain now, remember?" He laughed. "Question – you know that business a while back with the English guy who drove his car into the Dreisam…"

* * *

Richard put the phone back in his pocket, poured two cups of coffee and joined his other partner-in-crime at the window.

"Look, just think about this. Jack Jeffries…" here he paused, his glance out at the horizon accompanied by a self-congratulatory nod, "… I'm impressed that I haven't completely lost my touch and remembered that name, was over there on a business trip. He's a British citizen. He's in a smart suit, in a lease car – which Marcus will have taken in. It would have marked the guy out as being successful and not local."

Michael looked into his coffee. "Am I now mis-remembering, or did he have his own business over here?"

"He had his own wife over here, more to the point."

The cup, which had been heading towards Michael's mouth stopped halfway. "Did I misunderstand, or didn't Tillman just mention a gay bar, judging by your response."

Richard smiled. "Oh come on, Michael; how many gay or bisexual men are hiding in plain sight? Besides, our dear fellow cabal member might have been looking for someone to hide out with. Much as I hate to admit it, Marcus is a good-looking guy. If it's latent in you and you're on an overseas trip... what an opportunity. No strings attached." Richard shook his head, partly in admiration. "I've got to hand it to Marcus; he found a Hydra." He took in Michael's frown. "A many-headed monster. His original plan might have been to find a safe-house or to kill the guy and get back somehow using the documents etc. Then he finds out the guy is married so he has one over on him and might have planned to blackmail him. But then he guesses the physical side of marriage was probably not all that for Mrs Jeffries. She would be needy, horny and with her husband out of the way, she would be well-off! Let's have a look."

Richard returned to the laptop, followed by Michael. He tapped on the keyboard, waited a few seconds. "Aha! Mighty – an IT company." A couple more clicks and he leaned back in the chair, gesturing with upturned palm towards the screen. "Right, do you still have that Creditsafe password?" He smiled, reflecting upon how useful the cabal had always found access to directors' personal lives.

Michael ferreted around in his wallet and handed over the log-in details, which Richard entered. Again, he nodded towards the computer. "Christine Jeffries."

"Could be a sister?"

Richard tilted his head in acknowledgement and again pointed at the laptop. "True – but we have the world at our fingertips here."

A couple of minutes later, Michael put down the coffee cup with a bang. "It's Marcus!"

Richard responded without taking his eyes from the screen, on which a page from a local online paper was showing. "I tend to agree. The lack of details about the marriage to Joost de Boer, a supposed friend of her dead husband; the lack of a picture on the company website when we read that he's a non-executive director – in fact the absence of pictures anywhere in this day and age. Then there's the failure to land that ground-breaking deal. Above all, there's this." He continued to read the article, a small piece, but with a striking headline: *SECOND TRAGIC DEATH ROCKS AMBITIOUS I.T. COMPANY.* "The tragic suicide of the girl in Accounts." The two compadres exchanged a knowing look. "I think we know where we're going next." Richard stood purposefully while Michael headed to a drawer-unit. "Have you got the necessary?"

"Of course." Michael examined his Glock 19 handgun, likewise its magazine, which he slotted into place with more than a hint of satisfaction.

"No, you idiot." Richard knew it was neither the tone nor the language that anyone else could dare risk with Michael, but their bond had survived far worse than that. "That might bring us some information, but not as much as we will get if we coax her." His friend continued to look puzzled. "I meant the IDs."

"Ah."

"Yes, we're going down the route of encouragement rather than terrifying her."

Michael looked again at his gun. "I always found the latter worked quite well." He grinned as if at some favourite memory.

"Did you never read that Aesop's Fable – the wind and the sun were arguing about who is the stronger and decided to resolve it by trying to get a traveller to remove his coat? The wind blew as hard as it could, but the man just pulled his coat tighter around him. Then the sun shone brightly and the man removed his coat."

Michael stood for a moment, looking in bemusement at his friend. Then he weighed the gun in his hand. "No, I preferred the Grimm Brothers."

This time they both laughed while Michael rooted around in the same drawer before producing two plastic cards.

"I think we're going to have to make some assumptions, perhaps presumptions, in order to get where we want to be," said Richard. "Our beloved Marcus will not have laid us any Grimm-like trail of breadcrumbs." He turned to leave and then turned again, smiling in advance of his next comment, "Oh, and try to sound more German – remember we're fresh from the airport."

With that, they headed out.

Chapter Twenty-Nine

The sight of the two grim-faced men at her door spooked Christine, as if two of the Four Horsemen of the Apocalypse had arrived. She knew the other two would follow; these rather cruel faces would not be the harbinger of anything good.

"Mrs Jeffries?"

The accent, with its Germanic inflection, took her by surprise and brought with it immediate bad memories, though they were drawn from a different well of thoughts.

"Yes – how may I help you?"

"Um, if we may…" They gestured towards the interior of the house. She stood her ground. "Ach, please excuse." The speaker reached into the pocket of his bulky winter jacket and produced an ID, which he handed to her. She read the details while he introduced himself. "Polizeihauptkommissar Tillman Hoffmann of the Federal German Police. Here is my card as well. There's a number on it. Please feel free to call it. We will wait out here. I do apologise. I understand you might feel intimidated by our sudden appearance, but we're here in relation to your husband's murder."

That final six-letter word blurred her vision, indeed all her senses. She looked up. "Murder? He died in a car accident."

Now the other man stepped forward, though not before giving Hoffmann a look that verged on reprimand. He offered his ID as he spoke, which revealed his name to be Ulrich Berger.

"Please, before you or we go any further, feel free to close the door, to call that number and confirm our identities. Please forgive my colleague misspeaking. However, we have come over here especially to try to help you."

"I wasn't aware I needed help."

"Would I be right in assuming you and your second husband are no longer together?"

"I'm sure that's my business." She disliked the peevish note in her voice but felt defensive and threatened, perhaps more by circumstances now than by these men but by them too, nonetheless.

Berger raised a hand in his own version of a defensive gesture. "With all respect, this could be and quite probably is our business too. Would it surprise you to know that there is no Joost de Boer in Holland matching all the registration, employment, passport application and residential requirements for the life story of your supposed husband, but there is one on the Dutch Register for Deaths for 1964?"

Christine felt her arms fold across her chest in an involuntary movement, almost despite herself.

"The wonders of the dark web. That you were taken in by a conman does not make you a member of a unique club." Berger had taken over the reins of the conversation, his method a more eloquent one than his fellow officer, the darkness in the other's eyes absent from his. She wondered whether this would turn into a good cop, bad cop routine. "That he became your husband still doesn't grant you exclusive membership. That he wormed his way into your organisation," he said, giving her a knowing look, "well now, that's a matter that might best be kept from the public gaze. We work for a division of the police that specialises in such secrecy."

As if on cue, a woman walked past on the pavement. Her head turned in curiosity towards Christine, who raised a hand in acknowledgement and then gestured for the two men to enter her house. The irony did not escape her; she had allowed someone in before but through a combination of desire and despair. What love-children that had spawned!

They sat down, she offered coffee and they accepted, civility itself. It was a masked ball at which everyone was observing the rules of etiquette while seeking a glimpse of a dark underbelly of impropriety. She sat and awaited their advances.

Berger spoke: "First, please forgive me – us – for not having offered our condolences for the loss of your first husband, Jack."

She nodded, feeling some appreciation for what seemed to be genuine contrition and sympathy but still hurt by the reminder that there was a second husband. Hoffmann's jaw flexed and in a moment of distraction, as her mind sought some form of comic relief, she assumed he must be the ventriloquist, though it was already obvious Berger had the brains. Despite his ready smile and calmer tone, still he filled her with dread, seeming astute, intelligent, probing. There was something wandering in the shadows cast by his apparent friendliness.

In another time, place or world she might even have considered him attractive, though as she had acknowledged to herself just minutes before, look where her tastes had brought her. "So, Mrs Jeffries, is your second husband now your ex-husband? Did you divorce?"

"Actually no – well, I applied, but the parts that required his signature became an issue."

She felt concern, but again Berger raised a hand. "I wouldn't worry; the marriage will be annulled without question, given he is existing under a borrowed name."

"Did he have a tattoo?" It was the blunter Hoffmann. Christine forced herself to sit stock still. Surely this could not be mere coincidence. Had the police been monitoring social media? Indeed, what about her phone?

"Yes, he did. Some sort of weird triangle and circle, but I'm not sure what it was."

"On his left shoulder?"

"Yes."

"What colour hair did your husband – your second husband – have?"

"Do you mean, was he greying?"

"No, I mean…" Hoffmann gestured towards his body. "Excuse the question!"

"He kept himself clean-shaven. Why?"

The two policemen exchanged looks. "Thorough in everything," said Berger, his mouth turning down in a gesture of reluctant approval accompanied by a slight nod. He turned to Christine. "We believe he has been using alter egos to prey upon other desperate women and had dyed his hair blond. I will admit you have to define *desperate*."

Berger seemed to take a deep breath before continuing: "Under the circumstances, this will seem an insensitive question, but was there any chance Jack might have been, shall we say, of uncertain sexuality?"

There are times in life when a trip switch needs to be hit, bringing everything grinding to a halt. For Christine Jeffries, now was one of those moments. It felt as if her recent past had been thrown into a grinder and fragments were being hurled out like pieces of shrapnel, each one causing a fresh wound to a different memory. Was this some sort of tactic employed by the police, coming at you from all sides till you lost your way and made a mistake? She needed to slow this down; put all the pieces together again. She would retrace her steps back to the front door and the arrival of these two strangers.

She raised a hand, bringing things to a temporary halt if only for the sake of her sanity. "Wait, can we just go back to your first comment please? You said my husband was murdered." Berger looked at her with just enough intensity that she knew she had made the right move so she pushed on. "I was told he died in a car accident, having been over the alcohol limit. As I understand it none of his papers were taken. There appears to have been no motive. It was an accident. Where does Joost come into all this?"

Hoffmann took over, though it seemed to her that Berger was a little irritated by the interjection. "We believe he got talking to your husband in a bar. He wasn't going by the name of Joost at that time. He had been in Germany for a business deal that went wrong and he had, shall we say, upset some important people. He needed a route out of the country, or at least somewhere back here where he could hide in plain sight. What better than with the widow by claiming to be a friend of the husband?"

Christine had to put down her coffee cup and saucer when she noticed them starting to rattle and thrust her hands firmly in her lap. It wasn't just past events; there was something about these two policemen that made her feel uneasy. The way Hoffmann's tone had changed when he spoke of the people whom Joost had upset. However, there was no denying she had slept with a man considered by the authorities to be capable of killing her husband. It froze her.

Suddenly, she wanted them gone. "Well, there's nothing I can really do or say. I have had no interaction with him since we split up six months ago. I'm sorry I can't help further."

"Just one other thing, Mrs Jeffries." It was Berger again. She knew this meant trouble because this time his words seemed to carry the covert threat, which was a staple of all crime movies, when the detective or villain is about to drop a bombshell; that ill-named *one other thing*. "A photograph of your husband's – your ex-husband's – tattoo has recently gone viral on social media. Would you be able to shed any light on that?"

"Gone viral?" She knew it sounded weak. They just stared at her. She couldn't be sure, but it seemed those two words, representing a lie, triggered something in the eyes of both men.

Now Hoffmann spoke and again she found herself wondering whether this was indeed a tactic of disorientation – a pincer attack: "Mrs Jeffries, if we found that anyone is obstructing this investigation, there are important people involved and it would not end well for those being obstructive. As we mentioned before, the absence of due diligence when taking a non-executive director on board would perhaps sound some sort of alarm bells ringing with other companies. I believe in England it's called a death knell."

Christine Jeffries cursed for all womankind her foolishness and weakness in having slept with a man who had walked into her life when she was all at sea. What had she done? Had she left that door ajar even now? Who else would come wandering through it? Where would it end? Eyes which had not seen through the lies of the last man to enter saw, with sudden clarity, the reality of Hoffmann and Berger, if indeed those were their names. And their English – now she thought about it, they were remarkably fluent for two policemen who had been sent over in the last twenty-four hours to follow up some leads. Of course, the German police would send over guys who were used to dealing with the British, but still…

And now they loosened the ground beneath her feet by smiling.

Berger spoke again, the closest thing to a good cop in that combination. "Well I guess we should be going, if you're sure there's nothing else." He made to stand.

"Wait." He sat again with a swiftness that suggested he had been expecting this. She continued. "You were right about the social media situation. I am actually due, in the next couple of days, to meet someone else whom I presume to be a victim of whatever his name is. She said there were others too."

"Well then I suggest you go. We would like to know her story too. Mrs Jeffries, we are policemen. We're not here to harm anyone, despite what you think. We just want to bring justice for the many lives this man has destroyed, including yours and most likely your husband's. It needs to stop. Do you have the address?"

"Yes, but not on me."

Berger managed to smile and shrugged. "Very well – I mean, why would you make a note of those details? I understand. In that case, we'll make our own way there. What time is the meeting?"

"It's looking like one o'clock the day after tomorrow."

Christine Jeffries took a deep breath, stood up, grabbed a piece of paper and a pen and wrote. She handed the sheet over to Berger. "I don't think my nerves can deal with wondering whether you're there every time I look in my rear-view mirror during the next couple of days."

Now Berger and Hoffmann stood, reached out to shake her hand. She reciprocated. They were not the sort to not have on your side!

"See you soon," she said.

"Oh no, you won't see us."

There was something chilling in the cheerful tone of those words.

Chapter Thirty

Forty-eight hours later

So how did you recognise terror after no previous interaction, no introduction, when it stood at your door? Well, there were the whispered words: "You have something we need," uttered with a finger to the lips in a hushing gesture, demanding silence. That had the desired effect; a violent courtship which brought Jessica into instant submission, a woman not easily scared, who had faced danger a number of times while in the fire brigade and seen its impact on others.

The eyes of her visitors might also have been enough, speaking of dark histories witnessed. Both of them were probably handsome, one in a granite obelisk sort of way, but what caused Jessica to cling rather too heavily to the door as her legs shook were the words, soft and sinister, the worse for being uttered by the one who looked more charming and intelligent.

"We need you to invite us in, without fuss, without making a scene. We believe we intend you no harm, but… that depends on you."

The pièce de résistance was the gun, the gun-barrel directed towards her, used with a flicking movement to point her back into the house.

Doing her best to give off an air of calmness, though she knew it was redundant, Jessica beckoned them in but they insisted she led the way, perhaps suspecting she might have made a run for it onto the street.

They wandered into the large lounge with its now paradoxically serene views across Bath.

"A lovely place you have here," said the charismatic one, as she would have to think of him in the absence of any name.

"Thank you." How weak and cowed her reply sounded to her ears and doubtless theirs. Jessica's mind was a contradictory mix of numbness and hyper-activity. She had clocked the Germanic accent and jumped to the only possible conclusion – that they were in some way linked with Max. If the online comments about the tattoo were anything to go by, they might be ex-Stasi. The prospect of that knock at the door might have been the soundtrack to everyday life for anyone who failed to buy into the repression of the former East Germany. She shuddered at the idea.

Just for a moment, her thoughts wandered to her other recent visitors. During the course of their discussion, they had all settled, almost by default, on the moniker *Max* and Jessica had to wonder how difficult that must have been for Christine Jeffries in particular, who had married him in the surreal world that was her recent past. Certain lies could be forgiven, usually the ones told through shame or despair, but somehow a name embodied, represented, encapsulated so much. It was a disk, holding the core data of a shared life. It had to be the ultimate betrayal to discover that it was a scam, that when you had cried it out in ecstasy you might as well have been swearing or calling out a bingo number.

Her visitors sat and, in a somewhat abstract moment of role-reversal, beckoned her to do the same. Distraction afflicted her again – it seemed to have become her defence against the chilling realities of that day – and she wondered whether the seats were still warm from the previous visitors. The artist sometimes known as Max certainly had a way of getting people to gather round his works!

She waited but was close to being unable to take their silent stares any longer. She suspected the outcome of everything depended on whether they were avengers or protectors.

The Obelisk lifted the gun; she froze but he merely holstered it. She welcomed its disappearance from view. Then he spoke and she noted the depth of his voice; how it simmered with anger. "As my colleague said, we believe you have something we need."

She knew already. There was little point in playing ignorant as there was every chance they would respond by playing hardball. "Are we talking about Max… Joost… Tony the Tiger?"

It gave her some pleasure to see how she had taken them aback; the way that they glanced at each other and then looked back at her with smiles. There was, however, some confusion in their expressions.

Mr Charisma frowned. "Tony the Tiger?"

"His username on a dating forum. I don't know if he has others."

Now The Obelisk spoke: "You're already doing yourself no harm at all… provided you continue with such plain speaking."

Jessica sensed a sea-change in their attitude and if she could help them perhaps they could help her. They seemed the sort of people who might have something appropriate in mind for revenge. All of them were probably on the same path if not the same team.

She pushed on. "Already you have what I have, those names – his alter egos – under which guises he targets certain women for money."

"Given the long discussion you have just had with three other women, I doubt that is all the information you have." It was Mr Charisma, as probing as she had assumed he would be.

"Oh, believe me, you're welcome to have what I have. You see, I have a sick sister, whom he took advantage of and left for dead, perhaps even tried to kill, just a few days ago."

Again, the visitors exchanged glances. She hadn't expected to be on such a quick equal footing with them, if indeed at all. It was true what people said – knowledge was power.

The Obelisk leaned forward, elbows on his knees. "So tell us what you have, apart from a need for revenge."

Jessica leaned back, realising the body language spoke of defensiveness, perhaps fear or an attempt to keep the distance on which he had just encroached. At the same time, it bought her a few seconds for thought because she was just about to take the biggest chance of her life; far bigger than starting up her own business. She held her silence a moment longer, fighting the destructive impulses of her conscience, because dependent upon her success, looking at these two guys, might be the life or death of Max.

Who was she kidding? Avengers or protectors – either way, death was the only sentence they would pass.

She closed her eyes for a moment, forced herself to picture Katherine bleeding from self-inflicted wounds, in all manner of pain, physical and mental, her head perhaps being forced below the water; tried envisaging what these men might inflict on Max. Then as ever, practical, pragmatic Jessica stepped forward, the firefighter, not the businesswoman. When confronted by a fire, you had only one choice – you put it out. Extinguished it. She remembered seeing these two at the door, her visceral reaction, the sight of the gun. She could not obstruct them now. In fact, she wouldn't put it past them to hunt down Katherine, maybe even force Jessica to take them to her and threaten to take her life unless she complied.

Opening her eyes again, she guessed they had probably been staring at her the whole time, though it had been in reality just a few seconds. "Exactly that. What are your plans?"

Now Mr Charisma spoke: "For your sake, as well as ours, it's probably better if you don't know."

"Well, as you said gentlemen, what I have is a need for revenge but not the means. I assume that you can help me."

Mr Charisma sat back and smiled. He had the ability to make that facial gesture spread to his eyes whilst still conveying a chilly reality. "That depends on what you're going to tell us."

"Behind the username of Tony the Tiger, he hunts down his victims particularly on 1-4-Me.com. I'm sure it's not his only source of income, as doubtless you already know." Suddenly Jessica's stomach lurched. She raised her hands in sudden awareness. "Of course – Christine Jeffries! How else would you have happened upon my address?" Their respective attempts at enigmatic expressions confirmed her diagnosis. "I thought at first you had just tracked me down on social media but now it all makes sense. Her jumpy behaviour here today…"

Jessica didn't like the way Mr Charisma tilted his head, hoping it didn't bode ill for Christine, so she pushed on: "Oh, she said nothing, but I could tell she had something on her mind – saw how she glanced towards the door from time to time. She probably thought you guys were going to burst in."

The visitors nodded and stayed silent.

"Anyway, it is my intention to try to lure him to me on that same website."

Both of her guests – she'd been about to label them unwanted, but it was no longer strictly true – sat up straight.

Mr Charisma asked: "Do you think it will work?"

"Well, what else have we got?"

Yet again the two men looked at each other. It verged on a tic. Whatever they had done in their lives, the most meaningful and formative parts had been spent together, all of which gave credence to those online observations about the Stasi symbolism of the tattoo. She could guess who would have played bad cop. There was also a cruel irony in their kinship, given twins were said to feel each other's pleasure and pain. Sometimes she believed the pleasure had been all Katherine's and the pain, including mopping up, all her own. This day, this moment was perhaps the ultimate case in point.

Mr Charisma continued: "What else indeed! Our very words only the other day." He paused. "So how do we play this?"

"I set up a profile and play the recently divorced woman with a couple of kids, left a large sum of money by my ex-husband. Then all we can do is wait. You could help me; provide me with a suitable profile picture. I'm sure gentlemen like you must know of some Eastern European beauty who won't worry about image infringement for a suitable sum of money."

"What then?" asked The Obelisk.

"As I said, we can only wait."

"I don't like it – it leaves too much to chance."

"Look, I think my sister was his source of income recently… it would have been to the tune of thirty thousand pounds if I hadn't managed to step in." The men looked at each other and The Obelisk let out a soft whistle. "She's no longer on the scene. As far as he's aware she's dead. He'll be on the prowl. Don't forget, I know his username. I will seek it out and make my interest in him known. Let's see if I can draw him in."

"But once you do, how can we trust you? You'll have him then."

She leaned forward, fingers clenched. "I'm sure the memory of your gun will help me keep my focus and my word. But please remember this, gentlemen – I want revenge, not justice." Once more the men exchanged a glance and smiled. "Perhaps you don't know how it feels when a…" she paused, feeling the hand of some spirit on her shoulder, urging caution. She had been about to say *twin* when it occurred to her the two guests were probably not aware of that fact and there was no unequivocal need to reveal it to them at that moment. It might be her trump card for reasons as yet unknown. Yes, the way ahead was as vague as that but why show these vengeful birds-of-prey every break in the trees? Revenge had many faces, though the irony of that image given the circumstances was too much even for her to take in for now.

She realised they were looking at her in anticipation. "… when a sibling is harmed."

The words came from the heart, they told of her pain and anger, but only Jessica knew they were spoken by the injured sister.

"No, but we know how it feels to be betrayed by someone who is as good as a brother."

Mr Charisma put his hands on the arms of the chair as if preparing to stand. "Well at least we have a plan. How will we stay in contact?"

"Yes," chipped in The Obelisk, "we're not doing it through this fucking… sorry, through this social media thing."

Jessica almost smiled at the man's awkwardness for having sworn in front of a female, incongruous in someone who had pointed a gun at you. She responded: "Please make a note of this mobile number. It's my sister's number. I have the phone. If it isn't you, it would only be Max, but as he thinks she's dead, that's less than likely!" Jessica had a sudden thought: "By the way, what is his actual name?"

There was a silence before The Obelisk spoke. "Again, perhaps it's better you don't know. No matter what people think, suffering and guilt are eased by the lack of a name."

"Is that how it worked in the Stasi?" It was out before she could prevent it.

To her relief both men laughed, but no answer was forthcoming.

Now Mr Charisma stood. "Miss Dawes, it has been a pleasure to do business with you."

Once again, Jessica closed the door, this time on the most unexpected of visitors. Her plan for a little game at Max's expense remained safe, while he most certainly did not.

Chapter Thirty-One

He'd had to get out again; his refuge had become a prison. There was a new understanding now of the different types of silence. Life was teaching him to think more deeply than before and he saw how so much that should have been obvious had passed him by to this point. There was the stillness of the dead; the potential isolation that was the world of the deaf; radio-silence; the life beyond the boundaries of civilisation – and then there was that unnerving peacefulness, which was no peacefulness at all, filled by the accusing anger of the wind and the distant sea.

All of them, with the exception of the deaf man's lot, had formed the backdrop to his life for the last twenty-four hours. There had been something else too and it had been the most challenging of all – the accusatory muteness of the murdered that, in a damning paradox, screamed louder than any living being in torment.

The day before had been the toughest he had known – which was saying something when you had grown up in East Berlin! – waiting for night to fall while half-expecting the form beneath the blanket to move. Part of him had almost wished that it would; that her blood was not on his hands. Twice in the matter of three days, Fate had played its trick on him and forced those very hands into fatal activity.

Fate… fatal

Was the universe laughing at him? And who was he kidding that Fate was to blame for any of this, except perhaps on that fateful night when the Berlin Wall had fallen.

Fate… fatal… fateful

At last, in those small hours when the only activity on roads and lanes is the scurrying of foxes and rats, he had managed to drag the body…

… Margot…

… into the 4-wheel drive and set off with huge caution – he'd never known a darkness like it, though he needed to be grateful for that. Reaching the quiet cove where she had told him she had a boat, he had headed into the alien world of the sea, a place that spooked him at the best of times, never mind when you had such a passenger and all around was that sound of wind and water, restless and accusing in the night. He'd felt like the ferryman on the River Styx, except she had paid with her life rather than a penny. Having weighed her down with some rocks she kept by the front door, presumably for decorative reasons but which had now found their true, dreaded purpose, he had pitched her overboard, with relief but not without regret. Of course, his DNA was almost certainly on and in her, but they'd have to find her first – and then they'd have to find him. He intended to be long gone by then. Hopefully, out in that wild ocean, she would find kinship with many thousands of lost souls and provide dinner for thousands in shoals.

He knew that there would be an inevitable outcry when she was reported missing; someone whose book had sold in millions. All the more reason why he needed to be away sooner rather than later. The aforementioned radio-silence would be setting off alarm bells with her agent, who might show up at any moment.

Hence his driving now across the island in that same 4-wheel drive towards the port of Tarbert. He had pulled on one of her puffer jackets and her woolly hat, plus a pair of shades. At a glance he might have been mistaken for her. Indeed, that was his hope. He wouldn't be stopping to talk with anyone locally, but he would have put money on somebody in this one-eyed place recognising her vehicle and clocking that it appeared to be driven by a stranger to the community.

It was a trick of the stark remoteness of those western isles that distances felt greater. Already, nearing Tarbert, he felt the chances of being seen as an outsider were diminished. Yet in complacency lay danger. He needed to keep alert.

Once within striking distance of the port, he parked up a distance away from the harbour.

There were one-and-a-half bars of signal on the phone; better than nothing. It had pinged a couple of times during the drive. Now he saw what he had feared – an email from her agent, asking if everything was okay. His one consolation was that the woman was almost certainly based in London. A glance at the email footer confirmed that. She could fly up but would need a few hours. Hopefully by then his ship would have sailed. By Hebridean standards, the weather was calm.

Next, he couldn't resist trying to open Pandora's box. Was there anything in the news about the death of Jessica Dawes?

The signal was frustratingly slow so he couldn't be sure that everything he needed to find would be visible, but there was certainly nothing in the main news. Of course, although she was a successful entrepreneur, she might have been a medium-sized fish in a small pond and not known nationally.

He wanted to smash the phone, with its constant matey robotic apologies that *oops!* or *aw snap!* something had gone wrong and he would need to reload. However, his blood did chill when he at last got through to Fire-Dawes to find the website was down due to essential maintenance. He read between the lines – the business was on hold. He didn't know how many people she employed and chastised himself for that particular failing. He should have learnt by now, the devil also lay in a lack of detail.

Spilt milk! He shook his head and focussed again. The only thing of relevance at that precise moment was the email from the agent. He needed to be on his way.

It was probably roughly half a mile to the ferry. He removed the puffer jacket, stuffing it into a rucksack he'd found in the cottage. Peeling off the hat revealed a head of hair the same colour as Margot's. She'd had plenty of dyestuffs lying around. It seemed old habits of vanity died hard, even amongst reclusive millionaires hiding from the media.

What was it about boats? If he'd thought he'd been spooked before, that was nothing compared with the forty-minute wait at the terminal, which seemed to last three times as long. Once underway and on deck, he started to get a better signal and was taken aback to find no news of the suicide in any of the local publications for the Bath area.

This couldn't be allowed to continue. Mastery was meant to be his in his dealings with women. Instead, they had him unnerved, though the fact of them being dead might have played a part in that! He needed to move on; had other fish to fry. What was done was done. This lack of news could only be good. There appeared to be no sort of manhunt, at least not by the British police. Whether a certain couple of former East German officers were seeking him… he doubted they would ever stop, though it wouldn't be their priority.

The loss of thirty thousand pounds still ate at him. Sure, he knew he had plenty of funds tucked away, both as investments and pots, but that wasn't the point. This had become about the power, his ability to take what he wanted from women, whether sex or money, and in Jessica he had reached a new level in the playing for both. The others he had seduced might have been as productive in due course but she had given it all, in all senses, straight away. Though he knew her neediness and insecurity could be irritants, her lust and the fruits of it would have more than compensated. She would have opened doors, although he would have needed to tread with care as he went through searching for other possibilities…

He forced himself to stop thinking about it, wasting time, but his beloved nemesis Fate wasn't having it and tried taunting him with images of a far wealthier woman now lying weighted down by stones at the bottom of the Atlantic. However, in many ways that was an easier loss to digest. She could never have been his cash-cow. He knew her already as a woman who would want a partner by her side and with enough media commitments that her man would have had to appear in public. No, she had served a purpose – until she had started probing.

Right – in a strange way it felt energising to be angry now. It was time to put that frustration to some positive use. He logged into 1-4-Me.com and was surprised to find a message from Tanya, from some days before. Then it dawned on him, there was no reason to be surprised at all. That had been his conscience speaking; haunting him – no denying.

He read the message: *Hey, where are you? Why aren't you answering my texts? Need to see you.*

He couldn't be sure his state of mind wasn't imbuing those final four words with more cryptic meaning than they, in truth, possessed. Whatever; it would have to wait. He wouldn't risk answering her from this phone, just in case any GPS settings might give him away. He noted that there was no message from anyone else and wasn't sure whether to be pleased or not.

Then a lips emoji flicked up in his list; he had caught the attention of someone new – Rachel. There was a message too!

He tapped on the profile picture. Hello! What the fuck was a girl like her even doing on a dating site? Reading the immediate details, he thought he found the answer: age – thirty-two; widowed.

He started reading her profile: *I'm aware how I look – I'm not a shrinking violet. Don't make the mistake of thinking I'm some bimbo after your money. My late, darling husband was a very successful entrepreneur and has left me way too soon, but very nicely off, thank you. No, I'm taking my first steps into the world beyond bereavement and am seeking companionship on that journey. Anyone interested will need to take my kids on board – I love them to death, but I'm ready for someone new; someone who will set my pulse racing again. Is that you?*

184

Whoa!

He gathered himself together, forgetting for a moment that was just her profile, not the message, which he flicked onto now:

Hello!

The impact of that alone, with its unconscious echo of his own response just seconds before! Fuck it! He was caught between the devil and the deep blue sea across which his eyes stared now as he looked away from the small screen which had transfixed him. He wanted to answer but what if she asked for his phone number?

He needed to think fast; didn't want to lose this chance.

Now he reminded himself that she had messaged him. He needed to calm down. She was interested. Strange, given his profile picture was a stuffed tiger. He remembered the lack of insistence on a recognisably human picture had been the main reason he'd chosen this site. Anyway, maybe she had read enough in his profile to find him worth pursuing.

He thought on his feet and responded: *Hi! Flattered you've got in touch directly. Huge apologies, but I'm on a plane and we've just received instructions to switch off mobile phones.* He made a quick calculation. *Should hopefully land in six hours. I'll be in touch then. Hope you'd still like that. T.*

He assumed that might pique her interest and give him time to find, at the very least, an internet café and to pick up an unregistered phone.

For the second time in the last forty-eight hours, he struggled to hurl something into the sea, but he reckoned that was the safest place for the phone. Apart from anything else, it would be out of his reach, so he couldn't act on any stupid impulse, such as contacting her again. Her beauty hadn't faded from his imagination even as the boat docked in Uig on the Isle of Skye.

* * *

When the alert popped up on her phone, Jessica needed to sit down before she could open it.

"So it begins... or ends," she whispered to herself. Her heart was thundering. At that moment she would have loved to just back away from it all. The two visitors had shown her the darkness of the path she was treading, along which the lights had now run out, leaving it disappearing into shadows – but with them as guides, there could be no wandering from it or turning back. She knew that now.

Jessica wondered how exactly Max had incurred what she assumed was the wrath of two such formidable beasts. Despite even gaining the upper hand at times in her short dealings with them and although she had held back a key fact – that of being a twin sister – she had huge doubts about ever trying to outsmart them. It was arguable whether the person without a gun ever truly had control over the one who did... well, it wasn't even really up for debate.

She clicked on the message. So he was flying away somewhere or perhaps flying back. Then again, he was a professional liar. All she knew was she felt relief that no further response would be needed for a few hours. She could try to compose herself.

A ghostly counsellor whispered in her ear that if she weakened, she should try remembering her misguided, sick sister lying in a bath of blood and having her head pushed under the water by this latter-day Casanova.

She was shocked by the knowledge that it wouldn't help.

Chapter Thirty-Two

He was taken aback to notice his hands were shaking as he prepared to tap at the keys. Of course, it could have been down to the strong coffee he'd ordered in the café, but the new, reflective Marcus realised that would be mere self-deception.

He thought of Margot's weighed-down body. Her absence would be noticed soon enough, though he hoped for a couple of days' grace. He was pretty sure no-one had paid much attention to him on the ferry. Years of experience had taught him to clock the positioning of CCTV cameras and he had pulled on Margot's woollen hat again to cover as much of his head as was possible without looking suspicious. Likewise weighted with a rock taken from the clifftop, the rucksack containing her puffer jacket had joined its owner and her phone at the bottom of the ocean when the coast and the ferry-deck had been clear. He remembered – the irony of it – looking through closed-circuit footage in the depths of the Stasi headquarters; the unidentified man in the jacket and hat would cause confusion, assuming the authorities even got that far.

Yet here in the café, there was little sense of security or comfort. It seemed to have departed with the steam from his coffee. The beast now dogging his steps could not be so easily shaken off, this awareness that he would no longer hesitate to take an innocent life if it stood in his way. Perhaps it was simply that he had to recognise it for what it was – the monster born from his own ambition. Back in Berlin, it had been easy to operate under the cover of constraint. You were part of the system. Deception, torture, the death of innocence – it was just part of your job. You were following orders, protecting the State. Those whose lives sieved through your fingers like sand… well, they were enemies of the people and democracy. You were entrusted with the welfare of an ideology. Now he was reduced to saving his own skin.

He glanced up, almost expecting to find Jack Jeffries, Csilla Molnar, Jessica Dawes and Margot Foye sitting at a nearby table, sipping coffee and watching him.

Here in the corner, he ensured his screen was hidden from prying eyes as he accessed the distinctive website. Still he could hear their voices; his menagerie of victims at the adjoining table.

Yes, he's really fucked up, hasn't he?

Quite a trail of bodies now.

It's going to be his undoing. This is not the German Democratic Republic, where murder can earn you vouchers for food, or medals.

He had to stop for a moment, pressing a thumb and forefinger to his eyes, rubbing them in exhaustion before trying to focus again on the screen.

They were right, of course, those coffee-lovers from the other side. He *had* fucked up. So many deaths; such a spoor for the authorities to follow – and not just them, but a couple of former East German coppers too! Even if they didn't yet know the same person was responsible for the killings, they would soon work out it was one guy who kept vanishing into thin air. He wasn't Jack the Ripper, who had achieved such legendary status that even Marcus had heard of him from beyond the Wall and had revelled in the chance to go on one of the Ripper walks when he and the cabal had made their way at last to the legend that was London.

However, that analogy did stop him in his tracks. He could be Jack the Ripper. He could disappear. The realisation set his fingers trembling again. This Rachel might be his chance.

Where did she live? He checked again and knew that address was slap bang in the middle of London. In so many ways that was a perfect foil if Michael and Richard were looking for him. The worst place to find someone was in a crowd. Retreating to more remote, rural spots left you nowhere to hide and people were quick to spot something out of the ordinary, hence his caution on Harris, whereas weirdness and diversity were the very lifeblood of a metropolis like London. Besides, though he would change in some ways, he still had business to attend to, he had a life to lead and where better to that than in the febrile melting-pot of England's capital, where anything went?

For a moment, he recalled the time spent with Christine Jeffries; the rewards it had brought him, in effect being a kept man. Now he reflected on it, it had probably been the finest of times, with power both in the bedroom and the boardroom. He knew that in due course he would feel the urge for a few forays into the world of commerce again, but lying low for a while would be advisable and in London, with all it had to offer, including a multitude of hiding places, it might just work. His short stay in the Hebrides had revealed a world for which he wasn't made.

He looked once more at the picture of Rachel. Here was an added benefit. She was a slut. He knew to recognise one now. There was a big chip he carried into every game, never failing to pick the right number or colour.

This was more like it. He gave a tight grin. Time to get moving again. To feel better.

He tapped the keys: *Hi, so sorry about that. Are you still there? Wouldn't be surprised if you're not – looking the way you do.*

* * *

Jessica's body went into spasm as the phone gave its incoming alert. Since she had put her business on hold, there hadn't been many calls or messages. Given she had worked so hard to establish herself, it was of huge concern to her. That brought with it more than a frisson of guilt and shame under the circumstances. Plus, it struck her again – her wealth, ambition and drive carried, at least in part, implied responsibility for this whole sorry affair. It caused her much disquiet that she resented Katherine for making it so. That resentment was a flying, buzzing, nipping insect that wouldn't leave her alone.

She assumed her regular immersions into these murky pools of thought were what caused her startled reaction to any phone activity now. Had she become the ultimate corruption of Pavlov's Dog?

It was him!

She waited two minutes, which seemed an interminable countdown, before responding with trembling fingers: *Hi – no, I'm still here. So where have you been – I mean the flight?*

Had it been flight in all senses?

She could see he was typing. Up it came.

Ah, just got in from Boston.

No waiting this time: *Wow! I'd love to go there. It's on my bucket list. Where did you stay?*

* * *

He thought fast – wracked his memory: *Faneuil Hotel.* For all he knew, she'd be looking it up right now. *You would love it there – Quincy Market, the fact that you can walk everywhere and pretty much do the whole city.*

She came right back: *So where are you now?*

189

London. Shit! He'd hit the *send* button too fast. What if she wanted to meet?

It was worse than that. *Give me your number – I'd like to speak with you, if we're going to meet.*

She wasn't hanging about! Again, he needed to be quick on his feet. *As you can probably see, I'm contacting you from a computer. My phone's gone.*

Back came *??????* followed by *But you contacted me from a phone which you said you were about to switch off. Are you telling me you don't want to meet me after all?*

Fuck! She was quick on things, or at least fast enough that he was making mistakes. He would need to up his game… or give it up. Why didn't he just do the latter?

He looked again at her profile picture and made that most male of mistakes, listening only to the Y chromosome. *No no no! My phone was on the last dregs and needs charging. I didn't mean I need a new phone. Sorry, I'm just jet-lagged to hell and need some rest.*

You must know your phone number. I can call you in a few hours. Boy, she was either very keen or he needed to drop her now. So why didn't he?

His hands hovered over the keys as he considered that last question to himself, which might even have been rhetorical. It wasn't as if life hadn't presented a few challenges for a while. He couldn't blame boredom.

He gave a literal shake of the head as he remembered she wanted an answer… and he was going to give one. There would be only one winner of this contest and it couldn't be her. *Believe it or not, I don't know it. It's a damn work phone and I can never remember it.*

He banged his palm against the table, remembered where he was and raised that same hand in apology, while once again cursing this woman for his actions. He needed to move on now, not draw attention to himself.

* * *

He had *LIAR* written all over him. It might as well have been tattooed next to his Stasi symbol. She knew by instinct he was her man…

That's a first, Jessica, even if you weren't bisexual came the taunt from the shadowy empty corner that was her love life to date, the voice being that of her sister again. *She closed it out as best she could.*

… and could only assume the recent events were getting to him. He was making so many mistakes. But she didn't want to scare him off and needed to meet him – unfortunately – so decided to throw him a rope. *Hey, that's okay.*

Don't worry — I'm being too pushy. Look, here's my number. Call me when your phone has recharged, likewise your own batteries.

Virtual silence. More silence. Had he gone? Decided he had screwed up and this wasn't worth the effort? Or had she been the one to mess things up? Her experience on dating websites could be summarised in one four-letter word beginning with Z. Her questions might have seemed too probing.

If she'd thought the minutes before his last response were long, the five that passed now were interminable. And then…

Yeah, I'm sorry. I'll do that. Give me three or four hours.

You've got it.

Hating the enforced chumminess and flirtatiousness of that last exchange, she watched as he left the conversation. Had her chances gone offline with him?

* * *

He sat staring at the new phone at Hopwood Park Services, losing track of the time. So much thinking; so much thinking. The drive down from Glasgow had passed in a blur, though not so much that he had failed to observe the speed limits. Interaction with the police was the last thing he needed. Paranoia was in the mix now — he had no idea whether they were on the lookout for an ancient Mondeo, though common sense suggested they would have no reason yet.

He hated this; not knowing what the hell to do next. Along the way, at a couple of service stops, he had glanced at the rolling news on TV screens. No murder in a Bath hotel — in a bath, for that matter. No mysterious disappearance of multi-million selling author Margot Foye.

The immutable fact of those incidents in his recent history made him want to drive on at speed, meet this woman, this Rachel, date her, hide with her. She had shown keenness in giving her number when he had given all the wrong signals. On the downside, she'd had him making mistakes. Was her beauty a distraction to be avoided? He seemed to have wandered too often of late from his usual firm footing of objectivity onto the tracks and unstable pathways of passion. She was a complication, a maze he didn't have to enter, nor was she the only hot girl in the world.

He needed to get back to the container on the farm, spend the night there and see what the morning brought.

Now the imp on one shoulder reminded him of the thirty thousand pounds that had slipped through his fingers. Sure, he had money invested, plenty of it, but he needed spending money. As he thought again of Rachel, he wondered whether he had started, in some perverse way, to rather relish the dangers of this… he'd been about to call it a game, which spoke volumes for his state of mind. If there had been a good spirit on his other shoulder, it might have reminded him of how close he came to being seen at the hotel in Bath. That would have sent the pieces flying from the board.

Time to head for a safe haven.

Wasn't that what he had considered Harris to be?

He would get to the farm. He could change cars too.

Given those thoughts, he couldn't quite fathom the number he found he had keyed into his phone when he looked down, as if his mind belonged to one being and his hands to another. His thumb was poised over the green button, though the way he was feeling now, it should have been red.

He hit it.

Ah fuck it!

Of course, he could have hung up and of course he didn't.

She was speaking.

* * *

She might have believed she knew her limits and levels of exhaustion, but it was only when the ringing of the phone found her scrambling from the blackest pit of sleep that Jessica truly understood just how worn out she was. Her squint at the screen was probably superfluous. It took a while for the lack of a contact name to register with her; he hadn't given his number and she didn't doubt he would be calling from some pay-as-you-go phone. While the chill spread through her stomach, she noted the time. About four hours had passed, of which she had no recall.

She took the plunge: "Hello?"

"Hi, it's me."

So it was. Already the voice was seared into her consciousness.

"Hey." She'd never been an actress, so had no idea where the reserves of coquettishness came from, with which she imbued that single syllable. "Where are you? I can hear a lot of noise there."

"I couldn't sleep, so I've wandered out to a café."

This was surreal. The voice of a man who had tried to kill her sister. The man other men wanted to kill – she assumed. He was making no attempt to hide the Germanic inflection. Perhaps he was tired; after all, he had flown in from Boston.

Wait, what the hell was she thinking?! Who was the exhausted one here? He hadn't been to Boston, at least not recently, and had got confused with Faneuil Hall. If you had just been there, no way would you make that mistake.

She fought to retain the hints of flirtatiousness. "So if you couldn't sleep, how are you feeling now?"

"Well let's just say I'll probably sleep like a log later."

There was no time like the present. She couldn't drag this out. "That's a pity. I was hoping we could catch up." She swallowed hard. "Perhaps in a way requiring no sleep."

The pause spoke volumes. "Oh... well, I... why not? Sure."

"Where are you at the moment?"

"I'm in Bath."

If he was playing a game, looking to unnerve her, he had just put her in check. She sat up straight. "Bath?"

"Yes – it's where I live. It's why I'm so tired. By the time I'd driven back from the airport, I'd woken up."

She was tempted to ask him his address, see whether he was lying and call his bluff, but was alert enough to realise it would have been foolish, coming from someone who had pretended on her 1-4-Me profile that she lived in London. This wasn't the time to scare him off, despite her own horror at being within a million miles of him.

* * *

It was at this stage that some atavistic impulse, some reflex from the gene pool, stopped Marcus. His old Stasi self kicked in. He recalled the number of women with stunning looks who had crossed his path on dating websites, masquerading as British girls until you introduced yourself, at which point they confessed to being from the old Eastern Bloc countries, longing for a caring British man – for *man* read *passport*. This Rachel certainly looked the part, those cheekbones, the pale eyes. Or what if this were a set-up — the work of Michael and Richard?

And what if it weren't and he was going to walk away from this bombshell? Besides, the accent he'd just heard contained no trace of anything overseas and her command of the English language, spoken and written, was excellent, including not forgetting the definite article! Despite everything, he had to smile for a moment as he remembered the English courses he and the rest of the cabal had taken before the fall of the Wall, in the hope that one day they might be in the West, and just how far short of fluent they had found themselves to be once the opportunity came. That was something else he had worked on much harder than them in subsequent days. Seemed it had always been his intention to hide in plain sight, merge, mix in, both offline as well as in the shadows of the worldwide web. The other two had continued to rely on mafia-style processes.

So, time for a reality check. What did those two dinosaurs know about Tony the Tiger, or about 1-4-Me.com? To them, the internet was a spooky labyrinth and social media was a joke, a passing phase — not that he wasted masses of his time on the latter; for him the dark web and the dating websites were his screen-world. As for Michael and Richard though, it was as if, in their minds, the Stasi and communism had lived forever. They had never listened to him. That ignorance meant the chances of them having seen his viral tattoo were slim and as for setting up something on a dating website…! They weren't subtle, certainly not Michael. If they'd had a sniff of his whereabouts, he'd have known it by now. He didn't doubt they still searched for him but by old-fashioned means, and he would continue to evade their grasp.

Nevertheless, he would be careful. He needed to be. Like it or not, that stupid bitch Jessica had thrown a huge spanner into the works with her photograph of the tattoo. He'd need to have it removed or perhaps adapted. If in the meantime Rachel decided she was frothing for him, it would have to be with the lights out!

But again, that viral posting was never the work of his former cabal brothers. For them, a virus would still be something you defeated with medicine and if he was wrong, he was still ahead of the game now, thanks to Margot's naivety, in knowing about it.

"Are you still there?"

Her words broke the train of thought. Back to what had blood in its veins for now. "Where and when?"

"Well, I imagine tomorrow's going to be a problem now. You must be so tired and you're miles away."

"Bath's not that far from London really." He paused. "And you look worth the exhaustion."

"Oh… okay." He could tell he had wrong-footed her, cutting to the chase. "Um, do you know Camden?"

"Only too well." He did; loved the place. It suited him too. In that throng of alternative beings, he could observe all comings and goings at the designated meeting place.

194

"There's a club not far from the lock, actually called Lockdown; why don't I meet you in there? There's a new multi-storey car-park near there as well, which makes life a bit easier – you know what Camden's like!"

He was thinking this over, but it was evident his silences were discomfiting to her, because she continued: "Are you sure tomorrow's OK? You still seem a bit uncertain."

He liked her unease; it gave him the upper hand. "No – no, not at all. I look forward to meeting you."

"I'll wear a red dress and…"

"Don't worry," he interrupted, "I'll recognise you." Once seen, never forgotten. "Shall we say 9pm?"

* * *

No sooner had the call finished than she ran to the bathroom and was violently sick. She couldn't help wondering whether this same febrile state had afflicted her sister every time she met what she believed was the man of her dreams, or in the case of Max, nightmares. Yet she was only too aware her own nausea had a very different origin. She knew nothing of the horrors still to come but come they would and she was the gatekeeper about to unleash them.

After her previous conversation with Max, she had called Mr Charisma and The Obelisk. If definitive proof were needed that those guys were not German police officials charged with bringing Max to the judiciary, but rather had their roots firmly in the UK, it was the speed with which they had suggested the rendezvous at Lockdown. She hadn't expected that she would need to drive all that way, but part of her acknowledged it might be for the best. Her nerves were already frayed. Why sit for longer than necessary in Death's waiting room?

She picked up her phone, which once more took a supreme effort, went through the futile exercise again of hesitating before calling.

The other phone was answered.

"It's done."

Chapter Thirty-Three

Some things didn't change. Though he loved Camden, the parking was as bad as ever. Of course, he could have gone by Underground but preferred having the world at his fingertips, though that world was limited right now to his unregistered mobile phone. Still, if she decided to cancel he would at least pick that up before he reached Camden.

He had checked online and saw that there was indeed a recently built pay-on-exit multi-storey car park just down the road from the club. The good thing about those new car parks was that they were well lit – a positive in this instance at least, though it would have suited him less in the old GDR when he rarely wanted people to see him coming. Also, they were more spacious and built to take the larger modern car. Trouble had less chance of creeping up on you or scuffing your alloys, unlike that appalling car park in Windsor that which he'd had to utilise when meeting Tanya.

He was confident he hadn't been tailed, the more so because he had organised a rental car just in case. Likewise, his trained eyes could tell there was no welcoming party awaiting him as he drove in and parked in what was for him a typical slot, near a fire escape.

His phone chirruped with a text. *Running late.*

Recidivist mistrust kicked in straight away – was this a trap? He looked around the car park and suddenly those swathes of concrete felt exposed. He knew he might be overreacting, but decided he would rather be in the confused hedonism of the club, from which he could hear beats pulsing into the night air even now. He texted back: *See you in the club.*

Back came a response with a speed he knew was beyond his own typing skills but was the norm for the Instagram generation: *I hate walking into clubs on my own. Where are you?*

He looked around again, a slave to his suspicions, but seeing no lurking forms approaching he got out of the car. *Fourth floor of the multi-storey by the club.* Now he glanced down into that parking level below till he saw what he needed. *I'm in an orange Jeep Renegade.*

I'm in a Volvo XC60. Wait for me. It would be nice to walk in together.

He didn't bother replying; was already checking that the magazine of his pistol was full and the safety on. With that, he locked his car and headed off to the fire door, positioning himself so he would be able to hear any approaching engine.

* * *

She didn't know it was him for sure, but her partners-in-crime – *in-death?* – had emailed her various pictures of him, which combined with Christine Jeffries' photo meant she saw enough of a likeness in the driver of the Audi that drove past at what was pretty much the designated time. Also, that car park was expensive and less popular than it might have been, so there had been no other arrivals for quite some time. Party-animals tended to get taxis and the Tube. It was never their intention to drive home.

She waited a while and then sent her text: *Running late.*

The ensuing short, written dialogue felt like an excerpt from someone else's noir movie. Unfortunately, she had been cast in a bit part and too soon it was time to set off…

… which was when one line of text chilled her blood: *I'm in an orange Jeep Renegade.*

Was he onto her, or was this just the liar in him coming with irresistible force to the fore?

Oh God! She was going to have to trust the plans that were in place.

She had to take strength from knowing one part of that arrangement was just for her. The Obelisk and Mr Charisma knew nothing about it. She was pretty damned sure The Man Sometimes Known As Max didn't. It would be her moment. God knew why she had written it into her script — it was… just something she needed to do. Even if for only a second, she wanted to embrace another dimension. Be her sister, as it were.

She drove in, spiralling up, rather than down, to Hell. She saw the orange Jeep and clocked that there was no-one in it, and while glancing through the concrete supports, she saw the next floor up and the Audi. It, too, looked empty and sure enough, as she crawled towards it, parking a couple of spaces away, further scrutiny confirmed that it was.

This spelt only trouble. She wanted to drive away but that was never an option to her sometimes-obtuse soul. Besides, there were a couple of devils on the lookout for fallen angels that night. Still, it took all her strength to open her door and get out.

She needed some idea of where he was. That was the whole point if her plan, her mad, dangerous plan, was to have the impact she intended — he had to be watching.

She needn't have worried.

* * *

With the door cracked open, he listened to the distant engine; its change of tone and gears as it turned onto successive ramps. He hated that its approach filled him with a sense of foreboding rather than intensifying his excitement. Hot, rich Rachel had made the first move, not vice versa. Perhaps this change of dynamic had thrown him. He'd been used to selecting the next target. Was someone now playing him at his own game but with a much more dangerous motive?

What was that old saying: if it seemed too good to be true then probably it was? And was there a part of him, a canker that still lacked a sense of entitlement, of self-worth? That was something the German Democratic Republic ground out of you and though he'd had status, it counted for nothing here in the former west. When your position in life was built upon a foundation of terror you could achieve much, but never fully shake off the sense of a knife waiting to plunge between your own shoulder blades.

The sound of the rubber tyres squealing on the concrete as the car turned on the ramp shook him, accompanied as it was by the memory of a screaming mouth far underground in a cell in Berlin.

He squeezed his eyes shut for a moment, trying to clear it of this alien negativity.

She was heading towards the car he'd pretended was his. He pushed open the door a fraction more and peered with caution at the Volvo, always bearing in mind that she might be looking in her rear-view mirror. She had slowed and was taking in the orange Jeep, judging by the silhouette of her profile. Then, to his surprise and shock, she carried on past, turned up another ramp and swung in to park on the other side of his Audi, a couple of spaces further along from it. This obscured his view and if he hadn't known better, he might have believed she had the makings of a good Stasi agent. Then again, what if she were taking her instructions from just such a one?

He allowed a small, stifled laugh to escape; pure nerves.

As the engine stopped running, he closed the door behind him with a swift but gentle movement and raced down the nearest ramp to the floor below. He could still see her car; saw movement as she opened the door, though as yet, frustratingly, he caught no glimpse of her.

At last he heard heels on concrete, saw them from his lower vantage point move around the back of his car and stop. He was growing increasingly suspicious; the way she seemed to be scrutinising the car was hardly the behaviour of someone heading for a hot date. Then again, perhaps she had stopped to apply lipstick! Plus, the killer heels he could see were, for sure, those of someone looking for a night on the town.

She stepped into view…

… and he knew he would never be at peace nor sleep again.

What the fuck! What the FUCK! WHAT THE FUCK! This couldn't be… no fucking way!

He'd left her dead!

There was no Rachel – that much was clear – but what was happening to him? He buried his head in his hands for a moment, fingertips pressing against his forehead as if he were trying to perform an exorcism, then looked up again.

He didn't believe in ghosts. Given his history in the cells and interrogation rooms of the Stasi, the Fates would never have allowed him to shut out the restless, vengeful spirits of the victims if such things existed. Nor did ghosts drive cars. No, he must have failed to kill her. If so, then her very presence here raised questions and opened doors of far more frightening potential than anything the underworld or his recent imaginings could conjure. One thing was for sure — that she was here was no coincidence; no fucking way!

But she had been dead. Given all those lives which had ended at his fingertips, he knew a corpse when he saw one… and yet he had read stories of people revived after minutes under water. Now he thought about it, it hadn't been that long afterwards that the hotel staff had come knocking on her door.

Yet she'd cut her wrists too!

It was all too crazy.

He stared at her face — one of the hardest things he had ever done. It was her. If this was a doppelganger, who had found her? It couldn't be. In reality it didn't matter, because the pertinent question was *why* and the most likely answer was *revenge.*

Then again, he would have put money on Jessica Dawes not having the intelligence to put this together.

Put what together?

Of a sudden, his blood was chilled by a thought that would have seemed ridiculous and beyond his wildest imaginings at any other time yet had a fiery cogency under these circumstances. If you took the name Rachel, and shortened it to Rache, it was the German word for revenge!

He shook his head; he was overthinking things.

Michael and Richard.

No! Banish that thought. How the hell would they have known anything about her and vice versa?

On the phone she had sounded nothing like Jessica. Okay, it was possible to disguise your voice but he couldn't let himself believe that Miss Looney Tunes was capable of this Machiavellian plot.

The heels moved again. He had lost track of time, but these myriad thoughts must have been raining in with the velocity of machine-gun fire, because surely only seconds had passed.

Still hidden from her view, he looked around in swivelling desperation. What to do, where to go? If he moved, he feared the cloying silence of the car park would give him away. How he now longed for some stinking old, ill-lit, noisy version. He wanted nothing so much as to just head for one of the doors, yet there remained a part of him that thought if he could follow her, he might find out what this was all about, even though that was the least practical thing to try.

All of this was overridden by the dark knowledge that if this were some sort of trick, then his cover was blown. Were Michael and Richard involved after all, a nightmarish possibility? If so, then his old world was no longer a refuge. That being so, then someone was going to pay for it.

There was one option left; one piece, which could be removed from the board right now. Supposing his former collaborators – *friends* was no longer appropriate, if indeed it had ever been – were at play here, then Jessica was a thing of no consequence; a pawn. In fact, he would be sparing her a much worse fate. His old cabal buddies never left any detritus that might lead to them.

With that, Jessica's fate was sealed.

He reached into his pocket and grasped his gun. It was fortunate the safety was on because his fingers convulsed as he discovered what she had been doing for those few seconds before stepping into view.

The text alert of his phone pierced the stillness.

She looked across and down; straight towards the space he occupied, drawn by the sound of both her text and, if she had but known it, her death. They stood motionless, trophies in a silent glass case, stuffed and caged by forces beyond their control. He saw the horror in her eyes, but then, with an admirable courage that rather threw him, she gathered herself together and spoke: "Hi Max."

He opened his mouth to respond but could think of nothing to say. She seemed to take strength from this and continued: "Did you manage to wash the blood from your hands?"

He found himself looking at his fingers for a moment then back at her. A peculiar smile was forming on her lips. "Who are you?" He knew the question was absurd, but still, he couldn't allow himself to believe. "Who are you really, Jessica?"

She waited before replying, her eyes fixed on him. "Oh, I'm Jessica. If you only knew! But I could ask the same… Max…" He watched her feeding on some reserves that he could only envy right then. "… or is it Tony… or Joost? I'm sure there have been other alter egos."

That threw him, leaving him speechless. It was also a mistake, confirmation of who she wasn't, if not who she was. She wasn't some innocent. Still the face was Jessica. But the voice…? And the knowledge making a stand behind the fear in her eyes.

He didn't have time for this shit; for feeling unnerved. Time to redress the balance. He drew the gun from his pocket, raising it with deliberate slowness till it pointed at her chest.

Despite her attempted poker-face, he saw the impact of the barrel in her eyes. That was more like it. Ghosts didn't fear guns. Walking back up the ramp, he took slow paces towards her, gun-arm extended, though he found he had to fight to keep his hand from shaking, likewise his voice as he spoke: "So what's this all about?"

"I could ask you the same thing." Hers was a deceptive calmness. "You know, if you hadn't pulled a gun on me, you could have pleaded innocence…"

"To what? And I never plead." As he appeared to have been set up, he was taking no chances. "Throw your bag over here and take off your coat."

"Take off my coat?"

"Don't play fucking innocent with me! You could easily be wired for sound."

She took the bag from her shoulder and made to step forward but he gestured for her to remain where she was and slide it to him. A quick glance inside revealed there to be no recording equipment.

Next, as she removed her coat, he saw that she was indeed in a red dress. He pushed on. "Turn around."

He knew from experience that this instruction filled people with so many emotions from unease to downright terror; saw confirmation of that in her eyes, heard it in her response.

"Why?"

"Just do it." He wasn't up for giving answers right now but also enjoyed this little bit of payback.

Jessica turned, all the while trying to keep him in her view over her shoulder.

He stepped forward, watched her start to flinch and pressed his gun into the back of her neck. Right now, he knew she believed these might be her last moments, so it was difficult to tell whether the gasp that escaped her lips as he ripped down the zip of her dress, rather than pulling the trigger, was relief, surprise, shock – likely a mix of all three. Having checked for the possibility of a wire and finding none, he stepped back a few paces again.

Under other circumstances, the impact of that outfit on her figure, the flesh revealed as he unzipped the back, might have sent a twitch into certain key areas, but not today; not tonight.

"Turn again." Now he gestured to her hand with the barrel of his gun. "And the phone."

That seemed to shake her. "Really? It's my lifeblood. All my contacts are on there – and loads of photos I haven't…"

"… posted online." He silenced her with an abrupt movement of his finger to his lips, though the slight desperation in her tone had made him feel better; stronger. "No, your lifeblood is what you will see trickling across the concrete here if you don't do what I say." He pointed, "Again, slide it to me."

She obeyed and he didn't hesitate to crunch the gadget with his heel. She didn't evince dismay like some pathetic idiots, whom he had seen looking aghast or bereaved when their selfie-sticks broke, but still, he had hurt her. It was a relief to return to a world of concrete; one on which you could crush things.

He pushed on, knowing time was probably of the essence here. "Okay, so what was with the performance?" She frowned and said nothing. "Oh, come on! The borderline autistic stuff when we were dating… having sex," he gave a rueful smile, "though that, to be fair, was when I felt I saw the real you. Ironic, eh, on reflection? So again, who are you? I don't think you're police. Maybe a private detective. If so, I've committed no crime."

"Well, as I was about to say before you started destroying my property and making me half-undress, you could have pleaded innocent to targeting surprisingly naive women for their money, notably Bella Fisher, Tanya Collison, Christine Jeffries—"

"Oh boo-fucking-hoo!" He had heard enough. "Women sitting on piles of undeserved wealth who wanted fucking and got exactly that – fucked – in all senses."

"Precisely – from a certain point of view."

That threw him for a moment, but then he pushed on. "And as you're standing here in front of me, seemingly alive and well, clearly with something in mind—"

Her turn to interrupt. "Yes, justice for your attempted murder of my twin sister, Katherine Dawes."

The nascent admiration he'd started to feel for her courage at gunpoint was an irrelevance, just like that. Everything was overwhelmed by a tsunami, dragging with it the wreckage of his life. It was suddenly all in pieces, surging past in broken, irreparable ruins. Everything and nothing made sense. His jaw dropped open once more. She had his attention now. Boy, did she!

"Your *twin* sister?" he looked away, then back at her. "This is bullshit."

"Well then tell me why – why would I go through all that, pretending to be autistic? Just why the hell would I bother?"

"You tell me." He tried to regroup. "Perhaps you were bored; thought you would get more attention if you were pitiable. Maybe it's a perversion of yours."

She lifted her arms and he raised the gun, which had been heading in a gradual downward trajectory, but she merely extended her wrists towards him. "You're the one talking bullshit. Do you see cuts on my wrists? Do you really think I would have gone to those extremes? You know it's not true and that you've done something abominable. It's even in the air – just now, when you came closer, I picked up the scent of some product you use, perhaps aftershave or shower gel. That smell was in the corridor outside Katherine's hotel room and inside when I entered. They say smell and music create indelible memories."

He couldn't deny the logic. As if he was having a sudden moment of enlightenment on a very potholed road to Damascus, he felt it might have been good to just talk about it; no lies. The moment passed – real life took hold.

"Well, I suspect she would have been better off dead. Her life must have been a mess with you looking after her." He enjoyed the flash of something in her eyes that might have been anger, "Because I assume you were and that you're the high achiever she pretended to be; that it was your money she took. At least I must have made her feel better about herself than you did."

He was taking some shots in the dark here – an ironic image under the circumstances – but in many ways it wasn't difficult to piece together the back story now and the hurt in this woman's eyes spoke of barbs hitting home. He decided to fire further arrows, sharpened in his imagination. "Yes... yes, if I wasn't going to kill you this evening, we could spend some time around the fireside, and you could tell me tales of what it was like to protect someone you held to be so stupid... If I wasn't going to kill you."

He raised the gun and once more enjoyed the response. Funny how any smart-arse became less cocky with the 'O' pointing at them.

They were interrupted by the sound of a car engine from a floor below.

Marcus grinned. "Well, that solves a problem as I don't have a silencer with me." *Try getting smart with me now* – he'd not seen that look since the darker times in some of the cells in East Berlin. "Listen to the approach of death."

"What... no... no please!" She'd gone as pale as the ghost she was supposed to be.

He made a flicking gesture with the gun. "Go lie down on the other side of your car."

She was shaking. "Please, you can't mean it! Haven't you had enough death?"

"I was born in the German Democratic Republic and was a high-ranking member of the Stasi. That should tell you everything you need to know in answer to your question. And in a country where those lucky enough to have a car had a Lada, you can imagine how convenient the sound of backfiring engines was for assassins. I doubt this one will backfire, but I imagine the noise of the engine in this enclosed space will be good enough cover."

She surprised him, not for the first time, and stood her ground. "Well then you're going to have to shoot me where I stand. If I'm going to die, I'm going to do it on my terms."

The approaching engine was growing louder, though still a couple of floors below. He could not afford to wait.

As he levelled the gun at her, she threw her hands out towards him. "Wait, please! You don't have to do this!"

What was the matter with him? Why didn't he just pull the trigger instead of shifting on his feet and saying: "Oh yeah?"

She swallowed hard. "Katherine didn't die."

Of course! Her words of a few moments before came back to him.

"I know." He enjoyed the look on her face; the disbelief. He'd played it well thanks to the poker face with which life had imbued him.

"What do you mean?"

"You spoke earlier about the *attempted murder*." He felt pleased with himself. Despite the desperation of this little maelstrom of circumstances in which they found themselves, certain faculties had remained fine-tuned. Though the news of a twin sister had almost blown his mind, he had clearly retained enough of his wits to absorb and reference key details. Something had been niggling at him about her words – some flaw – and that was it.

His eyes must have glinted a diamond-hard gleam at that moment because now she laid a different, desperate hand of cards on the table: "And I have money – lots of it. At the end of the day, that's what it's all been about, hasn't it? Please."

"Oh yes, of course, stupid me." He slapped the palm of his left hand to his forehead in mock exasperation. "And the authorities won't be all over that like a rash. Everything – your accounts, your business, your hard drive."

Louder still grew the engine. He needed to get this done yet he couldn't help but lift his head, nostrils flaring. He still had his pride and this bitch wasn't going to emasculate him further. He continued: "I don't need you in order to make money. I'll close off this old world and set up a new one."

As her hands dropped to her sides, he didn't bother asking her to raise them again. "I have no doubt of that."

The strangest look crossed her features now. Impossible though it had to be, there might almost have been sadness in her eyes and he felt its impact in his own frown, the pity in his heart as he raised the gun. "I'm sorry."

"So are we, Marcus," said the voice of Beelzebub from behind him.

* * *

She had seen them approaching. Even under such circumstances, standing in the line of imminent fire, she was hardly relieved or reassured and besides, what guarantees did she have that they wouldn't wipe her too, from the disk recording these events for the gods? Leaving her alive was a risk. A risky disk. Yet they had given their word and for some strange reason she believed they would keep it.

After all, their world lay in the shadows even though they lived in the sunlight and her death might have shone a light into corners best left hidden. Besides, what threat was she to them when they knew she would never find them, but they would always find her? Just one misplaced word might be enough.

Spotting them, she had tried to keep Max, or Marcus as she knew him now, engaged, though her pleas for her life had been genuine enough! Marcus – would it make his death tougher or easier to take, knowing his real name? In many ways her game with him had worked. From the beginning she had wanted revenge and when the idea had come to her, some days before, of arranging to meet him here, her hope was to see the shock in his face when confronted by a ghost. It would justify her actions; confirm that he was her sister's nemesis. However, in the cold light of day or the soulless glow of the car park's fluorescent lighting, she could no longer put hand on heart and swear her motives were so altruistic. She had wanted someone to pay for her humiliation as well but it didn't sit quite so easily when you saw the nature of the debt collectors.

Now she watched him turn, swivel a hundred and eighty degrees, arms outstretched; a psychotic, gun-toting weathervane. Taking the belated chance to obey his previous instructions, she crept back and threw herself down behind her car. From that position, she saw his feet turn again in her direction. Oh God no! Was he seeking her as some sort of hostage?

There was a sound like a stifled, explosive sneeze. She saw the back of his leg erupt in red; heard his scream, watched him thump to the floor. A loud report, presumably his unsilenced gun, ripped into her eardrums, followed by another. She saw what she thought were The Obelisk's legs stagger. Another silent bullet made its mark somewhere as once again Max… Marcus screamed. Now she heard running feet, presumably Mr Charisma, as the other two in this unholy triumvirate had taken hits. She realised she'd closed her eyes because she heard but didn't see a thudding impact that might have been a boot against flesh, then another.

"Nee, so leicht geht's nicht!"

She opened her eyes in time to see a foot stomping down, crushing Max's wrist, the hand still wielding a gun now forced to release it. Had he tried to kill himself? She had some rudimentary German – *it's not that easy.*

The Obelisk was wounded but it appeared not to be fatal. He staggered over, kicked into Marcus' ribs three times, four, five. She should have been pleased but the brutality was almost beyond bearing. She had to force herself to think of her sister's head being pushed beneath the bathwater.

They dragged Marcus to his feet. His screams and groans were terrible to hear, particularly as she sensed they were more about the prospect of things to come. A blow landed and they were cut short.

At last she dared to stand, easier said than done on her shaking legs, but she forced herself up. They were already dragging him away. Only now did it register with her that the noise of the approaching car from before had stopped, because an engine kicked in again, breaking the newly fallen silence. It approached, turning up the ramp onto their floor. Someone was in for a horrible surprise. Would it be a fatal one?

It became clear soon enough. The driver got out in a hurry, opened the boot and in went Marcus.

Given the shock and horror of the moment, Jessica was thrown at first by her almost abstract, tangential realisation that returning to the world she knew and plunging back into her business would be a must. She'd have to keep busy, very busy, if there was ever to be any hope of shutting out these images, at least for a time each day. Exhaustion would have to be her Benadryl because tonight, sleep had also been murdered. Nothing in her everyday work would faze her again after this.

If she lived.

That last eventuality seemed in sudden doubt as Mr Charisma headed towards her, gun still in hand. For the second time that evening she uncovered reserves of courage, perhaps from her fire-fighting days, and stood her ground as best she could, swallowing hard as he stopped before her. A sudden, apologetic look softened his features as he glanced at the gun before placing it in his pocket.

"I'm sorry, I didn't mean to intimidate you."

"Oh, you know, just another shoot-out in a Camden multi-storey." She wondered where the dry wit came from but it was probably a fresh bloom drawn out by the light of hope that she might now live. She looked past him at the car.

"Once you told us about this place, we got here early to check it out, decided it would be too quiet for… activity, shall we call it, of this sort. The car served a dual purpose, covering the noise of what might have gone on and…" he gestured behind him, "… well, you can see its other use." He seemed vaguely embarrassed, which struck her as surreal.

Her chin quivered as she spoke: "It nearly provided cover for my own death… he was using it to… he was going to…"

With a movement that startled her, Mr Charisma stepped forward and put a calming hand on her shoulder. "I'm sorry." He paused. "I have to say, I don't understand why you insisted on this means to an end; why you put yourself in this danger. I guess you had your reasons and that's not my place to know – though perhaps I can guess." Now he looked round at the car as he continued. "But look, he won't trouble you – won't trouble anyone – ever again." He turned back to her. "Reassure your sister of that too." The smile that followed was rueful. "This has been a lesson for us about moving with the times." He pointed towards The Obelisk, who was sitting in the back of the car tying a piece of cloth around his leg, and his smile grew. "A painful lesson."

"What will happen to him – Max… sorry, Marcus?"

He took his hand from her shoulder, though without any aggression. "Really, it is better you don't know. I know you cannot stop the engine of your imagination from running but I have no intention of fuelling it."

She felt herself slump. "Look, thank you, for what it's worth."

"Take consolation from the fact that you didn't ask to be part of this."

"I'll try." Even as she said it, she knew the words were empty.

He turned to go but then pointed to blood on the floor. "If I were you, I'd get the hell out of here. You're not on CCTV. There's no need for the police to know anything."

"But what about the women who were his victims – I mean the ones I know about? Are they not due some recompense; some payback?"

As he faced up to her again, his eyes brooked no contradiction. "They kept their lives and if I were them, I would say that is reward enough, allied with new-found wisdom, particularly about dating websites." He half-turned, then turned again. "By the way, it's not just women who have suffered. I doubt strongly that Jack Jeffries simply lost control of his car."

That stopped her in her tracks. While she absorbed that piece of information, Mr Charisma was on the way back to the car. His words made sense; best to be away from this bloodstained field of nightmares, in body if not in mind.

She made her way home, once she had avoided trailing her tyres through the patches of blood, a manoeuvre that, months later, defied recall.

* * *

The warehouse, the money-pit into which the erstwhile cabal had sunk funds in the expectation of a distribution deal with a German pharmaceutical company, had been chosen because that particular industrial estate bore a resemblance to some dark imaginings from the mad corners of Goya's mind. It was devoid of

208

both visitors and light at night; perfect for activities in the small hours, minus any security. Thus Marcus' prolonged screams were heard by no-one and their echoes, which danced in the shadowy corners, might indeed have been the souls of those he had killed, calling for release from Limbo. He was in neither a position nor a state to appreciate the irony that his most recent victim had not managed to scream.

Chapter Thirty-Four

Five years later

In the end it had proved too much.

Not the rekindling of her business. She had been astonished to discover how few days had passed since the beginning of the whole sorry affair, how stress and fear created different concepts and laws of time in a manner which would have intrigued Einstein. Her reputation had proved sound enough that customers had remained loyal during the period of supposed website maintenance. Yes, the odd opportunity had gone astray, down mainly to her ignoring any phone calls except those from…

How surreal did this now seem?

… from Mr Charisma, The Obelisk and… Marcus.

She had shuddered at the knowledge the latter was unlikely to be calling anyone soon.

Ever.

She hoped the others wouldn't be getting in touch either.

That was the problem. She could no longer imagine the life she'd had before; the one in which Katherine played a daily part. Max… *God, that name might as well have been her own surreal tattoo!…* Marcus' fate weighed heavily on her and her sister was a permanent reminder of it. Worse, she found herself resenting Katherine for it.

Masking her actions with apparent altruism, she helped Katherine to find her own place, telling her she was bright enough to make her own way. Jessica implied that her own efforts to protect, or perhaps overprotect, her sister hadn't exactly ended well. She assured Katherine the allowance would continue to come through and if Katherine so desired they could meet every week and talk through any issues. Given that Katherine was a talented painter, she suggested perhaps she could look to make her mark in that area. Her sister's howls of laughter at the brilliant but totally unintentional mark-making pun meant nothing to Jessica until she looked it up later and found it to be a technique used in drawing. Such intellectual differences further emphasised that a parting of the ways might be no bad thing, though then again, she might just have been seeking excuses.

It had been like watching a child going off to big school, seeing Katherine take her case out to the taxi, her features a mixture of fear and anticipation. There was no denying the weight that lifted from Jessica's shoulders as she closed the door. She had made Katherine swear never to reveal what happened – there was huge selfishness in that on the one hand, but also a desire to try to expunge the whole sorry episode from her sister's mind.

In the weeks before that departure, not everything had run smoothly. There had been an incendiary discussion when Jessica had touched on what she saw as her sister's promiscuity and the latter's apparent belief that uninhibited, rampant sex was a concomitant by-product of love from early in a relationship. In the end, Katherine had agreed to tubal ligation, which was a partial solution only. Since that talk, when guilt tapped Jessica on the shoulder from time to time, she argued, as she had with her sister, that people's ability to conceive children was overplayed and mawkish, overshadowing their inability to raise them correctly in a dangerous world.

How paradoxical then – she chose to ignore the adjective *hypocritical* – that the thought of uninhibited, rampant sex had just caused a peculiar and wonderful lurching in her stomach, of a sort she'd not experienced in, well, too long, perhaps ever, though she did recall how success at work had once engendered a strong sexual need in her.

When an opportunity for overseas expansion of her business had emerged, it marked a quantum leap for her company. She couldn't help it now, the childlike excitement as she looked around her. The whole thing had been exotic from the moment of arrival. There was the architectural grandiosity, yet small-town charm of Munich. The Hotel Muenchen Palace was a wonder in itself. Hans Schulze had recommended it; likewise, the fabulous restaurant in which she now awaited his arrival.

Hans Schulze – what would he be like? On the phone, he sounded like a dream. It hadn't taken much conversation for her to feel like she'd known him forever and that the lesbian side of her bisexuality had been nothing more than teenage confusion brought on by reading the poetry of Sappho. He was clearly a man who kept himself to himself, because searches on the internet revealed little. The company appeared to be prospering but such images as she found were not particularly enlightening, indeed just the opposite as most were taken at outdoor events where his love of Terminator-style shades was apparent. Even on the website, where his few co-workers were pictured, the couple of shots had him in safety gear, helmets, goggles, that type of thing. She had wanted to quiz him about this but embarrassment had prevented her, not wanting to come across as some teenage stalker with a crush! Also, the irony didn't escape her – after what had happened five years ago, the fact of her chasing down a man online verged on doublethink.

She gave a rueful grin. His voice had been so evocative, which was ironic, given she'd have thought a Germanic accent would turn her blood cold. Time clearly did heal.

She glanced at the menu and her mouth watered. There was also no denying that other parts of her had moistened too. Boy, she was shocking herself now with the lewdness of her thoughts! There had already been more flirtatiousness over the phone than was business-like, but hey, what was a girl to do? She felt that after everything she had been through in recent years, she owed it to herself to live a little.

Was that Katherine tapping at the Gothic windows of the restaurant? She did her best to ignore it.

She wondered whether a keen skier, which he professed to be, had a supreme butt to match. Then she put down the menu with a slap, shocked at her own shamelessness but sporting a broad grin nonetheless.

And then in he walked.

Stop all the clocks!

She had to call back her entrepreneurial alter ego, who had risen from the table and was wandering away, leaving only Miss Let's-Dance.

He raised a hand in apology, although he wasn't late. "Very ungentlemanly of me to leave you waiting."

"It's not a problem." *Get a grip, Jessica!* She stood, moved towards him and he planted a kiss on both cheeks before gesturing her to sit again. "That's a lovely aftershave." *Get a damn grip!*

"Thank you – and for taking the time, Miss Dawes, to come here to Bavaria."

"Not at all. Thank you for the opportunity – potential opportunity…" she raised her hand. " Sorry, that was presumptuous."

But she knew – she *knew* – business was just a bedroom away. *How do you know, Jessica? Where's the experience you're drawing on right now?*

She looked around. "Some place!"

"Un Profumo d'Italia – some of the best food in Bavaria, even if it is Italian! And for me tonight, the best company."

She looked down, feeling the unwanted attentions of a blush. Was that a first?

He glanced around, signalled, then turned to her as the waiter approached. "Shall we have a glass of champagne to toast…" he paused, "… opportunity?"

She smiled, opened her palms in agreement and gave a considered response, not sure whether his comment had been a touch mocking. "We can certainly drink to the chance of it."

He gave her a knowing look and winked. *Knowing* – an interesting concept, as there was undoubtedly something about him that had her believing their paths had crossed. Yet they had not and she came to the conclusion her conscience was trying to offer her a defence; after all, who…

Katherine

… slept with men on a first date?

The waiter had brought menus and Hans pointed to one of the main courses. "The best pan-fried calf's liver you will find anywhere, if that's your thing of course, and I certainly recommend the sea bass ravioli as a starter."

The menu might as well have been written in Gaelic or hieroglyphics; such was her inability to focus at that moment.

The champagne arrived and was poured at the table. They watched it settle before drinking. Hans pointed to it. "Perhaps a suitable metaphor for how we're both feeling this evening."

She laughed and heard the girlish peal in the sound.

They lifted the glasses and Hans said: "To Fire-Dawes – great name, by the way."

She responded: "To Schulze Sicherheit." A beautifully resonant silence then descended for a few seconds, so she pushed on. "So, do you live in Munich?"

"Not right in the centre, but I'm in Neuhausen, which is beautiful and not too long a commute into the centre. On occasions like tonight," he winked, "so I can enjoy a drink or ten, I stay at a hotel near here. It's not as magnificent as yours, but if you're here for just one night, why not live it up?"

She smiled and gave a little nod. "Why not indeed?" Never had three words from her carried so much nervous expectation.

The food was exquisite and so was he. The business talk passed in somewhat of a blur, helped on its way by delightful wines. It felt they had known each other a thousand years.

She found herself struggling with the concept of running health and safety training for an overseas company but he insisted: the basic rules of saving lives didn't change and once she had familiarised herself with German and European legislation it would be no problem. She had come so highly recommended, he explained, that he couldn't overlook the opportunity. She asked by whom and he listed several people, most of them clients she recognised. It was flattering.

He looked at his watch. "Check with them in the morning if you don't believe me."

She was struggling with something else – the wine. She wasn't a heavy drinker as a rule and if he had asked her at that moment to turn up at work naked except for a Hi-Viz vest, she would have done what he asked.

A crazy, rather warped thought crossed her mind; was this how Katherine had felt on every date? If so, no wonder her life had followed its clifftop path. Despite all the references and contact names he had given, one thing hung like a fine mist over their evening together, the fact that they were meeting because, to put it bluntly, they wanted each other. Her phone records showed well enough that their conversations had increased in length beyond any business requirement.

There was more of her sister in her than she had realised.

The hours had flown by but then midnight struck and the carriage awaited. Sadly, he offered to call her a cab and she had no choice but to accept. Also, she couldn't deny she was feeling much headier and more exhausted than she had anticipated.

Note to self – Jessica, if you really want to get on in business, learn to drink.

The sad footnote was that now she must have seemed like just another drunken British woman, not the siren he might have imagined, luring him to a shipwreck. The only dangerous rocks in their evening had been the ones in the bottom of her post-meal gins. Of course, when she had been in the fire brigade, drinking had played no part in her working life so she'd never developed much of a tolerance for it.

As they stepped outside the restaurant, she felt ashamed of her drunkenness. By the time the taxi arrived she was leaning on him for support.

What was the matter with her? She couldn't even remember the name of the hotel.

Hans got in beside her. "You're obviously a bit the worse for wear. I'll come with you, just to make sure you get back safely."

In the rear-view mirror she thought she saw the driver give an old-fashioned look.

Chapter Thirty-Five

Five years earlier

They looked at him hanging there, parts of his body livid, eyes smashed shut, feet twisted and lifeless on the floor. The weight was supported from the wrists by the two ropes they had strung over the girders of the warehouse roof.

"Just like the old days," said Michael through gritted teeth, some sense of pleasure evident despite the frustration.

Richard stared at the red-and-white dappled marionette; his eyes thoughtful. "Except the type of people we were dealing with back then would have cracked long before this." He took a piece of paper from his pocket. "Anyway, I think we need to stop looking back, discard the false nostalgia. Judging by this list, the important people in his life are all involved in IT and software, not to mention hacking – it will be like communicating with ghosts." He flicked the piece of paper with his free hand. "I think we've found our new modus operandi. We've been dinosaurs too long and he has proved it, one way or the other. We can't say he didn't warn us."

Michael looked at his bleeding knuckles. "I've always had a lot of admiration for the dinosaurs. One hundred and sixty-five million years they ruled this planet."

Richard brandished the piece of paper in Michael's direction. "Pay these people twice what he did and you can rule the Jurassic, Triassic and Cretaceous periods." Now he looked again at the lifeless piece of meat hanging in front of him. "I think we're done here. After what he's just been through, I don't think there's much more to be had. Maybe another name or so, but we have enough here."

Michael wandered over and pulled Marcus' head up by the hair. It was impossible to tell whether the bloodied eyes were open or not. "They bred us tough, didn't they – the DDR? I wonder how he felt, being on the other side of the…" he paused, looked around at a table of instruments, "… the other side of the blowtorch. Well, if we're done…" He pulled the head up higher to expose the throat and hefted the knife he was holding in his free hand.

"Wait!" Richard raised the palm of his hand as an apology for his semi-abrupt tone. "I was just thinking…"

Michael pointed towards Richard with the blade but was grinning. "You think too much. Then again, you are the brains."

"I'm just not one hundred percent happy with this outcome. As a cabal we swore to protect each other. I'm not sure how I feel about taking another brother's life."

"What? You'd be doing him a favour now."

Michael was still holding Marcus' head by the hair. To Richard, the way he shook it as he spoke, he might have been Perseus displaying the head of Medusa. Then he thought of Salome and John the Baptist but dismissed that image with a dry grin. His conscience might have been pricking him, but this was Marcus the Might-be Murderer. "I know, I know; maybe I'm feeling that misplaced pang of nostalgia again. Who knows how many of us are left – the old Stasi?" He looked up, then at and through the warehouse structure to a land beyond the Iron Curtain and another more famous wall; a place, a homeland, which like those literal and metaphorical barriers, no longer existed. He was struck by a sudden, unexpected and unwelcome sense of displacement and homelessness. Looking at Marcus, he couldn't help but wonder whether their pursuit of him had been truly just about revenge, or did they hate him for having moved on? When you lived in a world where all the inhabitants were criminals or liars, who had any true right to sit in judgement? Was the reality that he and Michael were scared of being left behind by their rebellious, factious brother?

He broke off, perhaps uncomfortable with that alien sense of inadequacy, bringing his thoughts and feet back to a damp concrete floor where they felt more at home and just in time to see a gleam in Michael's eyes. It was a flame that chilled, likewise the words that accompanied it: "Well then, let's take a certain amount of revenge for the women he has cheated and the one, at least, we know of that he has tried to kill."

The facts were incontrovertible, if somewhat convenient for Michael as an excuse for revenge. "Okay, I'm open to suggestions."

"Besides, there must be justice; punishment for his betrayal of the cabal."

There was the truth of it. Richard raised an eyebrow. "That… for certain."

Whether what happened next woke Marcus from his unconscious state, or whether he had been half-awake and playing dead, it mattered not. His screams reached the very edge of the industrial estate but as before there was no-one around to hear them.

* * *

The next morning, standing just apart from the crowd that had gathered near the cordoned-off maze, Richard turned to Michael. "I love this place. Remember when we first came here on the recommendation of the guidebook? Such peace and tranquillity." Michael nodded in silent agreement. "And do you remember, it was Marcus' logical thought-processes that cracked the maze. *'Just keep the hedge to your left all the time and you will end up in the middle.'*" He smiled at the remembrance.

Michael stared straight ahead, watching the activity. "Yes – typical of him to spoil the fun." Two men in non-contaminating protective clothing walked past carrying something in a plastic bag and he watched them as he continued. "Guess it helped us last night though. Ironic, hey?" Richard stared straight ahead. "Oh well, he won't be showing his face here again."

Michael laughed at the brutal underlay to his own comment. Richard shut him up with a nudge. Joviality was hardly an appropriate reaction at that moment with a Forensics team active, observed by a sombre-faced public.

Now Michael frowned. "But… I'm still not sure it was the best idea – leaving evidence of our activities, and I don't just mean those bits." He pointed towards the Forensics team.

"As I said, it sends a message to various people and finding this puzzle within a puzzle gives us a guarantee of it hitting the press. The Stasi association was already out there on social media – we haven't been approached, so I think our tracks are well and truly covered. Anyone who has been dealing with Marcus will know someone capable of this is not to be messed with. In terms of those names we have on the list now, we'll approach them anonymously. Only the toughest nuts will respond," he said, patting Michael on the arm, "which is exactly what we would want, eh, my friend – people of the right mindset!" He took in Michael's nod of agreement and turned back to watch the activity. "And last, but not least, it reminds both Miss Dawes and Mrs Jeffries we're not to be messed with. Both will know they've had a hand in this. Both have hidden things that they would prefer not to see surfacing again."

Michael stared straight ahead as he spoke, which gave his next words a peculiar added emphasis. "And if the rest of the body surfaces? I mean, I enjoy the thought of the pain he's in…"

"Assuming he's alive."

"But if he does reappear?"

Richard turned to his friend. "Then we would know for sure the gods are against us and we might as well give up. But show me the man who recovers from that and I'll show you a god indeed!"

* * *

Detective Inspector Morris looked up sharply as Detective Sergeant Billings burst into his office. "DNA results?"

The agitation on the DS's face was misleading. "No sir. He's nowhere to be found in the records."

Morris slumped back in his chair. "Great – so what we're left with is a nose and a tattoo." He thought for a moment. "Okay, looking on the bright side, someone suffering those injuries shouldn't be difficult to find. They're bound to have checked into a hospital or… somewhere."

"Nothing so far, sir, believe it or not. Maybe they didn't survive the bleeding. I mean, clearly this is symbolic, sir, so the actual body might have been dumped somewhere. This looks like a message to someone else from the perps."

"Great. So why did you burst in so excitedly just now, Billings?"

"Well, sir, I went to have another look at the tattoo; I mean, it's unusual to say the least." In his excitement Billings sat himself down without any invitation. "The thing is, sir, you know I'm a believer in scanning social media – nothing escapes its gaze one way or another – and I decided to do a bit of research. Well about a week or so ago, guess what — the tattoo, or a replica of it went viral."

Morris sat bolt upright. "You are kidding!"

"No – somebody posted a picture of it; still attached to the owner by the way, unless there's more than one and it's some sort of organisation or club. Anyway, whoever posted it was asking whether anyone knew what it was; what it represented. There was all sorts of conjecture, but it came down to someone recognising it as being…" here he paused, "…potentially a Stasi symbol, although adapted."

"Stasi? What the fuck…? Who posted the picture?"

"Looking into it right now, sir, though initial searches suggest it was a false account. We're not sure who set it up."

Chapter Thirty-Six

Post-Munich

Despite the lights and smiles that greet us, we are born into darkness. The umbilical cord is cut, but soon the manacles are fitted.

This now was the literal embodiment of that metaphor in all its horror. Regaining consciousness to find you cannot see, while pain tears at your shoulders. A flail of the arms reveals that you are suspended by them, the metal clanking telling you that the chains are very real.

Blind panic indeed!

You scream, while somehow knowing you are far from help. Memories stagger towards you in the darkness, tattered and vague. And you struggle – how you struggle! – to recognise them; to understand anything that might help you deal with the dread.

Jessica lurched to an upright position to relieve the pain. The chains held her firm, but she needed to shift the weight from her wrists. Her legs shook. No hint of light breached the blindfold. Indeed, if her eyelashes had not moved against the cloth, she might have believed she was indeed blind.

While a part of her fought against the claustrophobic dread and silence, another was clutching at the volcanic debris of puzzle-pieces that fell around her. Slowly a picture formed – the restaurant, Hans, the light-headedness which she had assumed was the result of excessive alcohol. Now, another '-ol' word flashed before her like the lights from a visual migraine – Rohipnol. She cried out, knowing already it was a wasted effort, but needing to break the smothering silence: "Somebody… please somebody… is anyone there?"

The lack of response was a given.

Was he watching her? She tried not to let her imagination run away with her, but in that black void she had no other company. Was she in some dungeon in the middle of nowhere? She had no benchmark for such a thing.

It didn't feel as if she had been raped. If that were so, it almost made it worse with its suggestion of a calculating, manipulative captor.

There was neither sound, nor breeze.

How long had she been here?

How long would she be left here?

Was this where she would be left to die?

The shadowy shapes of taunting questions were performing a ritualistic dance around her in the dark, whispering these chants and threats. One stepped forward to terrify her – *you do realise, don't you, that you haven't been gagged because no-one can hear you?*

The idea of being trapped in sealed boxes underground or in windowless rooms had always terrified her. It was part of her motivation for joining the fire brigade; to help others who might have found themselves in that dreadful position, perhaps trapped in a hotel room or apartment while flames destroyed everything around them. She had been able to understand the mind-set of people who had chosen to throw themselves off the Twin Towers rather than die in a flame-lined coffin. Get up and out into the sunlight. Die beneath the sky…

She forced herself to break away from those horrors and tried imagining instead a rescuer on his white charger, but it seemed that he had sold his horse!

She was here in this terrifying place through her own fault, having developed an anonymous crush – a perhaps fatal attraction – for Hans, knowing full well there was every possibility that their contract would be put in place with a loveless screw; sealed with a French kiss. Sitting alone at the dinner table in that upmarket restaurant prior to his arrival, she had already acknowledged a certain envy of her sister, whose psychological weakness had led her down so many sexual avenues. Jessica had watched too many Nordic noirs in which the suave protagonists became twisted perpetrators, their smooth tongues proving ultimately an abrasive instrument of torture.

But why her? Why had she been targeted from so many miles away and lured to this… this what?

Which was when something occurred to her and, despite the hopelessness of it, she screamed.

And screamed again – and again.

* * *

Five years earlier

DI Morris looked up as once again his door was pushed open without invitation by DS Billings. He leaned back in his chair: "I really must remember to remove that drive-thru sign." Billings looked puzzled and then shamefaced. "I'll forgive you this time if you've actually got some information for me."

"My apologies, sir." The DS fell silent.

"Well, carry on – you don't need my permission to speak, just to come in."

"Sir, you remember I said the accounts that posted the photo of the tattoo on Instagram and Facebook were using a fake name?"

"Yup."

"Well, there was some interesting interaction." Billings paused.

"C'mon Billings, cut the theatrics."

"With a Christine Jeffries."

Morris drummed his fingers on the desk for a moment, then something clicked. "Oh – Christine Jeffries! Wasn't she the one whose husband died on an overseas business trip?"

"The same, sir."

"I remember for a time there was some vague suspicion he might have been murdered and there was a watch being kept at ports and airports for someone who might have been involved, but it was all broad brushstrokes and no details. In the end they decided to stand everyone down and the death was judged to be accidental, self-inflicted drunk driving."

"Anyway, sir, *interaction* might be overstating it but Christine Jeffries made an interesting comment. She wrote…" Now Billings read from a piece of paper in his hand. "If I read this symbol correctly, it translates as 'predator'. Would you agree? See my message." He looked up. "That's it, I'm afraid, sir. I guess at this point they continued their conversation, if any, via Facebook Messenger. But at least we know the tattoo seems to have prompted an interesting reaction. It suggests Christine Jeffries might know the former wearer, or at the very least something about the significance of the symbolism."

"And taking it further down the line, admittedly along an ill-lit path, that means neither of them can be ruled out as the person who removed that tattoo and, likewise, the nose. I know that's stretching it, but we don't have much else. Well done, Billings. It's certainly a strange, almost clandestine comment for someone like Christine Jeffries to make. I assume it is the same woman who lost her husband – it's not exactly an uncommon name."

"There aren't many posts on her account, sir, but from the few pictures it looks like the same woman. For example, there are a few posts about French Art and she was, or is, a lecturer on that topic when she's not attempting to run her dead husband's company."

Morris jumped to his feet. He could tell the DS was getting a buzz from the results of his research and rightly so. He remembered well how it felt to put something in front of your commanding officer that might be a game-changer.

"There's more, sir. I had a forage online and a relatively short time after her husband's death - about a year - Mrs Jeffries married a Dutch guy and then made him a non-executive director in the company she'd inherited."

The congratulatory hand Morris placed on Billings' shoulder might as well have contained a medal or an enlarged pay-packet, such was the beaming grin from the junior officer. "Well hopefully we can find out now quite easily who Christine Jeffries was talking to online." He paused for a moment's reflection. "We'll have to tread carefully of course. Your... let's call it research, hasn't exactly been standard police procedure and we don't want to earn ourselves an even worse name by seeming to be trawling through the public's social media discussions. I'm not sure where this is leading us, but it's good to have a direction, even if it's a circle."

* * *

For Christine Jeffries, unexpected knocks on the door had become the new laxative and on this occasion the sight of another two unknown men in suits brandishing police IDs was like an added diuretic.

She had invited them through into the lounge once identities were established – under the circumstances, the names Billings and Morris were almost antidiarrhoeal! – and in response to their worryingly insightful conjecture, proceeded to deliver a selective version of events. Yes, she had spoken with the woman who had posted the picture, as anyone would have done under the circumstances, those being that her second husband had a very similar tattoo.

That was as far as it went. She had no idea where he was now. Back in the day, once she'd become aware Joost was possibly taking advantage of both the company's expenses and perhaps of more than one of the women responsible for them, she had finished with him. As far as the business regarding the death of the girl from Accounts had been concerned, tragic though it was and although there had been nothing anyone could prove, the mere fact that it had become a matter for conjecture was enough for her not to want Joost around. That was it. She had filed for divorce and had no idea how long that process might take in relation to a husband whose whereabouts were a mystery.

The irony was, if ever a reminder had been needed never to betray her German interlopers, it had been that latest knock on the door; the terror in the possibility it might have been them again. When the discovery of the tattoo and the nose...

The thought of it chilled her, as did the idea of her inadvertent involvement in that act of butchery, presumably performed by the two Germans – surely that couldn't be coincidence.

... had hit the news a couple of days before, she'd wondered how the other two victims of Marcus' attentions, Bella and Tanya, were feeling. They had exchanged numbers after their meeting in Bath as a gesture of support – a gathering they had all agreed, if anyone asked, had never happened – and she had contemplated calling them, before deciding the less interaction the better, for all their sakes. Apart from anything else, who knew whether she was being observed or her calls intercepted. She would put nothing past those two – Berger and Hoffmann, or whatever their true names were.

She had also considered calling Jessica Dawes, but what stopped her in her tracks was the truly blood-chilling realisation, the gruesome possibility, that Jessica might have been involved in that act of savagery against her will, in whatever remote or inadvertent way, or indeed that she too might now be dead. Surely though, the latter would have been in the press somewhere and there had been nothing.

As she spoke, she realised just how much of a block she had tried to put between herself and the recent past, as she dragged banished memories back in the wrong, bloodying way across the barbs of the exit barrier.

Once the officers had departed and she had managed to control the tremors of shame and horror convulsing her body, she'd thought again about calling Jessica, even had her thumb poised above the green call-button before she changed her mind. Instead, despite her previous doubts, she had called Tanya and Bella; advised them that their names had been drawn into the conversation by the police, who had found out the identities of anyone contacting Jessica about the tattoo, but she had denied ever meeting them. She suggested similar denial was the best course. If for some reason Jessica tried to involve them, it would be her word against all of theirs.

Christine might have reeled in those blood-stained recollections, but to create the pretence of a spirit of co-operation rather than obstruction, she had given the officers some photos of Joost. It had been interesting to note that none of them revealed his tattoo – he'd been careful in a way that she'd never suspected and why would she have done? – but she confirmed it was very similar, possibly identical.

There had been a peculiar moment of reflection, one through which the multi-threads of guilt and hope interwove, as she had wondered whether the man she knew as Joost was still alive, despite all probabilities being to the contrary. But in the end it mattered not. She would deny any wrongdoing and if her conscience plagued her in the small hours, she would appease it by remembering Csilla Molnar, misguided and corrupted by that man – perhaps worse.

Thinking about her female employees – she shook her head at the abstract concept of that terminology – her mind wandered to the enigma that was Natalie Savage.

Victim or villain? Christine had needed to acknowledge that she was in no position to be judgemental, given her own fallibilities. She had taken time to reflect on her melodramatic gesture of hurling that ring into the PA's garden on what turned out to be the last night she saw Joost – she had to stop to recall just how long ago that now seemed – and decided to let sleeping dogs lie.

That analogy brought her a blessed moment of abstract relief and she reached down to stroke Tyson, the ultimate example of such a beast!

No, nothing good would have come of digging too deep into that set of circumstances. It had become apparent Joost was no longer a feature in Natalie's life – not that Christine had known it for certain before – because there had been something indefinable in the girl's eyes in recent times that spoke volumes. For once, Christine realised she held all the cards. If the PA wanted to keep her job and her above-average salary, then she faced a stark choice. What could she say or do? The answer was, she said nothing and carried on performing at her very competent best. For more than one reason, that silence suited Christine just fine.

Returning to the key protagonists, she knew that Jessica Dawes was a strong woman and likewise a wealthy one, making her very much the mistress of her own fate. Christine would not beat herself up too much over the nature of that destiny.

And yet – as she had turned her back on the still lake of deep secrets that was her past, Christine didn't hear the tiny splash of a pebble landing in the distance and only later did a weak ripple lap against the shore, representing that briefest of moments when she had to acknowledge to herself that it might be better if Jessica were no longer alive.

God – what had she become?!

She downed the last of her vodka, perhaps the third or fourth that day, before pouring another and continuing to contemplate that question.

* * *

Morris shoved the door open, threw himself down in his chair and puffed out his cheeks, before springing straight back to his feet again and crossing to his whiteboard. Billings had followed him in and been about to sit but took his superior's lead and stood.

Morris gestured towards the board. "Okay, the first time I really feel the need to use this so far."

With the marker pen he drew a big question mark in the middle of the board. To the right of it he wrote a list of names, *Joost de Boer, Christine Jeffries, Jack Jeffries.* To the left he wrote *Tattoo.*

He looked at Billings and tapped the question mark with the pen. "I'd love to be able to draw lines connecting some or all of these. We don't have much – really, we don't." Now he tapped on Christine Jeffries' name. "After our discussion today, I believe she hasn't physically harmed Tattoo-man in any way. This may sound ridiculous but actually I think she is too classy to have done that. She seemed more embarrassed about the fact that she had got involved with Joost de Boer at all."

"I still felt she was holding something back, sir."

"I know what you mean. I just wonder whether she was, as I say, a bit ashamed that she had fallen for his charms. Sometimes people try to block things from their memory. She may have been selective in what she was prepared to say and what might bring her shame." Again, he gestured towards the board. "Okay Billings, as we're standing in front of a door, a locked door with no sight of a key, we're going to look under every flower-pot. We don't have much, but I'd like you to find out who investigated Jack Jeffries' case in Germany and make contact with them. I want to know exactly what happened. See if you can organise a conference call once you've found out the officer in charge. It all just seems full of too many holes."

Though he wasn't old school, nor any kind of Luddite, it still threw Morris that, in no time, the call was scheduled for an hour later. So much was at your fingertips these days; it didn't surprise him that there was an increasing tendency for thriller writers to set their stories back in pre-internet times, where the logical mind of the maverick detective could still be the guiding light, rather than the one emanating from the computer screen.

However, right now in the black-and-white universe of hard facts rather than the grey world of literature, he was delighted to have Ulrich Jauch on that screen.

"Greetings Kriminalkommisar Jauch. Thank you for making the time."

"No problem – and please call me Ulrich. I'm intrigued – you have my attention. Why is it you're wanting to know about the Jack Jeffries case? What's the fire that made this so urgent?"

"I'm not sure it's a burning issue, but there is rather a lot of smoke."

There was silence for a moment.

"Interesting!" Jauch contemplated what he had heard. "So, in this case you're starting in the middle of the maze trying to work your way out for a change." Morris and Billings both laughed and Jauch reciprocated with a smile. "Bet you didn't expect that either – a German with a sense of humour."

Morris liked his counterpart. You needed to be able to laugh in their job, even if it was often graveyard humour.

Jauch continued: "So a nose and a piece of, you believe, someone's shoulder with a tattoo that you think might be an adaptation of a Stasi symbol." He leaned back. "I don't know if anyone's told you that Germany unified quite some years ago."

Morris let the sarcasm pass. "Well, you see the thing is we believe the owner – let's call him the victim of a crime – may have been a man of unknown origins who became involved with Christine Jeffries, the wife of the very man we're here to discuss."

Jauch leaned forward again. "Now that is, once more, very interesting. Was the DNA on any records?"

"No, but perhaps we could send a sample to you."

"You can if you want and I will certainly have it looked into, but I have to tell you DNA samples of ex-Stasi members… well, let's just say the data may be thin on the ground."

"Yeah, I understand." Morris paused. "Tell me please, what exactly happened in the aftermath of that incident with Jack Jeffries? I know the police here, the authorities, were keeping an eye on airports and docks for a little while but not for long."

"Well, there was no other DNA in the car but because of the level of alcohol in Mr Jeffries' blood and the proximity of the incident to Freiburg, I decided to head into the city and ask a few questions; whether anyone had seen anything. The reason the British authorities were looking for someone was that a couple of locals in a bar known to be a popular gay hangout had spotted someone very like him talking with a good-looking blond guy. That in itself is not enough to launch an investigation, especially as they didn't appear to leave together. Of course, there are ways and means... and toilet windows!"

Morris couldn't help but warm to his sometimes-acidic counterpart, who continued. "The reason it became an investigation was because the man working behind the bar that evening didn't turn up to work the next day. The locals said it was a little strange that he seemed to know the blond customer, referred to him as Dimitri apparently, even though none of them could really recall him drinking in there before. Doesn't mean he hadn't, of course. But who knows – was he paid for his silence, was he some sort of accomplice in the cunning murder of Jack Jeffries?" Jauch paused. "Though the motivation for that remains a mystery, unless it was indeed to target the widowed Mrs Jeffries. Was he silenced in some other way as a potential witness? Did Jack Jeffries perhaps pay him for silence of a different sort? He might have been paranoid about his inclinations becoming public knowledge. We issued as good a description as we could of the employee and the blond customer but neither materialised and the hunt was called off by the powers that be in the absence of a strong reason to suspect any wrong-doing." He looked thoughtful. "Those last words can also be a good disguise for closing a file that looks impossible to solve."

Silence fell. At length Jauch glanced at his watch. "Is there anything else I can help you with – not that I've been of huge assistance to this point?"

Morris smiled. "Plenty – and nothing. I will call if anything springs to mind. Thank you, Ulrich."

Morris moved the mouse. "I can't help feeling *disconnect* applies on more than one level here."

Billings nodded and Morris turned to address him. "So, where do we go from here?"

The DS smiled and shrugged his shoulders. "The pub?"

Chapter Thirty-Seven

Despite everything, she must have passed into unconsciousness, because the sound of a door opening woke her. She tensed.

"For God's sake, why are you doing this? Why? Please?"

She heard footsteps, firm but irregular, moving across the concrete floor towards her. They stopped behind her.

Hands pressed against the back of her head. The knot of the blindfold was undone, and it fell away. She blinked, tried to turn her head, but it was held firm. The sight of the sparse room panicked her tongue into activity again: "Please, why?… mmmm!" The words were stifled as the thick cloth of the blindfold became a gag.

"You can't guess? It's all been banished from your memory that quickly? Your screams of moments ago told me otherwise, as does the little pool on the floor, but if you need some help…" Now she felt breath on her neck. "What about the after-shave?" He laughed.

She recognised Hans's voice but also for what it was now; for what she knew it to be – the voice of Marcus. Ambition and lust had blinded her, weakened her senses on the phone in recent months, and in the restaurant. Oh God! She realised too, with hindsight, that he had always been some sort of chimerical monster in her psyche; a vicarious experience based on her sister's pain. Then, to put it mildly, other distractions had prevented her really absorbing anything about Marcus in the car park in Camden – he'd been wearing a woollen hat, his voice had echoed in the empty space… oh, and there had been the little matter of fearing for her life as the gun barrel pointed at her. Add to that the approach of his two captors, plus the fact that much of the beating they inflicted had been hidden from her view, both by her car and her closed eyes.

He walked past her and she noted the limp. She'd missed that too in her desperate need for some excitement, or he had disguised it somehow.

As for the surroundings, it looked like a hotel room without a soul. She'd stayed in more welcoming bothies in Scotland, known for their lack of facilities, even though there was a bed, a table with a laptop on it, a washbasin and toilet. The presence of those fittings only served to deepen her panic. This was somewhere someone was planning for her to stay. On reflection, the only thing that kept if from looking like a prison cell was the computer.

He crossed to the washbasin, ran some water, and soaked a face-cloth in it. Now he turned and, using the damp cloth, wiped diagonally across his face, creating a pale stripe. She wanted to look away, but found she couldn't, both horrified and transfixed, as if he had peeled away a layer of skin. Though self-preservation was her primary concern, a tiny part of her couldn't help but believe this was her punishment. Like everyone else, she had seen the news back then, five years ago; seen evidence of inhuman pain inflicted on a man which was partly her doing – and kept quiet. In the midst of this moment's horror, she wondered how the other members of the coven had dealt with it – were dealing with it still. They had never spoken again.

Her captor turned back to the washbasin, squeezed out the cloth, started again, this time burying his face in it before looking up and pulling at the corners of his eyes, allowing two green contact lenses to pop out.

There was a muffled gasp behind the gag as Jessica's ghastly imaginings stood before her at last as dreadful reality. A further groan was her smothered attempt at 'Max'.

If she thought she'd seen the most chilling sights, his smile put her right. He moved closer, held his face near to hers and ran his fingers across the bridge of his nose before turning his head to left and right, almost playful as he showed her the scarring and said: "Not a bad job in the end. It's not my actual nose, of course. I hid in a storage unit while that made the national news; hid my Phantom of the Opera face and tried to survive and then plot a future. Lucky – well actually not luck, as I had thought things through a bit – my place of refuge was on a fruit farm not far from the rundown industrial estate where this…" he paused a moment, because some horrors only fade and never die, "… this act was committed. They dumped me along a country road, presumably to die or suffer, not knowing they had taken me closer to the farm." Now he pointed again to his nose. "In fact, it suited me better to have a different nose. I've never been so grateful that some well-paid surgeons have, shall we say, needs and tastes that someone with contacts in the dark web had satisfied for many years while preserving their anonymity.

"Clearly my choice of nose worked, if your response in the restaurant is anything to go by. Un Profumo d'Italia – a scent of Italy; my little joke choosing that one." He offered his profile again with much theatricality. "Do you still like it?" Now he turned to face her and his deep stare froze her. "They cut off my nose to spite my fate, you might say. Well now the spite is mine and the fate is yours. Is it what you hoped for?"

The ground shifted again as he reverted to mock-civility: "Oh, how rude of me…" He moved behind her and once more she tensed, but he removed the gag. "… to ask questions if you cannot answer." Silence. "What, nothing to say?"

He was right. What could she say?

He was standing in front of her again and started to unbutton his shirt. *Here it comes,* she thought, but to her continued shame she had leapt to the wrong conclusion. He pulled it down to reveal the angry-looking crater on his shoulder where once had been the now famous tattoo.

It seemed he had read her features. "I know you think all men are after only one thing, but…" here he clasped his hand over his genitals, "… for some reason I will never understand, for which I am truly grateful, they, my brothers-in-arms, decided not to curtail any other activities. From what I remember through the haze of pain and my mind's attempt to protect me from the cruellest memories, I think they decided the removal of part of my features was sufficient; that I wouldn't be attracting any members of the opposite sex – of either sex – again." He pointed to the manacles. "A very neat little trick you played, handing me to those two butchers. That's why you're hanging here." Her eyes widened with fear. "Oh, that doesn't mean I'm going to take a knife to you – not right now. That's a decision for later."

His black playfulness was destroying her. She could do nothing but remain silent for now.

"I admit, it's not subtle, this torture. I just wanted you to feel how it was to hang there in total terror, unable to see – in my case because my eyes had been beaten shut. Like me, any screams from you will not be heard." He pointed towards the window. "I thought you'd like a room with a view. We are miles from anywhere and anyone, so feel free – scream away."

"Max, I…"

"Shut up – I haven't finished. And it's Marcus." His eyes brooked no argument. "Can you imagine what it is like," he said, pointing to a multitude of other scars on his chest, abdomen and back, some of them clearly burns, "to be taken to the border where death would be a welcome release, but not be allowed to cross?" For a moment his gaze shifted to some distant point. "Unfortunately it's something we understood only too well in the Stasi. If I had my time again, would I handle things differently?" His eyes returned to the here and now. "Probably not."

"I'm sorry."

She wondered whether she had ever, in her life, uttered other words that carried such sincerity yet were so lacking in impact. Whatever the rights or wrongs...

Were there any rights in this sad story?

... his scarred body was at least partly down to her and she would have to live with that.

Assuming you live.

Hanging in these manacles, her shoulders burning, terrified, she had the tiniest taste of what he had been through and was not proud of her role in that drama. Still, she forced herself to think of Katherine and that imbued her with some courage; just for a few seconds but enough to enable her to speak.

Words she regretted as soon as they were out: "Yes, this must be quite nostalgic for you – ex-Stasi – having a helpless person hanging here."

He grinned and once again it sent a shiver through her veins. "I will spare you any details but let me just say... you don't know the half of it; not even half of a half." He paused, again looked away, but this time through the window, clearly remembering something. "There's irony to this. Those victims of misnamed democracy, well, we used to play on the well-being of their families as collateral to get the information we needed." He looked back at her. "Remember this – when the target of our investigations was actually one of those other family members, we found that any person in enough pain would consider betraying those dearest to them." He laughed and the sincerity in that sound shocked her. "The people whose names I didn't betray five years ago to my two dear Stasi friends would be flattered to know just how much I endured in keeping their details safe."

He chose that moment to fasten his shirt again, as if the scars were paining and as if hiding the results of his torture might cast a blanket over the memories. He continued as he did up the buttons. "Of course, I had my reasons. One of the contacts has invested huge amounts of money on my behalf and I knew I would need that if I somehow survived the ordeal..." He paused and looked her straight in the eyes, "... which I will admit was not an expectation. The other has the greatest skillset where hacking and the dark web is concerned – much better than mine, which is not inconsiderable. Those whose names I gave are in no danger. In fact, they may make a fortune helping those two microorganisms, Michael and Richard, drag themselves out of the ocean and onto the land of progress." Again, he gave that disconcerting, panic-inducing smile. "Assuming I let them live."

Those words, echoes of her thoughts only moments before, achieved the impossible, filling her with deeper dread than she could have imagined.

He continued: "But regarding using family as any sort of collateral, well, in your case there's no point." He grinned. "I'm not convinced it would have that much impact if I decided to harm your sister; that you would care enough."

His bluntness shocked her but not as much as the possibility that he was right. He pushed on.

"Your silence speaks volumes – but I'm not after any information from you."

"What do you want?"

She would rather not have asked the question; the prospective answers terrified her.

He stepped forward again, directly in front of her, looking her up and down as if appraising her. There was that toying half-smile once more. She wanted, as a reflex, to fold her arms across her body and despite her position he seemed to notice, because he shook his head.

"Oh, believe me, if that was all I wanted you'd be grateful. I suspect that would probably be the outcome you'd object to least. After all, when did you last… what's that wonderful English expression… have it? You envied that about Katherine too. Anyway, I hope it tells you something about your position here that it's not on the agenda."

She did her best to hold his gaze, failed and stayed silent.

"Of course, before I saw you sitting at that restaurant table I could tell that you were someone seeking something but with no true idea what that might be; someone still looking for the true meaning of their life and just newly venturing down the road that led between their legs." He turned away. "But enough!"

He moved to stand in front of the window, seeming to take in the view. When he spoke again, there was a different cadence to his words and he kept his back to her. "Oh, it was hard. You have to remember, I thought they were going to kill me. When they took those first cuts, I wished they would."

Jessica knew to stay silent. Part of her was still hanging there in terror but another irrational instinct suggested it was not his intention to torture her, at least not physically.

He seemed to read her mind with such ease. "Believe me; I would have put no-one else through that." His head turned, so he spoke over his shoulder as if addressing her directly, seeking intimacy yet avoiding it. "No, if it comes to it, I will kill you quickly."

She swallowed hard. The fact that she'd been right about his intentions was scant consolation!

Now he did turn, went to the single chair and sat down. "I'm quite proud of my refusal to give them those vital names. No way would they lay their blood-soaked hands on my hard-won money."

Again she held back from making a point, the one where she might question just how difficult it had been to sleep with lonely women for money, staining your own hands with blood in the process. For now, she would abide by the same common-sense rule she'd followed when those other Stasi thugs had been at her house; the one where the person with the higher moral ground holds their counsel when confronted by a deadly weapon. Of course, *higher moral ground* was a loose term when both of them were standing, right now, in a shit-pit of her making.

He continued: "If I was going to die, why make life any easier for those two dinosaurs?" He smiled again. "Which is placing them further along the evolutionary chain than they deserve. No, my stubbornness was the balm to my pain as I sat in front of the surgeon. I mean a real surgeon, not Dr Death from Dresden.

"That other key contact I protected was the person who helps me forge new identities. I have several now. If you do walk away from all of this... keep walking. You will never find me." Now he laughed, "I think you wouldn't have a problem with that." He paused for effect. "But I would always find you. Nevertheless, rest assured, if you did try to point the authorities in my direction, I would know. You could never be certain I wouldn't exact revenge on that whore of a sister of yours."

She stayed silent, knowing he was trying to provoke a reaction.

Is that your only motivation? whispered her demons. Seemed they'd had no issue with accompanying her on her travels!

He stood; raised his hands. "What, no mock indignation? Have you finally acknowledged her vulnerability was not an excuse for her appetites?" He rubbed his hands together. "Believe me, in the bedroom or the back of a car, she knew such tricks that made even me wonder." He had walked across to stand in front of her again. "I believe you can now deal with the idea of her meeting a sticky end," he said, putting his hand to his mouth in a mock-conspiratorial way and sniggering, "a speciality of hers by the way – if it meant you could walk away from here."

A shudder passed through her, all the icier for the look in his eye and the casual thrust of his hands into his pockets. She fought against any display of fear but knew that was a lost cause.

Again, he strolled with insouciance around the room as he continued: "But I have no desire to waste my time in such pointless acts, so let's hope we can work this out. I have bigger fish to fry than the pointless harming of a slut." The pleasure he took from the repeated insulting of Katherine was palpable but still Jessica fought to keep her feelings to herself.

Why? The chiding voices were insistent. *Finding it difficult to deny?*

He pushed on; seemed not to need a response now. Had he read her encrypted thoughts? "And before you consign me to the ranks of the despised, let me remind you that you know I was unaware she had a twin. I never asked her to clean out your bank account." He nodded in acknowledgement of a latent question. "Yes, she was my target. I'm not claiming to be anything other than what I am." He raised a finger for emphasis. "But it was her cunning plan. I assume she took your identification before giving an award-winning performance of being you. Not quite the innocent you would have us believe."

She wasn't prepared to let him stand on some pedestal, even though he had touched on something disturbing; her sister's act of betrayal. "Well, your critique of my sister's duplicitous ways is masterly, perhaps accurate, but cannot hide the fact that you tried to kill her."

The inclination of his head, likewise the spreading of his palms, represented acknowledgement of that fact. However, he wasn't done.

"As I said, I'm not pretending to be some innocent. But *tried* to kill her." He accentuated the first verb. "Believe me, if I had wanted her dead, she would be dead. Nothing was calculated. She called me and I came but wandered into a burning building." He looked at her and grinned. "You would know how that can affect you."

"How did you..."

"Know about your previous career? You forget, you reference it on your website and I've had a bit of time to research you. Twice, in fact – once when Katherine was you, and once when I was Hans Schulze." He grinned, but his features turned serious again as he raised a hand with fingers spread. "Five years – it's also given me time to repent a little." He crossed the room to stand in front of her again, looked long and hard into her eyes and gave almost a nod of approval as he spoke. "But look at her needy cunning, waiting till I arrived before cutting her wrists.

Such a…" he made a thespian-worthy overdramatic gesture towards the heavens, "… theatrical cry for help."

"She's not well."

"If she wanted to die, she should have died. Believe it or not, I tried to help. I admit it was for selfish reasons. As it turns out – the irony of it – your arrival interrupted that."

She couldn't interpret the look he gave her and decided for the umpteenth time to hold her peace. He walked around behind her once more and she wondered whether she had finally pushed it too far.

He grasped her wrists – she gasped but heard a key turning in the manacles; felt her arms dropping to her sides. As feeling returned and she rubbed her wrists, he spoke: "I hope you're not going to try something so foolish as to run. Let me assure you, this forest stretches for many miles in every direction. You'll die of the cold before you can find a friendly fireside. Nor do I know how good your Russian is and in this part of the world," he said, gesturing along the length of her body, "a beautiful woman in a figure-hugging dress might be expected to show her gratitude for any hospitality." He pointed towards the seat by the laptop and indicated that she should sit down. "First things first."

From the window sill he fetched one of the bottles of water standing there and brought it to her.

"Drink."

Only now did she realise the full extremity of her thirst and she downed the half-litre almost in one. Smiling, Marcus fetched her another.

"How long have I been here?" Her question was greeted with yet another smile and silence, while her stomach gurgled as the fluid hit it. "On reflection, I couldn't have been here that long, otherwise…" she looked down at her dress, "… let's just say I would have needed the toilet."

Ignoring her, a response she found more than disturbing, he crossed to the window again, this time opening it with a key from his pocket. Reaching outside onto the ledge, he produced a small jar. Cold air from the forest froze her ankles. Producing a fork from a small cabinet near the washbasin, he placed both it and the jar by the computer. She saw that it contained anchovies.

"Quick protein fix," he said. "Eat some. You'll need it – we have work to do."

"Work?"

"Yes, and how long it takes depends on you." He gestured towards the fish. "Eat."

She did as she was instructed, her hands shaking, not merely from hunger.

At length he continued: "Okay, switch on the laptop." She was surprised, given the surroundings, that she could access the internet. "Satellite," he said as if reading her thoughts. "Have no doubts, we are as far from civilisation as I indicated."

He allowed that fact to sink in like a good interrogator before moving on. "I need you to blog… yes blog." The last two words were a reaction to her expression, which she assumed was some hybrid of puzzlement and amazement. "You do it every couple of days – let your fans know how well things are going for you. Tell them about your meeting in Munich three days ago." She looked up sharply. "Oh, I can assure you, I have kept you hydrated for the last couple of days – as I said, I needed you to be able to resume your day job!"

As she realised the comatose state in which she must have been, she felt sick, particularly at the thought of him ensuring her hygiene!

He continued: "And don't try anything coded, or any clandestine shouts for help, for I will recognise it." He had been walking across to the drawer unit as he spoke and now produced a large carving knife. "It might be the last thing you would type." Once more her eyes must have spoken for her. The mock sympathy and courtesy of his next words chilled her far more than the forest air. "Oh, I'm sorry; I didn't mean I would kill you. Literally, I meant it would be the last thing you would type." As he spoke, he looked at her hands and then at the edge of the blade. "Believe me, I know how it feels to lose vital things."

He came now and stood behind her while she wrote in her blog, *Open Dawes*, about her successful meeting with Schulze Sicherheit. She was about to post the message when he said: "Wait. There's something I need you to add." He looked at her hands. "Very well typed, given your jitters."

Now he produced a piece of paper from his pocket and started to read.

"One further thing – in keeping with my love of technology…" Pausing, he looked at her motionless if trembling fingers and the keyboard, gesturing. She typed what he had read before he continued. "I am changing the profile of my business to adopt more of an online approach."

Jessica looked up at him but the cold blue of his eyes was enough to make her hold her tongue, Again, the air that had brushed around her ankles earlier seemed tropical by comparison.

He read on – she typed. "Partly this is because the benefits of the aforementioned technology will enable me to move much more swiftly to meet your needs, but also, ironically, given the success of my meeting in

Munich, I have seen that the days of face-to-face meetings are numbered. Video conferencing and other technologies have rendered them so. The world is everyone's oyster now, which again is part of the reason for my final piece of news – I'm going into partnership with Schulze Sicherheit…"

Now her hands froze above the keys and her head shot round. "No fucking w—"

The knife slammed down, its point embedding a good inch into the table-top. In terms of focus, its impact was the equivalent of a magnifying glass on the sun's rays. Nevertheless, they held each other's gaze for a moment before she turned back to the laptop.

The devil's voice continued over her shoulder: "I will be setting up a new head office in Wroslow, Poland…" He stopped and pointed to the screen. "That's not how you spell Wroclaw – but then there are a few typos in that last part. I will allow you those on the basis of stage fright." He pushed on. "I will, of course, retain my UK office to support my existing customers there and grow the business. I look forward bla bla bla…" She looked up and he waved the piece of paper almost dismissively. "I can write the rest for you, plus make any corrections. Really I just needed you to sign in."

For the first time, she felt the old Jessica make an appearance, anger replacing fear. "As I started to say a few minutes ago, no fucking way! I worked hard to build this business – bloody hard!"

"I know the feeling." There was mock wistfulness in his response. "Imagine if someone just strolls in and takes it away."

"Don't make me laugh! You didn't have a business."

He gave a little shrug. "What I did was indeed my business." He strolled across to the window and gazed out. Jessica looked at the knife. "You can try." He turned and grinned. "Oh, no psychic powers – I just saw your reflection in the window." He walked back. "It made me think, where have I seen those features and a sharp object before? The Walton Hotel five years ago I believe."

The cat got her tongue for a moment, but she forced it aside. "It was no longer just your business when you involved my sister."

He took three sharp paces forward, reached into an inner jacket pocket and she wondered whether a gun would be making an appearance, so decided against her impulse to stand, but he just withdrew his hand. "What do you care about your mad sister? She's always been an embarrassment to you – a dirty secret. Wherever you could, you hid the fact of her existence. And another fact got to you; the fact that she outwitted you in closing one of your bank accounts. That really ate at you. It's why you contemplated letting her drown in that hotel, isn't it?"

"How dare you…!" She was lost for a continuation of that particular thought.

"… tell the truth? The bank knew nothing about her existence and you didn't enlighten them, did you? She was always an embarrassment to you."

"It was to stop her getting into trouble and—"

"Bullshit! You had important discussions going on about possible new contracts for Fire-Dawes and if the security risk that is Katherine Dawes was known about, if the possibility that she could render you the…" he made air commas "… *bankrupt twin sister*' got out, then important potential clients might be lost."

Now Jessica couldn't help herself and stood, looking to come around the table. "Look, I know she could be a loose cannon—"

"I think nymphomaniac was one word you used."

"Utter garbage! I never…" Did she? She might have thought it at times, but surely… then again, who knew what she had said under the influence of date drugs that night in Munich?

"Well, you hid that attempted suicide too – the shame of it! – rather than getting her to seek help."

"It was because I wanted revenge on you for what you had done. You didn't know I existed."

"Again, bullshit. Your revenge had a little but not much to do with hiding the fact that you had a twin sister. You hid it too from the two monsters into whose hands you led me. There, at last, she had a use."

For just a moment, yet inappropriate to that moment, she felt something – his power. He was causing her to doubt herself. "I…" she hesitated, "… my plans changed."

"Yes – and I can guess what to. You wanted me to believe I was seeing a ghost in that car park. It worked too, long enough to both bring you satisfaction and distract me from my own fate."

He stepped forward once more. Panicking, Jessica couldn't help herself and grabbed the knife. Then she swayed a little.

"Clearly not enough anchovies," he grinned, "and maybe a half-litre too much of the wrong fluid."

She looked in dismay at the empty water bottle, her last memories of the pavement outside the restaurant in Munich returning to taunt her as she slumped in the chair, while the knife slipped from her fingers and clattered to the floor.

He looked at the putative weapon. "Believe me, if you pick that up once more, I will use it to inflict on you the same torture inflicted on me. Your fire brigade tattoo would provide a suitable alternative." He gave her a knowing look and a wink. "Interesting hiding place for it." Now he looked once more into those distant ruins where he had abandoned but not forgotten his ordeal, and his features changed. "Even then, you will not be going through one thousandth of the pain I did at the hands of those butchers, my former brothers." His eyes returned to the present. "But I will admit making you dictate that blog a few minutes ago was some minor revenge. Of course, I could have written that myself. I just wanted to watch it dawning on you that you were about to lose everything." He sat down on the table and continued: "Because all that partnership crap is exactly that. You will be signing over your business to me."

She forced herself to sit up, looked him in the eyes and, as she said her next words, was surprised to find they weren't empty. "I would rather die."

"A thought, or words, you might repeat thousands of times in future." As if something had just occurred to him, he stood and turned his back to her. "Anyway, it doesn't matter whether you want to sign it over or not."

He reached once more into the inner pocket of his jacket, she presumed again for a gun. Turning back to her, he raised his arm, saying: "You already have."

Her eyes narrowed as she struggled to look at the object he was holding. He addressed it: "Did you get that?"

It was an iPhone and on its screen was an unmistakeable face – her own. Only the voice was different: "Hello, sister."

Chapter Thirty-Eight

This time when she came round, there was an initial misplaced sense of calmness as she found herself lying on a bed as opposed to hanging in chains.

Reality dawned all too quickly.

Waking in a strange place under the influence of drugs – it wasn't even the first time now! She had always prided herself on control. Memory mocked her once more as she remembered her nascent desire, before the meal in Munich, to live a little.

Yeah – well look where that has got you, taunted her Ghost of Christmas Past, whose name was probably Katherine. *Whatever self-delusional crap you choose to believe now, you know you came to Munich to sleep with a man you'd never met.*

She felt like she was fighting to stay afloat. Splinters of sentences floated by her; flotsam from the shipwreck of her life. Voices, one male and one female – her own – mocked her as she grew cold and started to sink.

"You were always a dirty secret. Even when she found you dying, she hid it from the world."

"… how many people even knew you existed…"

"… two abortions… the shame you brought…"

"… I couldn't tell the bank; couldn't let that possibility of a security breach be known – not when I'm running a business…"

"… she's a loose cannon… I'd have ended up looking after any children. I didn't have the time."

"… whatever the reasons for it, you were jealous of her passion. That's what made it so easy for me a.k.a. Hans Schulze to tap your Achilles heel."

"… why did you hand me over to those two torturers?"

"To avenge my sister."

"Bullshit! It was to satisfy something in you… I'd got inside your fortress… You could have just got in touch with the police. It was revenge, pure and simple. They didn't know about your sister."

"All my life I've had to cover up for your mistakes and sickness…"

"… tell a man you fancy you're looking after your sister who has Asperger's and you might as well tell him you've got an STD…"

But there were other voices too, interspersed, unrecognisable, repeating the same things over and again.

"Drink this… drink it…"

"Spit it out… here!"

"Sit here."

Vague memories of being manhandled.

She was awake now, any comfort in finding herself in a bed well and truly forgotten. Hope fled into the icy wastes that she could see beyond the window. She pushed herself into a sitting position and then stood, her legs shaking through a combination of sedatives and fear. The computer had gone; likewise, the jar of fish and bottle of water, though whether she would have drunk any was another matter.

Jessica crossed to the window and found no foodstuffs on the ledge outside. She tried the handle – it was locked. Outside, she saw wind blowing through clacking trees, but couldn't hear it in that sealed cabin.

She turned to face the room.

Which was when, to her utter surprise, she saw her travel-bag on the other side of the bed. She hurried to it, opened it, saw her passport and a flight ticket, both of which she opened. The former was hers, no doubt; the ticket – now there was something. She had bought an open-ended ticket; return date dependent on all sorts of things she couldn't bear to think about. This was not that ticket – it was one-way from Munich to Heathrow. What the hell!? Had this been done to taunt her?

She looked up. "Hello!"

Nothing.

"Hello… Max?… Marcus?!"

The silence was no surprise. So, this was it. The place where she was going to die. Jessica reached out to steady herself on the table and then crumpled onto the bed.

At length, feeling a little stronger, she picked up the chair by the desk and tried to smash it against the window. The muscularity from her years in the fire brigade seemed to have deserted her. Still, the chair broke into several pieces. Her hands went to her knees and she gave a wrenching sob. Spotting a narrow, slightly sharper piece of wood, she grabbed it and made her way to the door.

She had been planning to spare herself the despair of finding it locked. It was solid wood but didn't seem to be hermetically sealed. She tried jamming the piece of wood between door and frame with no expectation. It looked unconquerable but she had to try. She grasped the handle, intending to pull with all her might while she tried prising it open…

… the handle simply turned, revealing a world which, despite its bitter cold and a wind that obviated the need for a freezer, brought her an ephemeral joy. She allowed herself a few minutes of delight at the thought of having avoided a lonely death in that silent cell.

Death still beckoned, of course, but at least to some extent she would meet him on her own terms.

She would wait to see whether that low sun was rising or setting and then head south on the assumption that she was in the north, probably somewhere deep in the Taiga Forest. She looked at her dress, worn for a hot night out in Munich, likewise the fancy heels. Some graveyard humour surfaced as she thought of the crampon-like effect of those stilettos in the snow.

Jessica stepped through the doorway, staring out through the frozen landscape that would be her deathbed – which was when she spotted the tyre tracks leading to a battered Jeep-like vehicle parked off to the left! She hurried across; the icy wind forgotten. There were no keys in it.

She had to pinch herself, just to ensure this wasn't all part of the surreal dream to which she had awoken; a cruel, hallucinogenic joke played by sleeping pills. Reassured that she was indeed awake, the possibility of someone playing with her still existed. A thought occurred; she went back into the cabin and checked in the bag.

The keys were in a side-pocket!

She went back to the car, opened it and found a note: *Get yourself home.* To her continuing astonishment, at the turn of a key the engine started and the dashboard showed plenty of fuel. She wept, unable to stop for some time.

Someone was playing with her, but what did she have to lose, apart from those tears? She looked at the flight ticket, dated about a month after her arrival for her fateful meeting with the imaginary Hans Schulze. She had no idea what the date was now, but given all that had happened, plus the words on the note, she would just take a chance it was still valid. As for the direction or distance to

Munich – she had no clue, but she would follow the tyre tracks and hope they led her to some semblance of civilisation. She would change her clothes and be gone to wherever the devil was leading her.

* * *

The person watching her surreal departure into the snowy wastes that evening now had a call to make. It had all gone to plan.

Chapter Thirty-Nine

That knock on the door a year ago – how it had changed everything!

She stared down into the black coffee, her drink of choice for those nights when she didn't see him. That number was increasing, thanks – according to him – to the demands of the growing business. She feared sleep, which the caffeine held at bay, though the lonely doubts were almost as prevalent in her waking hours. As she looked into the swirling liquid, the artist in her saw a dark reflection of her new life. How different she had hoped it might be, but then again naivety had always been one of her many weaknesses.

Interesting that the only strength she recognised in herself, that artistic flair, kicked in now, spotting the symbolism in her whirling drink – at least some part of her was alive and well. The rest of her was exhausted; from not being herself or perhaps – the irony of it – from having to be herself. A bit of her had revelled in playing the part of her sister and the excitement of having to remember when to be her, in order to fool him. Maybe playing Queen Jessica had helped her to escape from being Princess Katherine the Failure, stepping outside herself.

Now she wondered, not for the first time, whether he missed it too.

It wasn't the same, maintaining this double-life for the benefit of the outside world, or rather the deception of it. He was her director now, reminding her, cajoling her, writing her lines and helping her not to fall over the furniture – when he was there. Looking back at her performance in the bank when she had gone on stage unprompted, she wondered just how the hell she had managed that. Strange the power that derived from the interaction of love, sex and obsession. Right now, his absences meant only one element of that formula was working and it was leaving her feeling inert.

Of course, she was more than happy for him to be running the show where the business was concerned. She'd never had a head for such things.

She should have known that someone as driven as him, who had survived the dreadful things she had unwittingly put him through with her damned photo, outlined to her by him in a way she would never ever forget, would make the business thrive and, of course, the price of that success was nights away.

She looked around at the well-appointed echoing house. It was hers…

It would always be Jessica's in her mind.

… for the moment, according to Marcus. He had promised he would buy her another, given the unhappy memories the place held for her, once the exact nature of her sister's fate was known. It hadn't become hers via a will, as they didn't know for sure whether Jessica was dead. Quite how that whole scenario would get played out – the concept was beyond her. Under current circumstances, surely it meant they would have to pretend it was her, Katherine, who had passed away. She had nothing to leave to anyone anyway, and they couldn't have two Jessicas roaming the earth.

Could they?

Marcus assured her that he had it all in hand. She would have to just believe him. There was no choice.

Katherine had to question how, even now, despite the parlous state her relationship with Jessica had reached, she could still grieve at the idea of her sister's death. It had to be something of a reflex, a reaction to her own current loneliness, given that Jessica had tried to let her die, according to Marcus. She wished she could believe it was an attack of conscience which had stayed Jessica's hand, rather than the idea of using her twin sister in her plan for revenge against the man who had driven a £30,000 wedge of banknotes between them. At first, blood being thicker than bloodstained water, Katherine had doubted Marcus' story; wondered whether it was in fact him who had left her to die in the bathtub. After all, it was him she had called, not Jessica. Yet as he had said, why would he do that to someone who had tried so hard to help him and might do so again in the future? Indeed, as he had pointed out, how could he have been there just moments before Jessica had turned up and not now be under arrest? He insisted he hadn't been there except possibly as a figment of Katherine's imagination, as her eyes strained against the water and the fading of her life, his presence at that moment her one wish. He told her he had arrived later at the hotel, delayed by the fact that he had been on the road and most of the way home, to be told by Reception that Jessica – as he knew Katherine then – had called down to say she now didn't want any visitors. That, he assumed looking back, had been the real Jessica making sure he didn't get the room number and therefore didn't find out there was a twin sister – buying herself time while she worked out a vengeful plan. Katherine realised later that she had never really asked him where he was that day.

His explanation made sense.

Didn't it?

Now the intensity of her concern for Jessica, her wish to know of her whereabouts or fate, dipped again as she remembered what she herself had been put through. That your own sister watched your life ebb away… it didn't bear thinking about – and why had she suddenly had a change of heart in that hotel bathroom and decided to help? Surely it had to be some sudden awareness that Katherine was more use to her alive than dead, as Marcus had suggested? Had it been as simple as Jessica wanting revenge on both of them, so she had condemned Marcus to his fate in that car park in Camden that evening, delighting in the impact his absence would have on Katherine?

And then there were the things she had heard on the phone, when Marcus had linked her into the conversation he was having with Jessica in the prison in the wilderness. The problem was that she had only vague memories of those words now. Perhaps that was best though. It might have sounded like a voice calling from the other side.

She squeezed her eyes shut as she remembered, in the months following her recovery from the failed suicide, how Jessica had lied again, telling her Marcus had run away. On reflection, it was no surprise that Katherine had been made to move out of the very house in which she now lived her empty life. As Marcus had said, in her sister's features Jessica would have seen her own guilt every day; the face that she had watched drowning beneath the bath water. Likewise, in that mirror of madness, Jessica knew the crime committed by her in betraying Marcus to his cabal would have shown on her own features. She had managed to hide the details from Katherine when they hit the news, pretending to be shielding her from the world outside. That state of affairs could not have continued for long. Katherine now knew that was why she had suggested her sister move out.

Now knew because Marcus had told her.

The knock on the door of her flat a year ago – she would never forget it – when a frighteningly unfamiliar face, but a voice that warmed her whole body, had appeared at her apartment. More lies by Jessica – so much for Marcus having run away, disappearing after his attempt to take her life had failed.

Katherine had let him in – to her home and her life again. His willingness to forgive her his pain had moved her. He told her about the horrors of the world to which the Dawes sisters had condemned him. Her skin and bones crawled with the shared knowledge and evidence of his surgery and suffering.

He had also been wonderfully honest, explaining the true background to his financial hardship, which he had hidden from her through shame; how he was from the old East Germany and had been a member of the Stasi, but had managed to escape to the West to flee the horrors of that regime. Of course, finding work had been hard. Then the Berlin Wall had come down, unleashing his former compatriots onto the democratic world. Once his tattoo had gone online – again Katherine shuddered on remembering her part in it – he found out the hard way that the Stasi always repay desertion, which they see as treachery. It was why he had taken on the name of Max some years ago – he had asked her to forgive that deception – seeing it as almost inevitable that one day they would come looking.

But it was when he said the words, *"it's as if the two of you deserve each other,"* that he had brought her to her knees, she now begging his forgiveness – and he had granted it, almost as simply as that. She had stayed on her knees – old passions and needs died hard! How she had missed him!

Then, over a drink, he spoke of the rest of his fight; of how he had decided he would no longer be the man in rags. He was determined to make something of himself. Friends had taken pity on him, pulling enough money together for him to have the surgery he needed, enabling him to show his face again to the world, with all the courage that entailed. Then he had worked hard and forged himself a career in futures. But for him, something else needed to be laid to rest and he explained his plans for other types of futures – theirs. He had told her to leave everything to him; to be prepared when the time came to travel to Munich on a passport that he would provide and to travel home on another – her sister's.

As instructed, on an agreed day he had asked her to listen in on her phone. She had heard everything that justified their course of action.

If only what followed had been as satisfying. For a time, while he ran things in Fire-Dawes, pursuing her love of art and the art of making love had been all she needed, but increasingly she was beginning to realise that one was nothing without the other and now he was seldom with her.

She imagined there were people for whom financial freedom and the chance to take coffee with friends would be nirvana – a minor point being that, for such a life one needed actual friends, not the art-club brigade.

The knock on the door! There it was again, only this time a different door, a little louder and not in her memories. She looked up. Could it be him?

No, Katherine, he has keys!

Besides, she remembered he was in Milan today.

Another knock, more insistent this time. Whoever it was, they weren't going away.

She got to her feet.

Chapter Forty

Once they had taken a quick drive around the building and estate, to check all was well and they weren't walking into a trap, they pulled up by the rusting roller-shutter door of that dilapidated monument to business failure.

Michael turned to Richard. "Not exactly – what do they call it here – Memory Lane, is it? I don't know how we ever let him talk us into this waste of money. There's fuck all here and this is one of the most depressing estates I've ever been on…" he said with an ironic grin, "… which is really saying something when you're from East Germany! I still don't understand why we've never sold it."

Richard nodded. "Well, those very reasons you've just given might have made it work. The place didn't cost that much, relatively speaking, in the larger scheme of things and there's no-one around to watch what you're doing at this time of night. A perfect setting for a bit of natural wastage – a damaged box here, a dropped pallet there and a little supply line of expensive pharmaceuticals for poorer countries. Plus, as I said before, Milton Keynes continues to expand and this real estate might grow in value."

"It would never have got past any of the GDP or MHRA inspections. We took our eye off the ball."

Another nod of acknowledgement from Richard. "So let's hope this new opportunity gives us a chance to cash in on our investment… at last." He paused for a moment's reflection. "I'm amazed she got in touch. Maybe it's a case of *better the devil you know*. Then again, there are devils and then there are devils. I guess it's cheap storage, we're useful contacts. Maybe she just wants us onside." Richard looked up at the building, still contemplating something. "She's a hard-nosed bitch. Look what she did to Marcus. She knew exactly what she was condemning him to, handing him back to us. She wanted a piece of him, other than the one her sister had, which cost her thirty thousand pounds – she wanted vengeance."

"Oh well, maybe we should have sent her the parts we had."

They exchanged a look.

Richard looked at his watch, wanting to move on from what were, when all was said and done, uncomfortable memories. "What time did she say she was meeting us?"

"Eight o'clock."

"Okay, let's go in and get the lights on."

"Yeah, but let's be selective with that." Michael grinned. "The place has been standing empty ever since we bought it. It's not going to be in the best shape. Let's leave the rats some shadows to hide in. Don't light up the racking aisles." He shook his head. "Fucking Marcus!"

They walked across the unlit, damp concrete. It struck Richard how certain memories were seared into your history. At first, the surroundings reminded him of his Stasi days but then, as he punched in the key-code, the sound of the roller-shutter door brought other phantoms forward and he half-expected Marcus' cries to emanate from the black space beyond.

He had a thought and turned to Michael. "Do switch on enough lights that we can see whether there are any bloodstains on the floor." Michael smiled in response and Richard found the gesture more disturbing than usual. He rubbed his chin for a moment. "Any joking aside, if we do manage to set up this deal, I'll have the place cleaned thoroughly. You just don't know what we might have missed."

"Richard, five years have passed since our – what shall we call it – little joke?"

His next question betrayed his nervousness. "It was definitely her you spoke to?"

Michael gave a somewhat disbelieving grin. "Whatever my faults, brother, I never forget a face and it was a Skype call. Believe me, I think to her that we're men who get things done. We could be useful for her. She certainly wouldn't want to cross us."

Richard set the door rolling in closure. The individual shutters settled. Now they stood in silence.

They had been through so much together over the decades, inflicted so much pain, but the silent screams in that space were worse for Richard. That bothered him. It had indeed been five years now. They'd had other adventures since then. He shook his head. "I think I'm either getting old or losing my nerve."

"That's not all you'll be losing."

The words hadn't emanated from Michael.

Despite the silence, they hadn't heard any footsteps.

Looking up sharply towards the dark space down one of the aisles, they saw the arm – and the gun – emerging from the shadows.

"Hello, brothers."

* * *

He stepped forward into the murky light, onto what seemed to him a suitably ominous, oppressive stage for this final act, at least the part these villains had to play. Their open, downturned mouths had transformed their features into two theatrical Greek masks of old.

"I thought I'd better introduce myself; figured you might not recognise these features."

"Marcus…?" It was Michael who spoke first, as he had known he would.

"Well done – ten out of ten."

"What's this all about?"

"Ah. Back to the bottom of the class."

"I wouldn't waste time protesting or begging." It was Richard's turn. As always, the more salient, reasoned response was his. "This is a done deal, I suspect."

Marcus gave a little nod of acknowledgment. "Insightful as always."

Michael looked backwards and forwards between the others. "But… but he betrayed the cabal. Everyone knows the punishment."

"I guess you were caught in a bit of a cleft stick. After all, you're not supposed to kill your brothers, but at the same time it would have been more merciful than the punishment you handed out." He pointed the gun towards Michael. "You can rest assured I will be more thoughtful." He enjoyed the dismay that registered in the eyes of a man who had never thought twice about ignoring that same look on the features of his victims; had thrived on it in fact. "But in many ways, I suppose you did me a favour. New identity…" he stroked his face, "… albeit I might have preferred to choose the manner of my facial restructuring. But now, if the authorities are looking for the old Marcus, they'll struggle.

"Then there's the focus it gave me. Rather than the slow milking of various cows, revenge gave me a target and a dairy farm of my own."

Richard spoke up. "You mean Jessica Dawes? How on earth did you get her back onside!? I mean, your cock might be big, but there are limits." Richard allowed a faint smile, incongruous under the circumstances, to cross his features.

Marcus grinned. "Oh, it's OK, the business has been signed over to me."

252

Richard frowned. "Again, I must ask, how did you win her over? I'll have to assume her invitation here tonight was to set us up for this..." he looked around, gesturing, "... farewell party."

"She had no input. She's not around anymore – I saw to that."

Now Michael chipped in, disbelieving. "But we spoke with her on Skype yesterday."

"I'm afraid you didn't."

"We did..."

"No, you made the acquaintance of her Zwillingsschwester."

"*Twin* sister?!"

It gave Marcus such pleasure to pull a mock frown, displaying false ingenuousness. "You mean she didn't tell you about her twin sibling Katherine, the one who emptied out one of her accounts on my behalf, masquerading as her; the one who read my script on Skype yesterday morning?"

The Greek tragedy masks were back in place, open mouths silenced for a moment.

He continued: "Of course as someone who suffers from Asperger's, she had no desire to run the business that her sister had built into a very healthy financial position, so was more than happy to sign it across to Schulze Sicherheit."

Richard nodded and even managed to smile. "Schulze Sicherheit – okay." That final syllable dragged out. "I can only applaud what you've managed to achieve, even though it is about to cost me my life."

Marcus knew he would have to be careful. Richard's acceptance of his fate was making him feel melancholy, almost nostalgic, and that way lay danger. He couldn't turn his back on everything, let it go. When they spared him his life, they had assumed it would continue as one of misery.

He pushed on. "Yes, Jessica's need was more for revenge than justice. She wanted to see me pay. I, too, didn't know there were two of them when I picked that profile on the dating website. In their own ways, they both had me fooled. I have said it to Katherine before – it's as if they deserve each other. A huge part of Jessica's delight must have been to see the look on my face in the car park that night. I thought I'd seen a ghost. That will have brought her so much pleasure.

"Anyway, as I was saying, Katherine had neither the desire nor the ability to run the business, which left a certain Hans Schulze siphoning money into an offshore account. And now that's done, the time is almost up. The course is run."

"Why?" Richard looked puzzled. "To continue your dairy farming analogy, surely Fire-Dawes and Schulze Sicherheit are your cash cows."

"I have learnt that a business is only as solid as its foundations and Katherine Dawes is built on shifting sand. She's fine for a picture in a blog or two, the odd event where she doesn't have to say too much maybe – I mean, she's not unintelligent – but it's time I was on my way." He looked at the gun. "Besides, I've found I'm bored."

"But that's a beautiful house in a lovely location in Bath. Surely that's a city one could get used to." Marcus was surprised there wasn't any undertone or hint of anxiety in Richard's voice. It seemed he remained a pragmatist to the end. Then again, he still suspected that was part of the plan, just to remain calm and talk him round to believing life was good. He was sure they'd love him to stay in Bath – a sitting target. "She's an attractive woman. You have her under your thumb."

"Believe me, you would need several thumbs. Her condition is unpredictable." Marcus looked around, into and through the darkness of their surrounds. "We would never have come to this place if she hadn't been so volatile; disobedient with her camera. Oh, I know you would never have stopped looking for me but you would never have found me and that I could have dealt with.

"Anyway, to quote the phrase I made Jessica use in her blog when she announced I was taking over Fire-Dawes – a phrase I love because so few people know the violent intent of the original – the world is my oyster and I have found that I do indeed need the challenges, the adventures, providing food for different sexual appetites. One more spontaneous wrong move from her and my story might have another ending."

"I can't help thinking, Marcus, your own impetuosity might bring you down. Talk about walking into the lion's den, what was all that with Jack Jeffries? What if the German Polizei had found you? They were hunting for weeks, though there was little to go on."

"And you know that how?" Marcus smiled, well aware his cabal family had eyes and ears in the German Federal Police. He was also impressed by Richard's continued attempts even in this dreadful place, Death's ante-room, to use tried and trusted psychological techniques to manoeuvre the situation – his use of Marcus' name being a bridge-builder. On another day, perhaps, it might have made some impression but there would not be another day… and the memories of pain in that setting ensured Marcus' continued focus. Standing in there in the dark waiting for them had been desperate and tough, despite the years that had passed.

As Marcus' question was, in effect, rhetorical, Richard continued: "Then this Dutchman walks into the life of Jeffries' ex-wife, surely not a risk worth taking."

"The German police were wasting their time. The morning they found Jack Jeffries, I had already leased a car and headed across the border to Zurich." He enjoyed the look of surprise. "I hung out in my hideaway on a farm near Newton Longville that you knew nothing about; the very same container you consigned me to later through your brutality." He paused, allowing the silence to work its black magic, a reminder to his former friends that this place and time had been his Hell and would now be theirs — they would never see the world beyond those shadows again. The fact of him telling them these details was proof that they would not live beyond that night. Then he continued. "All I needed was to find a gay man hiding in plain sight and store the details in memory only."

"Yes, that was clever of you, taking none of his documents so no-one could fathom the cause of his potential murder or the purpose of it."

"Exactly. Then, after a suitable period of time, I arrived at the door of his widow who wouldn't have had sex for some time, feeling lonely, abandoned, or to use the technical terminology, horny."

He glanced at his watch. "All this behavioural analysis, a sensible conversation laced with humour – it's almost like old times."

He was pleased to see he hadn't lost his touch when he killed them. He took Richard first, wanting Michael to have a moment when he knew his fate was coming and seeing the horror dawning in his eyes. Yet despite everything, there was immeasurable frustration in feeling nothing as he ended their lives, given the pain they had inflicted and the fate to which they had abandoned him.

The warehouse had been chosen in the hope that sounds of clandestine activity would not be heard. In that, it had proved very successful and no silencer was needed, which pleased him as he'd wanted this whole episode to go out with a suitable bang.

Likewise, it would take some time for the sight or smell from the fire to reach the more populated areas. He had toyed with the idea of just dumping the bodies in the nearby canal but there had been some good times too, so a pyre seemed fitting. By its hellish, flickering light he stared out west towards the place many miles distant where the final piece of this picture-puzzle would be slotted into place the next day. He would have loved to be there but really didn't have the time. He had a flight to catch; other places to explore, plus a half-mile to cover on foot back to his car. Having moved their car into the warehouse, he set off.

"Two down, two to go." He smiled as he walked away.

Chapter Forty-One

She was a sapling, rooted to the spot, trembling in an ill wind that sprang up whenever the outside world manifested itself. Yet had she always been this bad before she met him? One thing was sure – absence might have made the heart grow fonder but with him away, in mind and body she felt weaker than ever.

The knocking was insistent. It couldn't bode well. Perhaps it was the ghost of her dead sister insistent on revenge. She hoped that wasn't true, on more than one level.

She squeezed her eyes shut, still refusing to believe that he had ended that life, though why should she feel guilty when, according to Marcus, Jessica had tried to end hers?

According to Marcus.

Further knocking. Whoever it was, they weren't going away. Of course, it could have been someone concerned about her. After all she had rather dropped out of everything in which she had become involved for a while – art classes, writing groups, the café culture. With the possibility of some caring interaction, she found that her feet were shuffling forward. She was somehow disembodied and observed her hand reaching for the door latch.

* * *

He had a unique issue at airports, always needing to make sure that he was producing the correct passport! As he was leaving the EU this time, it required particular care. He couldn't help but smile as he remembered triple-checking that he had the correct ticket on the day of his last flight back to Munich. Even he might have had a problem convincing the officials that he was a female!

He had told Jessica that she was being held somewhere in the middle of the terrifying wilderness that is Siberia but in reality, after their night at the restaurant, he had driven her a much shorter distance, just three hours or so, to her prison in the snowbound Bohemian Forest. Fake government papers would have ensured his passage from Munich across the Czech border but being in the Schengen Zone had meant no-one stopped him, and if he had encountered any problems, worst-case scenario, he was confident the sight of a wedge of cash would have smoothed the passage. As it turned out, his sleeping passenger had remained undisturbed, waking in due course, in manacles, to be confronted by the nightmarish consequences of her actions.

He reflected on how much more your money could buy, depending on the history of a region. Back in the day, in Freiburg, he'd had to pay handsomely to cover his arse during the Jack Jeffries business, though to be fair, the person concerned had needed to quit his job in the SonderBar and disappear to avoid any questioning by the police about the blond customer called Dimitri. His latest contacts in the Czech Republic had settled for a lot less, even though they were watching over and sedating a victim, to be held safe and secure till he was ready to release her. Nevertheless, the money had assured their future financial health and hence their silence.

On his return to Munich, he had collected Katherine who had then flown back to the UK with him, posing, though not without obvious and understandable discomfort, as Jessica – it would have seemed suspicious if the latter hadn't returned from her overseas meeting. There might have been some business contacts looking for her. It was a risk Marcus hadn't been prepared to take. With Katherine's return, as far as the UK authorities knew, Jessica Dawes had come back to Britain.

One last move had been needed to complete his checkmate. He had headed back to Bohemia with Jessica's passport and her travel-bag, leaving them in the hands of his Czech associates along with instructions to await his call, probably in about a month.

He could only imagine Jessica's confusion when she awoke in her prison cabin. Being alive would have been enough of a shock. Finding her travel-bag, a flight ticket, a battered four-wheel drive car and passport would have rendered it beyond all comprehension. She would want to understand why she was still alive. His own revenge depended on it. Once she had hit a main road, the drive to Munich would have taken three hours at most. It wouldn't have mattered to Jessica that she hadn't bought that flight ticket. Once you had escaped from the nightmarish prospect of death in an isolated, freezing place, far from all hope – he knew that concept only too well – you would take whichever route out was available and then try to solve the puzzle from the warmth of your own home. This day, he knew the time of her return flight to the UK and found to his relief, courtesy of one of his hacker contacts in the airlines, that she had boarded it.

Marcus was pretty sure Jessica would feel driven to pursue those responsible in private once again – after all, her original need for vengeance had brought about this whole bitter affair, so there was no-one in whom she could confide. Broadcasting her shame in all its glory was not an option.

His own world was a distorted reflection of hers now, the difference being he had the power to choose his path. When you had hung by your wrists while every inch of your body was in pain and you knew your death would be your only freedom, but somehow the Fates showed you a dark road down which you managed to escape, you made sure to avoid the smallest mistake. Showing the wrong passport would count as one, hence his newly acquired paranoia. Now no-one would track him down. If for some reason Jessica in her desperation did call the authorities, they would be looking for the wrong man. Hans Schulze no longer existed.

In anticipation of take-off and the instructions to switch off all mobile phones, or at least activate flight-mode, he decided on a final glance at everything he was leaving behind, for some considerable time at least. He couldn't help but grin when he discovered Tony the Tiger was still being hit on! The chances of a response – zero. Fire-Dawes – he had left the website down for maintenance again.

Now, to his surprise, he found himself thinking about Mighty, and memories of Christine Jeffries resurfaced. Funnily enough, they were fond – at the end of the day, he had done her wrong and she had told him to get out. Given his subsequent experiences, that response seemed candlelit and harmonious! There were pictures of their time together that he would continue to cherish in his virtual scrapbook.

He flicked onto the website – they were still going and doing well enough, it seemed. Despite everything he had just been feeling, he couldn't prevent the slightest chill in his veins at the sight of the owner. Was that what a conscience felt like? He scrolled on down to the directors.

What the fuck?

Part of him felt a moment's panic but then his cranial calculator kicked in – the one that helped him to put two and two together and always make four. Well nearly always, though it had once let him down. Never again.

He worked out what must have happened.

We also ask that your seats and table trays are in the upright position for take-off. Please ensure all mobile phones are switched off or put into flight mode.

He smiled. He knew what his mobile phone would be doing later.

He was still in deep thought about the latest revelation when the stewardess stopped by his seat post take-off. "Champagne, sir?"

Now at last he relaxed, leaned back and raised his glass to the future – first to his and then, with a sardonic grin and bitter irony, to theirs; the Dawes sisters. They would have so much to resolve but never be able to – the house, the business, the lies.

* * *

Natalie Savage pushed the folder to one side and pursed her lips. She would never be free from Imposter Syndrome. Senior Director came at a price – your time was no longer truly your own and the direction in which that expanding company was heading was now something you were expected to advise on, rather than follow. Deep down, she knew any opinion she ventured in those areas would be ignored – tiptoed around by those below her who knew better.

Talking of whom, Gwen and Buck were still there. The latter was a geek, a software and hardware genius, and a barrel of fun. Any smoke and mirrors surrounding Natalie's sudden upward trajectory would have worked with him, because for him a chip was part of integrated circuitry, not something you had in a game. Gwen – well, that she had survived the whole sorry affair with the accounts fraud and failure to submit would have been a big plus. When Natalie's promotion had been announced, she'd made sure she congratulated her and pretty much just got on with things. Perhaps she had recognised a fellow survivor.

But Lancelot Greene? He had moved on. Could she blame him? To be answerable all of a sudden to your former PA would have been too much to bear, for Natalie too. His departure had suited them both!

She looked at the folder again and took a deep breath. It seemed in this company, the higher that people like her climbed, the more the lack of oxygen affected your conscious thought. The engineers were requesting her input on the planning of some new project. She was relying on memory at the moment, while trying to dig out notes she had kept when working for Lancelot. This was turning into a case of being careful what you wished for – better to have worked for it!

The trouble was that she wished for all manner of things in a materialistic way and was honest enough with herself to admit it. Her abilities in her new role had a low ceiling, but her bank account did not.

She'd done what she needed to do. Life was short.

She thought of Csilla.

Her phone rang. She didn't recognise the number and though she wasn't in the right frame of mind for a call, curiosity got the better of her.

Natalie could almost feel the blood drain from her head. She felt faint, tried to stand and gave up. The voice.

"You used them, didn't you? The files you'd kept."

As she tried to respond, her throat constricted; almost a visceral reminder of the last time they'd been together, though back then the choking sensation had been at her request and brought her warped pleasure.

His tone wasn't unfriendly; far from it – it was just one didn't often get to commune with the dead!

"I thought…" It was all she could manage.

"You're not alone in that – and as far as the rest of the world is concerned, I am. Oh, there are a couple of women who know different but that's the least of their problems. They won't find me and if they want to lead any sort of lives from now, they won't try."

"How did you… I mean, the tattoo and…" she hesitated to list the gory details.

"Don't worry, I have another nose you can rub in it." His laugh was disturbing, but then so was the fact that she found it comforting too. "So, what did you do to reach these dizzy heights? Senior Director, eh?"

She was regaining some equilibrium now. "As you said, I used what I had. My role was becoming stale, I had things I wanted to do. I assumed you were dead. My life needed a kick-start. I asked myself, how much would Christine Jeffries be prepared to give in exchange for my silence about the fiasco with the defrauding of accounts and her husband's role in it? This company is racing along. Information like that could give it a serious flat tyre."

He laughed. "Well done you! I'm impressed. We should talk again. Great minds think alike. I'll be in touch."

"Where are you?"

He was gone.

Once the disappointment had faded, Natalie found herself grinning. She believed he would indeed be in touch. Who knew where that might lead? An image of Bonnie and Clyde leapt into her head from nowhere and her smile broadened.

***

It wasn't exactly like opening a door to reveal a mirror. In a moment of sudden insight, his words came back to her…

"It's as if the two of you deserve each other."

… and she assumed her features now, full of horror and dismay, bore little resemblance to the one looking back at her in stony reproof.

"Hello sister."

The world was full of echoes and distorted reflections.

EPILOGUE

Sarah Kent called it an act of love. Others might have seen it as callous objectivity, the only love being of the tennis variety, the zeros in her commission.

She knew sales of Kingdom Cum would rocket again as a result of her actions. They would recover from the inevitable tailing off after their incredible peak when the novel had been serialised on TV. The short, passionate, moving and – key point from a sad, romantic point of view – unfinished piece she had found handwritten in a notebook under the mattress in the remote cottage on Harris was likely to garner huge attention for the author, the more so because she had vanished, perhaps even taken her own life. If the work was indeed being published posthumously, it could have the same impact as Thomas Grey's *Elegy Written in a Country Churchyard*, though probably with less long-lasting critical acclaim!

The mysterious disappearance of Margot Foye now guaranteed her scribblings and musings almost mythological status. As Sarah had said to the press, her client – her friend – had been making noises about the negative impact of fame upon her psychological well-being, hence her retreat to the Isle of Harris. It may have been that she had simply decided to run away from there too, though the absence of any withdrawals from her bank account for some time rendered that a specious argument and pointed to a much more gruesome possibility. People feared the worst. The irony was that if Margot then resurfaced, there might almost have been a touch of disappointment. Everyone loved a mystery or conspiracy theory. Who would have wanted Jack the Ripper to materialise and hang from the gallows?

However, as predicted by Sarah, the resulting novella sold like hot-cakes; an abbreviated, passionate, possibly autobiographical account of a meeting in a well-known bar in London between an author, at a time when fame was starting to take its toll, and a mysterious man possibly of Germanic origin, who knew her from her writing but not from Adam. There followed some moments of lust and passion worthy of her seminal work – in all senses of that word! That she had yearned to meet him again was clear from the text. So the impact when he did indeed turn up again at her door on a Hebridean island – well, it might even have moved the heart of Sarah Kent, had she possessed one.

But this news also attracted the attention of the police still investigating Margot's disappearance.

This was a case where it almost earned someone a pat on the back by default for not following the protocols of GDPR – paperwork of such biblical proportions that some officers had renamed it *God Don't People Rabbit!* There was only the lightest of reprimands for the owners of the club where Margot's star-crossed lovers supposedly met, when it came to light there were hidden CCTV cameras at the bar and police were able to watch actual footage of that fictional night, both what happened inside and outside the bar, on disks that hadn't been destroyed.

The biggest problem they would encounter was that it isn't only the dead who don't talk – of whom there were plenty, whose roles in that whole saga were likely to remain secrets forever, even if their bodies were to be found. Too many of the protagonists had concealed their shame, protected their reputations or hidden their own deceit and embarrassment with silence. Never had the last word of an idiom – *let sleeping dogs lie* – had a more appropriate double-meaning.

Plus, even if the police had a name for the man in the CCTV images, one of his many, they no longer had a face. They had parts of it but wouldn't know those were in frozen storage as part of another investigation!

It became apparent they had nothing to go on…

… until a police station in Bath received a call from a woman in Bath, a former businesswoman, who said she couldn't live with the consequences of her actions any more.

Author Biography

David Palin has an appetite for the dark and mysterious. Born in West London but now residing in Berkshire, he is intrigued by the things that hide, often in plain sight, in the shadows beyond the light of our everyday lives. From studying both English and German literature, he believes we are drawn to darker tales and imaginings.

All of this manifests in his work. Away from writing David enjoys sports, music, and the theatre — all of which have seemed like elements of a fantasy tale in our recent tough times.

Also available from David Palin

LET THE GAME COMMENCE

THE NEW THRILLER FROM
DAVID PALIN

Printed in Great Britain
by Amazon

42668497R00152